Star
Witness

Books by Richard Kluger

When the Bough Breaks (1964)
National Anthem (1969)
Simple Justice: A History of Brown *v.* Board of Education
(1976)
Members of the Tribe (1977)
Star Witness (1979)

Star

Witness

Richard

Kluger

DOUBLEDAY & COMPANY, INC.
GARDEN CITY, NEW YORK   1979

ISBN: 0-385-13505-X
Library of Congress Catalog Card Number 78–7760

For Larry, Myrna, Jolie, and Jennifer

"That woman is meant by nature to obey may be seen by the fact that every woman who is placed in the unnatural position of complete independence immediately attaches herself to some man by whom she allows herself to be guided and ruled. If she is young, it will be a lover; if she is old, it will be a priest or lawyer. . . ."

Arthur Schopenhauer

"It isn't that I think women are superior to men. It's just that they haven't had the opportunity to be corrupted by power. . . ."

Bella Abzug

"Remember, we're all in this alone."

Lily Tomlin

1

For all my simple tastes, decent values, and habitual consorting with the downtrodden, I was taken from the start by the very idea of going to work in so unconscionably refined a place.

I had often passed by the mansion on errands up and down that busy street without ever having paused to regard its elegance or wonder at its current use. There was no clue to its contents visible from the sidewalk, but I would have guessed, given the American fondness for misplaced grandeur, that it was now operating as either a funeral parlor or a cathouse. Despite the monumental solidity of the structure, one of the city's few survivors of the Federal period, it managed an inviting warmth. Its brick was of the mellowest terra cotta, its woodwork of a soft fresh cream, its roof of smoothly weathered slate, and the oversized pediment gave off a disciplined radiance from its gemlike oval fanlight. So lovingly had its former glory been restored to the exterior that, viewing it from across the way, one could all but hear the sibilant sweep of silk gowns over the parquet floors within. Wouldn't the faded but still pungent whiff of money, position, and influence intoxicate all who were connected inside? I was counting on it. So long as I was selling myself, why not trade for good goods?

Affixed to the center of the mammoth front door was the sole mark of commerce on the premises—a burnished brass sign, attached by small brass screws, stating with Spencerian flourish "Lamport, Kettering, Grier & Nightingale" and below that, in small yet commanding capitals, "ATTORNEYS AT LAW." There was no doorbell, no chipper little card announcing, "Open—Walk In," only a massive cast-iron knocker.

I rapped. It sounded like a twenty-one gun salute. No one came. Were they all occupied inside gilding cobwebs?

I tried again, with still more explosiveness. On my final volley the door jerked open with a suddenness that nearly sent me flying. "Sor-ry," said an apple-cheeked milkmaid in a demure outfit of knitted beige. "The phone was going crazy."

"Attorney Hill," I said with a smile of sisterly understanding, "to see everyone."

She looked properly opaque. Flippant plainly was not the spirit of the establishment, even among the young. "I beg your pardon?" she said.

"Tabor Hill," I amplified. "Mr. Lamport is expecting me at two."

"Oh, yes," she said, smiling back now, "I have you down." She led me across the foyer, a baronial expanse defined by high pearl-gray walls and rampant wainscoting of golden oak. The murky light from an immense chandelier and related sconces did little to display the intricate beauty of the vintage Persian rug. I was directed crisply through open french doors to the waiting room, where the decor was more determinedly, and dispiritingly, mercantile. Three balding black-leather sofas confronted the stone fireplace in a stolid horseshoe formation. The aqua rug had faded unevenly and was fraying in spots; the velour curtains of muted emerald seemed to harbor sufficient mulch to nourish several generations of philodendrons. And the walls were so mobbed with mezzotints of clipper ships and brigantines that the room took on an almost barnacled dampness.

The inevitable ship's clock on the mantel confirmed that I was on time. Too keyed up to fall into one of the sofas, too self-conscious to prowl around the room, I settled on pretending to inspect a portion of the armada on the wall. My head, though, was churning the alternate ways I might greet the formidable Maynard Stockman Lamport, Esquire, senior partner in Amity's ranking law firm, past president of the New England Bar Association, and impeccably pedigreed counselor to the vanishing remnant of local Congregationalist gentry. "Oh, yes-yes," he said after I had hung on the line for ten minutes before he picked up, "Judge Millis has spoken very well of you. You might come by—we're in the market for someone with strong credentials."

"Judge Millis is kind," I said.

"Let's hope he's being so to us both, Miss Tabor. Why don't you send me in a little background on yourself—and the judge says you did some writing for the *Law Journal*. I'd like to have a glance at that, if you can spare a copy."

"Of course," I said. "And I'm afraid it's Miss Hill—Tabor Hill."

"Right," he said, as if I had said it wrong in the first place. "We'll say a week from Wednesday—can you make that? Figure the better part of your afternoon. We'll run you down the line here if you and I both think there'd by some point to it, eh?"

"Wednesday would be fine."

"Did the judge mention we're a bit of a crusty outfit?"

"I don't recall that precise word."

"Old-fashioned, then?"

"Something on that order," I said. "The implication was hardly pejorative."

"I should think not—I happen to be his lawyer. Well, forewarned is forearmed, Miss Hill. Make it two o'clock."

I liked the superannuated sound of him. Perhaps I should curtsy on his threshold. God, I wondered if any children were still taught such small acts of civility. Who had the time and energy for it? Oh, how it all had changed even in my twenty-eight years on the planet. And how distant and ludicrous seemed the emblems of indulgence and refinement that had surrounded my childhood—hairbrushes with ivory handles, snow-white dresses so heavily starched they stood by themselves, a silver porringer with my very own initials on the handle in big loopy swirls, cloth napkins even with milk and cookies, and a genuine nanny from Bath who settled in with us in Farmington after the Second World War and failed famously to get me to curtsy right without falling on my can.

It was dear Miss Terhune who told me that Tabor meant something besides my mother's family name. To me, of course,

Tabor and Hill were as inseparable as bread and butter. I had always loved how they made me sound as much like a place as a person—a low-lying, rather bushy, and decidedly picturesque promontory in the midst, say, of the English Lake District about which Miss Terhune would regale me at bedtime. Then one day she explained that a tabor was in fact a thing as well as a name—a kind of small drum. Not long afterward, she produced a tambourine, painfully removed its bangles, and handed me "a tabor for Tabor." It was noted that we were both small, noisy objects and that sometimes people's names turned out to be remarkably apt.

Yet I escaped brathood, thanks to a set of parents who knew when to jolly me up, when to tamp me down, and when to leave me the hell alone. If I have never enlisted in the feminist commotion as such, it is not because I have been out of sympathy with sisterhood but simply that I have felt no need of self-affirmation by strident statement or collective act. I have been declarative on my own from the start.

My acceptance into full membership in the species, with a few minor adjustments for age and size, was initially the work of my father. Michael Hill did more than adore me as his tiny powder puff. I was something real to him, however miniaturized, and he loved to teach the world to me. The lessons were never candy-coated and, earlier than one might suppose, became both complex and sobering. Daddy was a ranking vice president of Hartford's third biggest insurance company, charged with administering an investment portfolio running into tens and later hundreds of millions of dollars. Bearing so grave a weight in so baleful an enterprise, he was afraid, I suppose, of being taken for a bloodless actuary. As if to compensate, he lost no chance to translate his workday numerology into games and pastimes of his own devising that won my rapid absorption. It was not the mirth they provided that bewitched me but the company. Daddy staked us out a vegetable garden, for example, off the sunny side of the back lawn and used it to instruct me in the basic principles of agronomy and bookkeeping. I was to pursue the welfare and disposition of every seedling we planted and keep track of the expenses in a little notebook I was always muddying. At the end of each growing season we counted up our crop and multiplied it by the prices at the farmers' market a few miles out in the country and the higher ones at the grocery in town ("more overhead," I was told, though the market looked loftier to me). Since, by my calculations, the earth and rain were free, not to mention Daddy's and my muscles, and only the seed and fertilizer were itemizable, our small patch of ground yielded a tidy profit. For the life of me I couldn't understand why the whole world wasn't out hoeing and weeding. Then Daddy, not ungently, broke the sobering news. In words of not more than two syllables, he explained the value-added theory of labor, fair return on equity, depreciation of equipment, and the inevitability of taxation, all of which, when properly taken into account, left us barely breaking even. In time he had me proposing that we cut down on carrots and scallions the next growing season and plant more tomatoes to improve our financial performance. "Tomatoes take a lot more caring for," he cautioned. I began to see all shortcuts to prosperity as perilous.

It was like that with father throughout my childhood. When we built a doll house together, it was done to excruciatingly exact detail. Each stage of microscopic carpentry was preceded by a litter of his worksheets as he fed me, in his chirpy fashion, fractions, ratios, percentages, the fundamentals of algebra, and the endearing virtues of the isosceles triangle. Because these puzzle-solving projects were invested with love as well as care and presented in terms I could grasp and in forms I could possess, the lessons imparted along the way were painless. As I got older, joy and purpose were ever mingled in my activities, though father's part in them receded. Thus, when I was given a pony for my twelfth birthday—a roan I of course named Tambourine and stabled a half mile down the road—I was required to chart its growth, diet, and exercise and meet the costs for feed, tack, stall, and veterinary care strictly within the budget provided for the purpose. Once, when I had the bright idea of our taking out a group policy on the lives of Tambourine, our scottie Leon, our canary Nellie, and other domestic creatures in the neighborhood, father went so far as to get out his calculator and tables and demonstrate that, given the limited life expectancies of the critters, within five years of issuing the policy his insurance company would either take a bath or raise the premiums so high that the family would have to hock the house to meet them. The latter was more likely, he said, in view of the relative financial strength of the parties. I said I thought that was a lousy way for a big company to behave.

Even game games turned to learning experiences. My brother Brownie and I rotated at trying to beat Daddy at chess —we did, too, but at such great intervals we always supposed he had taken a dive out of mercy—and mother would join us for intramural bridge tourneys waged with much solemnity. But father sportingly interrupted the flow of every contest to point out lethal moves of his we might have anticipated or alternate strategies to bring him down. It fell to mother to remind him we were only children and the games only games. He would say that so long as we were playing, we might as well do it right.

All this studied activity, it might reasonably be supposed, should have drained the spontaneity out of my brother and me, but I have no sense we suffered such a loss. The gain in intensity was not accomplished by derricking our delight in life's simple pleasures. What we did not do a whole lot of in our home was waste time. Even our skylarking had a point. Father's drill bore a single message to his offspring: What we achieved in any of our pursuits mattered less than the quality of effort expended. Not to try your best was the sin. The rule applied to boy and girl alike.

To ward off adolescent airs, I was not sequestered at Miss Porter's nearby harem for overprivileged maidens but left to cope among the children of commoners in the public high school. Aside from having the interior of my brassiere explored by an occasional boy instead of girl, I doubt that my academic training was much affected. Blessed with a retentive memory and precocious powers of concentration, thanks in no small measure to Daddy, I excelled in class. It was not that I never studied; rather, that I did so with discipline in order to be done as soon as possible. Other things attracted me more. Friends, first. All our hormones were raging, and with them endless curiosity about ourselves and one another and what the world held in store for us—and we, it. I was someone different each day—sometimes a pudding of insecurity, fastening myself for dear life to my pajama-party gang, and sometimes an unreachable princess of such bearing and exquisiteness that my feet scarcely skimmed the ground. Soon the posturing passed, and I functioned other ways. I won the town tennis tournament for girls (against, to be sure, diluted competition; the local *femmes athlétiques* were mostly off being preppies). I played violin, barely, in the school orchestra. I contributed two haikus and a fatuous elegy on the untimely passing of our family dog to the lit'ry magazine. And turned in a passable Calpurnia in the senior class production of *Julius Caesar* the day before being admitted to Mount Holyoke.

The play was the thing. In a way I have never quit that stage. Midway through my final scene, an un-Shakespearean twist caused the most mortifying moment of my young life. Lead-footed Kermit Zimmerman trod heavily on the trailing hem of my diaphanous blue dress while I was in motion and left me standing there half-unfrocked. Titters in the audience. Then snickers. Then gross guffawing. Oh, the urge to panic and dash for the wings. But something in me held. I rewound myself into the ungainly garment with a defiant dignity and went on with my lines, thereby shaming the hooters and winning far more applause at the close than my modest muse ever would have. Having survived, at so formative a phase in life, everybody's nightmare of a public disrobing, I have suffered only minimal discomfort ever since in facing an audience. No doubt the incident spurred my performing urge and helped shape my subsequent choice of career.

Throughout my coming of age, I was never treated at home as if I were among the anointed-in-training. My allowance was nominal, my wardrobe of superior quality but modest quantity, my access to the telephone and family cars stubbornly resisted, and my obligation to keep self, room, and possessions sanitary if not spotless remained constant.

On top of this was my mother's insistence that our family

owed something to those less fortunate than we and had damned well better meet that debt or suffer heaven's wrath—and her own. The former Miss Meredith Tabor of Croton-on-Hudson was no vainly bleeding heart. She had put in two years at nursing school in Maryland when she quit to marry father at the end of the war. Ever after she was haunted by visions of Clara Barton ministering to a wardful of low-moaning sufferers. Mercifully, her passion to comfort the afflicted never converted mother into a hovering parent. Beyond a modicum of maternal vigilance, her chief good work consisted of tireless labor in behalf of Hartford's largest private hospital, for which she was eventually rewarded with a seat on the board of trustees. (The sole perk this distinction granted her, so far as I ever saw, was access to the O.R. amphitheater, to which she was constantly threatening to drag me in the hope of sponsoring a career in neurosurgery. I always professed nausea when invited.) Mother was only slightly less devoted to the fortunes of the Farmington cell of the Republican Party, unswerving advocates still of abolitionism and trustbusting but otherwise pretty cautious people. She was off at some meeting or other at least one afternoon and evening a week, though never both on the same day. After a time, she became so adept at committeeing that the sessions were scheduled more or less at her convenience. Given her talents, I asked her why she didn't run for Farmington First Selecthuman (this being before the movement coined the hardly more felicitous "chairperson" and other execrable hybrids). She said it was because she was basically a quite private person and had no wish to take the guff that every surly taxpayer thinks it his or her sacred right to direct at the handiest official any hour of the day or night. "Democracy has a fondness for abuse," she disclosed to my stunned ears, "and a contempt for commands. At best, it's a matter of endless negotiation and bargained principles. I'd rather bake a first-rate cake." Still, I harbored the secret hope she would relent someday and pitch her favorite wine-red chapeau into the political ring (no small trick since the hat was the size of a medium-range UFO). How else would I ever get to ride shotgun with the chief of police?

8

At mother's instigation, I did volunteer work at the hospital on weekends and devoted alternate summers to some similar selfless cause. One year the whole family would spend July and August at our cottage on Cape Ann, and the next Brownie would be a junior counselor at a Y camp in the Berkshires and I would serve at a ghetto nursery in Hartford. By my college years when I traveled and studied in Europe these alternate summers, I had come to understand that mother's conviction in the matter was something more profound than *noblesse oblige*. Certainly her charitable efforts were never mere conspicuous altruism, undertaken to advance her stock among the resident aristocracy. On the contrary, she was so convinced that only blind fate, not divine mandate, separated the cream from the curds in the prevailing social order that she viewed any public exhibition of elitism as morally degenerate. Our family membership at the club sorely tried that standard, but mother justified it on the ground that Daddy needed a reliable place to golf—the public links being so crowded that the poor man never had time to line up his putts with the sort of micrometric precision he craved. Besides, the admissions committee had dropped its bar against Catholics, Jews, non-Caucasians, Martians, and even Democrat WASPs. But we did not advertise our ties to the clubby set. Nor was there any sweaty coming-out cotillion for Miss Tabor Hill, duly recorded on the society page of the *Courant*. My femininity was plain enough, a residual brashness not withstanding. I dated regularly and whom I chose from the time I was fifteen, provided only that I limited the habit to two nights a week, got home by midnight, and was prepared to be written off without a dime if I turned up even a teensy pregnant. Whoever said charity begins at home was not the Republican Eleanor Roosevelt at our house.

Technically—and not that it holds quite the historical interest of, say, Magna Carta—I did not surrender my virginity until sophomore year at college. It was not a grand passion. In fact, it stank. Some Amherst gorilla in whom I had detected a certain animal magnetism plied me with beer, hauled me off not forcibly to the local Birnam Wood, drilled me impatiently in a musky sleeping bag, politely did me with a finger,

9

and then rolled over unconscious, leaving me to paddle around in the wet spot. My only solace was that nothing, and I mean nothing, could have germinated as a result: I had been fortifying myself for years against the horrific event by inserting, applying, spraying on, and swallowing every known form of contraceptive plus a few I dreamed up on my own. Oh, the dread of disinheritance in a devout Calvinist princess.

That joyless initiation was not the forerunner to a career of nymphomania. If anything, I was tending just then in the opposite direction. Petting to climax was about the extent of my heterosexual activity—constraint that all but earned me expulsion from the more worldly campus set. In truth, I was stricken with a case of intense indifference to men in general (though not all in particular), and not out of incipient lesbianism, which, while not unknown at women's colleges, was not common at mine. Nor was the cause my discovery of the minimal delight produced within me by the phallus, at least as wielded by the fumbling young lovers of my earliest encounters. All that did was prompt the compensating discovery that I could derive exquisite satisfaction out of self-dalliance. And surely that was preferable to being banged by a boy I cared nothing for. (I have come to consider this rechargeable battery of ours to be nature's thoughtful equalizer for burdening womanhood with the lavish discharge of the uterine lining every bloody month. Not that the Almighty did a great deal better with the male genitals: there is hardly anything esthetic about the scrotum, and the shaft itself, even at its engorged mightiest, is at least as ludicrous as it is functional.) My estrangement from men, however, had far less to do with biology than with history. For the first time I faced the truth: the bastards had enslaved us from the start.

Even my mother. In her case, the victimization took the form of conditioned thinking. A woman of immense competence, she never let on to even dreaming that she might reach for the scepter instead of playing the offstage kingmaker. And heaven forfend if someone had suggested she serve as president of her precious hospital instead of its chief fund-raiser and bandage-wrapper. No, not her—she was too fucking demure for that sort of unladylike striving. Woman's job was servicing the menfolk. Always was, always would be. Anything else was downright unfeminine. And for mother, with her satin voice, honey curls, luscious boobs, and delicate fragrance, there could be no worse slur.

By the time Betty Friedan and her apostlettes started waving the torch, it was too late to rescue mother from her groove. Even as she recognized the legitimacy of the feminist uprising, she resented its not very subtle indictment of women precisely like her, the most able of the sex, who had never ventured beyond their subsidiary status for fear of being labeled perverse. For me, however, as for a whole generation coming of age just then, it was an awakening. I enlisted, in my fashion, by writing a poem at the end of my copy of *The Feminine Mystique*. It went:

> Jack and Jill went up the hill
> To fetch a pail of water.
> Jack fell down and broke his crown,
> And Jill called an ambulance
> And then filled the pail
> Quite competently.
> Imagine her surprise
> When she saw the pail
> Was filled with oil,
> So she bought the hill
> And then the next one
> And the valley in between
> And made a great deal of money.
> Jack died.

For the first time in my life, I no longer took for granted that marriage was the desideratum for every normal, healthy, decent girlchild. And the more I read during my college career, the grimmer the prospect grew. There was old Havelock Ellis, for example, likening marriage to prostitution, each being basically a sex-for-food transaction. I was yet more devastated by Emma Goldman's lamentation for that wretched refuse of the sex who find fulfillment only in utter dependency. Marriage, she wrote, turns woman into a parasite, "incapacitates her for life's struggle, annihilates her social consciousness, paralyzes her imagination, and then imposes its gracious protection, which is in reality a snare, a travesty on human character." Well, it may not have altogether quenched my own mother's social consciousness but it sure as hell incapacitated her for struggling out there in life's hard arena. Her obligation to gentility came first. How would she remain recognizable as a blossom if now and then she lost a few petals to the storm? She lacked the will to prevail—to fight to win; most women did. That was what I most envied in men. What's history but hormonal determinism? Was it possible, I wondered, to ingest just enough testosterone to turn myself into a fearless predator yet not come down with a hairy face?

Salvation, I decided by the close of my undergraduate career, did not reside in biochemistry. If anywhere, it was in one's philosophical outlook. I settled on at least one guiding principle for the future. I absolutely had to control my own mind, my own body, my own life. I could not and would not depend on anyone or anything else for my well-being. No man to validate my charms. No woman, bosom buddy or mentor, to judge my actions or inactions. No parents to shape me, however benevolently, in their image. No temporal power to manipulate me or ecclesiastical one to monitor my lapses. By the same token, I could permit no dependence on me, no shuttering of possibilities, no extra ballast or baggage—not by any lover who was less than whole (let him take his own shirts to the laundry) or companion or fawning acolyte or, especially, any issue of my womb whose demands I was sure would utterly consume me once I let the little bugger out to breathe.

Having thus claimed title to myself, I had yet to resolve what purpose on earth I was to serve. That I would ascend in my chosen field was of slight concern: I was young and sure the relationship between merit and reward was close if not causal. What field, though, should I choose? It was necessary to take stern inventory of my virtues and limitations. On inspection, the latter were more apparent. For one thing, I owned no face that would ever launch a thousand ships. A rowboat, maybe, if the oarsman were taken with laughing gray eyes set well apart, hundreds of small, even, perfectly white teeth, and enough cheekbone to outfit a Mongol horde. But my pursuer would soon enough discover the malformations: too much forehead, too little chin, rubbery lips that rarely rested, and hair so springy it would have gone unclaimed at Little Big Horn. The rest of me, too, while comprising a complete kit, lacked the lavish proportions of Aphrodite; all in all, I was more daffodil than American Beauty rose. But women admired mostly for their looks, I told myself, spend their lives preening when not worrying how long the bloom will last.

Other qualities commended themselves to my attention. Mostly these dealt with character. Here, too, though, I sensed my obvious deficiencies—or, to be more precise, an absence of extraordinary aptitude. I lacked the inveigling charm of a Cleopatra, the cryptic wit of a Gertrude Stein; I had little of the insouciance of an Isadora or the cosmic compassion of a Margaret Mead; my courage was dwarfed beside the grit of a Susan Anthony, my muse a stuttering apprentice beside the eloquent mastery of *Sonnets from the Portuguese*. That left brains.

I was certifiably book-smart, having been elected to Phi Beta Kappa at the end of junior year and pulled a *summa* in classics. But knowing *Oedipus at Colonus* by heart in the original and enough Thucydidean syntax to fill a trireme did not a genius make. Book-smart, moreover, was not street-smart; that would take some living. Meanwhile, the trick was to place my natural resources under a regimen that would somehow bear fruit. Mere brightness was not sufficient. Mere quickness was self-defeating. My guide at this critical juncture was the superb George Eliot, whose exhortation to any woman wishing to rise above the station of scullery ninny was engraved upon my plastic mind. The way up was paved, she wrote, by "accurate thought, severe study and continuous self-command." Indulgence and predisposition had to yield to total engagement and intense contemplation; professional competence, and then mastery, would follow. But mastery of what? Did I want to own the world or merely run it, save it or unlock its deepest secrets —and to hell with the consequence?

I took time to decide. It would not be correct, exactly, to call it an interlude. So consuming was the experience that I nearly had to anesthetize myself against human pain to survive it. Having taken several courses in psychology at Holyoke, I signed on for a year as an aide at a university-affiliated psychiatric clinic. A career in medicine or science seemed possible, and here was a way to wet my feet without soaking the rest of me. There was something else. As opposed to organic diseases that I could do nothing to combat, I somehow conceived that mental disorders were a pathology I could minister to by the strength of my own intellect—and without plunging deeper into morbidity than I had done in tending broken bodies at mother's hospital.

In fact, nothing had prepared me for the shrilly disorienting life on the wards at Mather Psychiatric Center, one of the nation's plusher lock-ups. Among the dozen or so most distinguished seats of higher learning in the Western world, Mather University ran the place as a self-supporting annex to its medical school, safe from degenerating into a snake pit so long as there was a supply of patients from families with enough income or insurance to pay the astonishing upkeep. There were no sadistic nurses or brutal orderlies but round-the-clock treatment and surveillance by doctors, nurses, therapists, trainees, and hot-and-cold-running social workers.

Perhaps it was because everything there was locked tight and the windows barred that I shared at once the patients' sense of isolation, helplessness, and fear. It was, after all, a kind of madhouse, although its inmates were considered more or less reclaimable. That made it no easier for me to confront a hallucinating schizophrenic, a screamingly abusive paranoid, or an *anorexia nervosa* gorging herself in the dining room and then hurrying over to the corner to throw up. Anxiety collected like spontaneous tinder in every part of the place, ready to ignite at the least provocation, especially in the adolescent wing. It never got really quiet during waking hours on that ward; shouting voices, crashing doors, roaring stereos, and accosted soda machines bespoke the inner turbulence riddling them all. In a single week, I found a girl trying to cut her wrist in the toilet with a drinking glass stolen from the dining room, helped pump out the stomach of a boy who overdosed on Decadril grabbed from the nurses' station, and beat out a mattress fire in the middle of the night. But I also did a hundred dumb and futile things because I wanted so badly to help.

My usual tendency to commiserate was misplaced in there and threatened to reduce me to dysfunction. I began to feel guilty that I was in control of my senses and they were not. The secret of survival was to learn how not to flinch before that daily sideshow yet not turn callous toward its performers. My ordeal intensified when I was pinned into a corner by a hulking twenty-year-old after a ward meeting one morning and rubbed up against hotly several times before they pried him off. The next day I began judo. It took three lessons to lose my scruples and decide that kicking a man in the groin (forward or backward—I learned both techniques), gouging his eyes with my thumb, or driving his nose bone into his brain with the heel of my palm was not fighting dirty if my life was involved.

By Christmas I knew that the healing of minds and bodies was not to be my profession. I either reacted overly to the plight of the suffering or I turned stone cold before it. Useful traffickers in mercy, I saw, hardly ever lost their gentleness to the disabled, even when openly provoked, or the hope that something of value might yet be salvaged from life for them. Such hope, and the patience to nourish it, eluded me. I applied to Mather Law School, a few blocks down the street from the mental hospital, demolished the law aptitude test, and was accepted in early April for the following fall. The decision seemed so natural I wondered why it had taken me that long to reach it.

2

A fulminating voice penetrated the waiting room. I looked out across the foyer and had a glimpse of a man in a sedate suit at the door to the firm's library. The source of his annoyance was evidently a book he needed that had been removed from the room in violation of the house rules. Whoever he was chewing out for having allowed the catastrophe—a powerless female, from the soft reverential sound of the response—was trying to soothe him by saying she knew where the wayward volume was, or might be. He told her to get it back fast and buzz him the moment it surfaced. My-oh-my, we are important, I thought. As if reading my mind, he looked over at me, then quickly dropped his head in embarrassment for having popped off in front of a stranger, and beat a retreat, two steps at a time, up the staircase at the rear of the foyer.

When his smoking wake had cleared, I drifted out to the secretary's desk and asked if I might wait in the library instead. She said that would be fine and was sorry Mr. Lamport was running late. "He's usually very punctual," she volunteered.

"Was that he?" I asked, indicating the stairs by which Mr. Important had fled. I knew it was not.

"Oh, no," she said, "he's an older gentleman. That was—" Propriety intruded. "That was someone else."

The library was done all in polished woods of black and brown. The mahogany bookshelves rose with their profuse cargo from floor to ceiling. I identified myself to the matronly librarian who was occupied proofreading a sheaf of typeset galleys and told me to make myself at home. I took her at her word and toured the shelves. They were excellently provisioned for a firm of that size. All the Connecticut case reports from the beginning were there, as might have been expected, and the New York and Massachusetts annals as well, which surprised me and suggested a cosmopolitan outlook. Similarly, not only were all the Supreme Court opinions on hand but also all the other federal reports for the twentieth century. And yards and yards of state and local statutes, standard and specialized reference works, and a whole section of periodicals ranging from the *ABA Journal* and *U.S. Law Week* to *Juris Doctor* and the Harvard, Columbia, Mather, and University of Chicago law reviews. How very enlightened. And now these learned counsel were even considering employment of a young female attorney.

It was almost precisely a century since the Supreme Court itself had denounced the wickedness of such a species and declared the strictures against licensing them to be entirely lawful. I drifted back along the shelves, the bindings of the volumes deteriorating as I went, in pursuit of the notorious opinion. It would strengthen my psychic armament for the impending encounter to read those heinous words anew. I located the volume. The opinion produced the same shock in me as when I first discovered it that summer before starting law school. Female attorneys were an abomination, the Justices announced in *Bradwell v. Illinois*, because

> . . . the civil law, as well as nature herself, has always recognized a wide difference in the respective spheres and destinies of man and woman. Man is, or should be, woman's protector and defender. The natural and proper timidity and delicacy which belongs to the female sex evidently unfits it for many of the occupations of civil life. . . . The fundamental destiny and mission of woman are to fill the noble and benign offices of wife and mother. This is the law of the Creator.

I had not known before then that the Chief Justice had a hot line to God. You could practically hear the Almighty thundering, "Chief, you tell the brethren for Me to give that Bradwell bitch the boot. If a fine woman like Eve couldn't keep My rules straight, what can you expect from the rest of them? And notice whom I gave the Decalogue to. The gals just weren't built to haul stone. You tell 'em that, Chief." Oh, the sly dogs! They had put us up on pedestals as so much sanctified breeding stock and then used that exalted status to tell us not to worry our pretty little heads about anything besides the propagation of the race. The legal profession calls that sort of reasoning from fallacious premises *post hoc propter hoc*. I call it bullshit.

Now if men were honest in acclaiming our kind and nurturing disposition, they would logically let women run things. Devoid of the savage male urge to dominance, we are natural negotiators and conciliators and arbitrators. Who better to serve as the magistrates of the world? The fellows would be free then to romp off and follow their predilection to pillage, get drunk, and club one another senseless.

Well, the Creator blinked and a hundred years passed, Mrs. Bradwell went up on my Mt. Rushmore, and I checked into law school with the unapologetic intention of tearing the joint apart. If lawyers had made America what it was, they could remake it into something finer—and I would be among them. The first asshole who tried to stop me would rue the day.

The day came soon. My first week there I encountered an adorable bonbon in Berger's *Land Ownership and Use*, the casebook in my Property course. "For, after all," the author wrote, "land, like woman, was meant to be possessed." Before our professor, a perfect shit of the let's-torture-the-rookies school of pedagogy, could open the day's discussion, I had my hand wigwagging. "I haven't said anything yet, Mizz Hill," he said, eager to get on with the morning lacerations.

"I know," I said. "I have a question."

"The powder room is in the basement," he said. "And we don't have to raise our hands in law school to be excused for matters of personal hygiene."

The class thought that rich. "I've already been," I said, registering no pique. "There's no powder."

"You'll have to take that up with the custodial corps, Mizz Hill. Now if you'll just let the rest of us get on with it—"

"I have a question, sir," I said.

"We have a question period at the close of the hour, Mizz Hill."

"I think the flow of the discussion would make it untimely then, sir."

Seeing that I wasn't going to quit, he glanced at the wall clock, sighed audibly, and let me say my piece. I read the offending line out loud and asked if it was meant to be a joke. A chorus of groans went up from the male students.

"I believe they teach literary criticism over in Wooster Hall," said the professor. "Myself, I wouldn't venture an opinion."

"The line, sir, is demeaning," I said.

"Then I gather your question is rhetorical?"

"Yes, sir."

"Well, in that case I'll answer it. I think Professor Berger thinks it is a witticism. Now may we—?"

"Is that your assessment of it, sir?"

The merest thread of smoke seemed to escape from his nostrils. "I have not given the sentence exhaustive attention, Mizz Hill."

"May I submit, sir, that's because you're not a woman?"

"I'm delighted you noticed."

Everyone laughed, but I had made my point.

I still got an A from him, no doubt because I deserved it, and that, after all, was what women were asking for—the chance to be rated on their merits and advanced accordingly. Aside from the supercilious attitude of a few faculty, I went unpenalized on account of gender. My real struggle was to hone a lawyerly frame of mind. That meant ridding myself of all those fatty deposits of sentiment. My year at the mental hospital had drained me of most excess emotion, but when presented with a dispute in law pitting, say, a penniless widow against a multibillion-dollar oil company, my bias was not yet toward neutrality. The point was for me to learn how to argue the company's side just as persuasively as the destitute woman's.

As it turned out, I finally absorbed the lesson in a single memorable class hour on Torts law. The professor hypothesized: a strapping fellow in the prime of life passes by a bubbling brook in which he sees a six-month-old infant drowning. Is the man legally obligated to rescue the baby? The question was put to me.

"He should be," I said, "but I suppose he isn't."

"And why do you suppose that, Miss Hill?"

"Because otherwise we could all go home."

"Very good, Miss Hill," said the professor. "Now suppose you try for something a little more substantive."

"Well," I said, "perhaps the river bed is nothing but quicksand."

"I said it was a brook, Miss Hill. Quicksand is unlikely under running brooks, as I understand it."

"Yes, I see. Well, maybe the child had bubonic plague and has been discarded."

"That's a bit better, Miss Hill. You seem to be shaping for us a sort of presumption-of-hidden-perils theory—a Bad Samaritan doctrine, if you will, that excuses missions of mercy not undertaken on the ground that things are not always what they seem."

"Something like that," I said unenthusiastically.

"The law is generally less subtle than that, Miss Hill. I think you are pining for the dying baby."

"No," I said, "I'm hating the son of a bitch for not plunging in after it, whatever the risk."

He laughed. He was human. The law was human. I felt better. "I didn't say this Hercules of ours let the child drown," he said. "I merely asked if he were under legal obligation to rescue it. Now let's just suppose that things are indeed what they seem in this instance. Wouldn't you be inclined, Miss Hill, to charge the man with something we might call neglectful manslaughter if he ignored his plain humanitarian duty and the child did indeed perish as a result?"

"Yes, sir."

"All right. Now suppose I alter the facts a little. Let us say it is a broader stream with a somewhat swifter current and the person in distress is a ten-year-old in possession of all its extremities. Is the would-be rescuer's dilemma more complex?"

"Somewhat."

"And if we make that stream a surging river and the endangered swimmer a twenty-year-old with leg cramps?"

"More so."

"And if we transport this grim spectacle to an oceanfront where amidst the tidal swell our passing Samaritan spots a three-hundred-pounder going under for the third time? Is he obliged, knowing that many a swimmer in such a predicament grows wild with panic and is prone to pull a would-be rescuer under the waves with him—is our passerby still obliged under the law to go help?"

"Plainly not," I said.

"As a matter of fact, Miss Hill, in none of these instances, from baby to behemoth, is our passerby legally required to intervene, any more than he would be liable to A if he came upon him being threatened at knifepoint by B and failed to jump in between the pair." He moved to the far side of the classroom. "The essence of the law, ladies and gentlemen, is not nuance. Imagine trying to formulate a descending scale of culpability the nearer this callous passerby approaches to circumstances threatening his own destruction. The law generalizes. Its temple is built of pillars that are tall and stout and capable of withstanding a great number of unforeseen stresses. It is left to judges and juries to apply the overarching principles of law to the facts in any given case, tempering their verdict when unavoidable by acknowledging the claims of the heart. Such claims, however, are ancillary to the guiding concepts of equity we try to isolate in exercises such as this, so may I ask you, Miss Hill, without fretting further about that waterlogged baby in the brook, to formulate a principle for us covering this predicament?"

I understood. "Under Torts law," I recited, "one is generally under no duty to come to the rescue of another."

"A model of economy, Miss Hill. But that still sounds mighty unkind and ungenerous to me. Would you tell us, as an encore, why it also happens not to be unreasonable?"

"Because the opposite rule would be unworkable. It would impute a selflessness to human nature unjustified by history."

"Quite so. One might go even farther, Miss Hill, and say that it would establish a standard of conduct certifying as villainous anyone who declined to behave in what would commonly be thought of as heroic fashion."

"I was about to say that."

"I have no doubt, Miss Hill. Thank you." He moved to the back of the room. "Having determined now that the law does not hound what we might call Bad Samaritans, let us consider what legal obligations are attendant upon those who in fact choose to go to the aid of their stricken fellow creatures. . . ."

It was all so clean and elementary treated that way, one manageable step at a time. There was a precision to the thought, a cadence to the language, a symmetry to the proceedings of the law that ought to have made its outcome inevitable. All that kept the whole system from being fed into the computer to provide instant justice, I shortly discovered, was the infinite variety, ingenuity, and perversity of the human intellect. Cases forever arose in which legal principles of apparently unshakable validity kept colliding with one another. The key to the study of jurisprudence, then, became clear to me: master the guiding tenets operative in every field, even when in unresolvable conflict, and be able to invoke them at will in assessing the relative strengths of each party to a dispute; it will do you no good at all to declare a stunningly equitable solution to any case without accounting fully for how you reached that blissful state of the art.

This insight placed me among the top dozen scholars in the class at the end of first year and put me on the *Mather Law Review*. Spurred by my own eminence, I devoted the summer to researching a note, those exhaustively annotated compositions that ideally encapsulate the entire range of controversy surrounding a given issue of law. I calculatingly picked a topic on which my *confreres* were likely to be least informed—"the tender years presumption" governing custody cases. Other things being equal or nearly so, the law awarded young children of a divorcing couple to the mother. What more "natural" subject for a female student of the law to probe?

My intentions, though, were subversive. I read, besides all the law on the subject going back to Hammurabi, a great deal of Erik Erikson and Bruno Bettelheim and Ruth Benedict and seventy-seven other authorities. What I came away with, no doubt to the astonishment of the *Review*'s editors and faculty advisers, nearly all of them male, could not be termed even remotely feminist in its bias. The law, I contended, was poorly equipped to distinguish between men suited to assume tender loving direction of their youngsters' upbringing—as I believe my father, for example, would have been—and those inclined toward but incapable of the task. The problem was complicated by millennia of cultural conditioning that demeaned child-rearing as unmanly. That was no more defensible in the last part of the twentieth century than to characterize bread-winning as unwomanly. Fathers deserved at least a fighting chance, before the law, to demonstrate their suitability as adult models for their children and not to be presumed less loving or supportive than mothers. This was nothing short of a crypto-feminist proposal, of course. I was insisting that real men (*i.e.*, decent ones, whatever their preference in rutting) did not discharge their familial responsibility with the final spasm of ejaculation, and the law ought to recognize as much in ways more positive than merely demanding financial support from them. The male editorial contingent perceived it as a peace feeler in the war between the sexes. With a few minor modifications, the piece was granted ten densely packed pages in the *Review* and drew wide and favorable comment as the latest word on the antiquated state of custody law across the nation.

I was gratified but leery. It was easy to get typecast as a potential expert on family law, a somewhat zestless and non-remunerative field into which many women attorneys were politely ushered. I therefore turned in second year toward what was classically regarded as male territory, and that puzzle-solving aptitude my father had so ardently generated in me throughout childhood now came to the fore. Taxes were an emotionally neutral province of the law. Few philosophers patrolled it. Solutions to its intricate problems were readily calculable without wizardry provided you (1) were not unnerved by the dizzying statutory language, which multiplied exponentially every few years, and (2) got the arithmetic right. Massive patience also helped. I earned A's in both the introductory and advanced courses, and decided that either I was more brilliant than I had dared suppose or the subject was less forbidding than its reputation. I delved deeper by editing a young professor's note for the *Review* on the latest bittersweet implications of tax-loss carry-forwards; the following summer I crowned my student law career by researching secured creditors' rights to full liquidation value in corporate reorganizations —a subject so arcane that only the redoubtable Rudolf Rogovin, former deputy chief of the IRS and the ranking Mather scholar on the subject, was equipped to guide my undertaking. Rogovin made an exception to his standing edict against students writing on tax law—the web of regulations was so thick and tangled, he insisted, as to disqualify all but the most fanatic explorers—and worked with me on the project intermittently during my final year. Only after he gave it his somewhat astringent blessings in the spring did the *Review* editors accept it. The piece appeared in the issue published the day I graduated, making me the only member of the class to have managed two substantial notes during my student career—no small feat. Some guy seated near me at commencement said that was pretty good for a girl. I gave him a farewell finger.

My virtuosity as a student of the law was not limitless, the triumphs noted *supra* to the contrary notwithstanding. When I was good, I was very, very good; when I was bored, I was rotten —or not much better than passing, at any rate. I brought up the bottom end of the top third of my class—a perfectly respectable showing but hardly glittering enough to earn a Supreme Court clerkship. My notes for the *Law Review* helped gain me interviews with half a dozen of the big Wall Street and Washington firms, which were falling over one another trying to hire any woman law graduate free of brain damage. Aside from feeling like a slab of flesh on the auction block ("Gather 'round, gents, and see the strong, sharp teeth on this comely wench—the undulating thighs—and yes, the large and well-developed brain, extraordinary in the female of the species"), I came away from my sessions with these immaculate operatives certain I was not destined for membership in their sanitized clubhouses. No matter how princely the wages—or "princessly," as one of the droller swells put it to me—I did not intend just then to place my services at their disposal. Corporate leviathans were as entitled to able counsel as any gap-toothed pauper, no doubt, but the bushes were full of candidates grasping for the assignment. I preferred to widen my knowledge while contributing to the common good. There would be time to grasp later.

I told Professor Rogovin of my hopes. Within the hour he had me trotting across the Amity city green to the chambers of Judge George Hightower Millis, one of the brainier members of the federal judiciary. Within the fortnight I had been awarded a year's appointment as clerk to his honor at the United States District Court for Connecticut—and never even batted my lashes to get it.

3

A former Greenwich attorney who served eight years championing the free-enterprise system on the state public utilities commission, George Millis had been rated sufficiently noxious by consumer groups to merit elevation by the Nixon crowd to the federal bench. While his opinions were not detectably partisan or doctrinaire, the judge nevertheless made it a point to learn if anyone he was considering hiring had a background patently offensive to the party. After nearly a decade of campus upheavals, the pool of clerkship candidates contained few who had not been tainted by the sin of idealism.

My own record disclosed the most tepid sort of protest activity. In senior year at Holyoke, I had joined in an antiwar rally at an air force base, where twenty-seven pickets, including the president of Amherst, were arrested for endangering the national security by failing to shake their tails fast enough when the cops re-routed the line of march. Also, I was registered as an independent. But Farmington Republican leaders vouched for my family's impeccable pro-Americanism, mother excitedly reported, and her own long service to the party more than compensated for whatever aberrant behavior was manifested by her daughter. I was furious when I heard about all this snooping around—how many points had I lost, I wondered, for not retaining my virginity at the age of twenty-five?—and hurt that I had not won the job entirely on my own. Most of all, I wondered why a federal judge with a lifetime appointment was soliciting the views of party hacks. I decided to ask him straight out before committing a year of my life to making him look good.

The judge's smooth, pink face recorded astonishment at my question. "I don't *solicit* anyone's views on anything, Miss

Hill," he said. "My private secretary routinely does a little checking into the character and background of people I'm seriously considering for employment. I am, after all, an officer of the United States government."

"In other words, your honor runs a security check?"

"That would be a substantial overstatement, Miss Hill. I'd call it a precautionary inquiry on a strictly informal basis."

"And I gather political orthodoxy is one of your honor's requirements for the job?"

"Are you asking me or telling me, Miss Hill?"

"I'm surmising—from field reports." My sarcasm brushed the edge of effrontery.

"Perhaps you know something I don't, Miss Hill. All I'm aware of in that area is that among those usually consulted as a courtesy are a few old acquaintances of mine of similar political philosophy. Others are asked as well." He took off his tortoise-shell glass frames and pinched the bridge of his nose. "And it's not necessary to call me 'your honor' outside of the courtroom, Miss Hill."

I asked him what he preferred.

"Well, you might try 'Judge Millis' for a starter—that's a favorite of mine. And before long I suppose you'll be cutting it to plain 'judge.' Otherwise, you're on your own, provided you maintain a modicum of dignity. 'Hey, you,' for example, is not acceptable."

He had me smiling despite myself. Whatever his flaws, pomposity was not among them. I nodded and said, "But surely, Judge Millis, you didn't think I was a hippie or a Yippie or some other exotic variety of revolutionary? Bomb throwers, sir, don't graduate from Mather Law School."

"Or write law journal notes on creditors' rights."

"That, too."

"Or call men of any age 'sir.'"

"Sorry—is that bad?"

"It just makes me sound like Mr. Chips or someone with gout. And I'm not old enough to be your father or, for that matter, young enough to be your suitor—which suggests to me we might have a perfectly uncomplex and highly productive association if you can manage to overcome your suspicion I'm somebody-or-other's functionary." His tilt-back chair squeaked as he shifted his weight forward. "Now your judicial views may differ from mine on many a score, Miss Hill—and that's fine with me. In fact, that's a large part of why you're here. If I wanted a clerk who thought just as I do, I'd buy a tape recorder and save the government one whole salary. But this can't be a one-way street. It won't do at all for you to deny me the privilege of reaching decisions disagreeable to you without your feeling I must be addled or a closet fascist or in somebody's pocket. I write my opinions upon due deliberation and without regard to any political fallout. The only place I've ever taken instructions from are the courts above." He gave his glasses a festive little twirl. "Now either you can accept my word on that, Miss Hill, or we can part company cordially and without further ado."

There were no smiles now. He was clearly offended. And just as clearly, I thought, he liked my cheek. But he was right. Either he had my respect as a defender of the laws of the land or he did not have it. I was not required to rank him with Holmes or Justinian—or try him out for size in bed. On the face of it, he was intelligent and forthright and had met my complaint calmly and unevasively. This side of heaven, I was unlikely to do better. "I'd be privileged to stick by our arrangement," I said, "if you really want someone who says what she thinks."

"So she does," he said. "So long as she also thinks what she says, I'll take my chances." He extended his hand.

It was as if my twenty-year education had been one long dress rehearsal for this opening number of my professional career. Even so, I was nearly overwhelmed by the challenge greeting me at the courthouse. The paperwork on cases awaiting disposition, cases docketed, and cases filed over the summer was of blizzard proportions. It was not just the quantity of the cases but their astonishing variety that induced dread over my competence to cope intelligently and speedily with them all. There was nothing for it but to plunge in, adrenalin churning.

My week never ended during that first month. I worked every day, slowing to half days only on Sunday, and two or three hours every night Monday through Friday. And through it all the only sound was of my own brain humming. The judge's chambers were the most eerily hushed quarters I had ever occupied, even though there were four of us squirreling around in there. God, how I wanted to whip out a jump rope one lunch hour, climb up on a desktop, and start hopping away for dear life. The debris would have taken days to settle.

At first I was assigned to screen newly filed actions and prepare a memorandum not to exceed two double-spaced pages describing for the judge the issues in dispute, remedies sought, and basis for the claim of federal jurisdiction. The last was especially important; any time I detected suspiciously soft grounds, I was to alert the judge with a red check in the upper right-hand corner of my memo. Those were the ones he liked best. "I'm the guy who invented the expression 'Let's not make a federal case out of it,'" he quipped. "Let 'em exhaust their remedies arm-wrestling with each other." He was less jocular when he picked up on a slight tendency of mine, common among beginning law clerks, to want to put on robes; it took the form, in my case, of judgmental language very subtly favoring one side or the other in my purportedly neutral outline of the issues. "I don't want evaluations—you're not a talent scout," Judge Millis said. "Stick to the claims of both sides. I'm the one who gets paid to weigh the merits." He did not have to tell me twice.

The grind eased up a little after the judge began hearing cases toward the end of September. I watched him in the courtroom when I had an occasional free half hour. He was a bulldog about expediting the legal process. Nothing irked him more than protracted pre-trial skirmishing among rival counsel that he thought intruded unduly on the court's time. "Why don't you fellows go out behind the woodshed and settle this thing?" he would ask occasionally after a fourth or fifth motion for delay of trial. Or when presented with a massive answering brief, he might say, "You fellows don't need a judge—just a bigger typing pool." Once the trial began, he was a whip-cracker all the way.

In time, he moved me up to screening pre-trial motion briefs and appending a note on recommended disposition—my first whiff of temporal authority. While most of the motions were mechanically disposed of, enough were not to teach me the dark arts of procedural legerdemain and how to be a star litigator without ever actually having to go to trial. As I demonstrated competence, and occasionally a flash of something more, at each stage of my apprenticeship, the judge promoted me to the next. At a pleasingly early date, he asked my view on the merits of several cases claiming federal tax refunds, a field in which he knew I had some professional knowledge. He received my recommendations without comment, even incorporated some in his opinions, but never showed me the texts until after they had come from the typist—a plain enough way of saying I shouldn't suffer premature delusions of grandeur. Once, though, I spotted a factual error resulting in a flaw in reasoning, and thereafter was shown all tax opinions in early draft.

Almost unaware, I was sopping up case law like a voracious microfiche. One of my main jobs was to check out the precedent cases with which lawyers love to lard their briefs. On investigation, however, few such cited opinions proved to be on the precise point of law at issue—and even those were wont to contain portions, which counsel of course omitted, at odds with the argument being advanced. The practice struck me as shoddy, even devious. Judge Millis was more tolerant. The adversary system required every lawyer, he said, to put the best possible face on his side of the dispute. It was precisely the court's job to determine when and if the parties were exceeding what the judge airily called "the P.L.D."—the permissible limit of distortion. And so I was the chief distortion-detector there that season, and as a by-product of that surveillance the names and holdings of hundreds of cases got imprinted in my skull against the day any one of them might be summoned to the rescue, like the U.S. cavalry, to help me win a landmark decision from the Supreme Court.

As a farewell project, the judge let me draft an opinion of real substance. Every clerk was given the opportunity before leaving but mine was more engaging than most. Actually, it was racy. The board of selectmen in the little Housatonic Valley village of Buxton Falls was outraged when the owner of the only tavern in town imported three topless belly dancers to improve his weekend business. The board promptly passed an ordinance banning all forms of public nudity, top, bottom, or any combination thereof, on the premises of any commercial enterprise in the community. The language of the law was so erotically explicit that I suspected the village attorney himself of a little lip-smacking prurience, to wit:

(a) "Topless" is defined as less than completely and opaquely covered female breasts below a point immediately above the top of the areola;

(b) "Bottomless" is defined as less than completely and opaquely covered human genitalia; human buttocks, or human pubic area, that being the lower part of the hypogastric region that from puberty on is normally covered with fine, soft, short hairs, whether or not such area is shaven or otherwise depilated.

Whatever the graphic qualities of this small-town Rabelais' pen, to me his handiwork was censorship. Any shapely girl who wanted to twist and twirl to the beat of tasteful timpani before an appreciative assemblage ought to be able to celebrate her bodily glory in said fashion. Wasn't free expression what the First Amendment was all about?

Mother Nature, unfortunately, had not been treated quite so generously by magistrates. Whatever it is people mean to express by taking their clothes off in public, courts and legislatures have long called it indecent and usually penalized it. But how is a living naked body on public display different from a painting of one? How can the original be sinful and its re-creation in oil a work of art? Why is disrobing in a park disorderly conduct but doing it to music in a theater entertainment? Who is expressing what to whom and why? And who is harmed and how? Judges have been befuddled from the beginning in drawing such distinctions. The Supreme Court had not been notably more lucid in laying down obscenity law than any other tribunal, but the Justices had spoken the summer before

I confronted the Buxton Falls case and had at least narrowed the definition of obscene conduct.

In their zeal I decided, the village bluenoses had drawn too broad a law. It is an absolute and outright prohibition, under any and all circumstances, of nude or semi-nude behavior in any public place or on any commercial premises in the municipality," I wrote for the judge. "It is not on its face limited to conduct which is devoid of artistic value, and it does not conform in its definition of obscenity to the guide lines for proscribable conduct articulated by the Court in *Miller*. Under this ordinance, critically acclaimed theatrical works, which include nude or semi-nude performers, would be disallowed. Such a sweeping prohibition of what the eye may behold within any community would appear to be as constitutionally infirm under the First Amendment as a comparable limitation on what a press may publish or a tongue may utter."

And that was how I struck down my first law.

It did not matter that the decree affected directly only a few hundred people in the boonies; in legal circles the opinion would be broadcast across the nation, and the principle it proclaimed the more firmly enshrined. I savored the sensation —the rightness of it, the intellectual satisfaction of it, the hard power of it. My sole regret was that I could not expect to play judge again for some little while.

At the end of the term I was summoned to his chambers by Judge Millis and presented with a thin gold bracelet devoid of decoration. Inside, though, it was inscribed: "TO T.H., A TRUE FRIEND OF THE COURT, WITH ADMIRATION AND GRATITUDE— G.H.M." I told him how terribly glad I was that he had not bounced me out on my rear at the beginning when I questioned his screening procedure. "I'm glad you did," he said. "Your successor is a spendthrift Democrat."

"They're a slippery type," I said, "and you can't be too careful with these young people nowadays—your honor." My throat caught.

He took my hand. "Knock 'em dead out there, Tabor—the way you did me."

I kissed his cheek. He had shepherded me through more

stimulating law in a year than I could have wrestled with almost anywhere else in ten. Then I cleared out my desk and walked five blocks to my new job. There was no one there to hold my hand, and no time—only clients, stacked twenty deep.

4

If I were ever to practice my profession as a ministering skill instead of an abstract science, I could hardly continue to view it as so many dispassionate words on paper, prompting in response from me only other words. A lot of people were running around out there in desperate trouble, and wanting nothing more for the moment than to help, I jumped out of the cookbook, one might say, into the frying pan.

The Legal Assistance Bureau, which described itself as "a private, nonprofit, charitable, membership corporation," was eager to have me. It ate up idealistic young attorneys, paid them next to nothing, worked them to the marrow for as long as they lasted, then shipped the hollowed remains back to the civilian world for rehabilitation or burial. But while you survived, you were in the thick of real combat every minute. And you always knew who the enemy was.

The clients were largely black and Hispanic, all of them poor and most only marginally literate. Few of them looked or sounded or smelled very good, and their woes did little to enhance their characters. Why on earth I should have expected these ignorant, impoverished, malnourished, and essentially hopeless souls to prove more appealing than the comfortable clientele I might have been serving in a commercial practice, I cannot think—unless I had read too many Robin Hood stories as a child and never stopped believing in them. Legend to the contrary, oppression does not often breed nobility in its victims—just anxiety, resentment, and despair. "The most we realistically expect to accomplish here," Arnold Berenson, the Bureau's director and chief attorney, said to me at the beginning, "is to cushion the fall of those trapped in the legal system. You can't remake their lives."

There was about as much heroism in the activities of the Legal Assistance Bureau as there was resemblance between Sherwood Forest and the city we serviced. Once, Amity had been the principal Atlantic port between New York and Boston, but then Amity Bay silted up and the town's glory days of sea-going commerce were done. The coming of the railroads revived the place, and Amity turned into the transportation hub of southern New England. Manufacturers flocked to the environs and tooled up the westering nation. Unpicturesque but bustling to near frenzy, the city made everything imaginable—horse carriages and velocipedes and melodeons, clocks and guns and girdles, fishhooks out of steel and boxes out of paper and boots out of India rubber and cigars out of Connecticut broadleaf. Then the Civil War destroyed half its trade. And other places made clocks and cigars better and cheaper. And the carriage trade moved west. Calamitous fires took their toll as did the flood of goods from Europe. Industry shifted its sweatshops to the union-free South, and Amity wound up an economic cripple by the opening of the twentieth century. It would recover partially whenever the country went to war and the production lines at the still remaining arms and munitions plants picked up their deadly hum. But the war business was not enough to sustain local prosperity, and so joblessness turned chronic, the mills were boarded up or torn down, the downtown shops cut back or went out of business, and the population changed radically. The old-line Protestants and prosperous Italians and Jews fled to Upper Amity and Amity West and a dozen other suburbs ringing the old core, and their places were taken by blacks and Latins with little capital and fewer skills. It was a pattern afflicting almost every old urban center in the East.

But Amity was blessed with a saving difference. It was the home of one of the great centers of learning in the world, a vital repository of civilization's archives—and one rich and proud enough to resist the bacillus of urban blight. Mather

University, founded 1703, was a subcommunity of some twenty thousand students, teachers, secretaries, cooks, janitors, grounds-keepers, private cops, and miscellaneous paper pushers, all needing to be fed, clothed, transported, amused, and otherwise attended to. For me Amity held much of the variety of New York and Boston but in miniature: international cuisine, live theater, unending film festivals, touring concert artists and jazz ensembles, old and new bookshops, art galleries, craft shops, coffeehouses, and hospitals for diseases common and exotic. There were even beaches within easy drive during warm weather and, if you were willing to risk a little hepatitis, a sprinkling of clams and oysters left in the Sound from the days when Amity was the East Coast bivalve capital north of Chesapeake Bay. It was by no means a beguiling place, but its energy, blend of color and speech and outlook, and involvement with the cultivation of the mind made it decidedly metropolitan in mood without the dehumanizing scale of the supercities. Personally, I've always preferred small peaches to big apples.

Given the historic tension between town and gown, Amity understandably refused to settle for deteriorating into a supply depot for Mather and its satellites. At the close of the Fifties, it elected as mayor a native charmer with the unlikely moniker of Bryan Orlando O'Brien, who promptly launched the most massive renewal project undertaken by any city its size in America. Using guile and grit to raise five hundred million dollars of public and private money, O'Brien gutted the worst of the slums, rebuilt the heart of downtown, and put up or helped renovate ten thousand dwellings throughout the city. For the black neighborhoods, there were a few showpiece community centers and day-care facilities, a job-training program, legal and personal counseling services, health clinics, and noisy efforts to combat racial bias in employment—"people programs," Mayor O'Brien had labeled them. Experts came to Amity from all over the country to view O'Brien's miracle. "Our goal is the world's first slumless city," he announced midway through his regime.

At its end, though, the federal money had all but run out,

new industrial development had not materialized, unemployment was rising again steeply as the building boom slowed, and the underside of the city had grown embittered. Most of the changes had been aimed at keeping the white middle class in town; the social programs had been more cosmetic than therapeutic among the hard-core poor. By the time I first came to Amity to work at Mather Psychiatric Center, crime and drugs were of epidemic severity in the slum neighborhoods, social unrest was general, and the law was viewed among the city's destitute principally as an instrument of harassment.

The offices of the Legal Assistance Bureau were in habitual turmoil. The converted five-and-ten that housed the three dozen or so staff people was broken up by partitions, but the sound of aroused voices, jangling phones, and chattering typewriters was forever jumping the inadequate barriers and rattling off the stamped-tin ceiling. It was muggy in the summer and drafty in the winter, the lime-green walls were blistering every few feet, half the fluorescent lights flickered constantly, the desks were dirty and dented, and the coffeemaker turned out something you would feed willingly only to a child molester. But a great deal of legal business was conducted. There was scant time for the sort of craftsmanship I had been trained in but also scant need; boilerplate was adequate for three quarters of the complaints we filed. Most of the other business was transacted by dickering.

The director, "Bad News" Berenson (so called for always predicting the worst possible outcome to any case and thereby minimizing the clients' expectations of a miracle), took one look at my background and shoved me into the front line in the family law section, where the assault was heaviest but most routinized. Within forty-eight hours, I was chin deep in divorce, alimony, paternity, child abuse, child neglect, child custody, and child support cases—and almost always eligibility for welfare ruled all other considerations, especially love.

After a month, I was up to maximum load: fifty active cases, forty dormant ones, and forty-five others under my supervision but delegated to law students and paraprofessionals. Under that sort of pressure, it was a struggle to show courtesy, let alone compassion, to the clients who, all but discarded by proper white society, could hardly wait to tell the woeful story of their lives to a captive proper white ear. There was a touching urgency to the garrulous ones, as if to say they had been beaten up and shaken down and ripped off enough and couldn't I please arrange for a little kinder fate from then on. Five times a day I wanted to robotize myself, avoiding eye contact and shutting them up when they strayed. But I was their lawyer, and part of my job was to restore their dignity. When I was not commiserating, I was flying like a shuttlecock between the office and the city hall annex where the welfare dispensers were installed, impervious to the collective weight of misery I bore. Cleverness was altogether wasted on this crew, so insolent in their studied obtuseness. Only Gandhian patience, politeness shading into ass-kissing, and outright pleading were useful weapons. You would have thought the money was a sacred public trust, the way they hated to part with it.

Before long, I was doubling as Berenson's assistant, supervising briefs in more than routine actions against the power centers who put our clients to the rack. We moved against the city housing authority for leasing apartments at prohibitive rentals to welfare clients; against the utility company for premature shutoff of service to delinquent customers; against the hospitals for failing to make abortions available to poor women at a realistic cost; against retail outlets for garnishing salaries of customers who refused to pay for merchandise that turned out defective; against the municipal department of corrections for the condition of the city jail, especially the women's section (open toilets, leering male guards, lack of medical attention)—against an endless skein of unjust practices. Berenson even put my knowledge of tax law to use by having me draw the final brief in a case the office had been pursuing on appeal for a couple of years. We were arguing that an income-tax refund could not be included in a bankrupt's estate and was properly excludable as a tax-exempt item of wages. I told Berenson I thought it was a poor case, but he had been deep into it for so long that his objectivity had deserted him; he badly wanted to get on the Supreme Court docket and had convinced himself he had a winner. He had lost in federal district court and gone up to the circuit, which merely affirmed; why he thought the Supreme Court would reverse, I couldn't imagine.

"Our briefs have been amateurish—no one's had time," he said. "You do it right."

Flattered as I was and excited over bringing a case that high, I asked Berenson to leave my name off the brief after I had put it in the best possible shape. He chewed me out for my loser mentality, said he had been a lawyer long enough to know the final disposition of any action was unpredictable, and insisted on keeping my name on the papers. Five months later, the Supreme Court declined to take the case. "Bad News" Berenson started calling me "Hardnose Hill" after that.

Most of what I did was nothing so exalted. It was the kind of nuts-and-bolts law I had not known before. I underwent on-the-job training in how to draw up contracts, affidavits, wills; how to draft complaints, answers, and motions, and, after I switched over to the criminal section at the end of the first year, how to move for a change of venue or request a continuance because of unfavorable publicity, how to frame *voir dire* questions to ferret out hostile jurors, how to make an offer of proof or get around the best-evidence rule. Even more practical, I learned how to talk dirty. Not that I cultivated the habit; it just came naturally in surroundings like those, where street talk and gutter language generated an emotional force that fastidious vocabularies rarely communicate. I had never exactly been quarantined from foul language, but it took a liberal education to enrich my deprived upbringing. Dirty bit by dirty bit, I began incorporating scatology into my daily dealings but with a discriminating feel for time and place. Shit, a little locker-room vulgarity among men had always been an accepted, even wholesome, form of fellowship; was I to be denied the same freedom of colorful expression?

My own susceptability to verbal entrapment was tested early. It was a game to the men in court, the judges not least of all, to see whether female lawyers could be flattered or abused into ineffectuality. Those who withstood the assault were quickly admitted to the fraternity; those who came apart were fair game the next time around. I was initiated one morning while seeking a postponement of an evidentiary hearing in a garnishment proceeding in Superior Court. Having briefed the motion and knowing that the better judges preferred to hear oral argument on the high points instead of wading through the papers, I asked to argue the point.

"Oh, Lord, must we?" groaned opposing counsel, a stout courthouse veteran representing a big appliance store that specialized in selling rebuilt refrigerators to blacks at extortionate monthly rates.

"I thought it might facilitate things, your honor," I said.

"It would facilitate things to proceed with the hearing," said my lumpish foe.

"Two of the garnishee's principal witnesses are currently unavailable, your honor."

"Sure, they're in the pokey. You can guess what kind of witnesses those are."

"I was addressing the court," I growled at him.

"Oh-oh, a veritable shrew," he said, lifting his massive behind out of its chair.

"Opposing counsel has a point, Miss Hill," said the judge.

"Better call her *Mizz* Hill, your honor, or she'll threaten us both with a rolling pin," Fatso put in.

The judge never blinked. "How long are your witnesses likely to be—out of circulation, Miss Hill?"

"Sixty days, tops—maybe less."

"Less if she bakes 'em a cake, your honor," Fatso persisted. "Unless she's one of these new women who can't cook."

I could not believe my ears. For the instant I saw no choice but to ignore the needling. The judge continued to. "And you say these are material witnesses, Miss Hill?" he asked.

"Definitely. Last time, I should point out, when Mr. Babcock requested postponement, the witnesses were available—as he no doubt knew."

"Who could resist the renewed pleasure of Miss Hill's company, your honor?"

Clearly the barrage would go on until I countered it. "Your

honor," I said, "counsel is evidently under the impression he is trying out for the *Ziegfeld Follies*. Perhaps the court can remind him they haven't been doing that extravaganza for some years now."

"My, how them ladies lo-o-o-vvve to talk," another courthouse regular sang out in burlesque of a minstrel-show endman. It was threatening to become a gang bang.

"Is your honor inviting audience participation today?" I asked, masking my outrage. "If so, I could phone a friend of mine who's awfully good on the harmonica."

Finally the judge gave a rap of his gavel. "Under other circumstances, Mr. Babcock, I'd be inclined to deny counsel's motion," he began in all sobriety, "but under these circumstances, I'm afraid I have no choice."

"And what circumstances are those, your honor?" Babcock chimed.

"Counsel has better legs than you," said the judge, deadpan.

"Then I'm going out and buy a petticoat, your honor," Fatso threatened.

"Wear it in here," said the judge, brightening his delivery, "and I'll hold you in contempt."

"Just don't hold anything else, your honor—us girls have to stick together."

The merriment was by now universal. It was like being trapped in a Marx Brothers movie and getting stuck with Harpo's lines. All I could do was honk once or twice and join in the merriment. To grouse would have been to surrender. And repartee would have been lost in the crudity of the moment. They were like boarding-school adolescents who had become so used to pulling their puds in private that they had no idea how to behave when the place went co-ed. Other women, I was told afterward, were reduced to tears by the ordeal. I held on, kept my head up, waited for the boors to calm down, and got my motion granted. On the way out I blew Babcock a kiss. He bowed back to me—or began to until the size of him intervened.

What threw me was not the sexual but the subterranean bond that allowed the men to cut each other to pieces in the courtroom and then a few minutes later trade smiles, hand-shakes, and dirty jokes out in the corridors, as if the earlier contest had been no more than pantomime. How can you be strangling somebody and then all of a sudden turn around and throw him a sweaty embrace? I told myself it must be something boys learn growing up and strapping on their oversized jocks and going after one another furiously till the whistle blows and then cheering the other guys afterward no matter how they feel or what the score was. Male radar seems to distinguish readily between temporary antagonists and blood rivals. I myself could no more do that palsy-walsy number after a case than caress a rattlesnake I had just been trying to kill.

It was bad enough when they played the buddy game out of court. One day it happened when court was in session, and they used me as the ball. I had joined Berenson in a discriminatory hiring case, and he was asking the judge's permission for me to participate in the oral argument. "Why, since Miss Hill worked with distinction for Judge Millis last year," said the judge, "I'd be pleased to hear from a young woman of her—her endowments." The man was a master of the sniggering *double-entendre*—Porno Pete, the wired-in young people around the courthouse called him while I was there. He turned to our opposing counsel. "Do you have any objection, Mr. Billings, to a beautiful young lady opposing you here?"

"Only if your honor is partial to her," said Billings.

"In the generic sense," said the judge, "as I am to any and all lovely members of the fair sex."

"In that case," said Billings, "I have no objection. If I had my way, in fact, I'd prefer that Miss Hill appear alone."

Berenson piped up, as if eager to get in the game: "Maybe you could work that out with her in private."

It got a laugh and the case proceeded from there, but it burned me up. I told Berenson afterward. "It was a cheap shot, Arnold. That whole business has no place in a courtroom. You were all like a bunch of teen-agers having a circle jerk over the Playmate of the Month. And I certainly don't expect you, of all people, to demean my status as a lawyer."

"Come off it, Tabor. Everyone was just horsing around."

"At my expense."

"We were complimenting you."

"Bullshit, Arnold. You were talking about me like the prime attraction in a cathouse. I never hear anyone talking about Handsome Harry Honcho, splendidly endowed boy lawyer. Either take me seriously or don't take me at all."

"I have to take you seriously—you're the smartest fucking lawyer in the shop."

"Don't butter me up, Arnold."

"I'm not buttering. I'm trying to get you into bed."

"Oh, Jesus."

That was when I moved over into criminal work.

My clients there were almost all black and all young and all male—and almost all guilty as hell. I spent the better part of a year out of my life plea-bargaining for their dumb asses—just why, I'm still not sure. Partly I was convinced the rest of us were as guilty as these hassled, abandoned, and desperate punks; partly I thought I could save a couple of their lives by getting them out of the jailhouse soul-shredder a little sooner. Just how misdirected my efforts were was suggested delicately to me by one of my more senior criminal defendants, a hospital orderly named Duckett Washburn. "You got your head up your ass, Miss Superfox," he said. "All you are doin' is puttin' the junior dudes back on the street, where there is nothin' good goin' down."

He was a dark, reedy man in his early thirties who had been charged with attempting to steal barbiturates from the hospital dispensary. He wore a sour face when he saw I had been assigned to defend him. I knew that his cousin had done time for taking part in a Panther shoot-out five years earlier and then moved to the Coast, leaving Washburn as one of the last of the aging black militants still in town; leadership of the now mostly amorphous rights movement had reverted to the older moderates and the professional Toms. "Which gives you more grief—my color or my sex?" I asked him.

He gave a small snort. "That's like askin' if I'd rather be gassed or fried to death. It's neck 'n' neck, lady."

I asked him if he knew the song "Woman Is the Nigger of

the World" and whether he believed any of it. He wouldn't say. I asked him whether he didn't think women had been enslaved every bit as much as blacks. He still wouldn't say. I asked him if he didn't suppose the fear of rape was just as universally intimidating to women as the threat of lynching and other condoned violence had been to blacks until people like him and his cousin and Martin and Malcolm had come along.

"What do you know about it?" he said after a minute. "You look like rich people to me—the precious flower of white civilization, growed in some big hothouse."

I had on jeans and a man's pullover sweater. "This is rich?" I asked.

"That is your power-to-the-people disguise, sister. I'll bet you bop down to the Good Will every mornin' for a fresh one."

"Suppose I told you I spent the longest summer of my life scared shitless in the fields of Mississippi trying to talk black farmers into voting—and getting myself kicked and punched and spat on—and told five times a day by snot-faced white trash that I was nothin' but pussy on the prowl to see how many nigger dicks I could blow because I had heard up North how big they were."

His eyes narrowed. " 'Sthat a fact?"

I crossed my arms over my chest. "I didn't say it was a fact. I said suppose I told you that."

"Then I'd say that was the smartest white trash I ever heard of."

"Fuck you," I said and headed for the door.

"Okay, Superfox," he said to my back, "I apologize. I thought maybe they'd send Thurgood Marshall to get me outa here."

For a while it didn't look as if Houdini could spring him. The hospital had had Washburn under suspicion and found the stuff on him when they moved in. But just before the trial was scheduled, a veteran black nurse came forward and said she had given Washburn the drugs and told him to take them to the next ward—a clear violation of hospital rules but no criminal action. His case was dropped.

42

To celebrate, he and his wife, Lenore, had me to dinner in their apartment out in the Gully, the largest black section in the city. Not only had it escaped the attention of the renewal authorities; it was also, despite its exceptional incidence of crime, arson, and garbage, of only the most marginal interest to policemen, firemen, and sanitationmen. Street lights and sewer lines and buses, to cite three of the more common urban amenities, were as scarce there as rose gardens, and the library, the school, and the post office had been neglected nearly beyond repair. A lot of it looked like London after the Blitz.

"Seldom is heard an encouraging word," sang Duckett, leading me through that grim scenery, "and the honkies remain far away." I asked him why he stayed there. "Actually," he said, "I got an application in at one of them condominiums goin' up beside the golf course—they call it the Grand Dragon Towers. You know the one? The doorman, they gonna get him up real nice in a sheet and a pillow case with them peek-a-boo eyes—very deluxe. Only I keep not hearin' from the management. Maybe your office could look into it. I don't like makin' accusations, but some friend told me the sign they got sayin' 'Niggers Keep Out' is wrote in Latin. Now that's the kind of class I want to be associated with, you dig?"

He got four stars for gallows humor. There wasn't much else to laugh at out there. He stayed, he said, because that was his turf and those were his people and someday somehow he was going to see it rebuilt. I said I hoped he was right. He said, "See, there's just one little problem. The government got plenty o' money to hand the Japs and Germans after shootin' their balls off fo' five years, see, so now we are swimmin' in Sony teevees and Panasonic hi-fis and Rabbits and bugs from the Fatherland. And there is billions to piss away chasin' gooks in sneakers through them jungles without nobody knowin' what it is they done to us in the first place, see? But let ol' Uncle Samuel spread a little bread on the needy brothers and sisters here at home and all shit breaks loose. Hell, we the enemy, too. We're entitled. Don't give me more of Lyndon baby's soul number. Just stop leanin' on us and give a hand."

I said I thought the hand had been given. Just the finger, he said. I said there had been a lot of things started. "Drops in the ocean," he said. "Meanwhile, the cities are gettin' blacker all the time but only the superstars get the money, and a whole new crop of kids is growin' without hope that anything real has changed—because nothin' has—so they drop out an' shoot up an' steal an' die young—or might as well."

I said I thought there was more than a little self-pity in what he was saying.

"You're not followin' me," he said. "We got to have the tools. Nobody makes it without the tools. Columbus didn't get nowhere till the queen give him the ships, right? It's like that. We got to have some basics. We got to have roofs over our head that don't leak an' ceilings that no poison paint comes off of. We got to have protein on the table an' clothes on our backs. We got to have some cops who are not on the take—an' some teachers who don't treat our kids like vermin. We got to have sick care without bein' hassled to death to get it. You understand what I'm sayin' to you? First we got to have a little peace o' mind. Second we got to have somethin' to do besides sweepin' up everyone else's shit. Is that so fuckin' much to ask?"

That was the beginning of the end of my career at Legal Assistance. It was plain that, as the guys say in the bunkhouse, I was pissing into the wind—laboring at the wrong end of the social process, trapped nearly as inextricably as my clients, and getting goddamned discouraged by it. The case load, moreover, was unbearable, and the quality of my work had tailed off accordingly. Try as I might, I could no longer pretend that I was performing a noble service by defending kids who, however understandably provoked, had turned into brutes. Vicious crime, even in vengeance against your tormentors, is not a justifiable way of life.

I confided in Judge Millis. "I think you've done your time," he said. "If you're not afraid of the idea of making an honest buck, I'd give my friend Maynard Lamport a call. His firm is looking for someone young and first-rate."

"And female?"

"He didn't put it to me quite that way."

"Then how?"

"I think he said, 'It could even be a woman.' Maynard's a little behind the times."

5

"I'm sorry for the delay," he said, not especially sounding it. "It was one of those things that couldn't be helped—a client died. They're doing that to me more and more."

I said I understood and was sorry. What was a wait of forty-five minutes compared to the passage to eternity? The corpse, on the other hand, had less cause for impatience than I, but it plainly would not have been politic to suggest as much. Maynard Lamport's lean, elliptical face, though more weary-looking than stern, was not a countenance that invited playfulness. He was all bones and joints and angles that badly wanted oiling and had not an ounce of flesh to spare beyond a modest wattle. His shoulders sloped so obliquely that they imperiled the straps of his decidedly unfashionable suspenders.

At first I thought it odd that a man of his age, bearing, and eminence would work in shirtsleeves, but it was warm out for a spring day and there was no air-conditioning I could see. Several of the windows were open and the curtains stirred peaceably. The room had an intimacy that survived its conversion from what had apparently been the mansion's master bedroom suite. The antique furnishings—a brass-cornered campaign desk with a strutted Windsor armchair behind, a painted yellow rocker, a maple cabinet that looked like Hepplewhite, a pair of wing chairs embroidered in flame stitch, a gateleg table in front of the fireplace—were almost certainly collector's pieces. The walls had been done in a soft sand color and fitted out with Audubon prints framed in beechwood. The obligatory diplomas, certificates, and licenses of his trade had been tastefully exiled to a far corner. Informal, though, would not be quite the word for the setting or the man. His serious gray suit jacket was stretched across the back of his desk chair as if ready to be donned instantaneously from a sitting position, should pressing occasion arise. I, apparently, was not such an occasion.

"Now that's something they don't teach at law school," he was saying. "Funeral arrangements. Every lawyer ought to take a crash course. I seem to spend half my week these days burying widows and executing their wills. Damned dreary business it is, too, especially when the survivors live out of town, show up late for the burial, and then bark at me for not having put mother to rest in the best damned casket money can buy. They figure that's the least they could have done for her, which is precisely what they had in mind. A lot of difference it makes to mother. If I had my choice, I'd put 'em all away in a pine box —that's what I've ordered. Simplicity and humility in the face of the inevitable, eh? Trouble is, I also represent half the damned undertakers in town, and if I don't order their A-number-one bronze sarcophagus, they think I'm Ralph Nader or some other wild-eyed defiler of the sanctuary. Half the times I'm tempted to take my business to Potter's Field."

"Not much of a client, I shouldn't think."

"Who's not?" he asked, looking at me directly now as if I had summoned him from a deep interior monologue.

"Potter's Field."

"No," he said, "I suppose not." I would not win him with tasteless whimsy. He reached for a folder with the material I had sent him and flipped it open. "A Farmington gal, I see," he announced approvingly. His forbears had been active abolitionists in their day, he said, and had directed more than one runaway slave to our town, a prominent station on the Underground Railroad. He wondered whether any of the blacks of the antebellum era had remained and put down roots. None that I knew of, I said. "Hartford's overflowing with their progeny," he said. "And we're not doing much better."

"You make it sound like the plague," I said.

"It is," he said. "I don't mean the people—I mean the problem."

"They didn't invent it themselves."

"I'm not suggesting they did. But they might take a more active part in overcoming it, don't you think?"

Those who were equipped were doing so, I said. "We seem to resent equipping more than a handful at a time, though. I'm afraid it's going to take generations that way."

"Why," he asked, "if you harbor such deep feelings on the subject, are you turning your back on these unfortunates? I gather you've done a great deal in their behalf at Legal Assistance."

"I've done my job, that's all—I'm not suffering from a Schweitzer complex. I don't want to spend my career serving a cause. I prize my individuality too much—and my professional aptitude too much, if you'll forgive me—to submerge them that way."

"In short, Miss Hill, you want to do your own thing, if I may be so inelegant?"

"In short, yes."

"That's good," he said. "Then you understand, I trust, we are not in business primarily to save the world? Some of our clients are very much capitalist exploiters, I'm afraid."

"I've heard."

"Does that bother you? You've been devoted, after all, to advancing the cause of truth and justice. Here you'd be paid to promote the personal advantage of the client, however admirable or loathsome. Might that not be demoralizing—or are you counting on the money to ease the pain?"

Subtle he was not, but he was fully justified in raising the point at once. Most women lawyers were not in it for the money or power; he had to find out early if I meant business. "I suppose there'd be a little transitional agony," I said, "but I don't really divide the world into good guys and bad guys. Everybody is some of both." It came out sounding rehearsed.

"Let me venture a thought that might reduce the agony somewhat." He flew out of the chair like a bundle of sticks and collected himself upright. "I do not hold myself responsible for the moral or social views of my clients. My services are not purchased to improve the buyer's chances of getting into heaven. Now that reality can prove a somewhat joyless taskmaster on occasion, but there is a compensating aspect to the work here, Miss Hill. Once you have taken on a client or a case, no matter how unbecoming, you are personally committed to the outcome. It is a test of your professional competence to prevail. The trial is never about some indifferent matter to the lawyer but always concerns himself—that's how Plato put it. It's your head on the chopping block, not just some blackguard's you'd as soon see done in. That way there's a constant challenge in the job and the obligation to yourself to perform with maximum craft—and guile if need be."

So all that was required to assure one's advance was a certain degree of insulation from the sons of bitches who paid the bill. "It's mostly a matter of discipline, I gather."

"That," he said, entwining his knobby hands and resting the cluster on the top of his chair, "and the conviction that you have a transcendant duty to provide your client with prudent counsel even when that requires placing his or her interest above those of the collective whole."

"My client, right or wrong—is that it?"

"It is," he said. "The wrong may need the counsel most. No doubt you discovered as much representing that unlovely bunch at Legal Assistance. The clients you'd encounter here are not as poor but otherwise no less deserving."

"But I didn't prosper from my clients' sins at Legal Assistance—I only tried to mitigate their effect. Isn't feeding on their low character somewhat venal?"

"It is—in the sense that every mercenary is, by definition, for hire. But the quality of a prostitute's services, if you will forgive me, is not judged more or less admirable according to whether her customer is an Eagle Scout or homicidal maniac. The venality rests in her purchasability. What saves her and us alike —us, more so, I should think—is the freedom to accommodate whom we choose and not every villain who walks in the door."

I asked if I, even as a newcomer, would have that freedom. He said surely, provided only that the client pay the fees and did not soil the furnishings. That left open the matter of poor clients who sought but could not afford my services. Did the firm have a policy on work *pro bono publico*—for the public good?

"Yes," he said. "No more of it than we need to salve our consciences."

I said I thought that seemed a bit stonehearted. "Even the crustiest Wall Street firms have been taking on a limited amount of *pro bono* work."

"The Wall Street shops operate on a rather higher profit margin than we—and presumably have more conscience-salving to do."

He was not without humor, just extraordinarily undemonstrative about it, as if the full weight of his Puritan ancestry would fall upon him the moment he favored an expression brighter than midnight. The firm would agree to release fifteen percent of my time to work with *pro bono* clients, he said, "in recognition of the legal community's civic obligations. But if you abused this arrangement—by putting in unbilled time after hours—you would be shortchanging both the firm, Miss Hill, and yourself. I say this not out of suspicion about your questionable character but from fear it is rather too elevated to pursue the profit motive with abandon." There was a difference, too, he noted, between my taking on clients who could pay nothing and those who could pay something but not the full fees. "As to your apparent strength in tax law," he added, "we would intend to make heavy use of it in the trusts and estates area, where I have been doing the bulk of the hard labor for the firm—and frankly, I'm growing a little weary of it. It is not exciting work, and I won't pretend otherwise. It just happens to be a mainstay of our prosperity. If you wish to share in that prosperity, you would naturally be expected to contribute to it."

Just how sharply that prosperity might alter my professional orientation was made dramatically clear when he mentioned the starting salary the firm was prepared to pay if the position were in fact offered to me: It was three times as much as I was earning at Legal Assistance, not counting such fringe benefits as group health insurance, a secretary, and a clean toilet.

Only one matter remained for him to explore with me. He did so with courtliness. "I hope you will forgive my antediluvian outlook," he said, "but I would be dishonest with you, and disloyal to the firm, not to broach the question of marriage and motherhood with an attractive woman in the full bloom of youth. The last thing I want to do is invade your privacy, but members of a relatively small law firm such as ours are subject to a certain degree of intimacy with one another in their daily dealings. In this case, I would be less than candid if I didn't admit our hiring practices have been ruled by a reluctance to take on skillful young women only to see their ambitions consumed by familial duties. Now I hardly demean that preference. It's simply a fact of life we can't ignore. The only woman now with us is a senior associate who joined us on a part-time basis seven or eight years ago in the trust department." He moved to the side of the desk and perched his bony behind on a corner. "I think you have my drift."

"You mean are my intentions honorable?"

There was the slightest twitching at the corners of his mouth as if he were struggling to suppress even the hint of a smile. "Well put," he said.

"I'm not celibate," I acknowledged, "if there was any question of that."

"Quite the contrary. It makes the subject I raise the more pressing."

I took a deep breath. "Well, I suppose I will marry some day," I said, "but it's not a project I'm actively pursuing. I value my independence and will not yield it to mere romance. Any man who wanted to marry me would have no doubt that my life could not be subsumed in his. By that token, babies are not a consummation for which I devoutly wish. If one materialized, I would arrange for its care and not conduct my life around its. My intention is to become a perfectly splendid lawyer at the earliest possible moment. I'll do whatever I must to get there—short of traveling horizontal."

He nodded and then massaged his jaw for a moment. "May I ask if you are presently—keeping company?"

"I am."

"Is it—serious?"

"The man and I have shared the place for about six months. I would call it a warm and open relationship."

"I'm afraid I don't know what 'open' means in that context."

"Candid—relaxed—unstructured. We go our separate ways when and as we like. I would give it another month or two, at a guess. But there will be no shattered pieces to pick up, if that helps answer your question."

"After a fashion," he said. "But it raises another one. Marriage can and usually does disrupt a young woman's professional life. I should think it would also bring emotional stability to it. However dedicated to your work you may be, Miss Hill, the heart, too, is a demanding client."

"Any man attracted to me rapidly discovers that I already have a consuming passion—and one intractable master is about my limit. That narrows my field for romantic involvement to a quite self-contained sort of man, confident enough of himself not to require a servile consort."

"I see," he said. But I did not think he saw at all. Had I said too much too soon? He followed with a probe to test the stridency of my feminism. "As a matter of curiosity, Miss Hill, can you tell me what you think an appropriate wardrobe for a woman attorney? This, I take it, is your normal outfit—surely you didn't put on your most decorous clothes to ease any lingering chauvinism among us neanderthals?"

Hester Prynne in the depths of her penance was hardly more somberly dressed than I. Probably (to be honest) because I have a presentable pair of legs, I am partial to skirts and jackets in my professional tailoring, except in winter when I wear pants, good gabardine or twill ones. For this occasion I had on an oxford-gray blazer, a white silk blouse with a touch of lace at the throat and cuffs, a tweed skirt, and plain black pumps with a nothing buckle. It was what I wore, except at home when I lived in jeans and men's button-down shirts. Thus, I told Lamport in all honesty, "Certainly not. This is about what I wear generally, although in court I like to add a flower to my buttonhole."

"Not a chrysanthemum, I trust?"

I smiled appreciatively. "I save the flamboyance for my delivery."

He nodded. "Well, then, no pants for you, is it?"

"I beg your pardon?"

"Pants, Miss Hill—you don't wear pants, you wear skirts and even dresses, I suppose?"

"I do have a dress but I never wear it. In fact, I don't remember what color it is. As to pants, I own several pairs."

"Would you wear them in here, Miss Hill?"

"I might, in the cold weather. I hadn't considered the matter. Is it important?"

A rasping sound came from his throat. "I don't know," he said. "I was wondering if such a get-up might not prove a distraction to clients."

"Odd," I said. "I've been told my legs are actually something of a distraction. Perhaps I should try metal braces and a wheelchair?"

He still wouldn't smile. I wondered if he were toothless. "Some of our clients are likely to be troubled by the novelty of a woman lawyer, Miss Hill. A woman in pants simply compounds the problem."

"You think it inappropriate, sir, for a woman to wear pants?"

"It's a matter of time and place, Miss Hill. One wears a revealing bathing suit on the beach, not to a church supper. How would you expect my clients to react if I were to show up here in a skirt?"

"I suppose," I said, "it would depend on how well you looked in it."

For a long, frosty moment, he sat there expressionless. Then he broke into a thrillingly toothy grin and laughed like hell.

They paraded me down the firm's letterhead—an encouraging sign since I never would have got beyond Lamport if he had taken an active dislike to me. I had tried to show him both respect and backbone; after all, I was not presenting myself as a recruit for dusting off the books. In return, he had shown me a pleasing if astringent vibrancy and authentic majesty that appeared unneedful of bluster to reinforce its sway.

Daniel Everett Kettering was another matter.

Where Lamport was brisk and sinewy, his younger cohort seemed under attack by suet in both body and mind. A torso that had once been muscular was fighting a losing battle against the encroachments of time and indulgence. Everywhere around the office there were mementos of his rugged forays of yore—a picture of him as a Marine, a photo of the 1948 Dartmouth football team, a mounted swordfish big enough to cut down a redwood, and a shelfload of golf and tennis trophies, plaques, and assorted bric-a-brac attesting to his prowess as a jock. His scalp, which I knew to be fifty-one years old, was sleekly black, suggesting the presence of a rug or heavy applications of Grecian Formula. His suit was cut too severely for his shape, his birdman glasses were too modish for his profession, and his language suffered from an excess of slang that suggested a doomed resolve to get with it.

His father, Kettering explained to me, and Lamport's had established the firm in the early Twenties and built it well and swiftly until the elder Lamport moved to the state bench "and everyone thought of this as Clark Kettering's shop after that." He folded his hands behind his head. "Dad was a great old bird. He wore plus fours on the golf course till the day he died. Taught me the game when I was ten. Wouldn't talk to me for two days the first time I beat him." He brought his reverie down from the ceiling and gave me a close look for the first time. "You don't happen to play?"

"Only bad tennis," I said. "Mostly I walk a lot."

"Tennis is my game. We'll have to get you on the court and check out this false modesty of yours."

"The truth is I'm only half-bad. Nice ground strokes, steady serve, fair anticipation—but no guts at the net. I'm afraid I'm going to get the thing rammed down my throat."

That got him philosophizing about how courage under fire in any sort of combat was mostly a matter of steeling yourself against the peril by assuming the other side was just as scared. "It's all a matter of believing in yourself." I agreed with that, I said, only there are times when it's hard to. The boys who fought in Vietnam, I suggested, were a case in point.

"If the country had supported the military wholeheartedly, Vietnam would have been an entirely different ball game. The flower children did us in, if you want my opinion. I'm afraid your generation had such easy pickings when it was growing up

53

that nobody in it believes the world is full of people who would just as soon see our whole set-up totaled."

"I don't really think you can blame anything on the kids—except the courage it took to tell the grown-ups they were losing their way."

"All the grown-ups lost, if you ask me, is control over their kids. We spoiled 'em rotten and turned 'em into potheads. There's no sense of authority left—nobody's held in respect, no person, no institution, not even money."

"Authority," I said, "is not a divine right in a democracy, Mr. Kettering. It's got to be earned. When it's used corruptly, it deserves to be hated, not respected. The only thing the people I went to school with thought Vietnam was preventing was a slump in corporate profits."

His large, fleshy face looked somber. "Different strokes for different folks, I guess. Me, I still love this country. There's never been any place like it. If everybody keeps knocking it, though, we're going to go down the tube before our time."

His country had suffered massive schizophrenia and a dozen other psychic dislocations from a hopeless war halfway around the world, urban guerrillas, political assassination, Watergate, rampant crime on its streets, violence in its media, inflation, depression, polluted skies, soiled beaches, bacterial waterways, shattered privacy, gross pornography, and the disclosure of a new cancer-breeding chemical every month, and this big lug still saw everything as black or white and good guys trying to beat off bad guys. "The only way to save it," I said, "is to face up to its excesses and deficiencies. Why assume that anyone who favors fixing the system is a less loyal or loving citizen than you are?"

He rolled his eyes upward, as if to say what a far-outnik this one was, and finally got us off into talk about the law and how the firm functioned. Maynard Lamport dealt with the dowagers, the doctors, the clergy, the idle rich, and the First Amity Bank. Kettering himself concentrated on real estate, superintending a couple of hundred closings a year that ranged from a twenty-thousand-dollar cottage to a thousand-acre industrial tract. "Sparky Grier's our resident politician," he continued, "and the only Democrat in the house—at the moment." But Grier was not precisely a red-hot radical; he functioned primarily as the conduit between the business community and the local Democratic bureaucracy, which had been in power more or less steadily since the Depression. Sam Nightingale was the office tweed, handling a large part of what legal business Mather University conducted locally as well as individual clients in the intellectual and artistic community. "He's so thick with the college crowd," Kettering said with a chuckle that sought to charm, "he's got ivy growing up the side of his desk." The youngest partner, Gilbert Serini, was the firm's way of recognizing that the ethnic composition of the area had changed significantly in recent years and with it the deployment of wealth. "Gil must represent half the legitimate Italian businesses in town—restaurants, building contractors, Bonaventura's supermarkets, that sort—plus a fair amount of *pro bono* civic and church work. Helluva nice guy." For a dago, he meant.

When I got to Earl Grier's office, he was busy conjuring on the phone about some kind of building-code variance. He motioned me to sit and held up his index finger to say he'd be just another minute. There was small mystery why he was called Sparky. His short auburn hair must have been flaming red in his younger days, and his small, deep-set eyes darted around in a sea of still prominent freckles. More than his ruddiness, though, seemed to have prompted the nickname. I sat listening to him poke and probe and parry while he alternated between dragging intently on a cigarette and manufacturing an elastic cat's cradle with a heavy-duty rubber band. And when the cigarette went out, he did a little discreet chewing on the rubber band.

"Yeah," he said to me after hanging up, "I didn't want that to go so long—and to make matters worse, I've got a meeting in our conference room in about ten minutes."

"Why don't I come back some other time when things are a little less hectic?"

"I don't think so. This is the slowest day I've had in weeks."

"Sounds a little frenzied."

"Not really—I'm pretty efficient most of the time."

"Just hopelessly overcommitted?"

He gave a nod and half-grin of concession, then reached for my background folder and flipped through it swiftly. "You seem to have excelled at whatever you've done," he said. "I can't think why you shouldn't be a big asset around here." And he shut the folder. Biff-bam-boom.

"If I understand the protocol," I said, "I have to be invited first."

"I wouldn't lose much sleep over that. We don't see many candidates with your credentials—that's one reason we do very little hiring. We'd all rather work a little harder than bring in mediocrities." He pushed my folder to the side, as if I was business already disposed of, but then had an afterthought. "How's your character?"

I found it a peculiar question to put to someone directly. It was unanswerable. Maybe that was why he asked it. "Innocent till proven guilty," I said, unable to think of something better.

"No, I'm serious."

"I don't go out of my way to kick stray dogs, if that's what you mean."

"That's good," he said. "Ever rob any banks, deal in drugs, or bomb the ROTC office at college?"

"I have never robbed anything, I have smoked grass on one or two occasions—and I went to a women's college that had no ROTC unit, but if it had, I would have been sorely tempted."

He grinned easily. "I see you and Dan Kettering are going to need a permanent peace-keeping force to get along." Then he ran a hand through that trim red corona of his and grew contemplative for a moment. "I've seen you argue a couple of motions in court, Miss Hill," he said. "You're good. A touch arrogant, maybe, but that's better than tiptoeing around like a bashful bride. I hope you'll get into litigation here. I need some help, for one thing. And even though the firm pretends it's allergic to courtrooms, more and more legal business is being generated that way. Every time somebody gets a splinter now, they're ready to sue the lumber company for ten million dollars. But let me offer you one small, serious piece of guidance, Miss Hill, if and when you join us. Don't embarrass the firm."

"I'm not sure I understand."

"I'd guess that, based on your background, you're going to want to handle a lot more *pro bono* work than my partners imagine. You're still young enough to think you're Joan of Arc —and maybe you damned well are. But you're not going to ingratiate yourself around here by turning the place into a one-woman legal defense fund for the grievously afflicted."

Sparky was a shrewdie, all right. No wonder he conspired with politicians half the day. "You mean I ought to do enough *pro bono* work to stay clear of purgatory but not enough to get into heaven without appealing all the way up?"

"That's about it," he said. "Seraphim make lousy partners."

"I'll remember that."

He left with me to go to his meeting and made a fleeting introduction to Gil Serini, the firm's junior partner, who said he wanted to say hello at least before heading off to a closing he could not avoid. "I read your piece on custody," he said. "First time anyone ever said not every mother is a Madonna." A rumpled man in his mid-thirties, hair tousled, tie askew, suit in need of a pressing, he emitted a boyish effervescence even that late in the afternoon. "Good luck," said Serini. "I hope we see you here."

"Thanks," I said. "Happy closing."

"They're all happy—as long as we get paid." And off he bounded.

I was down to the final partner.

Samson Nightingale was sleepy-eyed by the time I reached his office. That was a change from the last time I had seen him, striding angrily across the first-floor foyer after chewing out the librarian.

"Did you ever get your book?" I asked.

He looked defensive. "Yes," he said. "I'm afraid I got a little hot under the collar."

"Boiling, I'd say."

"I'm actually a pretty phlegmatic sort, but I had a brief due in court by five and was cutting it awfully close."

"The way I hear it," I said, "is that you enjoy picking on the help."

There was a second's hesitation while he decided I was kidding. I saw his eyes scan over me. The rest of his face was unremarkable, almost putty-like in its bland impassivity, as if it were waiting for age and adversity to etch character lines upon it. But the eyes were full of life when stimulated; they were large and hazel and wide apart and seemed to delve with an intense fixity that said there was a powerful presence operating behind them that could see farther and deeper than most mortals. "Well," he said, "all kinds of rumors spread when you carry a whip in your briefcase."

I smiled at being outquipped, and he asked me how I liked the physical arrangement of the offices. I said if he wanted my real opinion, I thought the firm's layout and decor were just grand "except for the first-floor waiting room—unless, of course, you're all in love with fraternity-house Victorian."

"I don't get in there very often, I'm sorry to say. A bit oppressive, is it?"

"All it made me think of was scurvy and hardtack."

"Perhaps you can do it over for us."

"I don't do rooms, Mr. Nightingale—I inhabit them."

He stretched the lower portion of his face in mock sorrow. "Forgive my impetuosity, Miss Hill. Some women, you know, actually excel in the decorative arts."

"Some men, too."

"But you were so forthright I thought perhaps you had some special competence in the area."

"Only ordinary good taste and refinement."

"In that case you'll be pleased to know that room contains about the finest collection of nineteenth-century maritime prints in the nation. The firm has standing offers from the Fogg and the Atheneum to sell it for a tidy sum."

"The firm ought not hesitate to allow the public to share in such a treasure."

He laughed and said it was plain I was a woman of strong convictions. Then he pulled a tobacco pouch out of his jacket, a muted green-brown herringbone, and filled his pipe in silent ritual for a moment that allowed him to retake command of the interview. "Tell me, Miss Hill," he said, "why does a spirited young woman like you want to work at a stuffy place like this—or perhaps you've seen enough of us by now to decide you'd rather not?"

"On the contrary," I said.

"Then what's the attraction? I understand that the money and perks have their appeal, but it's hard for me to believe they're decisive."

"Why? Is it odd for anyone to want to earn as much and work in as pleasant surroundings as possible?"

"No, not at all. It's just relatively rare that I hear of a woman attorney who's more interested in the plumbing end of the law business than the—what shall we call it?"

"The do-good part?"

"I was thinking of something like 'social improvement.' Yours has a negative bite to it."

"Isn't that what you wanted?"

"No, I'm not putting it down. I'm just genuinely curious when somebody breaks out of the mold."

"More would if the bars weren't so thick. Women work where they can, not where they choose. Money means power, and men aren't eager to share it."

"And is that what you want?"

"Certainly. I don't want to tilt at windmills for the next forty years."

"But you could go to work for the government or a foundation and try to shape things that way. Why this office? Nobody walks around here worrying particularly about how to benefit society."

"And why should I? Because I'm a woman? Don't tell me—man's the adventurer, woman's the nurturer, so any woman who's not literally stuck in the nursery should figuratively be out there being nursemaid to the world, right?"

"Look," he said, "I'm not trying to debate with you. I'm just wondering if you fully understand what motivates an operation like ours. In the beginning, at least, you'd have to do what you were asked. And most of that is making fat cats fatter. Is that how you want to put your brains and heart to work—helping clients use the law to the prejudice of the weak—or turn out plastic products nobody needs?"

He was plainly testing me. To respond with more conviction than I felt, I invoked the words of that revered counselor to the overprivileged—Maynard Lamport. "So long as a lawyer provides wise and faithful service," I said, "his or her clients' motives are entirely secondary. My commitment is to the quality of counsel I give. Why am I responsible for the social or moral values of my client? That's what divines are for."

His eyes started cauterizing me again. It was not a comfortable sensation. "You're telling me what you think I want to hear, Miss Hill," he said. "That's not good enough."

"I'm suggesting you may have been brainwashed into thinking all women lawyers ought to behave like Girl Scouts but it's okay for the fellas to pretend they're mean bastards since everyone knows law is only a game they're playing and after showers they'll all be good buddies again."

"All right," he said. "Can you play the game mean enough?"

"You bet your ass—Mr. Nightingale, sir."

His eyes flinched. "No matter what uniform you get assigned?"

"So long as it fits."

"And you think you can really escape moral responsibility for your legal activities when the clients you willingly align yourself with here are the most powerful and self-seeking elements in society?"

"No one says I have to represent hateful clients."

"Not all tyrants wear swastikas on their arms."

"Not everyone with power is a villain. A lot of despots are benevolent."

"Until the going gets rough."

"That's true of everybody. I've seen a lot of unpleasant poor people."

"They're unpleasant because they're getting their behinds kicked in by our clients, Miss Hill. It's something called survival of the fittest."

"What is it you want me to say—I'm selling out because I want to be with the winners?"

"Are you?"

By now it was evident that this frontal challenge was a basic part of the screening process. None of the other partners had done much more than exchange pleasantries with me; Sam Nightingale was the resident heavyweight. It was essential that I not become overheated. "I'd prefer not to dignify a loaded question with a direct answer," I said.

"You loaded it," he said. "I aimed it."

I eased out of my chair. "Do you mind if I walk and talk at the same time? My head needs the ventilation—I've been at this for a few hours now." He waved approval. "All right," I said as I paced, "let me be straight about it. Corporate law firms have powerful clients who didn't get that way by being Mr. Nice Guy—I understand all that. And that means you've got to do some dirty work if you join them. But their power and money mean the law practiced at a firm like this can be genuine craftsmanship—there's enough time and enough bodies and a high enough level of expectation. The kind of work that gets turned out here becomes the standard of the profession. It gets relied upon by judges and legislators and government administrators. And there's the opportunity for continuing relationships with the sort of people making the big decisions out there. I'd like to help shape those decisions from the start—that's how you change society, not just by reacting to as many instances of injustice as you can cope with that day. Sure, I want to be with winners, but real winners in my book don't gloat over the losers—they try to ease the pain. Real winners understand that if they don't try to spread their wealth and well-being, the lower orders are going to rise up one morning and beat their bloody brains in. I'd view it as one of my primary functions here to urge the practice of enlightened self-interest on the clients. To the extent I succeeded, I'd be relieving the subjugated masses, not just arming the willful exploiters. In the process of serving as this sort of farsighted intermediary, I'd get to use my skills creatively and be amply rewarded for it." I dropped back into my chair. "The defense rests."

He expelled a small cloud of sweet smoke and let it dissipate. "That's better, Miss Hill," he said. "I'll buy at least fifty-one percent."

"But I mean it all."

"Oh, I don't doubt it. I was commenting on its validity, not your sincerity."

"You think I'm a little naive?"

"I think you're rationalizing extra hard. The history of human behavior is against you. People in power rarely reform their ways willingly."

"I didn't mean I expect them to be thrilled doing it. It's a matter of seeing the handwriting on the wall."

"They'd rather buy the wall and slap posters over the writing. It may not be pretty, but it sure as hell relieves anxiety."

I shrugged. "Let's just say I don't accept the flat-out notion that I'm selling myself to irredeemable malefactors of wealth. Let's say I'm seeking a position to serve society by raising the consciousness of those who really run it."

"Even if they don't appreciate the favor?"

"Especially. They'd be the first ones to have their heads put on pikes if the revolution comes. I'm trying to stave off the revolution."

"Dan Kettering will be glad to hear that."

"I'm afraid I came over to him as a bit of a bomb thrower."

"But he likes your spunk—he's already had a word with me." He let his gaze drift up the wall behind me. "It's Maynard who's afraid you may be too high-powered for us."

It came without warning. I thought they might wait at least until I was out of the building before dissecting me. My face must have shown the surprise. I did my best to cover. "Like Tugboat Annie?" I asked with a mechanical smile.

"More she than Little Orphan Annie, I think he means."

"Was Orphan Annie whom you people had in mind?"

"Not at all," he said.

"Then why tell me that? It sounds like you're reading me my rights before I get booked. I didn't know I'd have to defend myself for—for being myself. And I don't think I'm going to. You've got my background there on paper, and seventy-three character references or however many there are, and I've spoken up frankly and fully here all afternoon. If that doesn't please you gentlemen, then—then it doesn't. But I'm not going to pretend to be what I'm not. They sell lollipops in the candy store."

"Miss Hill," he said, chill creeping into his voice, "I didn't tell you that as criticism. I told you because I think you'd be an asset around here."

I managed a half-smile. "But why tell me—Mr. Lamport is evidently the one who needs convincing."

"Miss Hill, I'm trying to gauge your character, not outwit you. My primitive way of doing that is to provoke you and see how you respond. Do you understand?"

I must have been under more tension than I had realized. All at once and more than anything, I wanted to cry my fucking eyes out. For half a dozen years I had been competing my butt off against men, one way or another, and worn my tough-cookie persona like a wetsuit, knowing that otherwise they'd ship me off for life to wash dishes. And now here was this perfectly pleasant guy calling me on it, charging me in effect with having overdone the number. Maybe he was right. Maybe I had lost something permanently. Maybe that was the only way. And maybe that was why I wanted to cry.

"Yes, thank you," I said after collecting myself. "I gather he means too high-powered for a woman."

"He didn't say. That might be a fair surmise, though."

"Would he be happier if I had curtsied? I thought of it, actually."

"He'd be happier if you weren't living in sin."

"No-o-o," I said. It came out a groan.

"I'm afraid so," he said.

"He thinks I'm a loose woman?"

"He thinks you are fornicating, Miss Hill. You told him so."

"Doesn't he do things like that? Surely in his time he must have—now and then, at least?"

"Mr. Lamport—I'm conjecturing now, mind you, since he isn't the sort to confide in these matters—Mr. Lamport copulates, he does not fornicate. Fornication is illicit. Copulation is —well, however great an ordeal it may seem for him, it is sanctioned by heavenly and temporal authority. Your activity, Miss Hill, is not."

"If you'll forgive my indelicacy, Mr. Nightingale, screwing is screwing."

"Mr. Lamport and the Pope, to cite two authorities at random, think otherwise."

"Which of them would you suppose is more sexually active?"

"Mr. Lamport. He has a most alluring wife."

"More's the pity," I said. "Look, Mr. Lamport thinks pants on a woman are a sin."

"On a woman he respects."

"Would he respect me more if I were chaste?"

"That or married. I think he'd be less concerned. Cohabitation is often associated with emotional volatility."

"And marriage isn't?"

"It implies a certain reconciliation of differences."

"I think Mr. Lamport thinks that if I sleep with one man I'm not married to, I'd sleep with any."

"Maybe. Or he may think that would be at the back of other people's minds—clients, for instance."

"Does anyone give the matter a second thought when an unmarried man is the subject?"

He shrugged. "I suppose not. We have a couple of them around here."

"Then I'm being told single women have lower characters than single men. That's actionable."

"I'm speaking informally."

"But honestly. A single woman is a temptress. A single man is a sport. Isn't that what it comes to?"

"Well—"

"Forgive me, Mr. Nightingale, but that stinks. Besides, whom I sleep with is my business."

"I don't believe Mr. Lamport asked you. He says you volunteered it."

"After a fashion. I was trying to be responsive."

"That may have been one degree more candor than you were called on for."

"I was indiscreet?"

"I would say so."

"What do you think he would have said if I told him I also smoke cigars?"

"Do you?"

"Occasionally. Schimmelpennincks, when I'm sweating out a brief. They're quite slender and elegant, actually. And never more than one a day."

"Well, I wouldn't go out of my way to demonstrate in my first week here, if I were you."

"Am I going to have a first week?"

He looked coy. "Unless I vote no."

"Don't."

He laughed. "You *are* a little high-powered."

"It's a defense mechanism, if you want the truth. I'm actually nervous as hell."

"You just fooled four of the better lawyers in town."

6

If my initial value to the firm could have been gauged by my proximity to the senior partner's desk, I was worthless.

They stationed me in a double office on the third floor, next to the men's john. The ignominy of exile was mitigated by several factors. For one thing, nobody but partners and their secretaries occupied the second floor. All of us underlings, including Alva Potter, the crotchety ex-alcoholic ex-attorney who functioned as the officer manager, and Estelle Pinkham, the fiftyish house authority on trusts and estates and the only other female attorney ever to grace the firm, were shoved upstairs. Our tight offices flanked what was once the mansion's ballroom and now served to house client records, photocopying equipment, bookkeeping, and the snack bar (duly renowned for its runny tuna-and-egg-salad sandwiches and tepid but palatable coffee). My officemate, an earnest young fellow named Stephen Balakian, in his fourth year with the firm, was no slouch, to judge by the volume of work that crossed his desk. Most of it was real estate and negligence, not very stimulating fare, as he himself announced every morning, but it was bread-and-butter business that he handled expeditiously and thereby earned steady advances in pay—of paramount consideration to a guy in his early thirties with a wife he wanted to please and a new baby. Continued perseverance could well earn him a partnership in three or four years and a ticket to lifetime security, even if he failed to establish himself as an authoritative presence or to bring in important new business. Low-level volume alone, though, might stamp him as strictly a functionary—a fact of legal life of which he was well aware. "I'm just waiting for the right moment to make my move," he would say periodically, as if he had a submachine gun stored in the closet ready for storming Lamport's office whenever his horoscope dictated.

Balakian's generosity of spirit brightened my first glum couple of weeks when I was loaded down with bushels of routine work that provided little opportunity to shine. "They're just trying to see if you can handle the stuff competently and reasonably fast," he advised. "Don't sit on anything too long or try to give it overly sophisticated treatment—nobody expects you to be the top expert in the world on anything yet. What they're looking for is a kind of wide-ranging awareness of the implications of whatever problem you're dealing with." That sounded right. On the other hand, I hesitated to set my standards along lines recommended by a spear carrier.

Lamport exercised his *droit de seigneur* and claimed exclusive use of my services for the first several months. I was saddled with a couple of dozen wills and estate plans, past and pending, and asked to evaluate them in light of current federal inheritance tax law. I asked him how extensive a report he wanted on each. "Whatever you think appropriate," he said without bothering to look up. I opted for the technique prescribed by Judge Millis—a two-page summary memorandum, raising questions without attempting to answer them.

"Why have you picked a uniform format?" Lamport asked me midway through the second week when he had had a chance to review the first batch of reports. I said that it had seemed a sensible and orderly way to proceed. "But the plans are of different magnitudes of complexity. If you force them into a mold, you shortchange some that need more thoughtful assessment and drag out some that can be disposed of in a paragraph or two."

"I thought I would attend to the more difficult ones in a follow-up treatment," I said, "pending your approval. I've framed the questions that I think need more extensive exploration."

"I noticed," he said frostily.

"I guess that was wrong."

"Not entirely," he said. "One can't very well provide answers till one has figured out the questions. But to be honest, Miss Hill, the answers are of infinitely greater interest to us."

"I just didn't want to go off on a wild goose chase without your seeing the direction I was headed in."

"You can assume my approval of whatever direction you pick —that's why the job was given to you in the first place." He handed my reports back. "You try these again." There was just enough controlled exasperation in his voice and gesture to scare the living cholesterol out of me.

The problem was that I was trained either to research a question to death or to deal with a familiar area of the law in sure, swift fashion. This project fell in between. Not wanting to devote my life to the task, I chose to concentrate on five of the plans and dispose of the rest in a succinct few paragraphs. Among those that I so dismissed, unfortunately, was Estelle Pinkham's proposal for the estate of an elderly wealthy industrialist, perhaps the firm's richest client, and Lamport thought it had been botched. And I had not detected the shortcomings.

"The trouble with generation-skipping trusts," he said dryly, glancing up from my approving commentary, "is that they have to be drawn with great precision of language in order for the assets to bypass the estate of the testator's spouse for death tax purposes. The IRS is poised like a jackal for the first sign of loose draftsmanship, eh?" It was a little verbal tic he had, half-interrogatory, half-accusatory. I nodded in mandatory concession. "Well, then," he said, "under the maximum-benefit trust alternative, the widow Begley is not going to be able to invade the principal and retain her trusteeship unless that invasion power is defined by an ascertainable standard. Do you know

Moore's article in *Trusts and Estates*—ran in '72, I believe. It's the definitive piece on ascertainable standards." I said I was familiar with the point in general and thought the proposed plan addressed itself to the issue he raised. "Where?" he asked.

I flipped through the document tentatively. It took a couple of run-throughs to find the spot. "Here," I said. "The language beginning, 'My wife shall have the right to invade, for her comfort, welfare, or happiness . . .'"

"Do you think that is a satisfactorily ascertainable standard?"

"I thought that was why the language was in there."

"No doubt," he said. "But does it serve?"

"I thought so." My head began to ache.

He looked toward the window like a weary schoolmaster confronted by an obtuse pupil. "Assuming you thought about it at all," he said. "The language must read, 'My wife shall have the right to invade, for the purpose of her health, education, support and maintenance in her accustomed manner of living . . .' or words very like those." He turned back toward me. "Now under the discretionary trust plan, which Mrs. Pinkham offers as the alternative, do you see any marked advantages or disadvantages? Your note is silent on that score."

"Well," I said, temples throbbing now, "the widow has substantially less power and the trustee a great deal."

"Yes, that is the premise of the arrangement, Miss Hill."

"That seems to me plainly a drawback."

His glance was back out the window. "Yes, but surely there are compensating features. The discretionary trust permits a far more flexible pattern of distribution to beneficiaries in need when they need it—"

"I am improperly prepared for this discussion," I suddenly blurted. "I deeply regret it."

"Yes," he said. "No doubt." He looked back slowly toward me. "Your comments on those plans which you deigned to examine in depth are quite helpful, Miss Hill, so I have little doubt of your capability once you address yourself to a subject. But a boat with an excellent sail and a defective rudder will not provide very reliable transportation."

"No, sir."

"In this firm, Miss Hill, you are judged by everything you do —not just what you happen to think is important."

"Yes, sir."

"Please familiarize yourself with bypass trusts and have a redraft of this instrument on my desk in seventy-two hours."

I did not sleep much during that command performance. And in the process, I managed to antagonize no fewer than four co-workers. I all but pushed Steve Balakian out into the hall while spreading the reference materials I needed over every available square inch of our joint terrain. "Only till Thursday," I promised him, and he acceded but not without a slight curdling in that sweet disposition of his. Mona, the secretary he and I shared, was considerably more put out. She was not a very enthusiastic worker, typed carelessly, and spelled atrociously, thereby doubling the time she took on any given assignment. She made it no secret, furthermore, that she did not enjoy taking orders from a woman, and when I sent up a distress signal that I would likely need her to work overtime one night or possibly two, she greeted it with "Oh, screw that—I've got plans." I tried to woo her over lunch. At no point did she make the connection between our out-of-office intimacy and possible on-the-job cordiality; back in the office, I was the enemy again. The other secretaries were scarcely warmer. Reinforcing that barrier was the attitude expressed to me by Alva Potter, more officious concierge than efficient office manager, who saw me and Mona return from lunch together and summoned me to his bunker at the other end of the floor.

"The lawyers here, Miss Hill, do not mingle socially with the staff," he said with Pecksniffian ardor.

"Where does it say that?" I asked, annoyed that I was losing time from my urgent task.

"It's customary," he said.

"Customs change—especially fatuous ones."

"We are not running a sorority house here, Miss Hill."

"Or the Third Reich, either, Mr. Potter. I'll take my lunch with whom I please."

"It is most unprofessional. Your effort to ingratiate yourself with the help is transparent and demeaning. Furthermore, if you want Miss Donadio or any of the secretaries to work overtime, you'd best file the request with me. I determine who works what hours among the staff. You'll find them much more responsive to my directness than your blandishments, Miss Hill."

But his enmity was nothing compared to the cold front directed at me by my sister attorney Estelle Pinkham, who caught wind of what I was doing to her draft of the Begley trust and assumed it had been my idea. I tried to set her straight and portrayed myself as a groping amateur responding to the order of a harsh taskmaster. "You do what you must, Miss Hill," she said, the air crystallizing about her.

I stayed up till five in the morning on the day my assignment was due, typing the final twenty pages of the ninety-six-page document myself. There was no word from Maynard Lamport till the weekend had passed.

"I counted nine typographical errors, six pages with badly smudged erasures, three with blatantly inserted words or phrases, and one split infinitive," he said. "One thing I do not tolerate, Miss Hill, is slovenly presentation of our professional services. It reduces the client's confidence in our infallibility and—as in this case—distracts from an otherwise first-rate piece of work." He noted the breadth of my smile and moved at once to check it. "I am required to forgive a good deal in this age of permissiveness," he said with profound sufferance, "but I can see no excuse whatever for the split infinitive except laziness or ignorance. Which do you claim?"

"Fatigue," I said, "to boldly dodge your indictment."

He grinned, gave his right suspender an approving snap, and thereafter played the genial tutor until I was sent off to work for Dan Kettering.

7

I had not expected my relationship with Jonathan Kenyon to survive that initiation period at the firm. Each of us had too much invested in ourselves, and too little in each other, to endure the strain.

Although we shared an apartment, frequent coupling, and a substantial portion of the rest of our lives, I hesitate to say we were lovers in a deeper or even sentimental sense. I think of our relationship as having been one of mutual convenience and esteem rather than a full-flowering partnership in which the whole is somehow different from the sum of the parts. I would not trivialize it as a casual affair, for there was between us real affection, real laughter, real caring, and, as with any two intimately affiliated people, real irritability. But there was never a time when we were consciously building something together, and each of us understood that the other could take a walk at any time. I found that freedom and unaccountability quite congenial, as I found Jon himself to be. However emotionally prophylactic such an understanding, though, it can never immunize you altogether from distress when your confederate turns elsewhere for satisfaction.

Jon Kenyon was five years older than I and about as decorative as a man should decently be. He was tall and lean and shaggy and full of himself and his mission to redesign the world. I think of him as always having worn the same outfit—a wide-wale corduroy jacket in tobacco brown, a rust-colored flannel shirt, a tie of patterned paramecia that bore no discernible relationship to anything else he had on, tan or olive or beige Levis, tattered sweat socks, and space shoes massive enough to kick down the door to Fort Knox. In his jacket pocket there was always a little sketchpad. He may not have

71

been the most accomplished young architect in America but few, I suspect, thought harder about their calling.

His basic trouble was that he was living in the wrong century. Too much of modern design he found cold, severe, shoddy, or mere novelty. Where purity of line and integrity of materials were invited, the results were often felicitous and Jon reveled in them and kept hoping commissions for such splendors would come his way, but they were invariably so costly that only the *arriviste*, the pedigreed, or the eccentric could afford them, and none of those sorts was likely to be captivated by contemporary architecture at its most austerely sublime. The merely decorative appalled Jon as much as the grimly functional: Each struck him as a waste. The well-designed object ought both to work and to please, he said; anything less was a contraption or a contrivance. He made me read his master's thesis in art history—"Ornament, Proportion, and Utility in Three Works of Christopher Wren"—to understand. "There was very little invention in the guy," he said, "and he could have crudded up everything with borrowed *schlagg*. But he didn't. He took only what he needed and he never overdid. He'd spend his genius on a single aspect—the proportions of the structure, usually—and render the rest as simply and economically as possible."

"Sure," I said, "but he'd be a dud with plastic, aluminum, and cinder block."

"No," he said, "that's the point. I think he would have worked with them and got the most of their properties. Like glass—he would have been marvelous with glass—but he would never have let it take over for his own sensibility the way so much chic-looking shit does now. Glass is a void, glass is a suggestion, a nuance, an implied projection of something more substantial, it keeps getting overused because it's shiny and cheap. It's an excuse for art, not a manifestation of it."

He took me on a tour of the Mather campus to demonstrate what he called the bankruptcy of American architecture. The passion of his outrage was as stimulating as anything about Jon Kenyon. "Old is not good just because it's old," he said. He pointed out only a single set of college buildings dating earlier than the twentieth century that he said were lovely as well as commemorative—Cotton Mather and Increase Mather halls, those matched brick survivors of Revolutionary shot and shell that were the entire institution during its first three decades of life. "The gambrel roof is what does it," he said. "It gives the whole a presence without letting it become ponderous. And notice how the pair of them vibrate together somehow." I suggested Tillman Chapel, with its Tudor minarets and milk-chocolate masonry, as a classic embodiment of Ruskinian Gothic Revival. He snorted. "It's a curio—that's all. In and of itself, it's just plain ugly."

What he abhorred most was the expensive neo-Gothic *kitsch* of all the dormitories and lecture halls erected during the first third of the twentieth century at Mather and several dozen other venerable universities that could afford fine materials and superior workmanship but would not risk imaging themselves in a way that reflected their function, location, or time, to say nothing of the spirit of their nation. That outburst of College Gothic bespoke not dignity or tradition but anxiety and pretension, he said, as if the university could not wait for recognition from the Old World and had to costume itself to speed the process.

At the end he took me to the one spot on the campus that delighted him. To me, the Burnham dormitories, vintage 1960, by Saarinen were no more than a series of linked boxes, like heavy rickrack, brutal rather than imposing in their sculpted squatness. Jonathan saw more to them and made me see it. The irregularity of the stippled stone-and-aggregate facing gave the construction a coarse grain that in itself, he said, lent character and strength. And the knife-edged facets of each unit were angled to produce the dramatic alteration of pale brightness and soft shadow that one finds in villages throughout the Mediterranean littoral. "It's the contrast that makes it work," he exuded, "the mesh of hard and gentle, of heavy and light. The whole thing has a kind of dynamic serenity Americans are incapable of admiring."

Jonathan rarely used language like "dynamic serenity" and similar oxymoronic horseshit that art critics, stock analysts, and other poseurs love to fondle. His down-to-earthness was his second most endearing quality. In combination with his sensitivity, imagination, and highly durable cock, that open naturalness assured me that I would not be used in bed as a mere receptacle for his frequent spasms of lust. Not that I would have consented to such a practice, but I had known a number of devotees of the kiss-feel-eat-hump school of lovemaking that, for all its civility, was little short of a regimental exercise in its unvarying itinerary. And I was expected to squeal and thrash in the bargain.

Jonathan was different. He was unhurried and unworrying whether he would stimulate an ecstatic response. He waited till we were both extravagantly lubricated and then lodged himself within me and remained there hard and deep and still and sent out soft ripples, and he did not quicken his own slow thick movements at my first climax but held back and guided me up and down and over until I had nearly had my fill so that his own ultimate letting go was a massive act of joint celebration.

Curiously, other bodily functions turned him squeamish. He excreted privately and protractedly as if in chronic dread of constipation—bowelomania, I called it, to his unamused distress. He would arm himself for that purgative ordeal with heaps of magazines, blueprints, and other absorbing literature and not emerge for what seemed at least an hour. He seemed to think the retention of so much as a single strand of waste matter within his lower colon would sully his entire gastrointestinal tract, foul his breath, and exude telltale traces of bacterial rot from his usually polished anus. Eventually I would yell something through the door about the local drug discount store running a special on nitroglycerin or whether I should inflate his rubber ducky in the event he had fallen in. A great shuffling of papers and general stirring within would follow. "What color star shall I put up on the B.M. chart, sweetie?" I would ask.

And out he would come, all grumbles at being unceremoniously dislodged and head wreathed in clouds of Glade or some other cloying sweetner to neutralize his fecal musk. He grew comparably addled at the slightest glimpse, whiff, or even suspicion of my menstrual blood. I think he thought it was heaven's way of leeching womankind for the primal sin and wanted to distance himself from any contagion in the flow. There was of course no sign of solicitude from him over my delicate condition, largely because of my own massive indifference toward it. But Jonathan declined to risk bodily contamination from me on those red-letter days. "It's unnatural and unhygienic," he said. "The Old Testament says so."

His professional performance was not so satisfying as his recreational one, but there were encouraging signs. He had come to Amity after four years of apprenticeship with a large firm in Boston and teamed with a couple of prominent local guys who split their time teaching at Mather's School of Design and working in the field. Most of what Jon did at first was mopping up for his colleagues. But then he won a competition for converting an old foundry a few blocks from the city green into an office building without destroying the character of the original, and a number of such restoration and modernizing projects began to come in to him. It was not precisely avant-garde, but it did spread his name and finally got him a major job, building a wing on the Jewish home for the aged. The wing was bigger than the original dilapidated structure, which Jon wanted to pull down as unsafe and uneconomical until what he called "the chicken-soup lobby" said that wasn't going to happen. I told him not to be abusive just for not getting his way. "Abusive?" he said. "Who, a good old *shaygets* like me?"

So positive was the response to his design for the old-age home that for the first time Jon had the luxury of turning down proffered commissions because he could not handle them all and was not ready to delegate any. One job he could not decline was the invitation by a divorced woman doctor to design a modern home on a pristine twenty-five-acre site in the Bethany countryside. He flung himself into the job with hyperkinetic fervor. Dr. Pamela Haselkorn had appropriated a quarter of a million dollars for the purpose, and since the land was there to start with and the house was to be a relatively small one, he was able to work with the finest materials. He must have made a dozen trips to the site and a thousand sketches before settling on the final design. It was a thing of such exquisite simplicity, so pure white and uncluttered, that at a glance you might have thought it altogether artless. All it was, was two stark steel-framed slabs for the floor and roof, supported by two rows of four steel columns; at each end, the slabs cantilevered out beyond the sheer glass walls of the house to form loggias. He had the steel sandblasted and spit-polished and painted flat white and the whole construction mounted on a set of recessed stanchions so that the house seemed to hover in the air. The glass walls, he said, were to frame and reflect that lush woodland setting and retain the severe lines of the composition. "Cold," I said. "Dynamic serenity," he said. "Besides, she loves it—every inch."

Of him, too—every inch—as soon became apparent. His visits to the country lasted longer as the project moved off the drawing board, and on his return he offered me only spent ardor and indifference. In a man whose seminal vesicles needed siphoning at least every second day, this abrupt departure from habit could not escape notice. And his action in the sack became labored for the first time. I said nothing. After all, neither of us was tethered. For my part, though, I never, as they say, spread my favors when I lived with a man. He was it, for however long it lasted. You could hardly call it monogamy, but it was at least a limitation aimed at heightening our intimacy. He went along, so far as I knew, until the arrival on our scene of the restless and rich Dr. Haselkorn.

Jon's entanglement with his client overlapped my own headlong involvement with Messrs. Lamport, Kettering, Grier & Nightingale, and I no doubt contributed to his waywardness by that sudden new devotion of my own. I have always been subject to spells of occupational excess, especially on encountering fresh challenges, when my glandular appetite tends to adjust downward temporarily. In this instance, my libidinal languor seemed to fan his already diverted fire. He came back to the apartment one night with a back raked by fingernail scratches. He made no effort to hide them. Quite the opposite, in fact.

"Do you want to talk about it?" I asked finally, after pretending for a while not to notice.

"Not especially," he said.

"Then why the skin show?"

"I guess I'm confessing."

"You've been confessing for weeks."

"There was no hard evidence before."

"But plenty of soft."

He grunted in acknowledgment. "All right, I'm balling her—and I like it."

"Good. I'd hate it to be one of those tacky beachboy/merry-widow things."

"It's not."

"You're not just her stud?"

"I like her as a person, Tabor."

"On top of which, she fucks like a wildcat."

"More or less."

"Lots of moaning and thrashing?"

"Some," he said.

"And being a medical person, she's clean, of course."

"Tabor—"

"How come she sliced up your back if she's a healer? She could lose her license."

"Tabor, cut the shit!"

"Me? What's it got to do with me? Ball who you want—just get your ass out of my face."

"When I'm good and ready."

"When I say so."

"You're over-reacting. It's not that big a thing."

"It's not? Tell me you're doing it just to protect the job. Tell me she's not going to pay your fee if you quit laying her."

"Okay," he said, "I'm telling you."

"Sure—and Chairman Mao's got a Swiss bank account."

"You heard that, too?"

But it was no good. I had run out of laughs. I told him I didn't want to cramp his style and conceded the stunting effect of my own behavior on his. He said he still cared a great deal for me and hoped his affair with the doctor would not drive a permanent wedge between us. On that note of sickeningly civilized discord, we agreed to separate for a few weeks and see what would come of it.

"I hope the house turns out the way you want," I said as he headed for the door.

"Sure," he said.

"I mean it, Jon. I know what you've got invested in it."

"Okay," he said. "And thanks."

"There's only one thing."

"Yeah—?"

"It's very handsome, the design—stunning and immaculate."

"Yeah, thanks, Tabor. I'll call."

"Only I wouldn't live in the thing if you gave it to me for zilch."

"Okay, okay."

"It looks so goddamned cold you couldn't get Eskimos to move in."

"Right."

"Or even their huskies."

"G'bye, Tabor."

"It would be like living in a world's fair pavilion with thousands of people milling around outside and pressing their noses up against the window minding your business. The house sucks, Jon, if you want to know—it's as inhuman as the designer."

"Tabor," he said, "you're a cunt." And he was gone.

I cried. I hated that word. It was the one form of Anglo-Saxon foulness I could not abide. It was so hateful a dismissal, so vile a refutation. Why had I driven him to use it? Because I preferred to feel bad than nothing at all.

By morning I had my mind back on other things.

8

The key to acclaim and advancement at the firm, I saw soon enough, was not how much I knew or how fast I learned but how pliable I felt to the shaping hand of each partner. Had I

78

displayed excessive competence or fed the suspicion that I was brighter than anyone there, I would have won only displeasure and envy. Their joy came in showing me how much they knew and how little I did. That meant, of course, a willingness on my part to stand corrected without becoming peevish or disconsolate. All that was really required of me in the beginning was evidence of enough native humus to nourish the hope I would flower beautifully with seasoning. There was an element of subterfuge in this, I will concede, but nothing essentially corrupt; mostly it was a matter of spending my energies most prudently.

The trouble working with Dan Kettering was that I was so busy telling myself he was a jerk that I nearly forgot my own ground rules. It was not so much his contention that I could actually learn something useful under his tutelage that I resented—man, after all, can gain much from intense observation of the ant. Most of what he had me do was routine real-estate paperwork that a secretary could have handled. But Dan was a stickler for proper form and petty detail, proclaiming to me with pride that no client of his had ever ended up owning the Brooklyn Bridge. There was not much mental discipline involved, yet I unquestionably absorbed enough about title warranties, easements, variances, quitclaims, leaseholds, and the like to think I could begin to cope passably with substantive problems in the field. I also picked up sufficient insight into the operations of banks to tell Dan how much I admired their gift of finagling a sanctified position in the community. "They actually make the public pay a premium for the privilege of getting soaked," I said.

"How so?" he asked, eagerly taking the bait. "They play by the rules."

"Well, if every bank in town charges the same interest rate for a mortgage, I don't quite understand why that's not price-fixing and collusive under the antitrust statutes."

He looked at me over the top of his birdman glasses to make sure I was serious. "I suppose that's a good question," he said, "if you don't know a whole lot about the banking business."

"Just that I have to pay them to use my own money."

"They lose money handling every check you write."

"But they make it off the rest I leave on deposit."

"It's a high-risk business. Their profits are measured in fractions of a percentage point."

"If the risks are so high, how come every serious loan has to be collateralized to the hilt?"

"Because banks aren't charities."

"Then why don't some of them maximize their business by charging slightly less for mortgages than every other bank in town?"

"Because high volume and high profits aren't necessarily related. At the moment more people want loans than the banks can make. Since the pool of lendable money is finite, the rates stay up. It's something called the law of supply and demand."

"I've heard of it. It means the public pays through the nose."

"Baloney. If you consider inflation, I'd say interest rates just now are a bargain—consumerwise."

"Except that the banks are sneaky about it."

"How so?"

"This point thing they charge at the closing. What rational basis is there for a one percent surcharge against the customer? What is it, a tip for the bank's graciousness in agreeing to take the borrower's money for the next twenty-five years?"

"It's a hedge against inflation."

"So much for bargain interest rates."

He began to splutter. "I don't think you appreciate the right of business to earn a profit. That's what it's there for. It's only doing its thing. Take away incentive and America's just another banana republic."

"Profit's fine with me, only it's got to be earned. Business ought to be required to deliver durable goods and dependable services before it gets rewarded."

"It does the best it can under the circumstances."

"The circumstances are called life."

"You're talking about relative values. If people didn't think they were getting their money's worth, they wouldn't buy."

"Unless they have no choice—unless the quality of everything has been debased to protect profit margins."

"Business has to survive however it can."

"That means the lowest quality it can get away with at the highest price it can extract. Once upon a time, it used to be the opposite."

"Cottage industry doesn't work any more."

"Right," I said, "only child labor in Hong Kong. So charge all the traffic will bear and *caveat emptor*."

"Is that so awful? The race is to the swift."

"And the losers starve?"

"The hungry have always been with us, I'm afraid."

"But now they turn communist and kill their exploiters—haven't you heard?"

"Yes," he said, "which is exactly why America has got to stay strong."

After a couple of weeks of such dialectics, I relented. Dan naturally assumed I had surrendered because of his devastating intellect. He himself survived, of course, precisely by not re-examining the basic premises of the system under which he prospered. That even Rolls-Royces required repairs now and then he would have conceded only grudgingly; that you could never get to the moon in one would have struck him not so much as a limitation of the vehicle as the wrongheadedness of the aspiration. So I stopped arguing and settled for doing his bidding. This consisted largely of making sure the files were in order for every closing and watching Dan fuss-budget with the documents like a gin-rummy novice arranging his cards after the deal.

Toward the end of my torpid tour of duty at his elbow, he assigned me a task that acutely defined the nature of my professional transition. I had passed from mending the lives of the destitute to tending the playing fields of the loaded. At specific issue was the future tax-exempt status of the Amity Lawn Club, Dan's tennis hangout. It was the sort of showcase problem, he explained earnestly, that meant more to the firm than the billable hours it produced. "A lot of high-powered types belong there," he said. "It's a tribute to the firm's standing that we're of counsel." How we had failed to land the Upper Amity Hunt Club, he did not say.

The feral federal government was making it harder than ever, it seemed, for social clubs to maintain their tax-free standing. New regulations imposed taxes on the outside business income of these elitist establishments—on the meals taken there, for example, by non-members or on rentals from social functions attended largely by riffraff—as well as on their invested endowments. And to certify the tax-exempt portion of a club's revenues, far more thorough records would have to be kept, like duplicate chits of member charges involving thousands of pieces of paper per month. "I doubt that it's worth it any more," I reported to Dan after surveying the IRS regulations and studying the club's annual operating statement. "The government is insisting on such meticulous record-keeping and proof of legitimate business or social purpose that the whole thing looks to be punitive."

"Goddamn pirates," he said softly.

"The upshot of the new regs is that the club can no longer subsidize service costs to members by laying off the losses against untaxed outside income."

"Bunch of bolsheviks," he said.

"Now I gather that all the members really care about is the overall cost of services they receive, regardless of the tax status of the place."

"Right."

"What I'm saying is that, all things considered, it's probably going to be cheaper to operate the place as a regular taxable enterprise that happens to lose money every year than as a tax-exempt entity with all the regulations and limitations that would entail."

He gave a bunch of little nods and pursed his lips reflectively. "Very good, Tabor," he said. "But I'm afraid you've left one thing out."

"What's that?"

"If we keep our tax-exempt status, we also keep our exemption from civil rights and public accommodation laws."

"Yes, that's right."

"Didn't you think that was worth mentioning?"

"I assume you knew that. My concern was with the financial impact of the new regulations."

"Yes," he said, "I'll grant you that. But the measure of an attorney's usefulness here is how practical his or her advice is. Does it take into consideration the real issues involved? In this case, the heart of the matter is not whether a change in tax status is going to take a few more dollars out of the members' pockets but whether it'll affect the whole complexion and purpose of the club."

"I thought the purpose was to eat, drink, swim, and play tennis."

"With congenial colleagues, screened for their compatibility."

"Oh," I said. "In that case we could have avoided the whole exercise."

"That's not so," he said. "The club's board of governors specifically sought our counsel."

"Okay. My finding is that the cost of exclusivity is going up."

"Now you've got it," he said. "Lay it on them for four or five pages."

"I suppose you'd like the main point put a touch more diplomatically."

"Check. Only not too cute—I'd hate the board to miss it."

"I don't do cute," I said.

As if a gratuity for my efforts in behalf of the gentry, I was invited to join the Ketterings in a mixed doubles match at the club the following Saturday with a partner of my choice. If I could have found a coal-black Nigerian in a scarlet dashiki, a Bombay untouchable with enough strength, or a kamikazee on a Kawasaki, I would have teamed with any one of them for the occasion. Instead I settled for a bearded Mather geophysicist named Jeffrey Kramer, a good friend of Jon's and mine, who had actually captained the squash team at Williams in his undergraduate days. Given Dan's competitive intensity, I thought it best to equip myself with a partner who would divert attention from my ineptness.

True to form, Dan had reserved one of the three courts

below the dining terrace—"the showcase courts," he would have called them—and was taking vigorous practice hits with his wife, Sally, a leggy butterscotch blonde, when we arrived. They were of course both all turned out in official tennis white, Dan in a shirt with one of those loathsome little alligators stitched on the left breast, the missus in a short skirt that displayed her well-toned flanks with every motion. I had been tempted to razor-cut a pair of old jeans down to mid-thigh length but decided that would so mortify Dan he would more than likely impale himself on the club flagpole. Instead I hastily picked out a pair of powder-blue shorts at Penney's and wed them to a man's old white button-down with the sleeves folded up neatly just above the elbow. Jeffrey, anyway, looked tennis in his Mather T-shirt and shorts and wrap-around glasses. His beard, though, seemed to trouble Dan until I identified him as a professor; my outfit he avoided altogether as beneath contempt and took out his displeasure, I thought, by strafing me at net at the first opportunity as if I were a Japanese infantryman and he were back on Iwo Jima.

Sally Kettering was perhaps a dozen years younger than her husband and as much better than I at tennis as Jeffrey was than Dan. That made for a close if not very picturesque match. Dan exhibited perfect tennis etiquette throughout. He checked the height of the net at the start, made sure the lines were brushed clean, opened a fresh can of balls before each set, had us change sides after every two games, and yelled "Let!" with gusto when a serve skimmed the net instead of the casual "Take another" on which I'd been weaned. Only his game lacked finesse. A large but no longer limber man, he tried to substitute power for speed and wound up overhitting half his shots and brewing a torrential sweat.

Sally, on the other hand, kept cool. She had a somewhat awkward but surprisingly swift serve, and while her ground shots were more chops than strokes, she seemed able to direct them to precisely the spot where Jeff and I would do an Alphonse-Gaston routine and let the ball skip merrily by. They won the first set, 6–4, and we struggled to a 7–6 victory in the second, at which point I was ready to pack it in—what could be nicer than a spirited contest that ended in a tie? I could nearly feel the steaming shower on my back. But there was Dan glugging some Gatorade and toweling down in readiness for "the rubber match."

Sally's serve went awry at the beginning of the third set, and with it her composure and Dan's temper. "Just get it in—and no tricks," he growled after her fourth double-fault.

"Just face front and fuck off," she said.

But they never recovered. Things got so bad that they were even banging my cream-puff serve into the net instead of putting it away past poor Jeff's splayed reach as they had earlier. We won, 6–2. Dan looked on the verge of cardiac arrest.

With true ungrudging jockmanship, the Ketterings insisted we stay to lunch on the terrace. Jeffrey and I had had vague plans for a picnic, but Dan would not hear of it, and there we were being fussed over by old black men in linen livery. Jeff wound up being interrogated closely on his work with atomic and thermal energy as alternatives to fossil fuel—Dan thought shale would serve fine if all the bed-wetting environmentalists could be caged—and I on the receiving end of Sally Kettering's rapier chatter.

"Dan says you're doing marvelously downtown," she said. "I told him if the lot of them weren't such cavemen, they wouldn't have been the tiniest bit surprised by a woman's performing their hocus-pocus quite as well as they."

"They've all been very generous with their time and help," I said.

"I shouldn't wonder," she said. "You're the most refreshing thing to blow through the place since the hurricane of 'Fifty-five. I just hope for your sake they remember to act like gentlemen." There followed a sly smile that translated freely into: Mess around with my man, such as he is, and I'll cut your gizzard out before you can holler *habeas corpus*.

So many friends of theirs came over and gabbed that she gave up on introductions and let me nibble at my chef's salad in peace while the breathless exchanges ran on unchecked by common politeness. I was plainly nobody of importance or Sally would have identified me, so the stoppers-by rattled away,

85

mostly about the quality and finances of the Amity Symphony Orchestra, which the Ketterings were apparently spearheading the drive to save.

"Super sound Tuesday night," one of Sally's cronies hissed, glossy lips flashing in the noonday sun. "Just promise me no more Beethoven this season—I'm still reeling from last month. Now I know why nobody does the First and Fourth any more —or was it those housepainters again messing up in the woodwinds?"

"Hell, the painters are stars," said Sally. "It's that one-armed chiropodist on first violin." She laughed wickedly and then told the interloper to be sure to bring her children to the kiddy concert that afternoon.

"Oh, my God, I forgot entirely. What are they doing?"

"*The Sorcerer's Apprentice.* Leon's conducting with a mop handle."

"Damn—today's the church carnival, and Betsy's part of the crew running the horror house. But you get Paul Newman to narrate *Peter and the Wolf* and we'll all make it next time."

Sally threatened to scratch her from the patron list and waved her on her way. "Some of these people don't understand we can't survive playing to half-filled halls," she told me, assuming my interest. "The truth is, it's a losing fight. The audience just isn't there any more. I guess everybody's got all the music they want at home on stereo—who needs real live artists? We're actually going to run pop concerts next year—you know, half Chopin, half Cole Porter?—to see if we can wrestle up some crowds." Her manner left little doubt she considered it her private orchestra, not a mere civic enterprise, and that Dan went along for the ride. "The poor dear's got a tin ear," she said and reached over to pat him on the wrist, "but he's game, I'll say that. I don't think he's missed a concert in three years— he says it's good public exposure. Trouble is, he keeps dozing off—did it right in the middle of Vivaldi's oboe concerto, can you imagine—and I've got to nudge him awake without being obvious about it. But he's been a treasure raising money from the industrial community. I don't know where we'd be without him—or who's going to do it next year. Dan's down to do the heart fund then—he does one big charity thing a year—the church, the party, the scouts, whatever. He may even do Gay Rights one of these years."

What infuriated me was not so much her galloping self-centeredness as the soaring presumption that we somehow had a shared frame of reference just because we were sitting at the same table. What church was she talking about, what party—as if there were only one right one of either? And how did she know if there was music in my soul or I could tell Vivaldi from Lawrence Welk? And maybe I was gay, for all her insolent majesty was aware.

My resentment must have shown as she spoke and at the first possible moment she was letting Dan know they had discharged their duty to his guests and it was time to get on with their tightly scheduled lives. "Do check the booze bin while I'm at the concert, Danny, and fill in if we're short. Remember, they're sixteen coming. I'm due at the hairdresser at four sharp, or I'd do it myself. And while you're at it, be a sweetie and see if you can pick up some tarragon at the market." She turned to me. "Don't you just adore tarragon?"

"I've never read him," I said and reached for my bag.

That was the kind of lawyer Dan Kettering was. All heart and intensely dedicated—to the manner of living his wife prescribed. The wimp. He should have re-upped in the Marines when he had the chance.

9

So palpable was the air of activity vibrating about Sparky Grier's desk that I expected to find relays of heel-clicking retainers servicing his needs. But there was only Sandy Weiss, in his fifth year with the firm as an associate and the odds-on favorite to become its first Jewish partner, and a highly competent secretary to keep that redheaded ball of nervous energy from self-destructing. Things piled higher and higher around him while he talked so incessantly on the phone that I wondered how he ever dug out. Until I worked with him during Weiss's vacation and was exposed to his commanding, and demanding, presence. His voice level remained modulated no matter how intense the business absorbing him, but there was a machine-gun delivery to his words that left little doubt in the tattooed listener that he had better heed them or risk permanent exile. Me he treated from the first with respect due a peer. In a way that was even worse than fear of being taken for a corner-cutter by Maynard Lamport or a halfwit idealist by Dan Kettering.

What kept Grier busy beyond the normal press of legal matters was his link with official city business. He, and therefore the firm, served as bond counsel to the municipality, one of two designated for the post, which made him an intimate financial adviser to the mayor and his team and, not incidentally, brought in a handsome fee to the firm every time Amity added to its bonded indebtedness. That responsibility and the skilled way he and Sandy Weiss had discharged it had made Sparky Grier an *ex officio* one-man shadow cabinet and troubleshooter *extraordinaire* whenever local political issues threatened to become even more irrational than usual. Such embroilment would have distracted many an attorney to the point of dysfunction; Sparky Grier thrived on the turmoil and his own quick wits. Just how quick they were was stressed to me my second day with him.

"Here," he said, handing me a four-hundred-page transcript of depositions, "will you look these over and see what kind of case we've got—if any?" The client owned a fleet of tank barges operating in and out of Amity Bay Harbor. One of the barges had blown up a month earlier while undergoing repairs in drydock for a leak that was discovered after it had taken on a load of Iranian Grade C crude oil from an over-full tanker. The client firm was seeking exoneration from liability in federal court.

If there was a field of law I knew less about than admiralty it could only have been property rights among the Cossacks. I knew starboard from port and stem from stern but beyond that I was pushing my luck. I had never studied the subject at law school and never had a case dealing with it while clerking for Judge Millis or working at Legal Assistance. And Columbus had never sailed the Atlantic before but that didn't keep him home, I told myself and plunged in. No more than two hours had expired and I had scanned about half of the transcript when Sparky summoned me. "Well?" he asked.

"I'm getting right into it."

"What's it look like so far?"

"Like I've got to look at it more."

"What's your first impression?"

"That I'm not familiar enough with the area to shoot my mouth off till I've thought about it some."

"I'm not after a closely reasoned argument, you understand."

"I understand perfectly, but I'll need a couple of days to familiarize myself with the particulars."

"I haven't got a couple of days, I'm afraid."

"Can I have overnight?"

The phone went off. "All right," he said, reaching for the instrument. "Be in here at eight sharp." Meaning that eighteen hours were enough for any dolt to master the subject.

It took me half that time just to figure out the essence of our client's complaint: Its management claimed not to have had "privity or knowledge" of the causes of the explosion on that dinky barge. The supporting depositions made the claim seem shaky at best. Something told me, though, that Sparky Grier was enough of a tiger to pounce on even vaguely promising bits of testimony and turn them into triumph. The truth proved to be more nearly the opposite, but being younger, hungrier, and more dewy-eyed, I thought it my duty to make caviar from seaweed. Sparky let me down easy.

"Yes," he said, "that's the heart of the claim—our guys didn't know why the ship went up. You read the testimony—did they?"

A thousand dots from sleeplessness dancing before my eyes, I consulted the clutch of notes I had scribbled down. "I think a case can be made that they didn't," I said. "The operations people didn't know that the Coast Guard had downrated the boat to handle only Grade D crude. And no one at Amoco evidently told the shipmaster that it was Grade C being put aboard the barge. And the maintenance people didn't know that a gas-free certificate hadn't been obtained from the Coast Guard before they began welding."

He put his feet up on a corner of the desk and twiddled with a rubber band impatiently. The gesture discouraged me. "Go on," he said.

"Well," I said, "that's the heart of it."

"Is it?"

"From our side."

"And how strong would you say our claim is?"

"I suppose it depends on how effectively our people testify."

The rubber band grew tighter around his fingers. "Did you happen to notice how much time elapsed between the Coast Guard's downgrading of the barge and the explosion?"

"Something like six months, I think." I looked at my notes. "Well, a few days less."

"Does that strike you as long enough for word to have circulated within the company's yards?"

"I guess so. But maybe the Coast Guard transmitted the news in some sort of inconspicuous or erroneous way, and no one noticed."

"Is there any testimony or other evidence in the record to suggest as much—or that the Coast Guard behaved in any way improperly?"

"None that I noticed."

"And this downgrading, what brought it on?"

"The company asked for a year's delay of the regular Coast Guard inspection. The Coast Guard obliged but downgraded the barge."

"Meaning what? What difference did it make that the barge could only take on Grade D instead of Grace C crude?"

"C is more combustible."

"So the Coast Guard imposed a routine precaution in response to a routine request by our people."

"So it would seem," I said.

"And whether or not the Amoco people told our barge people the grade of crude they were having transferred, wouldn't you think it incumbent on our people to ask?"

"You would think so," I said.

"And if you've had a leak from a tankful of highly combustible crude oil, wouldn't you want to take every precaution that the area had in fact been examined and certified as gas-free before proceeding with welding work to plug the leak? Wouldn't you, in fact, establish a rule that the presiding official at the site actually examine the certificate before allowing the work to begin?"

"I guess I would."

"And did our client do any such things?"

"Apparently not."

"And who in fact was the presiding official at the repair site?"

"That seems to be in dispute."

"You mean they're passing the buck back and forth."

"The testimony is open to that reading."

"And now I wonder if you'd like to revise your estimate of our case."

I gave a small sigh. "I guess so."

He undid the rubber band he'd been toying with and reached for an open book nearby. "The governing case is a 1946 Sixth Circuit ruling called *The Cleveco*. The relevant portion of the holding reads, '. . . knowledge means not only personal cognizance but also the means of knowledge—of which the owner or his superintendent is bound to avail himself—of contemplated loss or condition likely to produce or contribute to loss, unless appropriate means are adopted to prevent it.'" He flipped the book shut. "Even with well-heeled clients, Miss Hill, discretion is often the better part of valor. I'm advising that the action be suspended."

I sat there benumbed for a moment. Then I said, "Can I ask you a question?"

"Sure," he said, evidently not overwrought with displeasure.

"If you knew all that to begin with, why ask me?"

"On the chance you'd see something I didn't."

"And I didn't."

"You didn't," he said. "But I don't consider every hour we can't bill to a client a waste of time. You're learning. You knew nothing about the subject and you had only overnight to do the job. Six months from now, you'll do beautifully under similarly impossible conditions."

I smiled thankfully. "Just one other thing," I said. "If our client had such a rotten case to begin with, why'd you let them file the action on the barge matter?"

"See," he said, "you're learning already. The answer is that I did what I was told. They thought they might mitigate any future claims against them even if they didn't win exoneration."

"You mean they hoped to intimidate anyone from filing against them by establishing a record of non-culpability?"

He nodded. "Unfortunately, the record shows them to have been total incompetents in this matter. I'm telling them to pray a lot and if they get hit, to settle on the best terms they can scrounge."

He gave me a chance to redeem myself the next week. The matter appeared on the face of it to be as favorable to our clients, a pair of retired Amity policemen, as the earlier case on the exploding barge had been unfavorable; naturally, I smelled a rat.

It was the first time I had been called upon to defend cops, and I took up the task with measured zeal. Their complaint was that the city's pension and retirement board had erred in calculating the money due them by failing to include the lump payment for unused sick days they had received just before leaving the police department. That money, they said, should have been part of the annual average pay on which the pensions were to be based. The language of the contract between the city and the American Federation of State, County and Municipal Employees seemed airtight. "Average annual pay" was there defined as "the average of all compensation including but not limited to base salary, holiday pay, longevity pay, overtime pay, etc., which the employee receives during his or her three highest paid fiscal years." The actual money involved was only a couple of hundred dollars per man, but the principle thus established would affect every member of the force and eventually amount to thousands of dollars. As quasi-counsel to the city, Sparky felt he could not represent the cops directly in an action against the municipality but said he would try to arbitrate the matter without fee.

"The language of the contract doesn't specifically say that sick pay is included," he said. "It only says 'et cetera,' That's ambiguous."

He was testing me. "No," I said, "the language is crystal pure. It says that 'average annual pay' means 'all compensation including but not limited to' the specified examples. The examples cited are therefore only words of illustration, not of limitation. No one can reasonably argue that 'all compensation' doesn't mean what it says and say what it means. 'All' is one of the more serviceable words in the dictionary."

"All right," said Sparky. "I'll buy that. Why do you think the pension board doesn't?"

"I was wondering the same thing myself."

"Let's find out. You go have a sandwich while I make some calls."

"The calls sound more exciting than the sandwich."

"Then splurge on a turkey club."

"They make a mess."

"Ham and cheese, then. On me." He reached for his wallet.

"No way. I want to listen."

"I don't generally perform with a studio audience."

"I won't breathe."

He was both flattered and annoyed. "I don't know," he said.

"Pretty please."

He grinned. "Has anyone told you you're a little cheeky?"

"How else do I get initiated into the rites of the male power cult?"

"I don't remember that being one of the terms of your employment."

"It's the main one," I said.

He tossed up his hands, then fished out his cigarettes and snatched up the phone. His technique was so artless that I wondered how it buffaloed anyone. He opened with a pleasantry or two, asked after the other party's family, threw in a decoy *soupçon* of immaterial gossip, and then caught his prey off guard with the zinger. He put his question in a way that implied he knew a good deal more about the matter than was the case. The effect was to leave the respondent eager to enlighten Sparky and thereby enhance his own standing as a public-spirited citizen.

After the third call, he had the full picture. The swing member of the pension board was a dentist whose teen-age son had attended a party at a friend's home a few months earlier. The noise level attracted the cops, who said the kids were disturbing the neighborhood and were reportedly smoking pot. The kids denied the charge, but the police asked to search the house. In his parents' absence, the boy hosting the party felt that to resist was to confess guilt so he let the cops in. They found a boy and girl sharing a joint in an upstairs bedroom and a couple of butts in a living-room ashtray. All twelve youngsters were arrested, but the charges were later dropped because the police had failed to warn the young host he could refuse them entrance without a warrant. The pension-board member whose son had been included in the illegal bust knew enough about police procedure to seek to have the charge erased entirely from the boy's record since the fact of the arrest, if ever disclosed, might jeopardize his college admission and be prejudicial to his entire future career. The other parents joined in the effort. Since the kids had in fact been guilty of breaking the law, the chief of police got hot because on top of going unpenalized for what he viewed as a mere technicality, they now demanded that the records be rewritten out of consideration for their tender sensibilities. That the law provided for such expunging of arrest charges against minors was of small concern to the chief. "Let the bastards sue," he was quoted as having said. That would have meant petitioning the courts to have the records cleared and risking precisely the sort of publicity the families had hoped to avoid. When the chief remained adamant, the pension-board member struck back in the only way at his disposal—by voting to drop sick days from the salary base used to compute retirement pay and letting the department rank and file know precisely why. The cops fumed. "Let the bastards sue," the pension-board parent echoed the chief. The tempest was threatening to blow the top off the teapot.

Within the hour, Sparky was stroking the police chief's tail feathers. "It's no skin off my knuckles, Chief," he said, cradling the phone under his chin while he lit a fresh smoke, "but if you want to know how the ball game looks from the grandstand, I'm at your disposal." It was a probe to make sure he wouldn't get his nose broken for sticking it where it hadn't been invited. As Sparky had sensed, however, the chief was longing for someone authoritative to tell him what to do, and the mayor apparently had not yet heard about the impasse—or, having heard, was letting human nature take its stubborn course.

"I appreciate your annoyance, Chief," said Sparky, invited to go on. "The punks ought to have had their butts dented and here it looks as if they're putting in for their citizenship merit badges at your expense. The trouble is, you're backing yourself into a heads-they-win-tails-we-lose kind of situation if either of the cases gets into court. It's going to cost your boys money if the pension board's action is sustained, even though I don't think that'll be the outcome. But you never know. And if the board loses, the kids' parents may well decide to bite the bullet and take the story to the funny papers, in which case your guys wind up looking like strong-arm bozos pushing around a bunch of wholesome kids having a little fun in private. If you want my guess, I'd say the kids have been scared good and proper, Chief, and any further effort to humiliate them looks a little like overkill."

It flowed from him so matter-of-factly in such a low key that the words were hard to resent. Here was a square-shooting pal calling it the way he saw it. The chief capitulated to the logic of that sympathetic analysis. Without injecting an emotional note into the exchange, Sparky hinted that the chief had just made a gesture of Churchillian grandeur and offered by way of reward to act as informal emissary to the pension board to make sure the matter would be cleared up simultaneously at that end. The offer was taken right up, and Sparky de-escalated the negotiation by urging the chief not to bet on the Red Sox to win the pennant unless they found some pitching somewhere and fast. That was how Earl Grier practiced his version of *pro bono* law and still managed to collect power and get rich —by pulling strings when nobody was looking and not asking for medals afterward. People even liked him for it.

"Can I buy you lunch any day you're free?" I asked him when the show was over. "All it'll cost you is a ten-minute lecture on how the town really runs."

"Only," he said, "if you'll spring for a turkey club."

The problem with American politics, he explained to me the following week at the best table at the best restaurant in the city, is that whenever anyone really competent at it comes along, "he starts thinking he's Caesar and pretty soon the people want to make like Brutus." A classic case in point was Hizzoner Bryan Orlando O'Brien, who had presided over the renewal of Amity in the Fifties and Sixties and wound up more despised than beloved.

O'Brien had put together the pieces of his power package by the political equivalent of atomic fusion; he convinced each group in the community to surrender its hatchet and join the common cause, provided that all the others would. When the federal government witnessed that remarkable display of urban unity among normally warring tribes, it started to funnel the money in. And when the citizenry saw the rebuilding unfold largely on the strength of outsiders' money, they exulted and hoisted Boo O'Brien on his high white horse and urged him to ride. And the faster he rode, the more he liked it.

"But he made two mistakes," Sparky concluded. "He rode alone. Most of these guys do that—out of fear that if they delegate some of their power, soon the rest of it's going to be taken away, too. So they trust no one, surround themselves with yes men and incompetents, and sooner or later find the whole thing is out of hand." Still more important, what he had built was Showplace City, meant to please the out-of-town funders; the real problems of the community, despite the huge infusion of money, were barely touched. New stores and office buildings and garages went up, but nothing was allocated to attract new jobs once the construction dust had settled. New schools rose but not teachers' salaries; a new police headquarters was built but the cops' professional training continued to be neglected. Most of the new housing aimed at keeping the middle class in the city, not improving the lot of the poor who had no choice but to stay. "All they got were a few token low-cost units, a couple of playgrounds, and a cinder-block community center where they sit around complaining there's no decent work."

"If you saw all that," I asked, "why didn't you speak up and say the blacks were getting shafted?"

"Boo had stopped listening," he said. "All he believed were his own handouts—and his name on all the cornerstones. He said everything that was being done was for the benefit of the city as a whole, not this or that ethnic bloc. The only thing wrong with that was it totally ignored where the money really went. This wasn't a big relief melon being sliced up for the multitudes. There wasn't any money being put into the pockets of the needy for services rendered, like in the New Deal. And there wasn't even any semi-intelligent training program for jobs that really existed. Hell, no. This was private enterprise rebuilding the town with public capital. All that meant was that a lot of money that might have gone for urgent social needs got siphoned off as profits and pay-offs. And most of the rest went to skilled union labor that loves overtime and hates niggers."

"And how long does the hating have to go on?"

"Till whites don't feel threatened by blacks any more."

"But it's the whites who've been kicking black asses for ten generations."

"Of course—that's why the whites are so afraid."

"You mean of retribution?"

"Of course. It's guilt in its most perverse form. And the only reason we haven't made it up to them is that every one of them who gets to be something is one less for us to spit on—and that's bad, don't you see? Start treating jigs like real people and who's there left to lord it over? Not even women, any more. You're fixing us good, the bunch of you."

I was full of admiration for his savvy. He seemed to possess precisely the right blend of cynicism and conscience to broker a sweeping conciliation among the city's ethnic factions. "Why don't you run for mayor?" I asked. "You could change some things."

"Until they noticed. As it is, I get to move in mysterious ways and still survive. Martyrs aren't necessarily the most useful citizens."

"Don't you want them to name schools and stadiums after you?"

"A law firm's enough," he said.

10

I didn't even get to water the dracaenas in Sam Nightingale's office during my rotating apprenticeship. The reason, I was told, was neither personal antipathy nor professional ill regard—just that he had nothing much for me to do right then whereas he knew that Gil Serini was hard-pressed. "Could I have a rain check on your gifted services?" he asked.

"If I'm not tied up with the IBM account when you call."

"I think you'll find IBM uses house counsel mostly."

"I'm bringing them around," I said. "So far they've promised me the southern New England business after my first year here."

"Maynard will be pleased to hear."

"Does Maynard know I'm alive?"

"Sure. He says Miss What's-Her-Name did very well with me."

"For a sinner, he means."

"He doesn't say that—not any more."

"Well, if it comes up, you can tell him I've reformed."

Sam shifted gears. "My sympathies," he said gently.

"It's no big deal."

"I trust our righteous indignation wasn't a factor."

"No, just the workload. And that was only an accessory after the fact."

"Well," he said, "go help Gil save his love life and win yourself some Brownie points. The guy works harder than the rest of us put together."

If Maynard Lamport demanded patient industry above all from his trainees, and Dan Kettering, proper form, and Sparky Grier, speed and smarts, Gilbert Serini wanted, and needed, love. Or at least repeated reassurance that he was valued for his own gifts and not out of WASP condescension toward the strident ethnicity surfacing everywhere in the land. Gil joylessly called himself "the house paisano," though no one else I heard did, and referred to his clients as "the vowel brigade" because their names mostly ended in "a," "i," and "o" with an occasional "e" in there. Their money was as good as anyone's, he insisted at billing time without ever quite seeming to believe it himself, and he was almost apologetic that so much of their business was generated in messy trades like food and cement and garages, that they worked and lived in unchic neighborhoods, and that a disproportionate percentage of their legal affairs involved unsavory matters. "At least there's not a lot of matrimonial action," he said. "Murder, *sí*; divorce, no." After two days of that, I told him to stop putting down his people or I'd hand him a tin cup, tie a string through his lapel, and walk him beside me down Broad Street while I delivered the Gettysburg Address in organ-grinder dialect. He shut up. But the *angst* persisted.

This rampant insecurity of his had its productive side, as I learned when Gil set me to drafting a brief in behalf of his client, Dante Motors. The state commissioner of motor vehicles had shut down the auto dealer for a week and taken away its permit as an official inspection station because one of its salesmen had fobbed off a demonstrator model of a Plymouth Duster as a new car. Dante's defense was that its salesman had made an honest mistake and that once it had been brought to the company's attention, the customer was refunded the purchase price in full. Neither the state agency nor the Court of

Common Pleas to which the decision was appealed had bought that claim, but Dante felt it had to try to protect its name by seeking exoneration in the state Supreme Court. "It's hopeless," Gil told me. "These guys are very crummy cookies. They make your run-of-the-mill thieving car dealers look like choir boys. Believe me, I would have brought in character witnesses at the hearing or the trial but everyone we could think of was behind bars."

The net effect on me of this forlorn assessment, naturally, was intensified effort in the client's behalf. It was not those shady rats I was championing out there on the lists, as Maynard Lamport noted in our first interview, but my own skill at overcoming adversaries no matter how hopeless the cause or, for that matter, unworthy. The worst degenerates had their rights, and just because Dante Motors was not poor was no reason to deny them the most stirring and ingenious defense money could buy. In fact, their very wealth made it morally mandatory that they pay plenty, but they were entitled to their money's worth.

The case history revealed that the trial court had declined to intervene on the ground that the state motor vehicle agency's decision was a proper exercise of its administrative power. "And that's beautiful," I told Gil. The court was saying that this guy was guilty until proven innocent. Punitive measures had been taken against the car dealer for alleged "false representation" in accord with the state regulation, I noted, "but there's nothing in the record to substantiate the charge. When the law is assigning blame, 'false' doesn't mean merely 'untrue'—it means untrue by design, untrue by intent, with malice aforethought. See most recently *Sallies v. Johnson*—and there are about a dozen other cities I could give. What we're saying is that the state agency overstepped its statutory authority, absent a demonstration of your sleazy salesman's lying intent."

"Crazy," said Gil. "Write it up and say a novena."

"I'm allergic to incense," I told him.

"Then I'll get you a rosary."

"That's all right," I said. "I'm not much for jewelry."

Without supernatural goosing, the state Supreme Court

agreed with our brief. Gil was generous in advertising my contribution to the case, but I drew small elation from it. It was his client, after all, and the salesman, without much doubt, had lied through his teeth. But as these matters are measured, it was a full-fledged victory and earned me a case in behalf of a far more deserving client.

She was a legally blind, severely retarded, and multiply handicapped eighteen-year-old girl named April Landino, who had been expelled from the Amity Valley School for the Blind on the ground that she had not made sufficient educational progress in two years there to justify remaining. The school had arranged for her transfer to a state-run custodial institution—its way of saying the best that could be done for April was to warehouse her for life. The girl's parents, friends of Gil's, took the position that by admitting her in the first place, the school had created an entitlement to continue her education there until she was twenty-one. The school, for its part, said its staff psychologist had tested the girl when she entered and found she was functioning at the two-year-old level of development; after her second year there, she was retested and found to be at about the one-year or one-and-a-half-year level, and therefore ought to be transferred out. Gil said he was too emotionally clenched over the family's plight to handle the matter at maximum efficiency and, besides, his current load didn't allow the kind of all-out effort that would plainly be required to reverse the school ruling. She was my baby now.

I saw the girl once. It was enough. Her eyes were milky, her arms shriveled, her legs crooked, her feet clubbed, and not much else about her worked right. Yet there was sweetness in that small soft oval face that swept you up and left you appalled that God could visit such a fate upon an innocent. She touched my nose and mouth and breasts and hugged me when I left. The law proved less responsive to her plight than I.

I used everything I knew. Her best chance, I thought, was in federal court on a claim of violation of due process. The school, while basically private, received enough local, state, and federal funding so that its dismissal of the child qualified, I said, as "state action," the requisite for a claim of federal jurisdiction. The school had decided to transfer the girl after the psychologist's examination but without holding a hearing on the matter; when her parents complained, the school admissions committee considered the matter and reaffirmed the executive decision. The school had admitted that it could not measure the girl's academic progress, I argued, and absent such a finding, it could hardly claim conclusively that she had not benefited from her stay. All that the staff psychologist's test had indicated was that April's mental *capacity* had not improved, but that was not to say she had not learned and progressed *within the limits* of her capacity, much as any other youngster might learn without an altered aptitude to do so.

It was a good try. Both Sparky Grier and Sam Nightingale, whom I asked to review my brief after Gil, thought I had put up the best possible argument, and the judge had no trouble grasping my central point when I appeared in court. He just didn't think it had enough heft. "The court's scope for review of a school administration's findings in such a matter is very narrow," said the opinion. However apparently harsh the school's conclusion, it was not made arbitrarily or capriciously but in the belief that the facility could serve another usefully, more usefully than the plaintiff. Motion for injunctive and declaratory relief denied. April didn't even get court costs.

It was not as if those three denied years at the school would have made her whole or that anything much could have been done to reverse the ever outward tide of her life, but the loss of her case left me drained and disheartened. The law, I had by then learned, was at best fitfully merciful, but its back of the hand to April Landino made me wonder if there was much point in persevering. The weak and the meek might yet inherit heaven but I could not see that they were making much progress on earth, not with me as their shepherd. Was I destined, then, to larbor assiduously for those who least deserved my partisanship while attending such pitiable creatures as April Landino only rarely, and ineffectually at that? For days I brooded. They added up to a lost week.

To snap out of it, I went that Saturday morning to the

Mather Gymnasium, where I had alumnae privileges. I ran some on the banked track, flopped around on the mats awhile, and struggled halfway up the climbing rope before concluding I was no longer a sylph and had better begin undergoing this paratrooper routine regularly. As I was taking a final lap around the running track and wondering whether I'd have enough energy at the end to go down for a swim, I sensed a figure gliding up nearly alongside me yet remaining just a few steps to the rear out of easy view. At first I paid my shadow no heed; there were so many weekend runners out that there was nothing odd in one of them settling upon a pace that matched mine. After a couple of hundred yards of being tailed, though, I felt crowded enough to turn on my uninvited accompanist. "Oh," I said, "hello."

"Miss Hill, I presume," said Sam Nightingale, moving up next to me at an unstrained gait. He had on baggy, dust-colored sweat pants and a Mather T-shirt.

"Why were you hiding back there?" I asked, puffing by now from the ordeal.

"You seemed absorbed."

"Just numb. I've been at it awhile."

"I can tell."

"I'm afraid I sweat like a pig when I run."

"Ladies never sweat," he said. "They glow."

"I never saw a glowing armpit."

He grinned. "You do this much?" he asked, arms pumping with the nice hydraulic beat of a naturally coordinated runner.

"As little as I can get away with. But I think I'm going to change that."

"It's good for you."

"I know. So are lots of hateful things."

"Bodies that don't get used turn to mush."

"Is that *ad hominem?*"

"Hardly. You still look pretty trim to me."

"Don't look too hard—it's indiscreet."

"There aren't too many other sights out here, I'm afraid."

"Your mind is supposed to be on running."

"No, that's what I like about it—I do my best thinking all week when I'm out here."

"Let's not tell the clients."

He grinned and we loped a few dozen more yards in silence and then he said, "I have a confession."

"What's that?"

"I can't run and talk at the same time."

"Me, neither," I said, slowing. "I'm going down for a nightcap in the pool. Care to join me?"

"Thanks, but no—this is my thing. Anyway, the chlorine turns my eyes into fried eggs."

We had stopped. His chest was heaving just a bit. He studied the floor for a moment and then looked up. "Would you take it unkindly if I bought you a discreet cup of coffee after your swim?"

"I'd do nothing of the sort," I said. "Give me forty-five minutes."

When we met in the lobby, he had on a good shag sweater, well-worn jeans, and a look that said the exercise had agreed with him. I was bushed but pleased with my effort. "You can't punish yourself once a month or even once a week like that and get away with it," he said to me as we crossed the street and headed for a little Italian coffeehouse with a thousand hanging plants on the far side of the square. He said he tried to run three times a week faithfully, more if he could find the time. "It's easy to let yourself go at my age."

"Forty-one is not exactly Methuselah."

"Who said I'm forty-one?"

"I looked you up—I looked up everyone when you guys were checking me out."

"I guess that's fair enough."

"Nightingale, Samson Ernest. Born, Lawrence, Kansas, which I find a little hard to believe, by the way. A.B., Columbia; LL.B., Mather. Two years, assistant professor, Mather School of Law. Two years, assistant corporation counsel,

Mather University. Joined Lamport, Kettering & Grier, 1964. Named partner, 1967. Married the former Augusta Somebody."

"Lockwood."

"—Augusta Lockwood, 1958."

"Nineteen fifty-nine."

"Something like that. And from this union, one issue, Robert."

"Roland," he said, "popularly known as Rollie."

"Why just one kid?"

"Why more? His mother and I have other things to do."

"And what is it Mrs. Nightingale does, if I may ask?"

"Whatever she chooses—mostly painting."

"What kind?"

"Abstract, I guess you'd say. They're really giant exercises in pointillist coloration."

"Dots? She does dots?"

"Thousands per canvas—in fact, millions."

"Sounds—painstaking."

"Infinitely."

"And a little tedious."

"Some people think drawing up wills is tedious."

"It is."

"Maynard Lamport doesn't think so."

"Because he's a master at it."

"And Lee's a master at dots."

"Who's Lee?"

"My wife. She hates Augusta. Lee's her middle name."

"She hates Augusta and likes Roland?"

"I picked Roland."

"Oh. Well, it's better than Siegfried, I suppose."

"My grandfather thought so."

"Grandpa Rollie, huh?"

"No, it was Grandpa Aloysius. He named his son Roland."

"Oh. Well, I vote for Aloysius."

"I'll keep it in mind," he said, "in case we get a cat."

The coffee came, and we both fell quiet for a little. Then he said I had seemed blue around the office lately and he wondered if anything was wrong. I asked how he could tell since we saw so little of each other. He said even at a distance I usually seemed so chipper that my spell of gloom had the whole place practically in mourning. "One might call it an infectious personality," he said.

"Sounds dangerous."

"I wouldn't be surprised. We better detoxify you fast. What's up?"

I told him how I thought I had learned to insulate myself from the woes of people I served while working at the mental hospital and Legal Assistance but that all I finally succeeded in doing was running away from both places with a helpless feeling. And now losing the blind girl's case had put me back in the dumps.

"But you did an excellent job," he said. "Gil thinks so. The family thinks so. I read your brief—you threw in everything you could. It just wasn't in the cards."

"Maybe."

"There isn't any maybe about it, Tabor. You did what could be done. I think you are identifying too much with the client."

"Is that so bad?"

"Lethal. You can't function fully if you're overwrought."

"I was okay during the thing. It's just the after-effect."

"Shall I tell you how you'll know when you're ready to be a partner?"

"Please."

"When you feel no rottener losing a case you really care about than you're thrilled winning one you don't."

That sounded right, if icily algebraic. "But I'm not sure I can ever become that cold-blooded a technician," I said.

"You'll learn."

"Is it worth learning?"

"Unless you're a candidate for sainthood."

"Not consciously."

"Then learn."

"To be a hardhearted bitch?"

"Isn't there some territory between bitchery and sentimental slobhood?"

"Like what?"

"Like being kind and attentive but impersonal about it."

"Like a computer printout?"

"No one's going to mistake you for a computer."

"I don't know how to be impersonal, Sam."

"Then you'd better get married and make babies."

"I'd rather be a middle linebacker for the Patriots—whatever that is."

"Then stop dying for humanity. Someone already did that—it's a hard act to follow."

"And that relieves posterity of the obligation?"

"Cut the corn, Tabor. It's perfectly possible to be a decent human being without being consumed by sorrow for the world's injustices. All life's an injustice."

"Is that what they taught you out on the prairies? I thought that was big Bible country."

"That's why I left it," he said.

"For what—flaming perdition on the outskirts of Sodom?"

"Not quite."

"Then what?"

His brow thickened. "I don't know," he said. "Whatever I've wanted, I suppose."

"Sounds like nirvana among the heathens."

"I'm not sure I'd go that far."

"Then what—wealth, glory, power?"

"Well, let's say I'm working on those."

"And that makes you happy?"

His flow of aphoristic instruction had been turned back on him, and the switch made him uneasy. "Sure," he said, "more or less. I'm working at that, too—isn't everyone?"

"Some people don't know how. They're too busy beavering to look up."

"I guess so," he said.

"But you wouldn't know about that because you're getting what you want out of life—nice career, nice family, nice future?"

His eyes fastened on mine for an agitated moment and then hurried past. "Yes," he said, "pretty much."

"That's good."

"Why do you trivialize it?"

"I'm not—I'm just trying to smoke you out a little. Beneath that kindly and bantering exterior of yours lives a very guarded person."

"With people I don't know."

"I wonder."

"What?"

"I have a powerful suspicion you don't really want to know people much beyond exchanging amenities with them—that would complicate your life. It's easier keeping the world at arm's length."

That searing look of his caught me again and raced on, like a beacon piercing dawn fog. "That's a sweeping indictment," he said, "considering we've hardly ever talked."

"Sweeping indictments are my specialty. Also snap judgments—I'd make an ideal prosecutor."

"I'm not so sure," he said. "Some prosecutors actually weigh the evidence first."

"You mean I'm wrong about you."

"You're shooting first and asking questions after."

"I wasn't trying to do any damage."

"Then why fire in my direction?"

"I was trying to help, not hurt."

"And what makes you think I need help?"

"I don't know—just a hunch. It's not a sin—everybody does —at least a little."

"Including you?"

"Except me."

"Why's that?"

"Because I'm incurably honest with myself. I can stand a little self-inflicted pain now and then."

"You also seem fond of lacerating other people."

"That's a sweeping indictment," I said, "considering we've hardly ever talked."

"One goring is enough to tell," he said and managed a smile and reached for the check. "I've got to run."

I couldn't remember having come across another man who seemed quite so together on the surface and yet so transparently vulnerable.

11

"Hey there, Superfox—you really gone big time?"

I had to think for only a second, though I hadn't spoken with him in over a year. No one else called me that. "Duckett Washburn," I said into the phone, "the Red Cross Connection."

"Ex-connection," he said.

"You didn't get busted again?"

"No way. You are talking to Mr. Clean, the most antiseptic dude in that entire hospital."

"Beautiful. Can you stand it?"

"We ain't eatin' good, but I'm hangin' in."

"And the Gully—how are the brothers and sisters?"

"No one is stompin' at the Savoy. Everybody says it's all your fault for leavin' us flat."

"A body's got to live," I said.

"Not that good. You are collaboratin' with the enemy."

"These are my people, man. I'm nothin' but a closet Ku Kluxer."

"Shi-i-it," he said, "you the house nigger, ain't they told you?"

I laughed. "You're not far off."

He was calling to ask if I could represent his friend Andrew Wells, an oldtimer who ran a little used clothes shop at the lower end of Seaview. Kind soul that he was, Andrew had agreed to sell one of the more notorious hookers in town a fur-collar winter coat on layaway: ten dollars a month and after eight months it's hers. The shady lady paid up for three months, then changed her mind and asked for her money back. Andrew said no way, so she went down to Legal Assistance pleading poverty and got them to file suit.

"Heavy," I said. "And you want a bigtimer to whip ass at Legal Assistance."

"You got it."

"Over thirty bucks?"

"It could be more. Andy says there's somethin' about a federal truth-in-lending law that's got penalties. He's afraid they're gonna put him right outa business."

It dawned on me that this was the very first client who was all my own. He was not being dealt to me blind the way everyone had been at Legal Assistance or assigned to me by one of the firm's partners who was too busy to attend to the matter; here was somebody actually seeking me out, and it could not have mattered less how small the case was or that the client could not pay. All I wanted was to win. For months I had been assigned the most mundane legal matters to execute in the partners' behalf, thereby freeing them for more lucrative activites. I would draw a will for Maynard Lamport, search a title for Dan Kettering, take depositions for Sparky Grier, and draft contracts for Gil Serini, all with a minimum of supervision and even less contact with the clients. It was not very stimulating work but I performed it well and without whimpers. No one patted me on the head—or the fanny. I was simply sustaining the mandatory effort to master the hardware of the trade. A less exhilarating spell I had never logged.

Professional performance aside, I did not much ingratiate myself at the place. Perhaps from perversity, perhaps from that inner ease that spared me the need to cultivate the whole world as a friend, I balked at the regimentation and rigmarole that plague even the pettiest duchies. This willful streak rapidly separated me from the lower echelons, who hewed the line fastidiously, and soon enough riled the upper one. There was the maddening matter, for example, of my failure to hand in my weekly time sheet on schedule. Precisely how many hours I worked for which clients had to be recorded before the firm's bills could be dispatched in good order, but since those computations in no way affected the size or delivery of my own paycheck, the urgency of the need kept eluding me. Everyone else in the place, from Lamport down, handed in a timesheet first thing Monday morning detailing the previous week's work. Thursday mid-day was the best I ever managed—until Alva Potter, nearly hydrophobic at my temerity, threatened to withhold my salary unless I reformed. And I did—he had my sheet bright and early every Tuesday, plus a carnation for his buttonface.

The secretaries and other female functionaries were steadfast in their resentment of my professional standing, though I did everything short of applying Flaming Lust nail polish to show I was one of the girls, only maybe luckier in my genetic lot. My work got typed last and worst and sometimes not at all, necessitating deadline heroics on my part at least once a week. I made all my own phone calls, got my own coffee, and fetched what books I needed from the library myself. None of the men lawyers did. But instead of earning gratitude from the women, my considerateness only deepened their envy-born conviction that I was undeserving of their deference.

With my fellow associates, I was not faring a great deal better. Steve Balakian was less then enchanted by the noise, disorder, and cigar smoke emanating from my side of our office but feared I'd eat him alive if he complained to Potter. Estelle Pinkham, increasingly paranoid with every job I successfully finished, looked the other way when she saw me coming. Sandy Weiss, smart, svelte, and sexually predatory, thought I was antisemitic because I would not go to bed with him after our second (and final) date. And the others wondered how I got away with all the salty language on those puritanical premises and why I seemed to command so much of the partners' time. "I give massages," I explained. In fact, my personal relationships with the partners ranged from merely pleasant and informal with Sam and Gil to pleasant but formal with Sparky to cool and formal with Dan (whose invitation to a return match at his tennis club I kept dodging) to stern but avuncular with Maynard Lamport (whose distaste for my arrival in pants, worn only in cruelest winter, was unmitigated by the calendar).

The case of the fur-collar coat, then, mobilized me and, soon after I took it, developed into a more interesting contest. For one thing, Legal Assistance got a whiff of the plaintiff's occupation and backed off the case; one of the grubbier practitioners in town took it over, and the stakes escalated. The pulchritudinous plaintiff claimed her money back on the ground that Andrew had failed to tell her what part of the price represented interest charges. Since Andrew himself had never made such a calculation and said he was not in the credit business but only trying to accommodate the hooker, I made a cross-motion for a summary judgment by the magistrate and told my client to relax. "I would," said Andrew, a benign, pear-shaped hulk who looked as if he belonged on the prize shelf at a shooting gallery, "only this ain't the kind of suit I know good from bad about."

His caution was warranted. My motion lost. We went on the docket in federal court, and each side, for good reason, waived jury trial. As judge we drew the Honorable Bennett Spinelli, the most liberal jurist in the district. He would surely perceive the injustice of a hardened whore trying to wangle thirty bucks out of a humble shopkeeper with no tricks up his sleeve.

After filing the defense brief at the courthouse, I wandered down the hall to the chambers of my former master and patron, Judge George H. Millis. To my surprise, the judge dropped what he was doing and greeted me like a long lost wayfarer. "Look at you," he said, "all poise and propriety—an ornament of the profession." There was something almost proprietary in his pride at the sight of me.

"Judge," I said, taking his hand with a nod of appreciation, "you look fine yourself. And may I be so bold as to say how much I admire your recent courageous opinions?"

"I've never known you not to be bold, Tabor, so don't stop now on my account. And thank you. I did what had to be done."

In response to a petition by inmates of the old county rehabilitation center near Bridgeport, then under use to house prisoners awaiting trial, the judge discovered a compound of low, dusty, sweltering buildings honeycombed with dimly lighted, scarcely ventilated, seven-foot-square cells from which the occupants were freed for no more than three hours of recreation weekly. He ruled the facility a form of cruel and unusual punishment and ordered it closed. Shortly thereafter he issued a restraining order against construction of a federal-state six-lane superhighway, due to consume thousands of acres in the western sector of the state. Environmental studies would have to be conducted first, Judge Millis held, to assess the full impact of the roadway and its accompanying effluvia. The first decision outraged the law-and-order lobby, which yelled that jails were not health spas and their occupants (even those as yet unconvicted) not due any kindness. The highway decision outraged realtors, builders, the unions, the auto industry, and the whole Rotarian-Jaycee phalanx that viewed every stimulus to the economy as a blow for liberty regardless of who or what died as a result.

Taken together, the two decisions signified a new willingness by the judge to interpose the arm of the law between the powerful and the powerless in the absence of other restraints. George Millis was growing more compassionate with each ensuing term he sat, his character more substantial, his temperament more serene, his outlook more respectful of the rights of social classes besides those from which his clientele had come when he was in private practice. "You'll be keeping the law-review editors up late at night if you don't quit it," I said to him.

"I take that as a high compliment, considering the source."

"It was meant that way, but I'm trying to be at least a little discreet. Those couldn't have been easy opinions for you to write."

"They weren't," he said.

"I hope you didn't have to burn too many bridges."

His look implied I may have presumed one degree of familiarity too many; I was not, after all, any longer a daily intimate of his. "Judges aren't supposed to own any bridges," he said, "or so you once informed me. Sometimes I wonder who was teaching whom back then."

"The impetuosity of youth," I said.

"And the courage," he said and moved us off to other terrain. We spoke of my new life at the firm, my distress over its protracted program of apprenticeship, and the case that brought me to the courthouse. "Ben Spinelli's a lovely fellow," said the judge, "but for your sake I wish you were handling the other side. He's a bug on consumer law—and you're defending the captains of industry." I laughed and described my lopsided client, the size of his purse, and the moral caliber of the plaintiff. He was sympathetic. "But don't expect Ben to be," said the judge. "And I doubt you'll ever get her occupation into the record."

In court, opposing counsel played to the bench's well-known preferences. My Andrew was portrayed as a pinchpenny leech, draining the hard-pressed ghetto community for every foul cent he could. In this instance, he was said to have failed to tell the customer not only how much interest she was being charged but also that the transaction was noncancelable and that he was maintaining a security interest in the coat throughout the term of purchase payments—all technically true but substantively distorted charges.

"Plaintiff's entire case is a tissue of contrivance," I opened, "and a blatant attempt to qualify for federal relief on the slenderest of technicalities. The truth-in-lending requirements were never intended to provide an escape hatch for shady characters trying to avoid their legal obligation to pay."

"Objection!" roared the plaintiff's counsel. "The character of the plaintiff is irrelevant and immaterial."

"I did not address myself, your honor, specifically to the character of this plaintiff," I said.

"She said the plaintiff was shady, your honor."

"That is counsel's ready inference, your honor. I would agree that whether or not the plaintiff is shady in her normal pursuits is irrelevant, except perhaps as it might touch upon her veracity. All I meant, however, was that in this specific instance, to avoid honorably made agreements by seeking legal loopholes is a very shady practice indeed."

"I'll overrule the objection," said the judge, "but defense counsel is advised that the bench does not view actions to enforce federal regulations framed in the public interest as the pursuit of mere 'legal loopholes.'"

It was all downhill from there. Andrew was twice as eloquent, in his way, as his attorney when he testified that he had simply been trying to help out a customer and now was getting burned for it. Judge Spinelli, however, did not much take to either of us. His opinion found for the plaintiff. And not only did she get her thirty bills back, but her lawyer won his claim for nine hundred dollars' worth of expended time and services, on top of which Andrew was hit with a hundred dollars in fines and court costs. I was stunned but refused to slither into ignominy. All that wrongheaded verdict convinced me of was that idiocy thrives among ideologues of every stripe. Andrew, who lived hand to mouth, was wiped out. The black community had to pass the hat to keep him in business; I dropped in a hundred dollars from my own savings.

An invitation to renew my gratis service to the downtrodden arrived far sooner than I expected—and from a source I had supposed to be steeped in grief if not hostility.

"I am offering a once-in-a-lifetime chance to redeem your exquisite hide," Duckett Washburn came on.

"Buzz off," I said to him. "I'm convalescent."

"Hey, what they done to Andrew ain't none of your fault—everyone says that. Folks figure a white judge seein' two spades goin' after each other in his court must've flipped a coin to see which one to burn. All your huffin' didn't much matter—except otherwise Andy could've got burned even worse maybe."

"We should have won. The judge is sucking up to the liberals."

"Superfoxes ain't supposed to eat sour grapes," he said.

I laughed and then listened to him. The Amity Board of Education was about to vote formally to close down the Bethune grade school, a gabled, dark-brick building nearly a century old, which the black community at the downtown end of the Gully cherished as a neighborhood institution. To bring the school up to current safety standards would be too expensive, especially since there was room for the displaced pupils in other buildings in the city. But to disperse the enrollment would entail longer trips on foot over dangerous streets or busing to distant points that would lengthen the youngsters' day and expose them to a less protective environment. The Gully Association of School Parents, known by its acronym as GASP, was fighting the move. In a time of cautious politics, reduced public spending, and rising white resentment over black crime, this was about the only sort of issue that could rally the ghetto. The radical era had ended; now blacks were just trying to hang on to what they had.

"Why me?" I asked Duckett, whose wife, Lenore, was vice president of GASP. "Don't you guys usually do your own arguing?"

"We been—till we're blue in the face. Only the man—like he can't tell shit from Shinola, he can't tell blue from black, neither." GASP had petitioned the school board repeatedly, picketed, staged a protest rally in front of city hall, and spoken out at a public hearing on the question a month prior, but all the indications from the bureaucracy were that once the local residents had finished airing their displeasure, the school would be condemned. Behind the decision, GASP was convinced, was a typical white power play, and that was why I was wanted. The school stood directly next to a large, idle factory that Mather-Amity Hospital had bought and was in the process of converting into a major annex, about six blocks out from the main complex; the annex, designed to house the hospital's clinics, was supposed to serve the ghetto better by being sited within its borders. The problem was that there had to be safe adjacent parking, and the Bethune school was the obvious place to put it. Neither the university nor the city, which operated the hospital as a joint undertaking under the direction of the Mather School of Medicine, would comment on the parking-lot story. A well-connected white attorney, the blacks figured in their desperation, might be able to unearth whatever foundation there was to the report and, by exposing it, demonstrate that the purpose was not worth the sacrifice; in a run-down neighborhood, there were a lot of places to build a parking lot. "And besides," Duckett wound up, "our Eyetalian brothers are more disposed to hear the music when a representative of the horsey set is doin' the playin'."

Which was precisely why Sparky Grier urged me not to accept the request to serve as GASP spokesperson. "It's a grandstand play," he said. "Everyone on that school board will know you're connected with this firm."

"And what's wrong with that?"

"I thought you'd noticed—the firm is very thick with both the city fathers and the university. We have a prior commitment to them. And the profession gets a little irritable when the same firm handles both sides of a dispute."

"But neither the city nor the university is officially a party to this thing—only the school board, and that's a separate legal entity. Unless you're telling me the blacks are right about the reason for the closing."

"Did I say that?"

"Are they?"

"Why ask me?"

"Because you know everything. Tell me, Sparky."

"First of all, I don't know everything," he said. "I only know half of everything—and that's the half it's in my interest to know."

"You're filibustering—tell me."

"Listen, angel, suppose I knew what you wanted to know and suppose I told you, and suppose it was what you wanted to hear—then where are you?"

"I'd know my side is right."

"You'd also know that two of our more powerful clients had a vested interest in the outcome of the controversy—and that you were caught in an unquestionable conflict and therefore had to drop your client."

"Are you telling me that I can't ever handle a *pro bono* client's action against the city because you help peddle its bonds?"

"I'm saying it's a very sticky wicket. I'm saying the same

thing I said when you first came by. It's one thing to represent an isolated individual who happens to be indigent and has a legitimate beef against the powers-that-be. It's something else again to align yourself with action groups and lobbyists whose interests are diametrically opposed to those of our clients."

"So they are going to tear down a perfectly good school to make room for a parking lot—a couple of hundred pickaninnies can go somewhere else to learn, for all the good it'll do them—is that it?"

"I didn't say that. And you're not going to wheedle it out of me, either."

"You're being a bastard."

"And you're being unprofessional."

"I think I'm being highly professional. I'm serving my clients without betraying yours—and vice versa. If my side was wrong, you would have said so, and you never would have brought up conflict of interest in the first place."

He ground out his cigarette in annoyance. "You're going to wise-ass yourself into trouble if you're not careful," he said.

I fed him another cigarette and lit it for him. "I'll be careful," I said, "but don't you be a louse, Sparky, just because you know where every body is buried in this town."

He took a deep drag and said, "I got a meeting in two minutes."

"Smile," I said.

"You're some operator," he said and reached for the phone. "Shut the door on your way out."

Sam Nightingale was less forthcoming. "I'd tell you if I knew," he said, "to spare your hide here. The truth is the med school does a lot of its own maneuvering. Maybe they've got a deal worked out with the school board, maybe not."

"Could you find out?"

"Probably."

"Would you?"

"So you can stand up in public and roast the university?"

"Something like that."

"Does that seem ethical to you, Tabor?"

"Does demolishing a perfectly good public school to make room for some cars seem ethical to you?"

"You're comparing apples and oranges."

"I've done worse things."

"Well, don't ask me to help you."

"Right," I said. "I figured you knew where your bread is buttered."

"You're trying to con me, Tabor. It's not smart to do that to people on your side."

"But you're not on my side if I'm representing these people."

"Then don't represent them."

"Why—because they're making life a little uncomfortable for a rich, old university that should know better than to abuse powerless people?"

"No one's abusing them. The clinics are being moved to help them more."

"Well, it's sure as hell not poor people's cars that'll be parked in that lot, is it?"

"I don't know anything about it."

"You sound like those Germans living near the Nazi death camps. You don't know anything about the dirty work, do you, Sam? You think alma mater is the Virgin Mary!"

He held himself in check. "You just don't know how to take no for an answer, do you?"

"Not when I think I'm right."

"You're not right. You're just frustrated. You want to be a star and you think the firm is holding you back. But you're wrong. You'll do just great, but you've got to give us half a chance."

I flopped into the big chair in front of his desk. "Who's doing the conning now?" I asked.

"I'm talking straight, Tabor. I like you too much to b.s."

That slowed me. The man was touchingly up front. "You really think I should get out of this thing? I already told them yes."

"Do what you think is right."

"I think helping them is right."

"But you're not a sole practitioner. You've got to consider the consequences. If every interest group in town thought it could manipulate the big boys by hiring you, you'd have to beat off clients with a stick. Is that how you want to make it—by browbeating your partners into indiscreet revelations?"

"No," I said.

"Well, that's why these parents hired you."

"But they were smart. If the city and the university do have a stake in the thing, this is probably the quickest way for them to find out."

"No one said you had to oblige them."

"Even if they have a just cause?"

"And do you honestly think the city and the university don't also believe they're operating for the good of society?"

I was feeling outnumbered. "If I back off this time, Sam, it'll be even harder the next. You guys'll never let me handle anything even slightly controversial. It's always going to have to be for the good of the firm—meaning your long-standing clients."

"Does that seem so strange to you—or awful? That's what we're here for—to serve the clients."

"Maynard told me I could bring in the clients I wanted."

"Doesn't logic tell you that if a *pro bono* client is opposing one or more of our larger paying customers, you ought to steer clear?"

"No one's told me that's what's really going on in this case, and so long as no one has, I don't see the conflict."

"You're splitting hairs."

"And you guys aren't?"

"You know," he said, "I'm beginning to think you enjoy being difficult."

That wasn't it at all, though. Something quite different was happening. It was one of those moments that are usually hard to recognize until long after and it's too late to rechart your life. I saw this one for what it was but just in time. I had rounded a bend in the highway and there was a fork dead ahead. The road signs told me which way each fork went but not where it would land me. I could continue as I'd been going all my life—part pluck, part brass, but essentially programmed to please by excelling as polite society directed. Or I could veer off from that heavily patrolled route and take my chances going where I wanted and how. The risks and rewards of either route were naturally unknowable ahead of time, but I was getting tired as hell locked to the straight and narrow. I said as much of that as I could to Sam, adding that I didn't hold out any hope he'd understand on account of its being a woman's special problem.

"But you're about as independent as anyone can get," he said, "and still be considered domesticated."

"For a woman."

"For anybody. I wouldn't be surprised to see you swinging in here on a vine some morning."

"But that doesn't win me any admiration—it just makes me a little notorious because I want you to know I'm alive. In the pinch, I'm always a good little girl and do as I'm told. That's how professional women survive—on charm, ability, and compliance. Anyone who's really good and shows it gets marked as a ball-buster. Then it's just a matter of time till the fellas gang-bang her and dispose of her remains."

He thought about that for a while. Then he said, "I think you're overstating the case—that seems to be a trademark of yours. In real life there's a choice between slavish compliance and outright rebellion. No one's telling you not to get passionate about your business once in a while; otherwise, you're just a piece of high-priced circuitry. The question is when can you afford to indulge yourself. Now is too soon—that's all you're being told."

I wouldn't buy it. Either I was my own operative when I chose to be or I was their co-opted tool—and the sooner I freed myself from their clutches, the better for everyone. I told Sam and Sparky there was no way of knowing how often and how directly my clients and theirs might be in conflict, and all we could do was take each case as it came. In the matter at hand, the conflict had only been hypothesized; to confirm it would have proven my clients' charge. My goal, then, was to prevent conflict, not foment it. If that wasn't good enough for them, then I was prepared to separate myself from the firm then and there. But if they wanted to be fair about it, they would wait and see what developed and assess my overall contribution to the firm and not panic at the first sign of complications.

What was a momentous matter to me was only another skirmish in a war the blacks who hired me doubted they could ever win. Their principal goal was to keep the casualties to a minimum. At the GASP war council the night before the fate of the Bethune school was to be settled, the membership had all but discounted the expected loss. Most of the talk had to do instead with how to prevent the white owner of the biggest laundromat in the Gully from shutting it down in disgust over frequent theft and vandalism.

"I thought they were worried about losing the school," I said to Duckett afterward.

"They finished worrying that one. That's what they got you for."

It was the first time my picture made the papers since I graduated from Holyoke. The spectacle of a white woman with one of the town's top law firms accusing the school board of callousness and deceit toward her beleagured black clients invited comparisons to Harriet Beecher Stowe by the local reporter, who rated my performance incendiary, electrifying, and irrelevant to the outcome.

The board president, a beetle-browed goblin misnamed Valentine, took a torrid dislike to me. He was the sort of antagonist you loved to hate. "These parents plead with you not to ride roughshod over their vital needs and those of their children," I declared and got no farther.

"No one's riding roughshod over anyone, young lady," Valentine shot back. "We've thrashed this question over endlessly. It's a matter of safety and simple economics, and the Bethune parents know that perfectly well. Why they've brought you in here now to berate us is beyond me."

"I haven't done any berating, Mr. Valentine. In fact, you're not giving me the chance to speak."

"You said we're riding roughshod over these parents."

"I said these parents are asking you not to."

"It's the same thing, young lady."

"You may call me Miss Hill, Mr. Valentine."

"All right—Miss Hill."

"If it's a matter of simple economics, Mr. Valentine, we're wondering how it's cheaper to bus these children all over town —that's six buses at sixty dollars a day for a total of fifty-five thousand dollars a year—than to repair a building that's such an integral part of the community. Even if we assume the board's figure of a quarter million dollars is accurate—and there is reason to doubt it."

"What reason, Miss Hill?"

"Our own people come up with a considerably lower estimate. We think one hundred thousand is a bit much for windows."

"It's shatterproof glass. And if the children hadn't torn the place apart, we wouldn't be in this pickle in the first place."

"And if they had been properly educated, they wouldn't have torn the place apart," I said. After a stunned moment, my clients erupted in cadenced applause until Valentine gaveled them to death. "At any rate, Mr. President, a little basic arithmetic shows that the repair bill is no larger than five years of busing is going to cost—and by the sixth year the survival of the Bethune school will be saving Amity taxpayers money, not costing them."

Valentine was wagging his head. "Miss Hill," he put in as soon as I caught a breath, "Bethune is a substandard structure. Since you apparently have no idea what that means, I'll set you straight. To refurbish a substandard building is throwing good money after bad. New windows are not the answer. The school needs more than patchwork. It has a wood frame inside, which happens to violate present fire safety codes. And there are other things that violate the building code and state laws, like inadequate provisions for the handicapped. We'd practically have to gut the building to bring it up to snuff. The cost would be prohibitive."

"Other public buildings that went up before these codes were drawn are allowed to stand under nonconforming use. I have city hall in mind as a prominent example. Why are you singling out this school?"

"Because it's very old and very dangerous. If one child died in a fire that didn't have to occur, these parents would never forgive us—and I wouldn't blame them."

Fortunately, I had prepared for this moment by persuading my former roommate and still occasional companion Jon Kenyon to spend an afternoon looking over the school and making stress tests and other safety checks. "I would like to use this occasion, Mr. Valentine, to submit to the board a report by a licensed local architect of excellent standing that contends the Bethune school is structurally sounder than most of the new schools in the city—or almost any building that has gone up during the past twenty-five years. A minimum investment in repointing the brickwork would assure continued dry timber. The sprinkler system, it is also worth noting, is tested weekly and is in perfect operating condition, and the youngsters take their regular fire drills very seriously. And in the absence of concern by the city, these parents painted the entire interior of the building at their own expense last summer and repaired the toilet and other plumbing facilities—essential work which this board refused to authorize. All the signs declare that you are purposely letting this school run down, and these people who so badly want to save it are entitled to know why." I dropped Jon's report on the table in front of him.

"I'm not accepting any unauthorized report, young lady!" Valentine spluttered.

"I think the board may find it very enlightening."

"We've already been enlightened, miss."

"Miss Hill," I said. "Do I understand the president to be saying that too much enlightenment will cloud the minds of the board members?"

At which point one of the members said he, for one, was interested in seeing the report. That got Valentine even angrier.

"Mr. President," I said, raising my harpoon, "the parents of the Gully community believe that under the guise of benevolence, this board is trampling on their rights and interests. It is a community that badly needs what few institutions remain to it. It is a community that, for all its tribulations, has its pride still. And it is a community that believes it is not being told the truth by this board."

"I deeply resent that charge, Miss Hill," Valentine exploded. "Where do you get off making such a reckless accusation against this group of citizens who do their thankless job with devotion?"

"Their devotion is not the issue, Mr. Valentine. Their candor is. I ask you now to state for the record whether the Bethune school is facing demolition because other municipal institutions have designs on the property."

Valentine looked at his fellow board members and threw up his hands. "Do any of you know what she's talking about— because I don't."

"I'm talking about a parking lot for the hospital," I said.

"That's entirely out of our hands, Miss Hill."

"Not if you don't tear the school down. And if you do and that's what happens, you will have dealt in bad faith with this neighborhood and with these people and violated the trust they have vested in you."

Off went the flash bulbs and down I sat, and the board marched off to its executive session and voted, four to three, to junk the school. It was closer than anyone had expected.

The GASP people sent me a glowing letter of thanks for my effort and a twenty-dollar honorarium for my time. I passed the money in to Alva Potter, who noted that it was twenty dollars more than my previous outing with the black folk had produced. That sly reprimand set me to contemplating a way I could serve both my firm and my ghetto clients without continually shortchanging the former or bilking the latter. A stray thought sent me burrowing into the IRS regulations one evening after work and by morning I had formulated the first really bright idea to come to me since joining the firm.

Having lost its school, GASP was trying hard to figure out now how to avoid removal of yet another vital local institution —namely, the large laundromat located on the ground floor of an older housing development and open to the public as well as the tenants. Hundred of families in the area relied on the place, whose absentee white owner was fed up with the constant coin-box break-ins and busted condition of at least half the machines. He had warned the neighborhood to start policing the laundromat or he would close it down within the month. The easiest solution would have been to find a black buyer for the business, which would then almost certainly have been less subject to robbery, sabotage, and neighborhood resentment. The problem was to locate black venture capital for such an undertaking, which was far too rickety an enterprise to attract a bank loan. No one at GASP knew anybody who had enough money to buy out Whitey. That was where my scheme came in: The tenants, their neighbors, and other users of the laundromat had among them one common characteristic that, according to the federal tax laws at least, was a substantial asset in this situation—their very poverty.

"Your people may be in luck," I told Duckett Washburn.

"That'll be the day," he said.

"Not really. Here's the scam. A lot of the families using the laundromat probably have gross incomes below the tax exemptions and standard deductions they're entitled to. That means they're not taking full tax advantage of their poverty, if you'll forgive the crude irony. Now if the users form a cooperative partnership to buy the laundromat on credit and run it themselves, the income from the business would be sheltered against tax by their excess personal and dependency exemptions and deductions. The partnership could then use the entire net income free of taxes to pay off the purchase price."

"No shit?"

"Absolutely."

"You wanna run that by me one more time, sis?"

"Look, everybody is allowed a certain amount of tax-free income plus an allowance for certain basic deductions—for dependents, for health costs, like that. But a lot of your people don't make enough to use up their credits. So I'm saying that the difference between what they make now and their taxable minimum can be applied against the buying and operating of the laundromat. Dig?"

126

"You mean we get somethin' free?"

"Not exactly. It's sort of pay-as-you-go. After a few years, though, your people would own it outright if the business generates enough volume."

"And if it don't?"

"Poof—no laundromat. Whitey gets it back."

"We ain't got no risk?"

"Not really, if you mean money invested."

"Why should Whitey dig it?"

"Because no one's going to make him a better offer. The only thing is you'll have to put down a little something on the machines."

"How little?"

"As little as possible—as little as he'll take. That could be very little because of the benefits he gets. See, he'll take back a chattel mortgage from the co-op—which means he can reclaim the machines if you don't pay up—only you guys don't have any personal liability on account of—of—"

"On account of we ain't got no credit."

"Unfortunately true. But not a severe handicap in this case. Now since you're buying the thing on the installment plan, Whitey gets steady income from his investment without all the headaches he's got now. And the icing on his cake is that your payments show up on his tax return as a capital gain instead of ordinary income the way it does now, so he gets to keep more."

"That figures."

"Of course if your people run the thing into the ground, he's out of luck—and you don't have a laundromat."

He sat forward in his living-room chair, spread his legs, and started tapping his knees contemplatively. "You know what you're talkin' about, Tabor," he finally asked, "or are you jazzin' me?"

"Tax law is supposed to be my special field."

"I didn't ask you that."

"Duck, you're bein' impolite," Lenore Washburn put in. "Tabor come out here to help."

"It don't matter if she was sweet Jesus if she ain't sure what she's sayin'."

"You think she'd be workin' downtown at a place like that if she didn't know her way?"

Duckett shrugged. "That don't prove nothin' by me."

"Let me put it to you this way," I said to him. "Has anyone around here got a better idea?"

He gave a defiant little snort. "Now that's hittin' below the belt."

"I didn't take judo for nothing," I said.

Duckett scratched his head a couple of times and then looked over at Lenore. "What do you say, Mama—should we get out the Rinso and go into the bubble business?"

"It beats scrubbin' on the river bank," she said.

The Washburns confirmed my supposition about the income level of the neighborhood, the laundromat owner greeted my proposal with joy since he was preparing to sell off the machines for scrap, and within a week I had drawn the papers for GASP's spin-off—the Gully Neighborhood Bootstrap Cooperative. An hour after its christening, it was being called the Boot Coop.

The project won an admiring nod from the firm partners. "Tabor's gang," Sparky Grier told Maynard Lamport within my earshot, "is the only collection of welfare clients in America with a tax shelter." Alva Potter especially approved of the fifteen-hundred-dollar legal fee to be paid out of the co-op's first-year receipts for my part in dreaming up the concept.

I made a point of doing my own laundry at the place. "Far out," Duckett said when I showed up the first time.

"What's the matter," I asked, "you closed to whites?"

"Nope," he said. "You just gotta pay double—and go last."

12

Near the end of my first year at Lamport, Kettering, Grier & Nightingale, I moved out of the shadows and began to earn some of my salary.

From the start I had understood that nothing major would materialize for me at the firm unless I managed to involve myself in the business of the big-money clients. I was not required to sign them up or direct their accounts or go to bed with them, but one way or another I would have to help enhance their dominion. There was reflexive resistance, though, by both the partners and the more exalted clients to the attendance of a nubile and not very deferential female associate at their august palavering. And when I was first invited to join the huddles of these steely moguls, I could read their minds behind the furtive once-over: What's a bimbo like this doing in the locker room while we've got everything hanging out? Couldn't they afford to hire a man? Then I'd say something and they saw I wasn't there to crap around. Then I'd say something else and they saw I wasn't chewing gum. Pretty soon I wasn't a woman to them but a co-conspirator in whatever heist was on the day's agenda.

Maynard Lamport himself sponsored my initiation into the big time by involving me in a singularly delicate piece of litigation with the firm's premier client, the First Amity Bank. He himself planned to argue the matter if it ever got to court, but his consuming mission was to smother the thing before it attracted public attention and altered the bank's image from skinflint to dunderhead. What had happened was that the bank had made an ill-advised loan of $100,000 to a local fuel oil company but hedged its bet by having it 90 percent guaranteed by the federal Small Business Administration under a blanket agreement. By its arrangement with the SBA, the bank was required to obtain and file documents verifying the collateral securing the loan. First Amity's chief loan officer, however, obtained only a financing statement on the company's equipment and failed negligently to get hypothecation of any of the other assets. The bank, meanwhile, continued to pay its semiannual fee to the SBA for its guaranty, and the federal agency never questioned the legitimacy of the loan to the fuel company. Two years later, the company defaulted on the loan. When the bank asked the SBA to pay it the $77,000 still owing on the loan the agency said it would not do so because the bank had contributed so heavily to the risk involved by its negligence.

"And I'm terribly afraid the federal people are right," Lamport said in reviewing the facts in the matter with me. "The bank's behavior was unpardonable. And, unfortunately, the man responsible is the executive vice president, a fellow I've done business with for thirty years. His judgment in these areas is generally infallible. It grieves me no end to see a black mark go against his name in the twilight of a fine career." He leaned toward me. "Confidentially, I think he must have taken a kickback from the borrower—there's no other explanation." He sat back. "We therefore intend to handle the problem as quietly and expeditiously as possible. The question before us, Miss Hill, is not whether the bank abrogated its responsibility —that is beyond dispute—but whether the SBA can escape liability to the bank. You are to frame the case that says unequivocally it cannot. I expect the complaint to be so forceful that it will bring the government to its knees. We want this messy business settled, not adjudicated."

"And suppose the case law is against us?" I asked him.

"Find some that isn't."

The early returns were not encouraging. A 1961 decision in the Sixth Circuit stared me right in the face. By its failure to obtain the security documents, the bank was guilty of "substantial and fundamental nonperformance" of its contract with the SBA and gave the agency the right to rescind. At a glance, it looked like an open-and-shut case against us. But I was not paid for glancing. I kept delving and after a while the pieces I needed came together. Having received from the bank insufficient documentation of the collateral, the SBA had either to rescind its agreement or stand on it (so spaketh the Ninth Circuit in 1945). When it did not rescind during the two years following discovery of the breach, the SBA waived its right to escape liability (said the Fifth Circuit in 1944 in *United States v. Maryland Casualty Co.*). "The agency is therefore conclusively bound by the contract of the parties," I wrote in my draft complaint.

"Splendid," said Lamport, massaging his knuckles as he read over it. "And are you sure these cases are directly on point?"

It was precisely the question I myself had been trained to raise in Judge Millis's chambers when determining "the permissible limit of distortion" in the citation of precedent cases by not overly scrupulous advocates. "As sure as I can be," I said. "But I've attached copies of the opinions for your consideration."

"I'm sure you won't mind my glancing at them."

"Frankly, I'd say you're obliged to. One can't rely overly on aides still wet behind the ears."

He pressed his lips together at that disingenuous disclaimer. "Getting dryer by the day," he said. I took that to mean my ears, not his lips.

I flew to Washington with Lamport for a meeting with the SBA lawyers to head off a courtroom showdown. Beforehand, he squired me around the city for a thoroughly delightful evening, at the end of which I kissed him on the cheek. He was momentarily flustered before reverting to form. "Can you be up and ready by seven?" he asked. "I'd like to go over everything one more time before we lock horns with these fellows."

Mornings at seven I generally functioned at subzombie efficiency; this time I overcame inertia by the simple expediency of never going to sleep and showering intermittently till dawn when I swallowed half a pot of black coffee. Lamport, himself wan and mechanical at our session, never noticed the toothpicks between my eyelids. On the taxi ride over I thought I detected him trembling slightly. At our 9 A.M. meeting, he rallied and was quite as magisterial as ever. In the long run, he convinced the feds, the case would cost the government more to argue than to settle—and their prospect of victory was, at any rate, far narrower than ours. We left with their promise to think hard about a settlement. An hour later at the airport, Lamport suffered a mild stroke.

In the senior partner's enforced absence during ensuing months, I held repeated conversations with the agency and the bank, consulting at all points with the other partners. Negotiating with other people's money, I was unflinchingly fearless. In the end, the government settled for $57,000. The firm earned a fee of just under nine thousand. And I, upon Lamport's return to action with all faculties seemingly unimpaired, won his distinguished-service commendation and my first dinner invitation to his home. He had taken up a paternal regard for my progress. Over a nightcap (compliments of the wine cellar of a late client who had chosen that form of partial payment for the executor's duties), Lamport toasted my health and waived all future reservations against my wearing pants to the office. I said that if he would not interpret it as feminist militancy, I would just as soon stick to skirts. "If you will not interpret it as male chauvinism," he replied, "let me confess they make for a more pleasing sight." Only Mrs. Lamport kissed me good night, but her husband's handclasp bordered on an embrace. At the office the next day, he was of course as formal as ever.

Fate was my timely consort as well in a case involving one of Dan Kettering's stellar clients. Logan Marts, a chain of discount department stores operating in suburban shopping centers, functioned more as a landlord than a vendor by franchising out most of its space under subleases to specialty retailers and service businesses. Dan prepared all the subleases, including one with a savings and loan association for the Logan Mart at the recently opened Upper Amity Shoppers' Mall. Subsequent to the drawing of that sublease and without Logan or the savings and loan's knowledge, the shopping center signed a lease with State Bank & Trust for a branch operation and appended a restrictive covenant providing that the center would not enter into a leasing arrangement with any other financial or lending business. Believing it had a monopoly of its trade, State Bank spent nearly $90,000 preparing its leased premises for the gala opening of the center. Then it learned that Logan had subleased to the savings and loan, in apparent violation of State Bank's restrictive agreement with the center's management, and it sued everybody in sight.

The whole business proved a badly tangled net, revolving in large part around the question of who had prior notice of what. The deeper Dan got into it, the more distraught he became. "I don't see how in hell they can rope us into any of this," he said, eager for my aid now that the First Amity Bank matter with the SBA had established my credentials as a Tory in his view. "Our team did everything strictly according to Hoyle."

"Meaning you didn't screw up," I said.

"I sure as hell did not." He seemed on the edge of panic. "I treated this sublease exactly like every other I've done for Logan."

"That doesn't mean you still can't get banged up by the other guy coming across the divider." I flipped through the State Bank complaint. "Let's pull the thing apart for a minute."

"Okay," he said, "okay."

I spent another little while reviewing the complaint and then sketched it out for him. "Okay, State Bank says we violated their covenant with the shopping center. So we say that's impossible since our sublease predated their covenant. They say they couldn't have known about our sublease since notice of Logan's basic lease with the shopping center had never been filed in the Upper Amity land records. So we say that's certainly not our fault and, anyway, the center's failure to file doesn't cancel our leasehold rights. Besides, the bank should have known we were coming since our building is going up right next to theirs—and Logan usually subleases to some sort of a savings and lending institution. They say they assumed we wouldn't sublease to a banking operation because of their covenant with the shopping center. So we say that was an unwarranted assumption on their part and all the center really gave them was the assurance that it would not henceforth lease to a financial institution. That guarantee in no way affected Logan's prior right to sublease to whom it chose. All of which means Logan bears no liability whatever and if State Bank had exercised due diligence, it would not have sunk ninety thousand into decorating an exclusive franchise it never really had."

It was hardly an arduous workout in mental gymnastics for anyone with an even modestly analytical bent. But Dan didn't qualify in that category. "Hey," he said, pupils dilated, "can you get up in court and do it just like that?"

"Me? I thought Sparky did all the serious litigating around here."

"Sparky's booked for months except for real emergencies. He thinks this is routine."

"He's probably right. I don't see any zingers in there, but I'd have to check the whole thing out pretty carefully. Trouble is, I can't get to it for at least a week myself. Maynard has me on several things."

"I'll begin checking, then—if you get me started."

So Dan Kettering became my assistant while I argued Logan's case in Superior Court and got them off without a blemish. After the two-day trial Dan drove me home and came upstairs for a drink. And then helped himself to another. I guided him toward the door before things got out of hand. He insisted on a kiss of commendation that was unmistakably prurient; I did not respond except for a nudge across the threshold.

"You're a remarkable woman, Tabor," he said, his birdman glasses steaming.

"A remarkable lawyer," I corrected him. "The rest of me is a mystery wrapped in an engima."

The episode was not a total loss for him, though. Logan expressed its thanks by sending him a collapsible canvas summerhouse for his backyard; the firm responded with charges of $8,000, billed out half to Dan and half to me. Dan had the grace, at least, to propose that my billable hourly rate be jacked up 50 percent to reflect the improved caliber of my craft. Sanity forbade my pointing out that the increment still left my time valued only half as high as the partners'; my trajectory, at least, was headed right.

It was soon afterward that my knack for threading the heavily mined straits of taxation law was summoned in earnest to the firm's service. Gil Serini approached me with unaccustomed pride on a matter he was handling for the social betterment of the Italian-American community. Would I examine the details for him to see if there were any rotten apples in the form of tax repercussions he had not anticipated? I would and did—and found the deal downright maggoty.

The Vesuvio Club was a combination of fraternal, economic, political, communal, cultural, religious, and criminal interests centered in the Brewster Street area of the city, the heart of the Italian quarter for the better part of a century. In a sense, it was an oldtime political clubhouse, bringing its influence to bear on every important policy decision the city made. But it was something beyond that—a repository of the fierce tribal loyalty, manifested in all those convoluted blood ties and even bloodier antagonisms, that gripped the survivors of a steadily shrinking urban village. Here they conspired to grade the priests, to count the Cadillacs of their offspring, and to make sure none of them went hungry or died without a thronged, floral funeral. One of the mellow Sons of Vesuvio, as that all-male band called itself, had made a considerable fortune in the construction business and wanted to express his gratitude by a fitting gift to the community. He asked his fellow Vesuvians to tell him what sort of facility would be most useful. They conferred for weeks and then agreed: a home for aged and indigent Italian-Americans. Their benefactor thought that a fine idea and pledged an endowment of five million dollars. That they all wanted the undertaking to be carried out faithfully and without caterwauling was evidenced by the selection of Gil Serini, the brightest and best connected young Italian-American lawyer in town, instead of one of the casually trained oldtime practitioners. Besides, Gil's father was a pioneer Son of Vesuvio and his baby boyo had better keep his fee down to pocket change or ever after suffer the evil eye of the Brewster Street crones.

Gil's principal task was to fortify the operation against even standard plundering by friends and relatives of the donor, not to mention the more sophisticated connivance of administrators and hangers-on. To prevent padded budgets and exploited patients, he consulted the trustees and books of the Jewish home for the aged, the one for which my friend Jon had designed the large wing, and patterned the legal framework of the Sons of Vesuvio home after that avowedly philanthropic institution. Despite all the good intentions, that blueprint proved ill-advised. The nub of the problem was that the patients at the Jewish home were not free guests but paying customers, and the Sons of Vesuvio insisted on going the Jews one better: Every Italian oldster admitted would pay nothing whatever—or else the place wouldn't be a genuine charity. "I'm afraid your generosity is going to cut down heavily on the number of people your home can accomodate," I told Gil after combing through the projected operating figures. "Taxes will take a big bite out of your endowment income."

"What taxes? The Jews don't pay any taxes—and their patients have to fork over five thousand dollars a year. Ours are all indigents."

"The Jewish home is a break-even operation. They don't have any profits to tax."

"Neither do we. Ours isn't even break-even—it's all red ink. We have no taxable revenues."

"Oh, yes, you do," I said. "The Vesuvio endowment by your benefactor is going to throw off half a million dollars a year."

"But it's all going to run the home."

"Only what's left after it's taxed."

"But the club is a nonprofit organization."

"That doesn't make it tax-exempt."

"It's always been."

"Who says? Did anyone ever ask the IRS for a ruling?"

"Are you kidding?"

"Everyone in town knows the club is engaged in political activities, right?"

"Right."

"Then it's not tax-exempt. And since the maintenance costs to run the old folks' home don't arise in a profit-making venture, they're not a deductible expenditure. Which means instead of a tax-free income of half a million, the club would have to pay Uncle Sam—let's see—about two hundred twenty-five thousand dollars on its gross endowed income at current tax rates."

"Holy shit," Gil said softly.

I proposed that the problem be avoided simply by seeking an exempt status for the home as an entity separate and apart from the Vesuvio Club and then endowing it directly. No one at the IRS was likely to get upset if the place wound up being called the Sons of Vesuvio Home for Aged Italian-Americans, Inc.

"You saved my life," Gil said.

"What's a quarter of a million dollars a year between friends?"

"My neck," he said.

My reward for that dose of preventive medicine was a summons to Sparky Grier's office. He said he was glad to hear about the good works I'd been performing around the place because he needed my advice and was no longer hesitant about asking for it. He had a client in the liquor wholesaling business who had had a run of luck that was going to leave him with a taxable income, even after dollar averaging, of $400,000 that year. Naturally, this fortunate fellow was looking around for a tax shelter, and a friend had proposed participation in a real-estate deal he was trying to assemble. "It's a new medical office building—the guy says he has a number of specialists lined up already," Sparky explained. "My client invests a hundred thousand and on the accelerated depreciation angle he gets a write-off this year of three hundred thousand. Which seems to mean he'd save himself a hundred fifty thousand on the deal. Sounds very sweet." I agreed. "What's wrong with it?" he asked. I took down the numbers and told him to give me an hour to think about it.

"Unfortunately," I reported back to Sparky, "your client's friend is only dimly acquainted with the IRS Code. The basis of that peachy write-off is accelerated depreciation on real property, which just happens to be a tax-preference item. In English, that means his earned income, which was originally subject to a maximum tax of fifty percent, gets converted to ordinary income taxed at seventy percent to the extent of the tax preference items. Which means instead of saving a hundred fifty thousand in taxes this year, your client is saving a hundred fifteen thousand. That's not bad, only he's really going to take it on the chin if the office building defaults on the underlying mortgage—and given the profusion of office buildings with low occupancy rates in town, that's not exactly an impossibility. So let's be cautious and say there's a foreclosure in the third year. Your client is going to have to report as income the two-hundred-thousand-dollar difference between his previously claimed deduction and his cash investment—and he'll be taxed on it at the seventy percent rate. Result: Disaster. Read it and weep." I handed him my worksheet:

Tax in initial year if client
didn't invest in shelter $194,000
Tax with shelter investment
(including preference tax) 79,000
Initial tax savings $115,000
Less: tax on "recapture"
in event of foreclosure 135,000
Tax loss on transaction . . . . (20,000)
Add: cash invested in deal 100,000
TOTAL LOSS $120,000

"It just doesn't make any sense for someone with earned income to shelter it with tax-preference items," I concluded my lecture. "A straight-line depreciation would avoid the problem, but of course the write-off would be correspondingly lower—if you follow."

"Enough to take your word for it," he said. "Now all I need is a shelter that won't land my client up the river."

"Can I have a few days to think about it?"

"Why—it's my problem?"

"But I compounded it for you."

138

"That's crazy. And you've got other work to do."

"I'll do it in my spare time. It's the kind of puzzle I like to play with—if you'll let me."

"Gladly," he said and reached for the phone like an orphan for his teddy.

While I was experimenting with ways to keep the revenuers from carving up Sparky's client's windfall, Duckett Washburn called me at home one evening to report that everything was cool at the Boot Coop but a related problem was stirring. The apartments housing the laundromat were suffering from an advanced case of slumlorditis, he said. "Heat and hot water comes and goes whenever the spirit moves the owner, which is maybe Christmas Eve and Easter Sunday and otherwise it's like buyin' a lottery ticket and hopin' hard. He don't fix the windows or stoves or the iceboxes or the elevators or the toilets —or nothin' nohow. Our people have begged and pleaded with this shitface but he got roaches in his ears it look like 'cause it don't matter to him what they say. The tenants been belly-achin' to the city and picketin' the health department, so the landlord gets hit with a couple o' violations and prob'ly chucks 'em down the incinerator. So I tell 'em not to pay the rent and they don't—till the landlord buys himself an eviction notice and puts one mama and her babies on the street, and now the rest of them is shakin' in their boots."

"The landlord's a real prince," I said.

"Your average honky," he said.

"Probably better than most."

"Right—so he's naturally gonna grab any halfway decent offer for the rat trap?"

"If he's sane."

"So why don't we put the motherfucker outa his misery? How 'bout we expand the Boot Coop and buy up the apartment the same way and put it back in shape?"

"What are you going to use for money?"

"Same thing we used to buy the laundromat—your skull."

"My honky skull."

"Don't remind me."

"Don't hassle me."

"You are my sister, Tabor," he said out of nowhere. "I'm teasin', not hasslin'." The feeling of the man was unmistakable. It did not take a lot of words to register. "I dig," I said.

"Okay," he said, "then think us up an apartment house."

"I can't just do it with mirrors."

"You did last time."

"That was small. And your people had tax benefits they weren't using. A thing like this is a lot tougher. What you need is someone with a spare piece of change to sock in—someone with the exact opposite tax situation that can dovetail with your gang's." Someone, it came over me even as I was saying it, like Sparky's client. "And I might know just the pigeon," I said. "Don't go 'way."

"How can I?" he said. "You got the key."

I gave the next two days over entirely to the yoked projects. First I spoke with the slumlord to see if he would in fact sell out and how low. Quite low, as it turned out, since he was losing money on the building even as he was running it into the ground. The problem was his mortgage, but even that proved manageable. For one thing, it was held by the same savings and loan outfit that our client Logan Marts had subleased to at the Upper Amity shopping center, so I knew the people there from our adventures as codefendants. For another thing, the slumlord was ready to default on the mortgage, and so the bank was hardly adverse to someone else's assuming it under the same terms. Then I calculated, with Duckett and several of the tenants, approximately what needed to be done to restore the building to a habitable standard. And finally I did the legal carpentering. The Boot Coop was a general partnership; I proposed revising it to make room for limited partners who would agree to bear the cost of all repairs, replacement of machines and appliances as necessary, and of course the mortgage, in return for a fractional interest in the expanded enterprise. The lure for the limited partner was the provision that all of the depreciation, repairs, and other deductible expenses would be assigned to him so that the total deduction would come to at least twice the aggregate investment—in short, a tax shelter that allowed him both to do well and do good at the same time. And afterward, if and as operating surpluses accumulated, the cooperative members could buy him out for the sum of his collective investment plus interest at the prime rate.

Sparky studied my memorandum closely. "So," he said when he was finished, "you're up to killing two birds with one stone already. I'd call that advancement."

It sounded more facetious than sincere. "You don't like it, huh?"

"Like it? I think it's inspired. They ought to strike a medal for you over in the Gully."

"But?"

"But I'm not sure my bird'll go for it."

"Why not?"

"Because my bird is the type that calls your birds 'jungle bunnies.'"

"Tell him God is black and this is his last chance for redemption."

"He'll never buy it."

"Why not?"

"He'll say who's worried about a God who's on welfare."

"Tell him that's only on the seventh day—and if his number's up any of the other six, his ass is gonna be in the sling."

Offered the opportunity, Sparky's client loved the idea of becoming an overnight humanitarian and making money in the process. And the housing wasn't even interracial. All he asked was that his participation in the arrangement not be made public for fear that, as Sparky quoted him to me, "every deadbeat between here and the Zambesi will be over me like a tent." All that remained was for me to get IRS clearance. On investigation, this looked to be a thornier problem than the tax gambit in the original laundromat purchase. Internal Revenue rules prohibited business deals "the principal purpose" of which was tax avoidance. Would I have to seize wicked means to win a goodly end? Was Heidi about to slip into a negligee to ensnare Yankee Doodle? I was registering contractions of conscience every three minutes even as I plotted my course. But if I could not indulge in a little forensic pragmatism without accompanying fits of self-flagellation, how would I ever prosper at my trade? Avoidance of all deviousness was as much a form of fanaticism in the adult female, I concluded, as the preservation of chastity—and about as rewarding. Thus, with a relatively unpained soul, I insisted that tax avoidance was not "the principal purpose" of our rich client's participation in the deal; that was simply what attracted him to it. The business reason behind the revised partnership plan, I wrote the IRS,

> is the limited financial ability of the general partners to raise the funds needed to maintain the premises and repair and replace the equipment therein should the cash flow from the laundromat receipts and apartment rentals remain inadequate for those purposes. By enhancing the feasibility of this self-help enterprise, moreover, this agreement will improve the financial status and living conditions of the tenants of this low-income housing project and their equally destitute neighbors—an objective in harmony with the national policy announced by the President to help the impoverished help themselves.

Washington could not have agreed more.

Duckett phoned to invite me to the opening ceremonies of what he called "the gala rejuvenation of the fucked-over premises." I said I'd do my best to make it. "You got to," he said, "on account of it's bein' renamed The Tabor Arms."

"Get outa my face."

"No, I'm levelin'—you are our main man."

"Just pay our ridiculously modest legal fee."

"That's number two on the agenda."

"What's number one?"

"Namin' the place for you."

"No."

"Too late. I got the sign all ordered. Gold letters on black."

"It's not really going to say Tabor Arms?"

"Sure thing."

"It's—it's—professional advertising. I'll get in trouble with the bar association."

"They don't come around much."

"But they'll hear. Look, it's a wonderful gesture but I can't—"

"Hey, you are the one which led us out of bondage. You got to be big about it."

"Call it Moses Towers if you're doing the bondage bit."

There was quiet on the other end for a minute. Then he said, "You know, for a sister you ain't got much amazing grace."

13

"Very creative stuff," said Arnold Berenson, my former commandant at Legal Assistance, in connection with the funding arrangements I had worked out at the Boot Coop. "Some of our clients are involved. They think you're a girl Robin Hood."

"Just a straight arrow," I said. "What's up?"

He wanted to borrow my services for a brief that needed top-to-bottom overhauling. His bureau had filed in federal court to prevent the state welfare department from limiting the rate at which one of its clients could spend his own retroactive Social Security award. It didn't seem to be an especially difficult case, I told him. "But there's not much law on it," he said. "Besides, I want to win—we've been in kind of a slump lately."

The firm agreed to let me do the job provided it fell within my allotment of released time for *pro bono* work. They had begun keeping a jealous watch on how I allocated my billable hours—a distinct if perverse compliment. A week of evenings and a long weekend writing allowed me to finish up the brief for Berenson on schedule. He called me a few days later to say he found it just fine "except for one or two tiny things" and was going in with it. "What tiny things?" I asked. He wanted to reverse the order of a couple of points and strengthen the language at one or two spots. I agreed and proceeded to forget all about the matter until the following week when I got a call from the secretary of my other former boss, Judge George

Hightower Millis, former capitalist lackey turning compassionate Solomon. The judge wanted to see me in chambers at my earliest convenience. Consumed with curiosity, I made it in twenty-seven minutes.

Some of his chronic pinkness had been drained out of him. "Are you all right?" I asked after a quick exchange of greetings.

"I was," he said, "until I saw this." He handed me a retyped copy of the brief I had prepared for Legal Assistance on the Social Security matter. On the title page, it bore my name, among others, under the heading of "counsel." Berenson and his principal assistant had top billing.

"Oh," I said, "I didn't think they were going to list me. I was just sort of a relief pitcher."

"You wrote it, Tabor. The style, the organization, the thinking—it's not what these people usually come up with."

"A lot of people wrote it, judge."

"But you rewrote them all—?"

There was no point in being coy. "Okay, so I did. What's the crime? My firm knows all about it."

"The point is that so do I. And I feel terribly compromised by it."

"I don't understand."

"I'm being asked to adjudicate a matter of some magnitude in which the plaintiff's pleadings have been drafted by the best clerk I've ever had. Doesn't that strike you as a little too close for comfort?"

"I hadn't really thought of it. Don't you routinely hear attorneys you've known before you went on the bench?"

"Not routinely. I consider the circumstances as they arise—and the degree of intimacy that existed. Usually it's no problem—I've never exactly been one of your hail-fellows-well-met."

"How am I any different? I was only here for a year."

He was by the big bay window behind his desk and looking out now. "You're different because—you're different."

"Well, that's certainly edifying."

"It's not something I can quantify, Tabor, It's a matter of instinct."

"Look, I'll have them take my name off the thing. I'll call them and ask for a retyped page. It'll be here within an hour."

"That won't change the basic situation."

I thought he was being overly dire about the whole thing and said as much. "But you're the judge—what do you want me to do?"

"I'm going to withdraw from the case, Tabor. With luck you'll wind up on Ben Spinelli's docket."

"And without it we'll be dead."

"Somebody should have thought of that before the brief was filed."

"I guess nobody realized you'd officially entered your holier-than-thou period." It was an effrontery I felt I had to risk.

He jabbed both hands into his pants pockets and rocked back a little on his heels. "I'm not holier than anybody, Tabor," he said.

"You're sounding it."

"Listen," he said, "I have an old friend who lives just outside Marseilles for about half the year. That's where he is right now. Made a fortune in the semiconductor business when I was in practice. I used to represent him." And he wandered on about the fellow for a minute or two. The tangent seemed so oblique and his face so livid I really did wonder if he were ill. Slowly, though, the judge arrived at the point he was fumbling after. "At any rate," he said, "my friend spends the rest of his year commuting between a New York apartment, a suite at the Mark Hopkins, and a vacation home on Hilton Head Island—that's just off the coast of South Carolina, a bit above Savannah."

"I know where it is," I said.

"It's a lovely little house on the quiet side of Sea Pines. He rents it out part of the time—he's always looking to turn a buck—and he lets me have it from mid-May to mid-June. I pay him, of course, so there's no question of impropriety."

"What is it you're trying to say, judge?"

"I'm going down there for Memorial Day weekend. Come with me, Tabor."

It was as if those tiers of wall-to-wall books that I'd dwelled among that unforgettable year of my life had come tumbling down on me. The roundaboutness of the proposition could not veil the nature of the bargain he was offering. His sanctimoniousness had been merely a lancing prelude to his lascivious intent. The dashed look I gave him answered his invitation.

"There's something you should know," he said.

"There usually is," I said softly. "I don't want to hear it."

He came to the front of his desk and loomed directly over me. "My wife has been a certified manic-depressive for all twenty-nine years I've been married to her. She's suffered from the condition since adolescence. Neither electrotherapy nor chemotherapy has prevented her from getting worse—and Lord knows, I've done no better despite trying every way I know how. When she is well, she is a lovely woman—but she is not well very often or for very long. Two months ago she reacted badly to a lithium treatment. She's been at the Institute for Living in Hartford since then. They expect she'll be there till fall." His tone was flat and even as he spoke. "I've been faithful to her for a very long time," he said after a moment, "and I want you to know that. It would pain me for you to think I'm a lecher. But after all these years I feel entitled to a little happiness in my private life."

That stopped my tears, anyway. He was not complaining, just laying on me the extenuating circumstances. "It's funny," I said, collecting myself. "Here you are, the epitome of everything people are supposed to crave in this life—you've got power, prestige, security—the works. Yet you're reduced to—this."

"Is it all that tawdry?"

"No, it's just sad."

"I don't want sympathy, Tabor—that's not why I told you. I told you because I think you're entitled to know. Very few people do outside the immediate family."

"Still, I wish you hadn't."

"I couldn't have asked you without telling."

"Then you shouldn't have asked."

"But I wanted to," he said. "You're someone special to me, Tabor—you've been since the day you breezed in here and started lecturing me on right and wrong. You were totally impossible—and impossibly charming. I was morbid for weeks after your year was up." He ran a hand through his hair. "I'd always hoped there was a reciprocating fondness."

"Fondness, yes, certainly. But not ardor."

"I don't expect ardor. I just want to spend a few days with you away from everything and everybody."

"I see," I said noncommittally.

"Forgive me—I suppose there must be someone on your end who—who comes first. I just wasn't thinking much beyond my own situation. I shouldn't imagine that an attractive young woman could avoid entangling alliances. I never wanted to know about that side of you."

Entangling alliances. I'd made a mini-career of avoiding the very notion. At the moment I was perhaps even less entangled than I liked. My architect Jon had split with his doctor client when she threatened to sue him over that gorgeous but unlivable house he had built her, but I would not have him back under our prior arrangement. We saw each other now and then and remained friends and sometimes went to bed but not as lovers. It was the same with my geophysicist Jeffrey, the more prepossessing of those two good buddies who had drifted apart over me. And there were a few others I played with and left without pain on either end. Mostly I was loving the law, even when I was hating it. I did not have to concede any of this, though, to George Millis. I needed only take the out he offered. But I was moved enough to be straight. "There's no one special," I told him.

His look brightened. "Then come," he said, just managing to avoid a pleading gentleness. "It's lovely down there now."

"I—don't know. I don't think so."

"But why? Is it my age? Believe me, I'm not in the rocker yet."

"No, it's not that."

"Then what? Am I so physically repulsive to you?"

The poor man was famished for reassurance. "Not at all," I said. "You're quite nice-looking."

"Then what?"

"I don't know." I was standing before him now, moving my

eyes slowly up his torso till I was looking squarely at that wavy judicial head of his. "Yes, I do," I said. "It's you. I can only think of you in robes—or like this, surrounded by the emblems of your office. You're Judge Millis to me—not George. You're not an ordinary person. You're removed somehow—"

"Come on now, Tabor. You sound like a first-year law student."

"I guess part of me still is."

"Didn't you see enough flaws in me when you were here to convince yourself I'm mortal?"

"It's not that so much. It's that sort of insistent impersonality you manage—or maybe you just kept me so damned busy I never had the time to consider you as a regular human being. Can you understand?"

He smiled at the thought and shook his head and looked off past me for a moment. "Have you any idea how depressing it is," he asked, "to be considered a sort of semi-deity when you're beset by a great many distinctly ungodly impulses? Do you have any idea how often I've wanted to hurl the gavel at some jackass arguing his insipid head off in front of me and enter a summary judgment for the other side? Why on earth judges are so mindlessly exalted I'll never understand."

"Just federal judges."

"Even so—"

"Because there are almost no other categories left to respect. And if you turn out to have clay feet, too, then there's no one incorruptible."

"But that's an impossible demand to load on anyone's character. We're only human." He met my eyes. "Depressingly human, I'm afraid."

"The demand comes with the territory. So much is expected of you because so much is given to you. You can make or break the rest of us with a flick of your wrist—like Superman—so you'd damned well better be nobler and smarter and kinder than anyone else. Hell, you're the steady light that's supposed to see us through the storm—you're not allowed to blink or dim or go out." Why was I being carried off on heavy elegiac wings when all the nice man was asking for was a little ass? I

148

caught myself short and studied him for a moment. Yes, he was clean and good and served as best he knew, and everything else was freighted by my Marian attitudinizing. I gave him a hurried hug, half from gratitude, half from affection, and said, "I'd love to see Hilton Head."

We flew down separately, no doubt out of tacit allegiance to the Canons of Judicial Ethics. The final hop from Atlanta to the island on something called Florida Airlines transported me beyond geography. The place was all fervent green and enveloping warmth and watered throughout by ocean and lagoon and clear creeks and the arcing spray from a thousand sprinklers. The sky seemed so dizzyingly blue and bright and the air so soft and perfumed that I felt gauzily drugged in the daylight hours. It was not a displeasing sensation under the circumstances.

The house was modern, all glassed or screened or open, with its decks and porches fenced from the road and bike path that ran in front of it. Not far to the rear was the sea. Just the two of us were there, about as private as we could be. I wore an old T-shirt and short shorts and nothing underneath and felt overdressed. George Millis in mufti looked remarkably like any other middle-aged man of means and taste idling in the semi-tropics, but he was reserved from the first and hesitant around me and plainly fearful he had blundered in inviting me until I made him unwind beside me on the matted veranda. He took off his shirt and I mine and the sun baked our nakedness and I combed the hair on his chest with my fingers and got him to talk about how all he usually did there was fish for pompano and wide-mouthed bass. And then I was on top of him full-lipped and coaxing and he was responding in pleasured jolts. I undid my pants and then his and clung to his soaring spar until he groaned and rolled me over. He did not know how to love with his mouth or his hands—whether he had forgotten or never known did not matter—so I moistened him and stroked him and squeezed him in spasms and guided him to me and over me and into me. There was discovery and then fierceness in his delving and spanning, and I eased him and soothed him and rehardened that prong of commendable girth if not length until it could no longer forbear.

That afternoon we walked the clean wide beach where we could see the ocean surf and the tidal currents of Calibogue Sound froth together in the estuary. He knew the flora and fauna of the place by heart and tolled them for me as we went —the prolific mockingbird spawning the three litters a year, the gophering sand crab and its clever camouflage, the prickly ash with its anesthetizing bark, the flattened sea cucumber springing into a protective ball when touched. . . . There was nothing pedantic in his recitation, just an easy familiarity that made the marine life more inviting and a part of me. I asked him why the sand didn't give way underfoot as at most beaches; he said it was made from shells, ground up and atomized and churned into a kind of mortar by the endless play of the seawater. I picked up some of the shells and inspected them and discarded some for better ones as I came upon them, and kept gathering and depositing all along our route until at the end I was left with display-case specimens that I brought inside with us and threatened to sell in the lounge below the Harbor Town lighthouse. Over vermouth we watched the sound empty of its Sailfish and Hobie Cats and grander craft and the sun dwindle to a molten sliver and then die, and I was glad to be suspended in that seaside hideaway.

We took a light dinner of pasta and chianti at the dockside pavilion in South Beach and spoke gingerly of our work. He further disabused me of my reverence for his office. I may have continued to hold it in awe, he said, but the masses clearly did not. "You can see it in the courtroom every day in a dozen ways," he said not unwistfully. "They come in late, they wear anything, they talk when court's in session, they stand grudgingly if at all when I enter or leave—I'd like to hold the lot of them in contempt. I think it's just the prevailing mood everywhere. The country's restless, disrespectful of its own principles —lost, I'd even say."

"Wandering," I said. "All dressed up in double-knits with no place to go but the Holiday Inn and Burger King. Well, it keeps the GNP moving."

He nodded and then he said he found it interesting that

each of us had moved several strides toward the social view held formerly by the other.

"I don't think I've changed any of my basic thinking," I objected.

"Maybe not," he said, "but you've submerged your objections to the profit-seeking monster."

"Not to its more ravenous instincts. I'm serving their interests because it serves my interest."

"That's the usual reason."

"But my heart's not with them."

"They don't need your heart," he said. "They're not into hearts." He smiled at his own apt use of head-shop vernacular. "All they want is your brain, your mouth, and your fist. It's all quite insidious."

"What took you so long to convert?"

"When you're caught up in it, there's no chance to get out in orderly fashion. You either fall off or get pushed."

"I'm not tripping with them, though. I'm using them and their needs and rendering fair service in return. That's what being a professional means."

"I know all about it," he said. "It's just that I think you're a different kind of professional. I'm sure you can be as dispassionate as you have to be but in the long run, you've got to believe in the good of the cause or you'll wind up just another hired gun."

"But not every cause has to be equally good—I can't go out and pick my clients off the trees."

"But you can choose your part of the forest," he said. "If you try to play the whole thing, I think you'll turn into a raving schizophrenic."

The irony of the exchange was not lost upon me. It had taken a whole year for me to put partisanship aside and learn to be lawyerly without having to embrace or recoil at the preferences of the clientele. George Millis, on the other hand, had moved beyond the requirements of the marketplace and the hoopla of the arena. He was free enough now and secure enough to act the exalted magistrate and the disinterested shaper of universal equity. He thought that a bit grand when

I proposed it to him but conceded the basic point, and in another moment he had me assessing the federal judiciary for its current inspirational output. "Very low," I said. "I think it's the fallout from the Nixon-Ford appointments. You're an aberration." He wanted to know who on the bench I thought was writing instructive law. "It's hard for us capitalist tools to keep up with everything," I said, "but from what I see and hear, there's only Mernige and Weinstein and Frank Johnson and maybe Jon Newman in the district courts and Seitz and Skelly Wright on the circuits—and on top there's no one. In fact there hasn't been a first-rate intellect up there since Fortas fucked up and Harlan died. Powell and White can think but they're all over the lot. Brennan and Marshall are usually right and God bless, but the prose is leaden."

"And me?"

I smiled at him. "You're making excellent progress, I'd say, in view of your severe handicap at the start."

"Don't patronize, Tabor." He really wanted to know.

"Well, I don't exactly study every opinion you turn out nowadays—can you bear that?—but the ones I've read closely seem very sound on the law but rather uneven in their structure and language. Some of the time you seem to be backing into the decision—there's almost a defensive tone to the opinion, as if you're hoping no one'll notice or mind too much."

"You're not far wrong," he said.

"Well, it shows. I'd almost call it a hedging quality."

He nodded. "And you'd prefer everything to be *basso profundo?*"

"If you want to be heard."

"But I'm not running for anything. And some of the time the decision is a damned close thing in my mind."

"And everyone can tell."

"You're a very hard woman to please, you know?"

"Impossible," I said.

He was beginning to suspect me of totalitarian intolerance, he said, and I howled. "It's the cruelty of the young," he said, "a perverse idealism. You look at the federal bench and find

152

only a handful who aren't cretins. I look at it, knowing that every selection is a compromise, and I'm amazed the output is even half as good as it is." I told him youth must be served and he said he supposed so, and on that conciliatory note we walked back to the house and stretched out on the porch and explored each other languidly. It must surely have been the first time in his life he'd been laid twice the same day.

We hiked and biked and picnicked the rest of the long weekend, and I read on the veranda while he fished for a couple of hours. The brief separation gave us each some breathing space and kept the mood cordial and low-key. Toward the end he confided how much he missed the sort of easy companionship we had shared those three days—a void that was particularly dispiriting to him on top of the enforced isolation of his work. "It's one thing to be removed from the *sturm und drang*," he said. "It's another to be a hermit. You dry up inside." I told him he sounded sorry for himself and that I had found substantial comfort in self-reliance. "But you're free to move in whatever circles please you," he said, "whenever the mood strikes. I don't have that luxury. I'm a slave to discretion. My work is my life."

"And when you're not working?"

"I'm afraid not to, to be honest."

"You're doing fine here."

"Because of the company. If you'd said no, it wouldn't have been much of a holiday."

"That's terrible," I said. "There's everything to do out there —and you should do it as long and as hard and as often as you can."

"It's not easy alone, Tabor."

"I do it."

"You're missing the point. I'm under constraints—"

"I'm not exactly a wood nymph myself. I think you're copping out, your honor. There are always ways if you'll make room for them—and people who'd be glad for your company but are probably intimidated by your rank. Take a little initiative now and then."

He strummed his fingers on the table beside him. "I don't know," he said, "maybe so."

We went for a final bike ride and I ruined things by swerving to avoid an oncoming child cyclist, skidding on a wet spot on the path, and taking a hard spill that nearly fractured my goddamn ankle. He would not hear of letting me travel back home alone on crutches, though we had planned to separate in the interest of propriety. Fear of discovery at the northern end reintroduced the tenseness that had ruled the first few hours of our liaison, and we sat mostly speechless throughout the plane ride. Past Washington I perked up and reminded him with a smile of how he had said at our second encounter that prospects were excellent for an uncomplicated relationship between us. "I think I actually said productive and uncomplicated," he remembered. "I wasn't altogether wrong."

"No," I said. "And we're not going to get you reversed at this late date, your honor."

"I told you once—I'm not 'your honor' outside the courtroom."

"I'm just joking."

"You're not. You didn't call me George once the whole weekend."

"I didn't?"

"You know perfectly well you didn't."

He was right. It would have meant nothing for me to call another man by his first name. With a federal judge, it was a statement of endearment if not an avowal of raging affection. That I could so sharply separate the action of my loins from even that merest expression of tenderness troubled him, it was plain. "I just don't want to lead you on," I said.

"It's only a matter of being civil."

"It's not," I said. "It's more than that."

"Because I'm a high priest of the temple?"

"Yes."

"I thought we'd more or less got past that."

"I know," I said, "and that's exactly what I don't want you to think."

"Why is that? I had a fine time with you. And I'm not aware you were in great pain—until your bike crackup."

Oh, God. The dear man still had a hard-on. My solicitude had plainly fed instead of slaked his brush fire. I put my hand on his wrist. "I had a lovely time—George—really, it was crackerjack, okay? I'm not just saying that. But one reason was that it was entirely out of context—like a nonrecurring dream, do you understand? It wasn't a road tryout for the Broadway run. I'm sure that's not what you intended. You asked me to come, out of the blue you asked—and I did because I'm fond of you and you seemed to need someone so much just now. That was how I took it, and yes, I had a fine time. But I didn't want you thinking there could be more—that a relationship is possible. That can't be, for either of our sakes—you must know that."

"Why must I?"

"Because of who you are—and who I am. It would be compromising, to say the least—and ruinous, probably, when word got around. There's no way, George."

"Aren't you the little girl who told me only recently there's always a way?"

The hurt was all over his face. He had had a glimpse of something, a taste and a touch and a feel of something that restored him momentarily and now he saw it slipping away from him faster than the ground below us. And now I was sorry that I had been kind; all I had done was postpone saying no to him, and now that no caused twice the pain. "You're distorting," I said, "and beyond the permissible limit, I'm afraid."

He looked at me for a moment in chilled silence. "You are the most stunningly detached person I've ever known," he said. It came out sounding like a life sentence.

"You're wrong, George. I'm anything but detached. I'm just very cautious about my emotions. And what's happening right here is exactly why. I am the founder, president, and sole member of the Tabor Hill Preservation Society. If I weren't, I'd get demolished about once a month. Please understand. I'm not commenting on you—or your charms—or your manhood. They're all fine. I'm the one who's vulnerable—and uncertain.

I'm not emotionally equipped for dalliances—believe me—your honor."

I won Arnold Berenson's Social Security case for him, and Legal Assistance hailed it as a major triumph. The federal court opinion by District Judge George Hightower Millis was bland but unequivocating. It was my first victory in that tribunal, but I turned down Arnold's buoyant invitation to a celebration lunch. After reading the decision over twice all I wanted was to take a long, lonesome douche.

14

My father died at the beginning of that summer. I was unprepared for the event. Sixty-four years did not seem long enough to live for a man I had grown up believing an ageless wizard who could outsmart wind and rain and the actuarial tables by which he earned his living.

In a way he had been dying for ten years, my mother told me after he was in the ground. The company had advanced him as far as it had determined he should go, and he sensed that the rest of his professional life would be a slow but unmistakable atrophying of his powers. His investment recommendations were increasingly second-guessed by the supervisory committee, and his cautious attempts to dedicate a small portion of the portfolio to socially commendable projects like public housing—an impulse, mother said, born of admiration for the selfless aspects of his children's careers—were methodically blocked. He sorely missed my brother, Brownie, and me and our tumult; there were no grandchildren to build doll houses with or for, not yet at least, and mother's outside interests were not ones he shared. The sweetness went out of the man, and while he always displayed curiosity about my professional progress when I visited for the holidays or an occasional weekend, he had limited confidence that I would amount to a great deal in my chosen field. "If you don't excel," he told me about a year before he died, "they'll say it's because you're a woman. And if you do, they'll say it's because you're a bit of a whore." Aside from the indelicacy of the phrasing, I thought that one of his most sensitive insights.

I stayed in Farmington for a week after the funeral, helping mother not go to pieces. She said she doubted that she could live in that large white house by herself and supposed she would sell it unless I objected strenuously. The place occupied too large a portion of my memory, prompted too deep a longing for unreclaimable moments of laughter and discovery and small victories over childhood's chilling demons, for me to contemplate sensibly that further loss of life. I opted for delay, pledging to mother that I would weekend at the house throughout the summer while she shipped off to California to visit Brownie, now a Caltech biologist, and his wife of six months.

There were other assets as well, I had known as father's duly designated executor—I told him I would no more accept the title "executrix" than I would be classified occupationally as a "lawyeress"—and it was plain that mother's half of the estate, along with her own tidy family inheritance, would not leave her wanting for material comfort. But having subordinated her life to a family that had now all but vanished from view, she faced needs of another sort. "Lord, how I envy you," she said before we kissed goodbye. I knew she meant the absorbing nature of my work. "It's your fault as much as Daddy's," I said. She knew I meant the model of unexpended resources she had provided for me and that I had so utterly rejected. "What he wanted for his children was not necessarily what he wanted in his wife," was all she said, and the subject was dropped between us for good.

I returned to Amity and the practice of law with an inheritance of sorts that left me more financially but less emotionally secure than I had been. My father's end forecast my own as no other event could have, and time no longer seemed infinite. I would be thirty soon and on my own more than ever. Did I want that? Or at subterranean levels would I seek a man to replace the one whose seed had begun me and love had shaped me and death had left me lonely and disconnected? That struck me as both so possible and ignoble an urge that I retreated for the moment from all but the most casual contact with men.

The first few days back at the office, I spent my lunch hour roaming alone through the historic cemetery, called the Amity Burying Ground, a few blocks above the city green. Neither necrophilia nor morbidity drew me there, only the need for a brief retreat to order my head and its wanderings. Set off from the city streets by a high sandstone wall on all sides, the hallowed ground held the remains of eighteenth- and nineteenth-century lives under tree-shaded tombstones that spoke to me achingly as if with the single inscription I had come upon the first day: "Rest, loved one, thy sufferings are ended." Stone after stone promised resurrection as if life on earth were but a vast detention camp for ritualistic writhing until divine accommodations became available. I tried to imagine my own immortal soul unsheathed by flesh and bone and pictured only a vaporous thing of terrible fragility to which no earthly frame of reference could be applied. What function would that unemployed wraith serve? What pleasure would it be granted without countervailing pain? All that bland, disembodied bliss struck me as more an everlasting doom than a heavenly reward.

My head was so full of metaphysics and birdsong as I made my way through that arbor of death, I nearly marched right past Sam Nightingale, who was seated on a stone bench at the end of the walk I had just distractedly negotiated. "Trying the place on for size?" he asked as I seated myself beside him.

"No, nothing like that," I reassured him. "Just consulting eternity."

"What's it telling you?"

"That it doesn't have anything to tell me."

He propped a foot upon on the bench and folded his hands around his knee. "Sounds like rather a one-way exchange."

"Pretty much," I said.

"I'm intruding—forgive me. I thought you could stand a little nonverbal company."

158

"I probably can." Slowly I turned toward him and saw that he was concerned. "How did you know I was here," I asked, "or are you practicing up for Hallowe'en on Bald Mountain?"

Sam grinned. "Balakian told me. He said you were a little down."

"Aren't most people when a parent dies? Steve wouldn't know that, though. He wasn't whelped, he was extruded."

"Such ingratitude. The guy was sensitive enough to mention he thought you were overdoing it."

"That means he can't understand why I'd rather mope around a cemetery than have a cheering hamburger with him. And wouldn't you? Dead people are livelier."

"Steve's not all that bad."

"I wouldn't go much beyond that."

"I find him dedicated and quite agreeable."

"Not to mention waffling and petty. He also wears appallingly short socks."

He shrugged. "Steve's just a little too cautious for his own good. And short socks are not a really major character flaw."

"They are if you expect to make partner."

"I wouldn't put them at the top of the list."

"Bare male leg doth not confidence inspire."

"Have you passed on that little haberdashers' homily?"

"Hell, no. What's he got a wife for?"

Sam gave his head a disapproving little shake. "Frankly," he said, "watching you walk up this way, I thought Steve was right. You looked like you were on the way to your own beheading."

"I don't remember."

"No wonder—you were in a trance. Usually you take long, quick strides. I don't know another woman who walks more purposefully or less seductively, as if you're on a perpetual classified mission without much time to finish it."

"There usually isn't," I said and climbed slowly to my feet. "In here, though, speed is not exactly of the essence." I drew him up beside me. "Here, come tour Necropolis. I'll show you my favorite graves."

The bad-taste prize I had awarded to a banker's headstone

featuring an interlocking dollar sign and cruciform. "The gospel according to St. Lucre," said Sam. A strong runner-up for grossest grave was a Roman-style marble arch of triumph that rose to about the height of my shoulder above the bones of the thirteenth president of Mather University. "Better that," said Sam, "than a replica of the Cloaca Maxima."

I grinned and felt myself unwinding there beside him. The rest of the markers on our route I was able to examine with some detachment. In one stretch we came upon the consecutive graves of an eight-year-old girl, a woman who had died at just my age, and a seventy-nine-year-old who succumbed a month after her husband of fifty-seven years. "There's not a whole lot of logic to any of it, is there?" I said.

"For the species, maybe," he said. "For one being, none that I've been able to figure out."

"I guess maybe everybody ought to be ready to pack it in the day after next. It's all borrowed time, anyway."

"In a way," he said.

"Once you've decided that, you can go like gangbusters till you drop. I think that's what all the great people do. They don't waste their time worrying how long they've got left."

"And what do all the ungreat people do?"

"Figure there's not much point in any of it and just screw off waiting for the end." We moved on in silence for a while. Then I asked him if he ever thought about his own funeral and where he was to be buried.

"As little as possible," he said.

"But why? It's part of life."

"So is having a cavity drilled."

"You're mocking me."

"Not you—it."

"Doesn't the prospect make you sad, though?"

"Unbearably."

"So you run from it?"

"What else is there to do?"

"Stay and think what it means. You can't do it afterward."

"Well," he said, "I can't argue with that."

"I think maybe I'd like to write my own funeral oration," I

told him, "and leave enough to pay the leading lady at the Old Vic to recite it."

He grinned at the very idea. "But you wouldn't be there to enjoy it."

"At least I'd know what they'd be saying."

"Afraid to take your chances with history's verdict?"

"Not if I was sure it would notice me."

"Does it matter to you all that much?"

"Don't laugh," I said, "but I think it may." We walked on a few more steps. "That must sound screwy as hell to you."

"No," he said, "it sounds like someone furiously driven inside."

I nodded a little grimly. "You know what, Sam—sometimes I'm afraid of my own ambition."

"That's good. It may even save your life."

"For what, though?"

"I don't know—another day, another year—maybe until they cure cancer and constipation and everybody'll live forever."

"I'd rather flame out than become a long-term basket case."

"Sure," he said, "because you're still young and beautiful."

"I am not beautiful."

"Oh," he said, "my mistake. How about pretty, then?"

"Flowers are pretty, not people."

"How could I be so dumb?"

"I'm interesting-looking, how's that?"

"So is a praying mantis," he said.

"That's my league," I said and took his arm and steered us on till we came to a grave with the epitaph "Loved and esteemed by wife, children and all who knew him."

"What more can anyone want said of him?" Sam asked.

"That he used his time here well," I suggested.

"Could a man who won such devotion not have?"

"Sure. Give me a week and I'll find you a hundred lovable wastrels." Even as I said it, I saw where the loving wife and children of that esteemed corpse had been planted next to him. The whole loving family was side by side in the ground. Sam saw my eyes swell before I could avert them.

"Hurts, huh?" he said without smothering me.

"All that goddamned togetherness."

"Is that bad?"

I tried to sniff away the gloom. "Not bad—it's just not for me."

"Weren't you close to your folks?"

"Very. I even love my brother."

"Then why the waterworks?"

"I—don't know."

"Yes, you do."

"It's private—okay?"

"Sure," he said. "I just thought talking about it might be good."

I shook my head and we moved off toward the gate. Then out of nowhere I heard myself telling him, "He wanted me to marry and have kids."

"Your dad?"

I nodded. "He never gave me a hard time about it. He just said he hoped I could make room in my life for both the law and a family."

"Can you?"

"I don't know."

"Do you want to?"

"I don't know."

"Is that what sank you back there—feeling alone?"

"I didn't sink. It just got me down a little."

"Not having a family?"

"Yes, for crissakes!" I don't know why I barked at him. Probably because he was poking deeper than I liked. "Sorry," I said. "I'm not quite myself."

We passed through the cemetery gates, were assaulted by the city fumes, and headed toward the green. "I think you've got a lot of courage to go it on your own," he said, "if you don't find that patronizing."

"It's not courage—it's preference. And fear."

"Fear of what?"

"Of being a wife."

"What's wrong with wives?"

"They're auxiliaries."

"Some are, some aren't."

"Most of them lead second-rate lives—face it."

"So do their husbands. So does almost everyone. In fact, second-rate is pretty high. Not everybody wants to tear the world apart like you, Tabor. People recognize their limitations and just try to cope."

"But coping is all most wives really do. They're scared to death to try to be more than a decoration or a walking disinfectant."

"Mine isn't."

"Yours paints dots."

"She's a quite accomplished artist."

"Who says so?"

"A lot of people."

"Who—critics? Dealers? Does she show her stuff—does it sell?"

"She's—working toward a show."

"Then who says she's any good—besides her loving husband and a couple of dozen close friends?"

"People she's studied with."

"People she's paid, you mean."

"Well—"

"Look, I'm not trying to knock her—maybe she's a genius. But she's probably dabbling. She puts in half the effort a man would. The other half's for you and your kid. And half isn't enough. That's how come there aren't more than a couple of women painters anyone's ever heard of."

He thought that over and said maybe I had a point. "I also happen to think women have an inordinate fear of failing," he put in, "so they risk a lot less than men."

"It's not just fear of failing—it's fear of succeeding. It would turn their whole quilted world upside down. They'd have to kick and be kicked and not fall apart on contact. It's easier to take refuge in biology and sexual analogies. Wives don't do—they get done—and afterward they clean up the mess. Who do you think got out the mop and the Lysol when God rested on the seventh day after all that creating?"

"Mrs. God?"

"Exactly. And you never hear a word about Her. He makes all the noise."

We swung down treeless Willow Street for the final two blocks to the office. "I'll tell Steve not to worry himself over you," Sam said, "and don't abuse the poor guy for being considerate."

"I'll just buy him a pair of knee-length socks and a gallon of mouthwash."

"What's wrong with his breath?"

"Nothing I've ever noticed. But it'll get him plenty worried."

Sam laughed. What easy pleasure it was to turn that expressionless face of his festive. It looked at times as if it were almost begging to be transformed. He was still emitting snickers when we hit the last corner before the office. Then he slipped on the seersucker jacket he had slung over one shoulder and grew pensive. "Hey," he said, affecting jauntiness, "if you ever need a platonic ear to chew—so to speak—call me. I'm a summer bachelor during the week—Lee and Rollie are groupies with another family at Niantic. She likes to work out there. I go over on weekends."

"Thanks," I said, "I'll remember."

The following week I called him.

The seven o'clock news had been particularly cataclysmic that night; even David Brinkley's wry nasality could not minimize the disasters of the day. Suddenly a long, empty evening loomed. As a rule, I had no problem filling it with a dozen different things: Bach and the morning *Times*, a Thackeray novel, some reading for the office, a letter to my brother in our own inimitable code, the new *Scientific American*, practicing the flute which I had lately taken up, a call to a friend, watching *Masterpiece Theater*, scrubbing my clump of ringlets and drying them to a side of Cleo Lane. . . . None of those seemed appealing just then, except blowing on the flute, which I managed for twenty minutes before resigning in desolation and drifting toward the phone.

Even looking up his number seemed too studied. I asked Information for it, wrote it down, contemplated it (a profoundly uninteresting number), lifted the receiver, paused, wondered what I was doing and why, and dialed. It was busy. An omen. Probably yakking with the little woman. Accomplished artist, my big toe. I gave it two minutes and tried again. Still busy. The henpecked wimp. Well, maybe he was on with a client. Or his mother. Or broker. Or lover. No—no lover. He was too true-blue for that. His invitation to me was strictly good scout-manship. I dialed for what I decided would be the final time. He picked up after one ring. I said hello and that I hoped I wasn't bothering him.

"No," he said, "not at all. Just give me a clue, though."

"What about?"

"Who I'm talking to."

"Oh," I said. "And how many Circes do you invite to chew on your so-to-speak platonic ear?"

He was still for a moment. Then: "Tabor?"

"No, it's Yehudi Menuhin—somebody busted my bow and I'm sitting here on the window ledge."

He laughed. "You okay really?"

"Sure. How about you?"

"Me? I'm fine, thanks."

"How's the weather over there?"

"Oh—the usual fire and brimstone."

"Mmm, sounds steamy."

"You get used to it."

"Well," I said, "good night, Sam."

"Already?"

"I suppose I could do my Bette Davis imitation first."

"I'll bet it's hilarious." His gift for small talk had deserted him. My call was plainly unexpected and apparently more than a little unnerving.

"Actually, no, it's Ronald Coleman I do really well. Also Herbert Hoover—my Hoover's a knockout." Nothing came back over the line. "Well, sleep tight," I said.

"Hold on," he said.

"For what?"

"I—I'm just finishing up some office stuff," he said. "I'm a little distracted."

"No, you stick to business. I just wanted to say hello—and thank you for being a comfort the other day."

"Forget it," he said.

"Should I?"

"I—you know what I mean."

"Sure. Well, back you go to the salt mines." And I hung up, feeling dumb and rueful.

He called back in ten minutes. "Want to do something?" he asked directly.

"Like what?"

"I don't know. What do you like to do?"

"Ride a camel—hang-glide over volcanoes—tango on a skateboard—the usual things."

"Try again."

"Sit and talk with someone I like?"

"Better," he said. "Where?"

"I don't know. You decide."

"How about the Pilot House? We'll have a drink upstairs and count the waves in the harbor."

"Sounds breathtaking," I said. "What do I wear?"

"Whatever you're wearing now."

"That would be inappropriate."

He laughed. "Well, just anything, then."

"Sam," I said, "are you sure you want to?"

"Sure. I'm thirsty as hell."

"Won't tongues wag?"

"About what? A drink?"

"Look out the window, Sam. It's getting dark."

"It's a quiet place after the dinner crowd."

"That's my point."

"Look," he said, "if you don't want to come, forget it. But don't go through a whole big Jiminy Cricket routine for my benefit."

"Relax—I'm just trying to be considerate."

"Who of?"

"Both of us, okay?"

"What is the big deal about two business associates sitting down in a public place and having a drink together?"

"Nothing," I said, "as long as they're associating over business."

"I'll bring a will, two contracts, and a calf-bound affidavit. See you in half an hour."

Despite his bravado on the phone, he was smoking a cigarette and looking a touch peaked when he drove up in his tuckered Saab. There was a nice, old-shoe feel to the car that perfectly suited its driver. I took one look at Sam and said maybe we'd better just go for cones at Baskin-Robbins. He said that was most unbusinesslike, ordered me to hop in, and gunned us off into the gloaming.

Perched at the edge of the Amity Harbor Pier, the Pilot House presented its customers with a two-story-high, floor-to-ceiling panorama under glass of sky, water, recessed cityscape, and the soft running lights of seacraft gliding smoothly toward their evening berths. There was just a handful of people in the lounge and no one either of us knew. Sam relaxed and we listened to the piano and sipped the house wine from a half-liter carafe he had ordered us when I said I drank nothing hard. In a while he began to open up some, but his discomfort was transparent from the stinginess of his disclosures.

He was the product of what by my lights was an exotic union between a Jewish psychologist and Methodist nurse who had met on the job at the Menninger Foundation in Topeka. "They raised me as a hard-shell Jungian," he said, "and in all my childhood fantasies God wore a long white coat, blew smoke rings from a pipe the size of Gibraltar, and was a helluva lot more concerned about dreams, neurosis, and repression than good and evil. I reached adulthood pre-shrunk." When his parents split, Sam moved at the age of twelve to Evanston with his father, who joined the faculty at Northwestern, where he passed an unspectacular career. His mother took a job in a hospital at Yakima, Washington. "I saw her about five times after that. It was nothing personal. She just resented the hell out of me as living testimony to the sorriest chapter in her life. And I wasn't really thrilled that she had all but abandoned me. Since I happened to be a carbon copy of her from the neck up, my father never could look at me for long without wanting to reach for an andiron and lay it across my jaw. We were never exactly close."

Not surprisingly, Sam ended the odyssey of his dispossessed boyhood by coming east to college, staying for law school, and creating a new life for himself as far as geographically possible from both his parents. The magnetic V. Judson Prettyman, then dean of Mather Law School, provided a surrogate father for him, inviting Sam to join the law faculty after his hypermotivated academic performance, and when Prettyman moved on to the university presidency, it was natural that Sam would become enmeshed in the legal affairs of the institution. He had what he called "a very cordial, very informal, very discreet" association with the college since joining the firm, undertaking such tedious but altogether essential matters as restructuring the retirement fund and planning the university health-insurance program in coordination with the school-run hospital. He also functioned *sub rosa* as a kind of legal gunslinger for the school in problems it wanted kept out of the papers, particularly its disputes with the town. "Which may explain," he said, "why I haven't been at liberty as yet to call upon your skilled services."

"Your hard luck," I said.

"So I hear. I'll try you at the earliest opportunity."

"Try me now. This is supposedly a working session."

"Try you on what?"

"On whatever you're working on and can't figure out."

"I'm always working on lots of things."

"Try me on the hardest one."

"I can't really do that."

"Why not?"

"It's private."

"So is everything else at the firm."

"Some clients are more private than others—especially if they have a half-billion-dollar endowment."

"You both need me," I said. "Spill it."

He tried to hold me off but I kept worming away until he finally pledged me to confidentiality and sketched out the project currently confounding him. It was nothing more exotic than the perennial collision between the city and the university over the disproportionately small contribution that Mather made directly to the municipal coffers each year. Indeed, almost all of the tax dollars that Amity gathered from its largest, richest, and most eminent freeholder came by the indirect route of property levies against the school's employees. And the more the university expanded, the more property it absorbed and transferred to tax-exempt status—and the narrower the city's tax base became. Mather naturally claimed that it contributed mightily to the prosperity of the town by the millions it distributed to its suppliers and the goods and services purchased by the members of the academic community. The town countered that the more Mather grew, the more municipal services it required from a shrinking municipal budget; besides, much of the wealth being generated by the school was siphoned off into suburban communities, where a lot of the faculty resided and a growing number of service industries were locating. At that moment, more than one third of all the property within the Amity city limits was tax-exempt, and very few new ratables were going up or on the drawing board. Faced with choosing between severely reduced services and bankruptcy, the city was putting intense pressure on the university to share its wealth or be left with a wasteland for a domicile.

"What remedies has the town got," I asked, "besides suicide?"

"Political muscle," Sam said.

"To do what with?"

"Tax the university into the ground."

"But the university is tax-exempt."

"They can unexempt it. There's nothing in the state or federal constitutions guaranteeing exemption to private institutions. It's just a courtesy, extended on the theory that churches, hospitals, and colleges serve the highest public ends. The city's lobbying like crazy to get the legislature to rewrite the exemption statutes—they'll take a little at first if they can just get the principle established. Then they'll take what they need—and more. Fortunately, the governor and about a third of the legislature are Mather people—and the rest think maybe they'll get

169

honorary degrees if they hold back the tide. Meanwhile, the city's stalling on every piece of construction the university wants to put up. All I've got to do is come up with something that'll yield the city some revenue and not put the college in hock."

I promised him I would work on the problem. "How's two weeks?"

"Take three," he said, laughing at my impertinence.

"You think I'm kidding?"

"I think the wine is doing you in."

"I'm a very quick study."

"Oh, I'm sure," he said. "But even if you could speed-read the *Britannica* overnight, you'd have a little trouble with this. The problem doesn't lend itself to simple solution—unless the university decides to raise the tuition so high that only junior Mafia and sons of oil sheiks can afford to matriculate. All I'm looking for at the moment is a stopgap—a bone to keep off the jackals while we search for something definitive."

"Then a bone you shall have at once," I said. "The rest of the carcass will take a little longer to deliver."

Our talk remained mired in this meringue-like substance, but there was a pattern to it that deepened with the evening. I initiated the topics; he responded with caution, as if to disclose more of himself than he had to would present me with too plump a target to skewer. His reserve was well advised, for what little he chose to reveal suggested a career in passage of such limited scope and infrequent exultation that I was saddened by the exceeding tameness of the man.

We stayed till the midnight closing, and then he drove me home. In the parking lot he sat frozen to the steering wheel for a moment after cutting the motor. "Thank you for the company," I said and touched his wrist lightly. "There's no need to walk me in."

He looked straight ahead for another moment. Then he said, "I enjoyed being with you. I'm glad you called."

"You don't look it."

"How do I look?"

"Perturbed."

"That means I'm thinking."

"Don't think too much—you'll ruin a perfectly good time. And look at all we accomplished. I'm already apprenticing on the firm's richest client. I think I'll put the evening down on my time sheet and give Alva Potter a heart attack."

He frowned at me. "You've driven up the guy's blood pressure fifty points—let him die in peace."

"I can't—he's a mean little shit."

"That's his job."

"Well, I don't like being on his hit list."

"Then stop tormenting him."

"But he loves it. I've given new purpose to his miserable life."

"You're really dreadful," he said, smiling.

"I'm not going to sit here and get insulted at this hour of the night," I said, smiling back and reaching for the door handle. "Call me some time, Sam."

There was no smile this time, only the shared recognition that I had been the one to initiate the evening. He looked at me hard. "Will you come if I ask next time?"

"If I can."

He turned gently to me full face, hesitated, and then without grace plunged his head toward mine, hoping I would meet him halfway as in the movies, but I held my place and he landed on my shoulder and gave a muffled laugh at his own ineptness and kept his face hidden there.

"You want to kiss me but you're not sure I'll respond," I captioned the scene for him.

"The average fourteen-year-old's problem," he mumbled into my shoulder.

"Even fourteen-year-olds take chances," I said, "or they never make it to fifteen."

Challenged, his face found mine without mishap and we kissed long and full and with quite astonishing intensity. His splayed hands cupped my breasts and tightened around them almost harshly. I folded into his arms and we kissed another time and wetly and did not stop until a car door slammed at the other end of the parking lot.

171

I glanced back at him once before entering the lobby. He had latched on to the steering wheel again and sat there blankly contemplating the night. All those studied airy words of his, packed with coiled tension, reached me as a single coded message that he wanted something he had never had—and greatly feared he would be wounded seeking. I decided not to wave goodnight.

15

My bearded scientist friend Jeffrey Kramer came by the next night on a condolence call and stayed till morning. Sexual abstinence was not a prospect I entertained more gladly than promiscuity. Jeffrey, supposing me in mourning, had not anticipated any action. At first he kept his distance out of respect for the deceased; finding me near and warm, he reconsidered. Nothing, we decided jointly, could be more reverential under the circumstances than a life-sustaining dose of *coitus marathonus*, which he administered in a curiously syncopated style that I found pleasurable though not half so satisfying as the enduring feats of his erstwhile pal Jonathan. Other men as well—past, present, and future—were on my mind as my body was in the act. I was never a subscriber to the women's-dormitory jape that every phallus is more or less interchangeable with every other at performing its primal task; technique, after all, is what distinguishes our coupling from the beasts'. But Jeff's dutiful plunger, I must confess, took on a certain universality for me that night as I concentrated almost wholly on the sensation and as little as possible on its deliverer. I hadn't been as horny since finishing law school.

Whatever his limitations in bed, Jeff at least did not dry up and blow away as soon as he was released from my clasping custody—a habit common to the diminished lovers I had known. On the contrary, he was far more personable afterward, often providing me a giggling detumescence by narrating his latest misadventures in the world of science. On this occasion, his surreal narrative took on an added dimension for me.

Jeff had been tapped by the university to codirect Operation Bright Flame, a research project to explore alternatives to fossil fuels and nuclear power to supply the Mather generating station, a rapidly deteriorating installation that provided the bulk of the electricity throughout the far-flung campus complex. The plant, in need of major repairs, operated below marginal efficiency and was a drain on the university's financial resources. But before undertaking a major capital expenditure to fix it, Mather's guiding lights decided to set a select group of its stellar young scientists to work figuring out if a cleaner, safer, and, above all, more economical fuel source could be harnessed for the task. It was a rare instance in which basic and applied research were to be conducted simultaneously; the university, in effect, had turned over its largest single piece of mechanical apparatus for the lads to tinker with.

"All they want from us is a century's worth of discovery in eighteen months," said Jeff. "We're brilliant, of course, but that's a little farfetched. President Prettyman assembled the bunch of us in his office and read us our orders. He says it's the most important scientific undertaking with immediate practical implications since they built the bomb. Somebody said what about the moon landing, and Prettyman said, 'I stand by my estimate. The world will be watching you.' We've broken the whole thing down into four alternate power sources—the sun, the wind, the tides, and shit. I'm in charge of shit."

"Shit?"

"Shit. Human solid waste. Instead of burying it or dumping it in the ocean, we're burning it. Manure was a widely used fuel for centuries, of course. The human stuff naturally needs some treatment first, but you can't beat the price. And given the way our countrymen feed their craws, the supply appears to be limitless."

"So much for avant-garde science," I said.

"You're wrong," he said. "Shit is the new frontier."

You had to admire the guy's spirit. I just hoped their budget allowed for stall showers in or immediately adjacent to the laboratory. The irony of it was that Jeff had laid aside his efforts in nuclear energy, presumably the most modern of fuel sources, for these experiments in anal energy, among the most primitive of power packs. It didn't make any sense to me, I said, since I supposed that atomic energy was the most efficient source of fuel extant for generating electricity.

"It's not," Jeff said. "It's about the least efficient—on top of being the greatest hazard to land, sea, and air, and all that dwell therein." To create the steam to drive the generators to produce the electricity at a conventional power plant like the one Mather owned, Jeff explained, took temperatures of between one and two thousand degrees. "The fucking atom, though, doesn't know when to quit. It generates temperatures upward of a million degrees. That's like a thousand times more heat than anyone needs to run a Water-Pic or watch Captain Kangaroo. And naturally when they dump the superhot water, even after cooling, it screws up the ecology. They're sucking out a quarter of the Connecticut River upstate to run just one nuclear plant. The water they put back in is forty degrees hotter than when they took it out—that's murder on mackerel, trout, or whatever the hell used to paddle around in it. And when you're dealing with stuff that hot, all bets are off on conventional engineering. Last year one of those supposedly supertight plants in the northern corner of the state leaked three hundred gallons of contaminated steam. They said nobody was hurt, but how in Christ does anyone know that for sure?"

Then why, I asked, were the power companies sinking so much money into nuclear plants. "I don't suppose they throw their money away on purpose."

"It's not their money," he said. "It's your money. Every time they put up one of these multimillion-dollar monsters, they get to raise their rates. It doesn't matter how inefficient or potentially dangerous the plants are—the utility companies are monopolies and they're guaranteed a fixed return on their investment. So the more they invest, the more they make. An economical power plant is counterproductive to their goals—and the banks that fund the plants. That's why the power companies are never going to get into cheap fuel alternatives in a serious way. Windmills and solar energy and shit-burning—they wouldn't add big bucks to the plant cost. All they'd do is erode demand for the utilities' inflated product. That's why our thing is so important—no one else is going to do it except the non-profit sector."

It was not your usual post-coital fare, but I followed Jeffrey's revelations closely and the very next day pursued the matter. The germ of an idea was prowling around my attic. I called the one person I knew to be supremely authoritative on the subject. His office said he was vacationing in Nova Scotia. I asked for his number there; his secretary was reluctant to give it but said she would make an exception for me for the old days. I hesitated before dialing but only for a moment. Would he think I was fishing for an invitation to join him up there? Or that my heart had grown substantially fonder in the weeks since we parted? I would disabuse him of such notions if need arose, but gently; I did not crave him for a lover, but I assuredly could not afford to have him for an enemy. The call was a way to say I remained fond of him and still wanted to be his friend—but a distant one, necessarily. Judge Millis was surprised to hear from me.

"I never would have bothered you up there, George," I explained, "but I need three minutes of your counsel."

"I'll try—for you," he said, "but I'm not supposed to be in the counseling business these days."

"It's a research thing really—nothing even remotely litigious, I swear."

"I'm dubious," he said, "but go ahead. I'll stop you if it gets too close for comfort."

But he did not stop me. We talked for three quarters of an hour during which he offered me the distilled wisdom of his years on the state public utilities commission, which had as its principal function the setting of rates for the power companies. "They're mighty strange beasts," he said, "like something out of *Alice in Wonderland*. They're half socialist, half capitalist, and manage to combine the worst features of both systems

—gross ineptitude and unconscionable profits." The key to their operations was the law entitling them to tack on to their cost of doing business a guaranteed net operating income equal to nine percent of their "rate base," which was just jargon for the capital investment in all their property and equipment. And because they knew the rates they could charge were set by formula, the companies had no real incentive to develop more efficient power. "Why, they're blue-printing plants that are going to generate thirty to forty percent more power than their projected peak loads for the rest of the century," he said. And the bigger the capacity, regardless of public need, the more profits the companies reap. He cited a few of the more distressing rate decisions the state commission had been obliged to hand down during his tenure and suggested I look them up if I wanted chapter and verse. I thanked him for his generosity. He said it was his pleasure, asked after my ankle, added that he was glad we had had the chance to get to know each other better, and left it at that.

I than invested a week of evenings researching the subject at the Mather Law Library and took a day in Hartford to check out the cases the judge had called to my attention. A visit to the university's buildings and grounds department and a talk with a few unsuspecting members of the blue-collar crew manning the disintegrating power station yielded essential technical data. Then I took the whole mess of material with me to Farmington for a solitary weekend and drafted a fifty-page memo to Sam Nightingale under the title "A Modest Proposal of Mutual Fiscal Interest to City and University." The gist of the idea was a transaction of benefit to every conceivably interested party.

The university would sell its antiquated power plant to Yankee Utilities, the local electric company, for ten million dollars, or about what it would cost to replace the installation. The investment yield on the purchase price would in effect reduce the cost to the university of the electric power it would then contract to buy from the utility. Part of the savings would be earmarked to underwrite the research into alternate sources of energy that Jeffrey and his colleagues were conducting and that could thereby be sustained over a longer and more likely productive span. The utility, in turn, would agree to supply the university's power needs by any fuel source found to be economically feasible as a result of said research, whatever course the company chose to follow in the rest of its service area.

The university would benefit from the deal by not having to sink a lot of money into capital equipment and yet winding up with lower fuel costs (all things considered) and an enhanced research budget.

The power company would benefit by adding ten million dollars to its rate base and a guaranteed $900,000 to its annual profits—and it could readily supply the university's power needs from existing plants whenever the decrepit station went out. Hardly incidentally, the utility would pick up the biggest power consumer in the community as a new customer.

The city would benefit by adding a ten-million-dollar ratable to the tax rolls at a single stroke; that translated into about $250,000 in annual property taxes it had not been getting from the exempt university.

The banks would benefit from the interest they would earn on loans to the company for purchasing the Mather power plant—not to mention the prospect of higher dividends on their considerable stock holdings in the utility.

The environmentalist, anti-nuclear lobby would benefit by the sounder funding of Operation Bright Flame, shit and all.

And the firm of Lamport, Kettering, Grier & Nightingale would benefit by a fee that I recommended be set at $100,000 or one percent of the sale price, payable—in view of the nonprofit status of the university—half by the buyer and half by the seller.

It took me three nights to clean-type the proposal. I carried the top copy to Sam's office in person. "This may interest you," I said and dropped it on his desk.

"What is it?"

"Something."

"What kind of something."

"Something stimulating."

"I don't have time for games just now—what is it, Tabor?"

"Excuse me for breathing." I turned and headed for the door.

"Just tell what the hell it is."

"Just tuck it in your tucker bag and look at it when you're not having a hemorrhage." And I left.

He called me that night. "What is all this?" he asked with a gruffness that sounded all too genuine.

"What's it look like?"

"I'm not sure. It reads like a scenario out of the Hudson Institute or one of those whacked-out think tanks."

"Thanks," I said.

"Well, you asked."

"You needn't be quite so brutal about it."

"Sorry," he said.

"Okay," I said. "Now tell me what's so whacked out about it."

"For one thing, the university doesn't sell parts of itself to private industry."

"Why not—if there's a good reason to?"

"Financial pressure isn't a good reason. There's always financial pressure. By your reasoning, the university ought to sell off its whole plant and lease it back from a dozen landlords."

"Maybe it ought to," I said. "Has anyone done the arithmetic?"

"There'd be no point to it."

"Why—because renting would be undignified?"

"Tabor, you're being perverse."

"I'm just trying to make a point."

"Like what?"

"Like you can't solve tough problems with stick-in-the-mud thinking. Now what else is so damned whacked out about the idea?"

"Who says Yankee Utilities would pay anything like ten million dollars for a beat-up old plant like that?"

"Who says they won't?"

"I do."

"How do you know?"

"Because they're not in the habit of giving their money away."

"I happen to think there are sound business and accounting reasons why they'd consider the whole package very seriously. Besides, the worst they can say is no. Now what else is so wrong with it?"

"I don't know—probably fifty more things. I only glanced over it."

"Then I suggest you have the courtesy to read it over carefully before you badmouth me any more. Good night."

He did not call back that night. At the office the next day I did my best to keep out of sight; there was no word from him. His secretary finally called mid-morning of the following day and said Sam wanted to see me. I told her I was busy but could fit him in at four-thirty or so that afternoon or any time the next morning. Sam came on the line a few seconds later. "Now," he said.

"No."

"Why?"

"Because I'm busy."

"With what?"

"With what I'm doing."

"For crissakes," he said, "why don't you act your age?"

"Why don't you stop shooting from the hip at people who happen to show a little initiative?"

There was a pause, and then a quiet "Okay."

"Okay?"

"Yeah," he said, "you win this round. Now please haul your ass down here on the double."

He was adjusting the air-conditioner when I sailed in without waiting for his secretary to announce me. "Why don't you turn it off and open the windows?" I said. "Sweating's good for you."

He turned around slowly and walked back to his desk without looking up. "I had no idea you were an authority on so many subjects," he said.

"Don't be peevish," I said, "just because a girl does a little thinking for herself."

He scorched me with a tight, hard look. "How do you know about all this?" he asked, picking up my memo and rippling its pages.

"By making it my business to."

"No one asked you to make it your business."

"Not in so many words."

"Not in any words."

"Then say I volunteered—I told you I was going to."

"That was a joke."

"Sometimes my jokes are very serious."

"Yes," he said, "I see." He tossed the memo aside. "There's a lot of hard information in here. How'd you get it?"

"If you'd ever given me a chance to work with you, you'd know how."

"You didn't talk with any people in a way that would compromise the university or my position?"

"Your dual sanctity is preserved, I guarantee it. The stuff comes almost entirely from printed sources and my own noodle. What few conversations I held on the subject were thoroughly veiled." I propped my elbows on the corner of his desk and cupped my hands around my face. "Why the third degree if it's just a whacked-out idea?"

"It's not," he said. "It's a good idea. I wish I'd thought of it."

"Really?" It came out like a joyful squeal.

"Really. In fact, it's amazing. There are a lot of sophisticated concepts in the thing that all seem to mesh." He rolled the memo into a cylinder and gave me a friendly rap on the forehead. "A number of things need to be checked out very closely, but I've raised the general principle with the university comptroller and he doesn't see any overriding reason why we shouldn't explore it with the company. We've got a date over there the beginning of the week after next."

"Who's we?"

"The comptroller and I—and you."

I all but bounced off the wall. "You told them about me?"

"Against my better judgment. But then I figured if they hated the concept, I had the perfect scapegoat."

"You sly bastard," I said and punched him on the arm for want of a warmer way to express what I felt.

Sam got me detached from other assignments and told Alva Potter that I would be working exclusively with him for the next several weeks on a university project. There was just a week to redraft the proposal in a form suitable for possible submission to Yankee Utilities. That meant the best face had to be put on the condition of the univerity's power plant, silos of statistics had to be accumulated on the university's potential as a power consumer, and the whole proposal had to be couched in terms that suggested it was but one of many options the university was studying. Whether anything on paper would be handed to the company depended on how the exploratory meeting went. To strengthen our hand, Sam and I took a day to drive to Hartford to examine the records on Yankee Utilities. On the way, we rehearsed the proposition from top to bottom. The only real divergence of interests that we saw affecting the parties was the university's commitment to help develop a cheap source of power. Sam said the utility would never bind itself to converting even a portion of its plant to an economical system—"unless the alternative were a government takeover." I told him that without some sort of ecological sweetener in the deal, the student body would kick up a massive fuss and probably queer it. We both agreed the asking price ought to be something above ten million if the university hoped to net that much. "I was thinking of eleven and a half," he said.

"Eleven-eight," I countered.

"Why?"

"It sounds more thought out."

"That's what's wrong with it."

After we had crammed our carrying cases with every document they let us copy at the public utilities commission, I asked Sam if he'd mind detouring on the route back for a stop-off at Farmington.

"I'd like that," he said.

"The house is empty—and kind of messy, I'm afraid. I stay there on weekends."

"I wouldn't think you make messes."

"Well, not huge ones. My mother once fainted at the sight of a crumb. She had me trained that way, too, until I finally figured out that immaculate underpants and spotless coffee cups are not absolutely vital to a full and happy life. Now mother's convinced I'm disease-bearing."

He laughed. "Sounds like she gives you a gift certificate to get pasteurized every Christmas."

I played with the idea. "No," I said, "pasteurize is what they do to old Kentucky Derby winners when they stop running."

He considered that for a second. "No," he said, "You're thinking of lionize."

"How can they lionize a horse? Maybe you mean 'balkanize' —that's what they do to Kentucky Derby losers before turning them into horsemeat."

"You're talking about 'vulcanize'—which is why the meat isn't very tender."

"You mean 'Sanforize' to keep it from shrinking. What good's a small horseburger?"

"Or a big Warren Burger?"

"I prefer him to the Big Enchilada."

"He's been misunderstood at this point in time. Better a stone wall than a loose Liddy."

"It's all the fault of the Jews—they lost us Vietnam."

"No, they lost us China."

"No, that was George Marshall. But he saved Europe."

"So the French could spit on us for not letting the Concorde in."

"What's a little sonic doom between friends?"

"I CAN'T HEAR YOU!"

"I said the French won the American Revolution, don't you know?"

"And haven't won anything since. Besides, it wasn't the French. It was Pulaski."

"No, Pulaski's that film director who got mixed up with all the crazies. You're thinking of Kosciusko."

"No, that's a bridge between Staten Island and Warsaw."

"There isn't any bridge between Staten Island and Warsaw —it's a tunnel. And they just raised the toll to ten million kopeks."

"Think of the traffic back-up in the exact change lane."

"There isn't any exact change in Poland."

"I'm tired of Polish jokes. Name me a greater composer than Chopin."

"Irving Berlin."

"Not counting the Beatles."

"He's not a Beatle. The Beatles are John, Paul, George, and Ringo—no Irving—and they're all Liverpudlians."

"I thought John at least was Church of England."

"They took down the Church of England—or was that London Bridge?"

"London Bridge—is that the one that goes from London to Warsaw?"

We broke up and fell off our antic toboggan together and I kissed him and he kissed me back and nearly drove us off the road.

At the house I played back highlights of my childhood. I showed him the doll house my father and I had made in the basement and the overgrown site of our old vegetable garden out back, the little meadow beyond it where Brownie and I wrestled and showed each other our private parts, my mother's off-pantry retreat with its testimonial plaques for her community service, and the study where my father worked his calculators so zealously but never quite got the columns of his life to add up. Sam said he had never known a family life like ours and listened almost wistfully as I reconstructed it. "I guess I was emotionally deprived," he said when I ended. "Or maybe you people just had something very rare going on in this house —a kind of passionate involvement with everything you did— and each other."

"But there was room for each of us to be ourselves. Nobody ever smothered anybody else. They were just there as reinforcements most of the time."

He nodded slowly and lowered himself into our big living-room sofa. "I envy you all that," he said. "I think it probably had a whole lot to do with turning you into such a supremely confident person."

"I'm not all that confident. A lot of it's a front—I told you that the day you interviewed me."

"But you don't seem to be afraid of anything in life."

"It's not that," I said, dropping down beside him. "It's just that I still find so much in it that amazes me. I know it sounds like I'm a teeny-bopper but every day is an adventure for me. I don't mean that they've got to stage the aurora borealis or anything—it's just that there's always something if you take the trouble to look and feel—if you get out there and walk and sniff and live life. I still wake up sometimes and watch the sun rise, do you believe that? Everything is so perfectly clean and still and expectant. I've been going up to the attic here to watch since I was a child—there's a marvelous view. I think that's why I hope my mother never sells the place." I turned to him. "Do you ever do things like that?"

"Not for some time now," he said.

"Or like running in the rain," I flowed on, "or just being out in it. I love rainy days. Most people hate them. But getting wet is wonderful. Nowhere else in the universe gets wet, probably. When I was little, I used to think it rained only on me—as if it was all some sort of celestial special effect arranged for my benefit. I thought it was a privilege to get wet."

"Some people think wet is uncomfortable."

"Wet is life. Wet makes everything grow—bodies, too. Did you ever taste your wife's milk when she nursed your kid?"

He shook his head.

"Why not?"

"I don't know," he said. "I guess it didn't occur to me."

"The one time in your life you have a kid and it didn't occur to you even to try it?"

He shrugged. "She didn't nurse him for long, anyway."

"Did you watch the kid being born at least?"

Now he was downcast.

"Why not?" I was almost shouting at him.

"I don't know—I was too squeamish, I guess."

"You weren't too squeamish to screw her in the first place."

"No."

"You probably screw with the lights off."

He was still.

"Do you?"

"It depends."

"Have you ever tasted your own semen?"

He shut his eyes now. "I don't think so," he said.

"How come? Weren't you ever the slightest bit curious? It's the seed of your own body."

"Hey," he finally lashed back, "get off me. I tell you how lucky and terrific you are and you turn around and make me feel like a prize clod. Thank you very much."

He seemed such a lovely man in so many ways—bright and caring and generous and funny and honorable—that it pained me to find this flagrantly unexamined quality to his life. It was as if he could not unclench himself long enough to experience a thing openly and fully for fear he would not know how to respond. All head and quick intelligence, he was desperately bereft of sensuousness. "I wasn't trying to hurt you," I said. "I was just trying to show you."

"You can show without bludgeoning. I didn't know consciousness-raising was the latest form of sadism."

"You're being defensive, Sam."

"You're being offensive, Tabor."

In sudden supplication I brought my mouth hard against his and fed on his salty wetness and traded it with mine till his hands awoke and traveled to my temples and smoothed their way slowly down the length of my body and stopped at the thighs where he began to knead and dig and I moved his fingers onto my mound and he seized it and held it and encircled it and clutched it massively and I reached between his legs where he was large and warm and rigid and I rubbed it gently and then not gently and then hard and his hands moved inside and upon my flesh and enclosed my delta and I left off holding him and lay back and then prone while he found my drenched core and with every part of his hand stroked it and sculpted it and with the other held firm to my tuft and pressed and spiraled until I was breathing loud and fiercely beneath his quickening motion and aching sweetly and more and more and I was adoring those hands and who propelled them and what they were doing more and more and faster yet gentler and I released with an unchecked cry of happiness. And when I touched him I could feel the wetness there now through the cloth and told him to take it out and he did and I ignited inside at the sight of it and fell upon the surging mast and tasted it on top and bottom and every side and engulfed it and he cried Jesus and I did the rest with my hands while he thrust and speared and I caught the lavish flow in my palms and when he lay still at last I touched a sticky droplet of it to his mouth and made him taste it.

"What are we going to do?" he asked after we had been on the road back to Amity for ten minutes or so.

"Do about what?"

"About us," he said.

"What about us?" I asked.

"That's what I want to know."

"And am I supposed to tell you?"

"You can tell me what you feel—and what you want." He glanced at me and then away.

"I feel terrific," I said, "and I don't want anything."

His eyes stayed fixed on the highway for a time. "You know," he said after so long a spell I thought he was on to other things, "you're a certifiable Jekyll and Hyde. One minute you're a dewy-eyed ingenue who sounds a little like she's trying to crash the starting lineup at Walden Pond. And the next you're as cold and scheming as Lucrezia Borgia. That makes you a little hard to figure."

"Not really," I said. "I'm different things at different times, maybe, but everyone is."

"I try not to be," he said. "It's the difference between an adolescent mentality and an adult one."

"Maybe that's the trouble," I said. "Maybe you ought to let yourself out once in a while. You're all bottled up."

"How come any time I say something about you, it winds up coming back at me as a critical judgment?"

"I don't know. Maybe you need it more than I do."

"And is the improvement of Sam Nightingale a project of special interest to you?"

"Sure," I said.

"Then why didn't you say so?"

"I said so back at the house. Didn't you notice?"

He nodded slightly and retreated into his head for another little while. Then he said, "Tabor, why did you get into this thing with the power company and the university?"

"What do you mean? That's how I make my living."

"No," he said, "it was way above and beyond the call of duty."

"Maybe I want to be way above and beyond a hack lawyer."

"So you look for ways to impress your senior colleagues?"

"I wouldn't say that. I try to do the job when they invite me to. You just never invited me."

"And that bothered you?"

"Sure."

"Why? There's other work to keep you busy."

"Because you're the brightest one there—besides me."

"I'm flattered."

"And because I care for you, okay? Isn't that what you wanted to hear?"

He gave an emphatic nod.

"Isn't that pretty obvious?"

"Yes and no. You apparently care for a number of people."

"Sure—to differing degrees and in different ways. What's wrong with that?"

"I can't be that casual about my affections."

"I didn't say I was casual. I just don't let every friendship I have with a man turn into a trauma."

"Including ones with federal judges, I gather."

He flattened me with that. I swerved my head toward the passenger window and tried not to let him see. The quickness of that involuntary gesture was all he needed to know he had reached me. I just sat there, looking out, and considered the implications of his knowing. None of them was good. That the episode was a closed book in my head was immaterial now. I had done a favor for someone who asked it of me—someone I thought deserving; would I have to pay now for a tendered kindness? There was no point, though, in self-immolation. I tried a holding operation. "I don't really know what you heard or how you heard it," I said, "but I doubt that you've got it straight—if it's of any interest to you."

"Some city hall flunky saw the judge come back from his Memorial Day weekend at the airport accompanying an attractive younger woman on crutches. He asked Sparky if he had any idea who the bimbo was. The judge, you see, is known not entirely affectionately as The Saint among the native cutthroats. Sparky, of course, said he didn't know."

"Very damned decent of him. And then he ran to tell you."

"He told me only last week. He's worried about the consequences for everyone concerned."

"If he's so worried, why didn't he ask me what it's all about. He's making a big deal out of a chance meeting. The judge and I met on the flight, he saw I was indisposed and offered to give me a lift to my apartment. Period."

"And that's all?"

"Yes, that's all. I worked with the man closely for a year—what's so odd about his helping me in a moment of distress?"

"Nothing," he said. "It's perfectly natural—just the way soon afterward you won the case you briefed for Legal Assistance. The judge is a most considerate gentleman."

"A lot of people were on that brief."

"That's not what Arnold Berenson told Sparky. He said you whipped the thing into top shape but he still didn't think they had a chance."

"And so you and Sparky think I screwed my way to victory?"

He looked at me with narrowed lids. "The possibility occurred to him."

"And not to you?"

"I said we ought to reserve judgment. Sparky thinks I'm a cream puff."

"Sparky's got a Humphrey Bogart complex."

"Sparky's a tough guy to cross."

"I didn't cross Sparky—I didn't cross anybody."

"And you didn't shack up for a weekend at Hilton Head with George Millis?"

"Who said anything about Hilton Head?"

"You did, I'm afraid. You told one of the secretaries, and she told Alva Potter. Potter keeps the book on everybody. Sparky used a few intermediaries to find out where the judge vacationed. He apparently goes down to Hilton Head every year about that time."

"So you guys practically sicked the goddamn FBI on me?"

"The firm is allergic to scandal, Tabor."

I blinked back my fury. "The firm is a sanctimonious son of a bitch," I said. Then I fell still. Miles passed. We reached Upper Amity before either of us said anything more, and then I told him, "Sam, George Millis is a fine man. He has a disastrous domestic life, as you may or may not know."

"I've heard some things," he said.

"He asked me to keep him company. He was very lonely, and I was a former colleague. I tried to say no."

"But then you figured you might lose your case."

"That wasn't how it happened, Sam!"

"Circumstantial evidence to the contrary notwithstanding."

"That's exactly right."

"And afterward you realized the magnitude of the indiscretion for both of you and you haven't seen him since?"

"No," I said, "not once. It was just something that happened."

"Then how come your memo on the power plant was loaded with references to cases he was involved with as a public utility commissioner?"

"Was it?"

"You must think I'm still in kindergarten," he said.

"I think you should go fuck yourself," I said, "and thanks very much for the benefit of the doubt."

Our meeting the following week with the university and utility company officials hugely advanced the plan to purchase the Mather power station. The company thought the asking price of $11.6 million was about a million too high and would make no contractual promise to adapt cheap power sources developed by the university, but it did agree to consider any such new technology with care and take "every conceivable action consistent with prudent fiscal responsibility"—the language was viewed as of paramount public-relations importance—to apply the Mather research to its overall operations.

The wording, everyone present recognized, was merely cosmetic; in fact, the utility would remain free to use what sources of power it wished even if the university scientists all of a sudden figured out how to light up the city with five ounces of cow flop. That being so, the principals determined to speed up the negotiations in the hope of reaching agreement during the summer recess. The working proposition that Sam and I had drafted became the essential tool for forging the bargain; the basic terms of the transaction were made public as a trial balloon. The city administration, the media, and the business community all saw it as a piece of town-and-gown statesmanship of the highest order. There were no organized voices to the contrary beyond a feeble broadside from a local consumers' group and an astute article in the counterculture weekly tarring the university for yet another sellout to the mastodons of capitalism. Jeffrey Kramer called me the night the story hit the papers. "If I didn't know better," he said, "I'd guess that your fine Machiavellian hand is in there somewhere."

"I've heard some talk around the office about it," I said.

"Thanks for tipping me off," he said. "A thing like this could kill our whole research program."

"First of all, I'm not supposed to tip anyone off about anything. It's unethical. Second of all, I stuck my nose in it enough to be sure your end of the thing was protected. The university is supposed to use part of the sale income to fund your work. Doesn't that give you a lot more time and security?"

"Once the deal is consummated, the university can pack the

whole thing in any time it wants. It won't have a vested interest in what we're doing any more—it can use the bread to buy cuspidors for the ladies' lounge or any other damned thing it wants. They wouldn't do it right away but I think our days are numbered."

"I thought Prettyman told you all that you were working on the hottest thing since the invention of fire."

"He did."

"So?"

"So all he has to do is decide an electric paper clip is humanity's most pressing need for this week and pull the plug on us."

"I thought college presidents had high principles."

"Starting and ending with their own survival. The utility, at least, is predictable. They'll have the Mather station shut down by New Year's and be feeding the campus on pure nuclear power—unless the students threaten to blow the company up, and I wouldn't put it past them. They know chickenshit when they see it."

I told Jeff he sounded panicky and ought to view the transaction in its most promising light. He said I had gone establishment, or was well on the way, and he would say a prayer for my mortal soul, but its prospects for salvation were now slender at best. More harshly than necessary, I told him to tend to his shit-burning and not live my life or anyone else's. Our closeness, which to me had been so pleasant and untrying, was over.

The sale of the Mather power plant, pending state approval, was announced by the university's board of overseers at their summer meeting as "a regrettable but imperative step if the academic community's constantly growing energy needs are to be met in an orderly and economically unburdensome manner." I felt an undeniable giddiness because a deal of such magnitude between two normally torpid leviathans had been expedited just five weeks after I had proposed it. That such unaccustomed haste bespoke an uneasy conscience on the part of the university's governors troubled me little. I had tried to formulate the sale to foster the greatest good for the greatest number; if some of those it would touch were to be benefited more than others, that could hardly be avoided in the real world. And that was where I lived now. Maynard Lamport called me down to his office and, with the other partners in attendance, bestowed garlands on my head. My hourly billable rate was raised again; now I cost just twenty-five percent less than the firm's top price—more, it was whispered, than any other associate. Sam asked me to join him for a picnic lunch the next day to celebrate.

"I thought the firm was allergic to scandal," I said, sliding into his car. "Aren't midday orgies in the grass on the suspect side?"

He laughed and said the occasion was a special one and a little bit of fraternizing sanctionable under the circumstances. I said I thought that was rather an arbitrary and capricious standard. "Look," he said, glancing up seriously, "don't let me dragoon you into this."

His sensitivity to my banter suggested that pain persisted on his side as well as mine over the remonstrance I had been delivered for my lascivious and compromising behavior in the semi-tropics. "Oh, I'm all a-twitter," I told Sam. "I just can't resist labeling a double standard when I meet one."

Druid Park was surely the most secluded public place in the whole city. I had never been there, but Sam lived only five minutes from it and remarked that the gorgeous little rolling estate of two dozen acres, which had been willed to the town a decade earlier by one of Maynard Lamport's illustrious widow clients, would remain a civic asset only as long as the citizenry ignored it. A miniature gem of landscaping, the preserve achieved the illusion of sweep and distance by the way it rose and dipped in the manner of English formal parks. A fresh vista unfurled with almost every turn in the footpaths and walkways—a glade of splendid maples, a ravine beside a stand of blue spruce to suggest an opening in an untrammeled forest, a wide graceful slope fanning into a once luxuriant meadow now turned patchy green and hay yellow. We parked by the gatehouse, and Sam led me down into that improbable woodland as I voiced amazement with every advancing step. Aside from a pair of groundskeepers laconically trimming a hedge and a girl with a dog, I did not see another person in the whole place. A high stone wall surrounding the entire park added to its magical quality, as if the setting had been plucked intact from a storybook page and dropped as a grace note upon a besooted cityscape.

We settled under a giant white oak on a rise above the far side of the meadow. Its heavy lower branches dove for the ground like hungry tendrils and screened us behind a natural lean-to. You could see far and wide from there without being spied on. It was too perfect. Something in me stiffened. I was ready to repulse Sam's merest touch. It was a measure of his own emotional tuning that he sensed as much and made no advance whatever. That relaxed me, and we ate up our lavishly catered picnic basket by laughing mouthfuls. In between courses we pitched a Frisbee I had brought along, and he proved far more adroit at it than I. It was good to see him run over the meadow and sweat in the sun and feel his moisture next to mine when he took my hand to lead me up the hillock for our fruit and cheese. Even then, he did not clasp me to him. The air between us was still not clear, and I would take no initiative to filter it. Then, when we were packing up, he said simply, "Spend the night with me." It was neither an order nor a request but more as if he were reciting a song title.

"Sure," I said, "you and Sparky and the FBI."

He smiled and gave a little nod of acknowledgment. "Two's company, five hundred's a crowd, I suppose?"

"You could say that."

But we moved hand in hand out of our hiding place into the sunlight and circled the meadow in plain view of anyone who might have been watching. I took that as a far more potent declaration than anything he had yet said to me. Nothing was spoken for a while as we climbed the spine of the park's main slope. Near the top, he said simply, "Tonight—unless you have other plans."

"Tonight what?"

"Be with me."

The offhandedness had gone out of his voice now, but he was imploring, not commanding. "With you," I said, "alone?"

"That would be my preference."

"Just what sort of a woman do you think I am, Sam?"

"Not shy," he said.

"Not stupid or insensitive, either."

"I don't follow."

"Oh, yes, you do."

"You mean you don't want me to think you're an easy lay?"

"That's for openers," I said.

"But I've never thought that."

"Then what was all that about the judge and me—cryptic flattery?"

"I thought you were rather calculating with your sexual favors. I never said you were overly generous."

"But of course there'd be nothing calculating about my going to bed with one of the principals at my place of employment?"

He gave that little acknowledging nod of his that guaranteed he would never make a con artist. "I thought there was a difference between the two cases," he added.

"Sure," I said, "but indiscretion by any other name smells no better—haven't you been told?"

He said nothing and fell to brooding.

"There's the other small consideration of your marital status," I said to try to settle the matter. "I happen to have a thoroughly admirable habit of not sleeping with married men except under highly extenuating circumstances."

"How thoughtful."

"It's not thoughtful. It's self-protective. I don't much like providing a little action on the side for disgruntled husbands—that's their hard cheese."

"I'm not a disgruntled husband."

"Then why do you want to go to bed with me?"

He looked at me as if I were putting him on. "Because I'm alive," he said. "Because you knock me out."

The words were so open and direct I could not be unmoved by them. I tightened my hand in his until we came within sight of the gatehouse. "Do you make this sort of proposition often?" I asked him.

"No," he said. "I'm a tediously dutiful husband."

"I wouldn't knock it if I were you. Fidelity is a beautiful thing when it works."

"Then how come you don't try it?"

"I do—when I'm living with someone."

" 'See subsection A under "Temporary Fidelity".' "

"That's a cheap shot," I said, withdrawing my hand.

"And yours wasn't? What gives you the right to moralize when you've never had to reduce your options to zero?"

"But that's the way of life I've chosen. You chose something else."

"And I'm doomed to it, come what may—is that it?"

"I didn't say that. All I mean is that playing around is a very draining kind of game—unless you're a totally heartless bastard. And you don't happen to be."

"So it's me you're worried about?" he said.

"Partly."

"Don't," he said. "This is a separate part of me. It doesn't affect the rest of my life."

"What happens to Lee?"

"Lee's not here. Lee's not involved. I'm not taking anything from her."

"You mean you've convinced yourself of that."

"I believe it."

"You're kidding yourself, Sam."

"I don't think so," he said.

"I'd think it over if I were you."

"I've thought it over. It's been my major preoccupation for the past year, if you'd like to know."

I waited in the car while he stopped off at his house for a fresh shirt, and we drove back downtown to work the afternoon away. I phoned him after I figured everyone else had left. "Come at nine," I said, "and if you bring a toothbrush, don't bother ringing."

He was too eager to be artful and his energy too rapidly spent, but there was an excitement in him that he relayed through my every fiber. We slept bare and uncovered till he woke before dawn and brought me up with a steady skill and control that let us go off together quite grandly. Afterward, I made him a gigantic breakfast, and he ate it all. "One of history's great one-night stands," I said to him as I finished dressing for work under his admiring scrutiny.

"I'm too much for you, right?"

Actually, my bottom was a little sore—a souvenir of our combined ardor. "No," I said, "I just think it would get to be a very destructive habit—for both of us."

"We'll cut it off if we have to," he said.

"Sam, it's hard to let people in your life and then throw them out when it gets inconvenient."

"I can manage," he said, "if you can."

"You are consumed by a deep self-delusion."

"Play with me, Tabor."

"I'm afraid, Sam. It's too goddamned dangerous."

"For a little while—just through the rest of the summer—then we'll break. Think of it as an idyll."

"Think of it as insanity. The office'll pick right up on us—maybe they have already."

"We'll be careful."

"They'll fingerprint our bodies."

"We'll wear rubber gloves—and keep everything after hours."

"It's still dumb."

"Some things are, but they're still worth doing. That's your gospel, isn't it?"

I smudged on some gray eye shadow and grabbed my purse. "Summer's over on Labor Day," I said. "Okay?"

He smiled and hugged me and said okay. I sent him downstairs first.

16

My honeymoon with the black people of the Gully ended that sultry summer when for a time I was ranked a turncoat and a buttinsky and nearly pelted off those strewn and pitted streets.

A ghetto enclave amputated from the inner city by soulless urban planners, the Gully had historically been the camping grounds for the least fortunate elements of the community. Renewal bulldozers scooped out the severest decay to make way for a sterile concrete link between the shoreline interstate and the downtown shopping hub, thereby sparing the speeding motorist an intimate glimpse of slum life. Unquestionably, the gutted housing had been beyond rehabilitation and pains were taken to relocate the dispossessed families, but the balance of the Gully, sheared off now from the rest of the city by the highway spur, became an even more unsightly backwater. Landlords kept cutting services as rentals and population dropped, sidewalks crumbled, garbage proliferated, street lights dimmed and went out and were not replaced, and only rage grew and crime seemed a justifiable means of survival. The city, with its social services distant and its mind on practical amenities, had conducted triage and decided the area was beyond repairing. Those who were able abandoned the community as rapidly as they could manage, leaving as their legacy of despair boarded-up buildings to be vulturized and vandalized and finally put to the torch by the avenging survivors. The circle of devastation widened each month. My clients at the Boot Coop manned one of the few remaining outposts of semi-orderly settlement off of Seaview Avenue, the Gully's main drag, but even the two-story frame houses surrounding the apartment (renamed Jackie Robinson Gardens and not in my memory) were in an advanced state of disrepair.

To celebrate the Fourth of July that summer, arsonists in the Gully burned down three abandoned buildings and one partially inhabited one. The flames spread to a row of stores along Seaview that looters picked clean before firemen responded (and were stoned for their efforts until wary police moved in to disperse the onlookers). A pair of young looters was spotted and arrested with the goods on them; one of the boys was a close friend of the Washburns' son, Oscar. On the Saturday following, Duckett came by the laundromat while I was doing my things and put the arm on me to represent the boy. "He's a decent kid," Duckett said. "Never been in big trouble before this."

"What's wrong with Legal Assistance?" I asked him.

"Nothin'—except it's a machine, and you never know who you gonna get."

"I'll be honest with you," I told him. "I don't like looters—I don't like looters almost as much as I don't like rapists, which is one helluva lot."

"The boy made a mistake, Tabor. His folks 'n' me just don't want his life ruined for it."

"But if he did it, then he did it and he's got to take his medicine. Legal Assistance will plead him guilty and ask for leniency for a first-time offender. You say he's got no record?"

"Not much of one. They arrested him for arson once but never proved nothin'."

"Did he do it?"

"He says no."

"That wasn't what I asked."

"I don't know, lady, I'm not the cops."

"Don't 'lady' me, Duckett—I'm asking if the kid's straight, and you're telling me he's an admitted looter and maybe a torch. Well, shit, I don't feel like putting my services at the disposal of a punk, okay? To me that's subhuman conduct—I don't care how hard-up someone is."

"All the kid took was one lousy shirt and three pairs of pants."

"That's enough."

"Enough for what? For gettin' fucked over by the cops and every creep in the pen?"

"He should have thought about that first."

He just sat there burning while I hauled my load from the washer to the dryer. When I showed no sign of relenting and instead started talking with two of the black women doing their own loads, he got fidgety and then downright pissed at me. "I want to show you somethin'," he broke in and told the women please to mind my things while he shoveled me out the door.

We walked about five blocks and turned a corner onto an open lot entirely different from any patch in the whole Gully: it was green, in rows, and growing. At least a dozen people were hoeing and weeding and watering the site that must have occupied a couple of acres. I recognized some of them as Coop members, including Duckett's wife, Lenore, who had on a wide-brim straw hat and was fussing with what looked suspiciously like stalks of corn. Duckett confirmed it. "We also got tomatoes, okra, green beans, and cabbage sproutin' outa what used to be the usual tumbledown shit."

I expressed amazement and asked him how it had happened. When spring came, he said, everyone got antsier than usual as if the very existence of the Boot Coop had made them eager to create something living of their own. To feed that special hunger, they had gone out with shovels and rakes and hoes and their bare hands and excavated this unnoticeable lot that had been abandoned years earlier. In wheelbarrows they moved broken cement and brick and rock and asphalt by the ton to an adjacent open lot, and what they found beneath was bad soil—sandy fill with almost no moisture-holding capacity, according to some of the residents who were of Southern farming stock. "What the soil was missin'," Duckett recounted, "the people got plenty of." Even the most skeptical Coop members pitched in. One man who earned his living with a landscaping outfit borrowed a rototiller and churned leaf mold into the soil to improve its absorbent properties, and then they all helped fertilize it and divided it into family plots and planted it and watered it and prayed their asses off.

"I told Duck he's diggin' his holes so deep his corn's gonna be next year comin' up," Lenore put in by way of noting the problematic harvest. But lo, the garden began to sprout, and their hearts leaped, and every evening and on weekends that green place became the favorite gathering spot of the neighborhood. People shared the work and sang and gossiped, and Sundays there was a chicken and fish fry. Even the kids who usually burned up their energies on antisocial activities did their part. Organized into squads and shifts, they picked up the litter, helped tend the plots of older people, and guarded the garden against vandals and vegetable thieves. Oscar Washburn's buddy, the one busted for looting, had been heavily involved in this garden-tending corps, Duckett reported and wondered if that wasn't testimony of his decent character.

I surveyed the scene and found it immensely cheering. "Just one thing," I said. "Whose land is this?"

"Who knows?" Duckett said. "It was left to rot a long ways back."

"But even abandoned land belongs to someone. Maybe the city took it over on a tax default or a quitclaim or something."

"Beats me," Duckett said. "We're just homesteadin' it. No one's bein' put out."

"So nobody checked with the city to see if all this was okay?"

"Oh, sure, we checked," he said. "Eddie Milgram, he's the Coop secretary, he knows a lot of people downtown, right? So he asked around at the redevelopment agency if anybody minded we're doin' a little nice gardening, and they say fine and not to worry so long as nobody's occupyin' the premises. That was good enough for me."

"But there's nothing in writing, nothing formal, giving you the right to garden here?" I asked him.

"It didn't seem worth the bother," he said, his lean face perspiring in the sun. He mopped it with a handkerchief and tried to change the subject by asking Lenore where their boy was.

"And it didn't seem worth asking me my opinion, either, I suppose?" I persisted.

"Hey, no, tiger. This is a people's project, if you know what I'm sayin'—somethin' we just want to grow ourselves without all the horseshit forms to fill out and meeting with the man and waitin' till kingdom come. It didn't have nothin' to do with you. Hell, you want us to come runnin' for help every time we got to take a leak? I know better than that."

I brushed a bug from the back of my pants and squinted out over the scene. "Look, you guys, this is a beautiful thing you've done," I said to the two of them, "and I really dig the whole idea. Only I think it's probably illegal as hell and you may get your asses whipped for not playing by the rules. Now that's about what you must have figured I'd say, so you didn't bother asking even though I'm supposed to be your lawyer. Okay, that's your privilege. But if you didn't need me for that, you sure as hell don't need me to plead a kid guilty for looting—which happens not to have anything to do with the Coop anyway. So I wish you luck with the garden and the kid luck in court and I'll mind my own business from now on."

I went back to the laundromat the next Saturday as usual, but was cut dead by the black women. The Washburns had plainly ticketed me for ostracism. I did not pursue the matter that day. But I did not intend to match hostility with petulance. I came back the following Saturday and, after sustaining another deep freeze, walked over to the garden. Lenore was there in her big hat, ministering to a stand of tomatoes on the far side of the spread. I gave her a nonchalant wave and got a short hard stare in return. An older woman weeding a plot nearby accepted my offer to help. I must have put in the better part of an hour before I was rewarded with a cup of lemonade and a word of thanks. When the weeding was finished and not before, I left without fanfare. The next week, I read that the young looter I had been asked to represent was given a six-month sentence reduced to thirty days in the juvenile detention center because he had no prior convictions. I could not have done more for him. As it was, I had called Arnold Berenson to make sure Legal Assistance had a competent lawyer on the case. "That's the only kind we have here," he said and then proposed marriage. I demurred, noting he was already married. "I can fix that," he said.

A thaw had set in by the Saturday after that when I came to

the garden and was asked to judge a scarecrow-building contest the children were holding. I gave a mighty hug along with a prize ribbon to the brother-sister team that made the winner, and they squeezed me back and everyone clapped loud and I was no longer an unperson among them.

The only unsettling note on that otherwise festive afternoon was the prowling presence of cop cars. I had never seen any around there during daylight before. My surprise was less than total, then, when Lenore Washburn called me at work late in the afternoon on the following Tuesday and reported the police had ordered the garden closed up and served a summons on every Coop member within sight for trespassing on private property. Could I possibly come out there after work? I had planned to spend the evening with Sam at my place, but when he heard the news from the Gully he insisted I answer their call and asked if he could come along. "Sure," I said, "only you'd better take your tie off or they'll think you're the D.A. and plant you between the corn and the okra."

Lenore was still wearing a stunned face when Sam with his sleeves rolled up and looking as seedy as he could manage brought his Saab in for a dusty landing in front of the Washburn house. "What you got to realize about Duck," she launched in without preface or acknowledgment of the warning I had issued to them, "is he got himself enough pride to sink a battleship. Now you helped do that, honey—you brought him back from the dead just about—and I love you for it. Everybody here say you are too much and done a wonderful thing for us. Only you got to understand we want to be our own selves an' that's hard when you got the whiphand. Oh, it's nothin' you do on purpose, see, it's just you bein' smart and quick and strong-willed like you are, we naturally gonna hear you out and follow along. So Duck, he felt like he got to do the garden, it was such a good idea, you know? And nobody figure the po-lice gonna care nohow about us growin' some cabbages out in the middle of all that shit. Why, we doin' a public service!" She banged her fist on the rusty metal rocker. "Now why you figure these fuckers want to beat up on us? We the best-behaved folks in the whole goddamned Gully."

Duckett met me at the top of the stairs and took my hand. I said I was his sister if he was still my brother and he kissed my cheek by way of an answer and said, "You got to understand how it is." I said I understood if he did, and he nodded and we each cried for about ten seconds and I had my worst-paying client back.

The next morning I checked the city records to see who owned the land the Coop people had cleared and gardened. Tax payments on the property were nine years in arrears, nobody knew where the owner of record was, and although the city had not taken title to it by tax foreclosure as it was fully empowered to do, it was acting as the owner's surrogate in pressing charges for trespass under its general policing powers. I tried to see Kenneth Schoonmaker, the city prosecutor, before the story hit the newspaper on the ungreening of the Gully garden. But it was precisely for such media exposure that the police incursion had been planned. The first edition of the paper ran the item with a big picture on the split page. The Coop gardeners were labeled squatters and scavengers by city officials who said lawful means existed to redevelop unsightly areas, but citizens taking the matter into their own hands had to be prosecuted. Schoonmaker did not agree to see me until the middle of the afternoon.

"Business must be slow these days," I said, after remarking that I had not had the pleasure of opposing him since quitting Legal Assistance.

"A nice girl like you is a lot better off away from that zoo," he said. He was a top-heavy, silver-haired man of about fifty, with the strained self-importance of a smalltime martinet. Ten years in the same office left him believing his position had become a hereditary right. "As to our business being off, it's the first I've heard of it."

"I was just guessing," I said. "I couldn't figure out any other reason why you'd be bringing in my kind, sweet gardeners. I admit they're a lot easier to grab than muggers and arsonists."

"Still a tough guy, huh?"

"No, I'm genuinely confused, Mr. Schoonmaker. I really thought the city had a lot more to worry about than a group of well-behaved poor people trying to make constructive use of a worthless piece of land in the last place in town anyone's going to get exercised over."

He poked into the basket of papers in front of him for the ones dealing with my case, glanced over them for a moment to make sure of his ground, and said, without glancing up, "Miss Hill, if Thomas Edison had invented the light bulb in someone else's basement without permission, he would have been pulled in, too. It's the principle of the thing."

"Exactly—and that's what I don't understand. These are very principled people, not trying to put anything over on anyone. They were out there working in the open, hoping to save a little something on their grocery bills—which is hardly criminal intent—and improve the neighborhood at the same time."

He snapped his head up straight. "You must be pulling my leg," he said. "Your clients were occupying property that didn't belong to them. Now you're an intelligent young woman, and I think it's commendable that you continue to do missionary work among our colored brethren, but if you really want to serve both your clients and the community, you ought to make that gang out there understand the meaning of the law. It's not something they can just ignore whenever they choose. The fact is that what your people did is different only in degree, not in kind, from what looters pull. Taking is taking. And unless an example is made, I'm sorry to tell you that these monkeys are going to keep right on thinking they can walk off with every damned thing that doesn't have a Doberman tied to it."

"These monkeys," I said slowly, "have had their tails twisted around their necks by gorillas like you and me, Mr. Schoonmaker, since the day they were born—which is why I happen to still be working with them. You may think I've assigned myself the task of civilizing these people, but the truth is that they hired me to protect them from the tender mercies of the white man's law. And your present action is a case in point."

He listened to me passively. "Too bad I'm not the jury," he said when I was done.

"Curious you should say that. I was thinking you might be."

"I gathered you'd want to talk settlement."

"As a matter of fact," I said, "I've come to ask you to drop the charges entirely."

"Now I know you're pulling my leg, Miss Hill."

"It's immoral to prosecute these people for one of the rare accomplishments of their cheerless lives—and what's more, I think you know it, only I believe you're under extraordinarily heavy political pressure to bring the case because it's somebody or other's misguided idea of an object lesson."

He looked at me as if I were something under glass. Without registering emotion, he said, "There are two schools of thought about me, Miss Hill. One is that I've remained the prosecutor this long because I always take political orders. The other is that I've stayed because I never take them. If you expect to be a successful lawyer in this town, you'd better find out pretty damned quick which school is right. The charges are going to stick against your dark friends."

"I see," I said. "Then I'm going to ask you to recommend to the court that these people all be given suspended sentences."

He looked amused at the very thought. "If I were going to do that, why should I bother to prosecute in the first place?"

"For the reason you said—to make an example of them. And having done so—perversely, in my view—you'd be perfectly able to let them off with a warning."

"Your position is untenable, Miss Hill. And I'm afraid I have a meeting."

"I'd also like you to state in court that the city has no objection if the defendants continue to cultivate the property until the crops are in, provided that they petition at once to have title to the land vested in their cooperative in recognition of the civic value of their activities."

"Sure," he said, "and I'll be the guest of honor at the harvest ball. Is that what you had in mind?"

"It would accomplish a whole helluva lot more than a callous prosecution and spiteful punishment."

"In your eyes, perhaps. There are responsible and compassionate people who happen to see it differently, I'm afraid."

We were just going through the motions. "Suppose I said please, Mr. Schoonmaker? Suppose I said please don't do this and I'll get my people to make a full apology in open court?"

"First of all," he said, "Washburn will never do it—there's Black Panther blood in his family. The guy's a time bomb that's going to go off one of these days, in case you didn't know it. Second of all, it's too late for apologies. Prosecutors aren't in business to win apologies. I want a conviction and I'm going to get it. After that, you can cry your eyes out to the judge. Now I've really got to pack it in."

I nodded and stood up. "There's one other thing I'd like you to mention to your ring of advisers, Mr. Schoonmaker. If you pursue this case and humiliate these lovely people, I'm going to exercise every recourse at my disposal to force the city to meet its constitutional, statutory, and moral obligations to them, no matter how long it takes me or what it's going to cost the city."

He looked bored. "You have no recourse at your disposal, Miss Hill."

"You'll be able to decide that for yourself."

"My, my, is that a threat you're making to the prosecutor?"

"It's a promise, not a threat."

"Then you must know something I don't."

"I wouldn't discount that possibility altogether, Mr. Schoonmaker. I'm grateful for your time."

My bravura performance yielded precisely nothing. Schoonmaker went for broke, the Coop was hit for fines and other penalties totaling $1,500, and the membership was permanently enjoined from gardening the lot—the vegetables were to wither on the vine. It was a cruel, stupid, and needless punishment. Duckett and five other Coop men went to jail for thirty days each rather than drain the disheartened organization of its last cent to pay the fine. Their time-serving called the attention of the black and liberal-white communities to the injustice of the entire episode.

"The whole thing could have been settled reasonably behind closed doors," Sparky said to me after the trial, "if only you weren't too damned proud to come to me for help."

"Why should I have bothered you?" I asked. "They're my clients."

"But I know Ken Schoonmaker better than you."

"These things aren't supposed to be decided on the basis of personal rapport."

"Unfortunately," said Sparky, "they often are."

"And you own the franchise for rapping with city hall?"

"I don't feel proprietary about it—it's just how things have worked out over the years."

"Then it's about time somebody else set up a new pipeline."

"Tabor, you owed it to your clients to take advantage of every contact at your disposal. Your pride isn't the issue."

"No, but theirs is. I think I served their interests best by playing the thing straight and letting the city reveal the depth of its meanness and stupidity."

"Reveal it to whom? Your clients already know all about it."

"I happen to think there are a lot of relatively decent people out there who don't understand the impact of official daily viciousness on the powerless, and the city's got to be called on it."

"Even at your clients' expense?"

"It's at their expense one way or the other."

"And you think one isolated episode like this really demonstrates anything to anybody?"

"I don't intend to leave it at that."

"What are you going to do—drive a stake through Schoonmaker's heart?"

"I wouldn't waste the wood," I said and promised to keep Sparky informed before I turned the city upside down. He said he would appreciate that.

I took two weeks of vacation time during August and nights throughout the rest of the month to conduct my most extensive research project since law school. I spoke at length with the Coop leaders to be sure they thoroughly endorsed the scope of the action I was contemplating in their name. I scoured law reviews and journals and case reports. I gathered data from the city records and went and saw some things with my own eyes. And I huddled nights with my unofficial collaborator and summer lover who proved equally ardent at law and in bed. In the display of our feelings, Sam and I were confined, practically speaking, by the size and intimacy of the city to the four walls of my apartment. The research project relieved some of that trapped sense and even lent a vaguely ennobling quality to what was at bottom an affair far more carnal than spiritual.

We made a formidable pair of advocates, on paper at least. I kept casting an ever wider net in framing the case; he thought that a fatal mistake and urged a narrower and sharper focus.

What it all came down to was the equal protection of the law. The suit contended that the petitioning members of the Gully Neighborhood Boostrap Cooperative were knowingly, systematically, and continuously being denied their Fourteenth Amendment rights by the failure of Amity officials, departments, and employees to provide them services in the manner, amount, and quality of those available to most residents. How many and how often police and firemen were assigned to the Gully was inarguably far below the city average for the population density (tables were provided). Garbage was picked up there half as frequently (figures cited). Street lamps and sidewalks were not fixed for comparable stretches with anything remotely resembling parity. But the worst disservice of all was the municipal role in fostering the wholesale abandonment of housing throughout the Gully.

Within a half square mile of the Coop, we counted one hundred twenty-seven dwellings, from a one-family house to a thirty-family apartment, that had been abandoned in the previous five years. About half of them were still standing, luring assorted derelicts and presenting a constant threat to the security of its residents. The empty buildings and lots left after demolition were dumping grounds for garbage, attracting rats, flies, and other perils to health. And the psychological damage caused by such esthetic blight was contagious. Landlords witnessing the decline of the neighborhood elected not to throw good money after bad and failed to maintain their property adequately; real-estate values snowballed downhill accordingly. The city, in our view, was not permitted to be an idle bystander. It had a statutory obligation to enforce health and safety standards by adequately policing property owners. Where property was abandoned, it fell to the city itself to abate conditions that inflicted nuisance and danger. With an enabling law, it could order the premises sealed or continuously guarded, as the New York City and Los Angeles codes provided. Or it could order the buildings to be fixed up to code standards, as in Chicago, and take liens on the property. Other cities were empowered to take title to tax-delinquent buildings and then either demolish them, or sell them, or rehabilitate them with public funds, or turn them over to homesteaders. But what no city could do without breaking faith with its people and ignoring its very reason for existing, our complaint declared, was to do nothing at all—and that was exactly what Amity had done to this neighborhood: Let it rot.

Now, we concluded, the city had to fork over for its years of neglect. We entered a claim in behalf of our black clients for permanent depreciation in the market value of their property and asked damages totaling just over three million dollars. And to show we were not being just mercenary, we sought a mandamus order compelling the city to supply the same standard of municipal service in all categories to the Gully as it did to the rest of the population.

To Sam, our massive brief had become a metaphor for our affair—a baby conceived by our minds instead of our loins. And when it was delivered just before Labor Day, the promised end of our time together was at hand. He seemed suddenly listless and immensely sad as we walked together after work for the last time in Druid Park. The place was so still except for the shrill steady undertow of the insects that I had the sense we were moving through a landscape of long ago, before modernity had sullied it all. I asked Sam if he felt that, too. He said yes, in a way, but his head was obviously elsewhere and not to be summoned by my maundering.

"I don't want this to end," he finally said a minute later.

"What?"

"Us. I don't see the point."

"We're not going to end. Friends don't stop being friends just because they spend less time together."

"It's not just that. I don't know how to go from being so close back to a casual association."

"Casual may not be the word."

"Whatever it is, it's a great deal less than what we've had."

"Without bed?"

"Yes," he said.

"And without bed we're nothing to each other?"

"Less," he said. "Lots less."

"If that's what you really think, it's all the more important that we stick to the ground rules. Sex is lovely, and I've loved ours, but it's no basis for something deeper. Every animal in the jungle can screw. It just seems a lot more important to you right now because your ego is all tied up in it. I'm someone new and younger and forbidden, so your engine's been racing—and recreation's a marvelous thing. Everybody needs a little change once in a while. So you got your rocks off and Lee's coming back next week and you'll be getting it regularly again at home and our thing will—"

"Don't fast-talk me, Tabor," he said, "and don't try to make our summer into a stag movie. It doesn't become either of us."

"I'm just putting it all into perspective, so you'll stop gooping around like an undertaker. We've had a grand time and I don't regret a minute of it, but I won't have it ruined by your trying to protract it. That was never in the cards. We've got careers and private lives too precious to be thrown away on an indulgence. Take our thing for what it's been—not what it can't any longer be."

"Can you really program your affections that tightly? Can you just zap them on and off like that to suit your convenience? Or haven't you really had very much invested in—this—us?"

"As much as you."

"I doubt it. I'm afraid you mean a lot more to me than I do to you."

"How can you know that?" I stopped and took his hands and held him at arm's length and made him listen. "Look, will you, and stop pining for a second. I take whatever I can get out of life, Sam—I'm a real scavenger—and the things you've given me—all the warmth and kindness and passion and laughter—maybe the laughter most of all—I've genuinely loved, and I've loved you for them, and it's a self-pitying lie for you to claim otherwise at the last minute. But I'm not just a sponger, Sam, I've tried to give back everything I've taken from you and even more if possible. I don't know how to do anything halfway—haven't you figured that out by now?"

210

"If it's been so fine, why are you killing it?"

"Because I don't want it to become ugly and destructive. And I'm not killing it—I'm just de-escalating it. If something more was meant to happen between us, it still will. And if it wasn't, it won't."

"As simple as that?"

"Yes."

"I'd call it a death sentence."

"You're being a coward, Sam."

"Because I want something to grow between us?"

"It's grown all it can for now."

"I don't believe that."

"You don't want to believe it. We've got very different temperaments, can't you see? We're emotionally out of synch."

"I don't buy that," he said. "You're just ten times as demonstrative about your feelings. That's a difference in our styles, not our basic values. Our heads happen to work a lot alike—and that's nine tenths of it for me. The rest—well, that's why we're good for each other. You'd die rather than admit it, but you happen to need someone to shove you back in your place when you go spinning out of orbit—the same way I need to be grabbed by the shoulders when I'm burrowing away and to be stood up and shown what I'm missing. You've done that for me—you've changed me in ways I needed." He stopped well short of prostrating himself at my feet. "Happily," he wound up, "I haven't needed you to validate my sensitivity, intellect, and all-around humanity."

I wrapped an arm around his waist and gave him half a hug. That gift for smiling at himself, displayed at unexpected moments, was the man's most disarming trait. "Whatever I've done—or you think I've done," I said to him, "it's already happened to you. You've assimilated it. Sure, you're a different person for having known me—and me, you—but I'm not your nursemaid—or your therapist—or your private genie. My function in life isn't turning on Sam Nightingale to the glories of the universe he's been missing." I took my arm away. "You want someone to hold your hand, try your wife. Isn't that what wives do? I haven't heard you lodge any heavy grievances against yours."

"Because they're irrelevant."

"I can't think of anything more relevant. She's the one you're supposed to be sharing your joys and sorrows with. Have you tried? Or is she too weak to bring you up or put you down?"

"I'm not here because of what Lee is or isn't—or does or doesn't. It's because of what you are."

He was not going willingly out of my life. I reached for the big muscle in his upper arm and touched it and gave it a tender rub. "That's about the loveliest thing you could say to me." He turned slowly and gave me a single nod. "What you don't know, though," I said, "is that if you had any more of me, you couldn't stand it."

He threw a last look across the meadow. "You're probably right," he said. "I'm not sure any mortal man can please you for long."

"You think I'm just tired of you—is that it?"

"I think my flaws don't fascinate you any more."

"Your flaws are just fine, Sam. I love your flaws. But it's not you I'm talking about—it's me—my needs, my demands, my selfishness. I'm all wrapped up in myself mostly. I can't give you what you're after now—you or anyone. It's not a question of your pleasing me. The one you have to please is you. Please yourself and I'll be happy as hell. Don't wear yourself out carrying a hard-on for me because it's not worth it—I'm not what you think—I can't ever be what you think you need. You've got to be that for yourself."

There were definite tears in his eyes—of recognition, I think, or wanted to think, or had to think. He drove off right afterward to bring his family back from their summer away.

17

Directly after Labor Day, I showed Sparky Grier, as promised, the text of my 156-page complaint in behalf of the Gully cooperative against the city of Amity. He called me down to his office about an hour after I had given it to him. I waited while he finished flipping through it. At the end, he handed it back to me noncommittally.

"Dynamite, right?" I asked his poker face.

"You're not actually going to file it, are you?" he said.

"Day after tomorrow—when Washburn and the others are let out of jail."

"I see—a genuine media extravaganza."

"Sure. The whole point is to stir the conscience of the community."

"There are ways besides fruitless lawsuits."

"I don't think it's going to be so fruitless."

"I know a grandstand play when I see one, Tabor. You've manufactured this thing out of thin air. It may be good propaganda, but it's lousy law."

"It's not lousy—it's new."

"I've heard of ambulance-chasing," he said, "but this is the first time I've ever run into grievance-chasing."

"You don't question the social inequities we're claiming—you've told me so yourself."

"No, but that doesn't mean the remedies can automatically be found through litigation. Christ, the whole country's gone cuckoo expecting the courts to solve every painful problem. Beyond that, I doubt that your clients have proper standing, or that you've even got an actionable claim. If I were a betting man, I'd say you were going to get your ears pinned back."

"So I shouldn't file?"

"I think you'll just be spinning your wheels."

"Naturally that's a strictly disinterested opinion?"

"Pretty much."

"Good. For a minute I thought you might be concerned that I was embarrassing the firm."

"Cute," he said, twisting a rubber band in his fingers. "I've been consistent about this from the start, Tabor. And I told you again when you first took up with these people. This firm is not a social agency. It's had a special relationship with the city government for quite some time, and you don't have the right to jeopardize it just to get a little more mileage on your record. If you want to save America's soul, go run for Congress."

I took the complaint from his desk. "I'll count on your support if I ever do," I said. "Meanwhile, I'm filing on Thursday—and I'm sorry you doubt my law and my motives."

"Suit yourself," he said.

The suit commanded the lead story and a four-column headline in the paper. Duckett was on television news that night, standing in front of city hall and saying into the cameras, "The folks who run things here have finally got to understand we're people just like them—we got the same rights and the same needs—only we're lots darker and lots poorer and lots angrier."

When I came in the next morning, the receptionist said Sparky wanted to see me first thing. "Don't tell me," I said, trooping in on him, "you think I'm hogging the glory and you want in as co-counsel."

"Not exactly," he said. "More the opposite."

"What do you mean?"

"The city wants to hire me as special counsel to defend against you."

"You're kidding."

"Not in the slightest."

"But I thought you said I had a lousy case."

"I did—and you do."

"Then why do they need you to defend?"

"They don't, but they think they do. They don't get complaints that long and that sweeping every day of the week."

"You mean they're nervous?"

"Evidently."

I gave a giant clap. "That's terrific," I said.

"I wouldn't celebrate too soon. City hall may be edgy about your little confection, but I'm not."

"I don't quite understand."

"I told you—you've got a weak case."

"But how can you defend it? In fact, I don't understand how they could ask you if they know I'm representing the plaintiffs."

He twanged his rubber band and fell back in his swivel chair. "You're a little slow this morning, Tabor."

"I must be. How can two members of the same firm handle opposite sides of the same case? It's unethical."

"Exactly," he said. "One of us would have to drop out of the case—or out of the firm."

The fog vanished. "Oh, wow," I said. "Right in the groin."

"I think it's pretty shrewd of them, as a matter of fact."

"But you can just turn them down and that'll end it."

"Or I could accept their offer and show you to the door—unless, of course, you decided to sell your clients down the river."

"Sparky," I said, "is that what you want—to get me out of here?"

"I didn't think you should bring the suit. I thought I'd made myself clear."

"You did—perfectly. But that wasn't what I asked you."

"But you went ahead with it, anyway."

"Because it was a matter of overriding importance in my view."

"Regardless of the firm's position?"

"The firm hasn't got a position—only you do."

"I was speaking for the firm in this connection."

"I don't think so. I'll tell you what I think. I think you resent me for horning in on your act. You're so used to being palsy-walsy with the boys in the back room that you can't bear anyone cramping your style. If you want me to leave the firm, just say so."

He sat motionless for a moment eyeing me—whether with

215

malice or dismay, I couldn't tell. "I'm going to make you a proposition," he said.

"Okay."

"If you don't like it, the firm will expect your resignation by the end of the week."

"I believe that's called an ultimatum," I said.

"Just listen to me," he said. "I will decline the city's offer to defend against your suit—and in fact I'll use my offices to try to work out a settlement that will please you if you'd like me to try. All you've got to do is one thing."

"What?"

"Keep away from Sam Nightingale from now on."

My whole inside stiffened. I tried to keep up a front. "Why," I said, "is he contagious?"

He folded his hands on the desk and leaned toward me. "Tabor," he said in a brittle voice, "I know what's going on. Everyone in the office knows—except Maynard. You've been seen together several times outside of the building after hours. And it's perfectly apparent from the way you both light up in here when you're with each other—how you look and talk and laugh and hang together—that the two of you are close. Just how close I don't know or care, but it's not what I'd characterize as a wholesome relationship in terms of this office and your own careers here—particularly yours." He waited to make sure the impact of his revelation had thoroughly stunned me. Then he straightened up and said in his measured way, "Sam Nightingale is a splendid guy—and a principal cog in this firm. I'm not going to sit back any longer and watch him make a spectacle of himself. As for you, I don't quite understand how anyone so bright and obviously competent can repeatedly risk her professional and personal reputation by indiscreet and offensive behavior." He let that cool for a moment before wading in again. "When you first came here, you told Maynard Lamport that you'd do whatever you had to in order to succeed at the law—except travel horizontal. I know that because he asked me what you meant. When I told him, he was dumbstruck by your forthrightness. I've spared him the news that you apparently didn't mean what you said."

He may have spared Maynard, but me he left bloody. I was trembling from shock and exposure. I felt ripped open, penetrated, and left to run bare through the streets. My private life had never before slopped over into my work or been anyone else's business, but here they had practically wired me for sound, blood pressure, and pelvic contractions. I struggled to get my vocal chords back into operation. "And I'm the heavy in all this?" I asked.

"Because Sam's a babe in the woods when it comes to this kind of thing," he said.

"I suspect he'd be interested in your view of the matter."

"If necessary, he'll get it, but for the moment you're the subject." He began to smoke a cigarette. "Your involvement with the federal bench I was willing to dismiss as a non-recurring lapse of judgment when it was called to my attention. But this consorting with Sam is different. It smacks of someone with bad character or a weak one—and if it's the latter, it's the only thing about you that's not stainless steel."

I hunched forward in my chair, propped my elbows on my knees, and made my hands into a vise that locked my head in place. Nothing was spoken for a while, and then I faced him, eyes brimming with hurt and fury. "So I'm a convicted scarlet woman, is that it?"

"I don't know about that—just a lot dumber one than I thought," he said.

There was no explanation I could make without implicating Sam. I had gone against my own better judgment in yielding to his wishes and permitting the affair, however abbreviated, and for that—and for feeling what I did for him—I was culpable. What burned me was that I was the only one professionally vulnerable to the consequences.

I saw no point in telling Sparky that my relationship with Sam had already been relegated to history. It would have been admitting too much too readily and conceding a guilt I didn't feel. Defiance, though, would have been equally useless. I was left with trying to squeeze what I could from a very parched turnip. As it happened, the situation was not without its saving element. I told Sparky I would not dignify his assessment of my character or Sam's by debating the matter in any way, but that he could be assured there would be no reason for his concern in the future. It was about as close to abject humility as I had ever come. The results were salutary. He said that was fine and he hoped the subject would never again arise between us—for if it did, there would be no conversations after it—and he would do his best to make the city government understand the profound implications of the pathbreaking action I had so brilliantly framed and brought against it.

18

Clinical observers studying me that fall at the outset of my fourth decade on earth might well have issued an interim bulletin warning against a condition of approaching turbulence. Not that I felt actively melancholy or even mildly headachy about how my life was churning along—just a touch uncertain about what I most wanted to harvest from my years in bloom.

In a way, it was a happy problem. I had become a victim of my own precocious performance at the law. Beyond any reasonable expectation, I had shown myself a spirited trooper at defending the resources and sanctuaries of the firm's propertied clients. Rewards had come promptly, with the promise of far greater wealth and sway if I remained loyal to the mission and overcame an ancillary reputation as a bitch in heat. But something else was also happening. I was getting my name and face in the media as a champion of the downtrodden. Worse yet, I was showing signs of addiction to their cause, which was plainly inconsistent with—if not directly opposed to—the one that paid my salary and kept the firm afloat. I hardly saw myself as a revolutionary, working to hasten the divestiture of rank, privilege, and wealth among their haughty possessors; instead, I had cast myself as a go-between at the interface of two worlds, striving to reduce combustibility at the friction point. Yet I sensed in the long run it was not possible to serve two classes of masters without offending both. For the moment, I was walking a high wire to growing applause, but every now and then I was starting to glance down—a sure symptom of a short life expectancy.

If my professional life was beginning to register early evidence of strain over the uneasy balancing act I had developed, my emotional life was transmitting similar signals of stress from sustained inner conflict. Perhaps I was vicariously sharing in my mother's loss of her life's companion. Or maybe my summertime with Sam Nightingale had offered me a not displeasing glimpse of the closeness I might myself enjoy with a wholesome, intelligent, and decidedly domesticated man of mature years. In fairness to Sam, our summer arrangement had amounted to a painfully cloistered affair, but even without generous dimension, our time together suggested he was someone it would not be hard to grow old with—no little virtue. I was not ready to begin growing old just yet, though, and the question of Sam's remaining charms, or absence thereof, had been mooted by circumstances. Still, I could not deny the void he left behind. Not that I was any more eager than ever to circumscribe my life's possibilities by regularly having to please or ultimately having to answer to another human being. Yet I wondered now whether my own resources were quite as bottomless as I pretended—if I was simply afraid to acknowledge a vulnerability to loneliness lest it open me up to disabling doubts of every sort. The difference in me was that I was finally willing to weigh at least the possibility of permanently sharing the divisible parts of myself with someone who could be tender and tart, teacher and learner, high wind and anchor all in one. Even the powerfully inclined, however, do not find such a parlay under "Situations Wanted," and my own inclination remained far from fervent. It was nevertheless a change, which I did not deny in myself—and thereby saved an exorbitant fee for psychoanalysis.

Sam had little to say to me that autumn and found few excuses to say it. What he did say came out frosted if not bitter. Whatever the words, his message was always the same: all right for you then. Soon enough to suggest either a saving resilience or a callous heart, his no longer requited passion became a crackling sardonic aloofness from me that I enjoyed all the more because it was so obviously labored. I cared for him no less than ever—perhaps even more, now that he had been officially proscribed—but there was no way to show it. He naturally mistook inactivity for indifference. At least he sulked with dignity.

That September, Jonathan Kenyon invited me to renew our volatile alliance. He had survived without me quite satisfactorily, he wanted me to know, and his career had actually prospered from protracted spells of celibacy. In fact, he found himself productive at work in inverse proportion to his screwing activity. Besides, he acknowledged, rounding up a good lay on short notice consumed more effort than it was worth to him now, and he was not yet any readier than I to forge a stifling union for the benefit of convenient copulation. It was a different kind of sustenance he claimed I offered him. "You make it all happen," is how he put it rather too glibly.

"What 'it'?" I asked, knowing perfectly well what he meant.

"It—all—everything."

"The smart money says I was never more than the whipped cream on your sundae."

"Could be," he said. "I know more now, though—who I am, what I want, what I can give."

"That's funny," I said. "I know less."

"Not a bad thing, maybe, considering where we're both coming from."

"Maybe," I said and suggested that we take it up again by stages.

"Suits me," he said.

I made him promise never to call me a c—t again no matter how grave the provocation and agreed to his proposal to cohabit, on weekends, anyway. Jon had bought a beat-up old Victorian with a witch's-hat turret in a remote section of Outer Amity and decided to live in it while putting the battered antique back in shape with his own hands. I was invited to keep him company throughout the process, sharing in the work to whatever extent I wanted in exchange for bed and board. The idea was not without its appeal but would have meant a half-hour commute both ways each day and a lot more isolated intimacy than I wanted just then. Weekends out there while the leaves flamed and the autumnal snap spiced our labors were charge enough. He was a wonder-working craftsman, all applied muscularity and pinpoint finesse, who even when he lacked a skill improvised with a zeal that drew me up in it as well. I played the all-thumbs apprentice helping him plane the warped french doors, plaster the high cracked walls, sand the scarred oak floors, restore the punctured bargeboard and the rest of the gingerbread that time had nibbled away, and paint the place a warm dove gray with white shutters instead of the puke apple green they had worn probably for ages. It was one big hormonal stir watching him spend his torrential energy and talent on that rambling wreck. I asked him why he didn't save the orgy for whatever he was designing at the moment.

"I'm burned out for a while," he said. "There's a lot of stuff in the works but it's all cranial, it's all on paper, and it's all coming out of my ears. Right now I need something I can touch—I need grain and texture—the bite of a nail in wood." He lighted a joint for us to share and we lay back amid the sawdust and dug the blended perfume of aged pine and good grass and earned sweat and October night air in the country. "Also, I'm bringing life after death," he explained, waving his hand toward the surrounding debris, "and that's a kick. And you're here helping—that's a bigger one." My resolve to refrain sexually evaporated in that sweet haze on our second weekend there together. How he filled me—deeper and wider and longer than any of the other men I had had—and how unfrantically and familiarly he worked me and brought me out of myself and meshed us and glided us and pounded us. We literally fucked the night away and slept midway through the next afternoon.

What lured me most to Jon Kenyon was not the virtuosity of his lovemaking, which turned me so malleable, or the sudden surfacing of his muse, which turned an ordinary moment electric, but the unharnessable quality of the man. It took the form not of a wild unpredictability but an easy, almost unnoticeable slipping away whenever his head required it. The change in him, by the time it registered, was startling. When he was really with me or beside me or in me, there was no mistaking his presence. But when he made one of his long, moody withdrawals, he might as well have been on Saturn's rings. I did not resent those periodic abandonments; they verified his insistence on an inner life I could never share and would not ask to, any more than I invited him to rummage through my own secluded recesses. What these episodes said to me about Jonathan was that I could never own him, never be absolutely certain of anything about him—and never know when he might dump me out of bed and go off with someone else as he had before. That unknowable ingredient made him as dangerous a lover as he was magnetic for me and required my withholding a still larger portion of my being than formerly from our renewed confederation. We remained separate sovereign states, however much of us might go into the merger. For all that my attraction toward him may have indicated a streak of perversity in me, it was by no means so pronounced as to amount to masochism. If there was to be another unilateral sundering of our connection, I was fixed on being the instigating party this time around.

One weekday night a little before Hallowe'en, Jon stayed in town late and had me join him for a supper at a Greek place we both liked. I asked after his work, but all he could talk of was a fellow he had found who did first-rate stuff with leaded glass. Jon had got him to promise to come out to the house the following weekend to see about redoing the badly broken windows around the front door. I wondered why he was so excited at the prospect; it was, after all, only a decorative detail. "No," he said when I asked, "it's more. It's like an overture. It sets the whole mood right at the threshold. Some details are extraneous—maybe most. Some, though, are the very essence of a thing."

"If you say so," I said. His physical, emotional, and financial investment in the house had begun to border on an obsession. I was not anxious to feed it.

"I guess you've got other things on your mind," he said, not missing my key.

"One of us had better."

"I suppose you think I'm overdoing it a little?"

"Why? Just because you eat, dream, and breathe the thing twenty-four hours a day? Any minute I expect you to drill a hole in its side and start screwing it." I shrugged at him. "It's just a thing, Jon, no matter how special."

"Things are how I express myself."

"Not totally," I said.

"You know what I mean."

"I know you're getting cuckoo over the place. It's a possession—that means you're supposed to possess it, not the other way around. Why does this thing matter so much? It's not as if you designed it or anything."

He speared the last few flakes of his baclava. "It's a declaration of values," he said softly. "It's how they made it and what they made it of. They used stuff to last—not green wood and plaster board and a staple gun. And they put it together to hold. Nobody does that now. Nothing holds—nothing stays. Instant effect is all anyone gives a shit about. Nothing's worth building—and it's nobody's fault and everybody's. But the house, this house—it's all still there, or almost—it's together a hundred years later, and with some hammering and freshening it's got more charm and grace and basic integrity than anything anybody's going to put up anywhere this year—or next." He pushed his plate aside. "I guess it's like a religious retreat for me—very humbling and very inspiring at the same time." He looked up at me at the end. "Can you understand that?"

I loved that fierce conviction in him when he talked about his profession. He was, if anything, more dedicated to his field than I to mine. There was no sneering at his esthetic pronouncements because he left you in no doubt about the rigor of his standards or that his accolade was never lightly bestowed. He did not merely like a thing or dislike it on Olympian whim; he always had reasons. Whether I agreed with them mattered less than trying to learn something from the way he applied his sensibility against solid shapes and hard edges.

I got one of those lessons from him after that dinner. Its subject was more abstract than concrete, but Jon insisted that was a distinction without a difference so far as the craft and vision that fashioned it were concerned. For a time, I had trouble hearing him because of who the artist was. The gallery a few doors down from the restaurant announced out front it was showing works by three new painters. One of them was Lee Nightingale.

There were four canvases by her. They drew Jon at once. I hovered uneasily to the rear. Sam had not lied: his wife painted dots, nothing more, nothing less. But in such profusion that they gorged the surface, thousands upon thousands of them, each an atom of pure color, mingling in a state of arrested movement that gave the composition a kind of pulsing intensity if viewed from the right distance. In each instance, the conception of the painting was identical. Near the middle of each glowed a ball of color, varying only slightly in size and location a few centimeters off dead center. In two of the paintings, that focal spot was more luminous than its surround and appeared to be the source of the soft figureless radiance that filled the rest of the canvas. In the other two, the core was less brilliant than the rest of the composition which seemed to be collapsing in upon it from the outer edges. The effect was monochromatic—a hazy royal blue on one painting, a deep umber on another—but examination revealed that the artist had achieved it by a painstaking application of the primary pigments in exacting modulated blends. There was no gainsaying the infinite care that had gone into the execution of each work, but beyond the technique itself I could find nothing very admirable in Lee Nightingale's labors. It seemed cold and almost mathematically precise—one large *trompe l'oeil* that, having been achieved once, was hardly worth repeating.

"Interesting," I announced to Jon, "but insipid. A computer could have programmed them all."

He kept looking at the paintings, up close and then backing away, with an intentness that tacitly argued their virtue. Finally he just said, "Whoever she is, she's amazing."

"I don't see anything even slightly amazing—except the artist's patience. They're just dots."

"But look what she's done with them."

"What?"

224

"I don't know how to put it exactly, but don't you get the sense of tremendous calm and yet really awesome power sort of locked there together in limbo? It's what she's done with the color—and the texture of the light. There's extraordinary control behind it all."

"Are we looking at the same paintings?"

"We're both looking," he said, "but only one of us is seeing. Give it a chance. You're too quick to dismiss her."

I took a step back in token compliance with his suggestion and looked again. It was still just pretty color with a blob near the center. "You're sure you aren't putting me on?" I asked.

"Not a bit," he said. "The more I look, the more there's in it. You can see each one as either microcosm—like a single cell of protoplasm just before it's going to germinate—magnified to the millionth power or as an enormous nebula way out there somewhere a thousand light years off. That's quite a thing—to be able to suggest a body of energy so miniscule or at the same time so vast. And the technique is so wholly rational, so calculated, it's hard to believe she can create that sensation of aliveness."

Most of me insisted what Jon was saying was unadulterated bullshit. His training and instinct, though, were such that I could not dismiss the possibility, however remote, that he was right and I was blinded, by predisposition if not an insensate eye, to the woman's gifts. "Different dots for different tots," was all I said.

Jon dismissed me as hopeless with the back of his hand and went to get the small catalogue of the show to find out more about the artist. While I was stewing in a corner, tall lean Sally Kettering, Dan's strident wife, came upon me with a restrained show of delight—of the sort you might offer on recovery of a lost pet cobra. I had not seen her since my command performance at their tennis club. She looked as cool and severe in a dark-green long-sleeved print as I had remembered her, though her honey hair seemed more plastically coiffed. She was with a girl friend no less expensively put together; the pair of them gave the impression of being out slumming.

"Ghastly, aren't they?" Sally asked me out of the side of her mouth, indicating Lee Nightingale's paintings. "I'll have to lie to her, of course. Candor is so awkward in this kind of obligatory situation."

"At times," I said.

"Maybe you like them?"

"Not very much, I'm afraid."

"Don't be afraid. Do you know Lee at all?"

"Not in the slightest," I said, beginning to get even more uncomfortable than I had been while Jon was gushing over her work.

"I hate to say it, but you're not missing a great deal. It's hard to get two consecutive sentences out of her. I've often wondered how a man as spirited and clever as Sam finds her the least bit stimulating. Maybe she's a marvelous audience for him."

"I'm afraid I can't help you."

"No," she said, "I don't suppose so." Her friend drifted off to another part of the gallery, and Sally turned to me with heightened interest. "I gather you've worked some with Sam," she pressed.

"Some," I said. "I've worked with everyone."

"Dan mentioned something about your having masterminded the selling of the university power station."

"That's overstating it a bit."

"Let's have no false modesty, Tabor. I say good for you. But I thought that was Sam's bailiwick."

"It is."

"Then how on earth did you storm it? Dan says Sam plays his cards with the university very close to his vest."

"As I remember, it just grew out of some offhand remark I made."

"I'll bet," she said with her glassy laugh. "Well, Sam's a doll —and don't you go getting him to fall for you because I don't know what we'd do with poor Lee if he ran off. On top of everything else, the dear seems not to have sold a one of her paintings, and I think this is the last week of the show."

"Perhaps her luck will change."

"Perhaps," Sally said, "but I don't believe in luck. Her stuff hasn't sold because it's no good."

226

The steely bitch. She spurred me to charity I did not feel. "Somebody may think otherwise," I said, gesturing toward Jon. "My friend is quite taken with her things."

"Oh, my," she said and gave him a scouring appraisal across the room. "I'd think a nice-looking boy like that would have better taste."

"Maybe he sees something in them we don't."

"Maybe," she said, brows arching, "but I happen to have some training in the field. I like to think I can tell artistic talent when I see it."

"Jon's an architect—a good one."

"In the modern idiom, I don't doubt."

"Not so much. He's taken with beauty wherever he can find it."

"A very practical sort."

"He says there's no other way to survive."

"Mmmm, he sounds eloquent." She turned away from him. "Well, I'm glad to see you're sticking with younger men."

"I beg your pardon?"

"You're at a tricky age, I think. A lot of women in their prime seem to prefer men rather older than themselves—professional women, especially."

"I hadn't heard."

"Oh, yes, it's quite common."

"I can't say that I pay much attention to a man's age."

"That's my point—one should. It's not very attractive serving as jailbait to senior types."

I looked up sharply. Her eyes skittered by me. "Is there something you're trying to say to me, Mrs. Kettering?"

"My name is Sally," she said, "and I just said it."

"You're not terribly subtle."

"Oh, my, and I thought I was."

"Is this some sort of game you play—dropping innuendoes till you get a bite?"

She managed an icy smile. "You're quite direct, aren't you?"

"I try to be."

"It's not always a virtue when someone's trying to help you."

"I think it's always a virtue."

"And I'm Shirley Temple," she said. "All right, I won't play games if you won't."

"Fine. Now what sort of help is it I need?"

"Advice—feminine variety."

"Oh?"

"Do you want it?"

"Depends what it is."

"There's only one way to find out."

"All right."

"Leave the firm before they throw you out."

I gave a small groan of shock. "Why would they do that?"

"I can think of two reasons. First, you're smarter than the bunch of them—they can't stand that."

"I wouldn't make such a rash claim myself."

"You didn't—I did. I know them. Only Sparky's in your league—and he's cunning, not smart."

"That's your opinion. And what's the other reason?"

"They all want to go to bed with you—and you're in trouble if you do or if you don't."

"Who said they want to go to bed with me?"

"No one said it—no one has to. But I've got eyes—and ears."

"It's news to me."

"Come off it," she said. "I'm sure Dan asked you long ago."

The bite of the black widow. "Look," I said, "I don't know what your troubles are exactly or how long you've had these fantasies, but I'm just a single woman trying to earn an honest living at the law."

"Very nicely put," she said. "Lee Nightingale says it another way, though."

The venom was spreading through me now. "Oh?"

" 'Honest' was not part of it, as I recall."

My temples felt hot. "I don't know what her beef is."

"That," she said, "is beneath you, Tabor. I would have thought you'd have the grace not to deny it."

"I don't know what this is all about," I snapped.

"Sam told her," she said. "Is that enough for you?"

I drew a breath and held on tight. Then I gave her the nod she so badly wanted.

"Personally," Sally said, "I think she had it coming. Lee's a cold fish." She motioned to the paintings. "Q.E.D."

"I'd rather not go into it if you don't mind."

"No, I don't imagine you would," she said. "Just one thing, though—tell me honestly that Dan hasn't propositioned you? He's tried almost everybody else in town—and nobody'll give him a tumble."

"Then what difference does it make if he tried me, too?"

"You know that old joke—maybe the law of averages is working on his side now."

"You're not really asking whether he tried me, are you? You're asking if he succeeded."

"Am I?" She feigned surprise. "Perhaps you're right."

"And why should you think that if he's such a loser?"

"The track record."

"His or mine?"

"Both."

I looked over for Jon to rescue me, but he was talking intently with the gallery owner. This woman in front of me was about the most unflinchingly oppressive creature I had ever encountered. Her wickedness gave her the strength of ten. "I don't answer impertinent questions," I said, almost stifling now.

"I guess we could debate who's the more impertinent."

"Look," I said, "I'll answer your goddamn question if you answer one of mine, okay?"

"By all means."

"Yes, he tried, more or less—he was half in the bag—and no, I didn't, not at all. I actually feel sorry for him, which is more than you can seem to manage. That's my question—what makes a woman shit on her own husband the way you do? If he's so pathetic, maybe you ought to sit down and figure out if it doesn't have a little something to do with you."

"Ah," she said, looking at the ceiling, "now I remember. 'Smart slut' were the words Lee Nightingale used. I'll tell her her generosity was misplaced. So nice to have seen you again, Tabor." And she was off in a puff of dragon's breath.

I was still ashen by the time Jonathan came back with the

news he had bought one of Lee Nightingale's paintings. "Very reasonable, too," he said. "What would you think about it in the dining room?"

"Get two, why don't you?" I said. "One for each toilet."

19

When a note from Jessica Lennox came in the mail the week afterward, I regarded the unopened envelope with displeasure. The address was local and foretold an invitation to revive collegiate comradery. A more dismal prospect I could not imagine.

The problem was not Jessie's charms, which I recalled as considerable, but the latent perils of female fellowship. Girl friends were a relic of adolescence and, in my view, properly consigned to that age of discovery and self-doubt. Even by the time I had gone to Holyoke, the idea of a bosom buddy made me uneasy. I had friends, of course, but I did not distinguish them by sex or calibrate them by degrees of mutual affection. There was just me and another unit consisting of all the other people in my orbit, some of them more pleasing than the rest but hardly objects to be collected or traded or purchased by behavior that compromised my self-respect. I sought neither preceptors nor shoulders to cry on nor models to emulate, yet I was not lonely in a world that kept beating on my door to peddle me its beauties and its terrors. I had just one dread—dependency on any other living thing—and conducted my life accordingly. Thus, I was forever vigilant against would-be intruders, however benign and of whatever sex. Jessica Lennox's note, though, had a pleasing air about it that eased my hostile predisposition:

Dear Tabor Hill,

Torrents under the bridge since last we met. Wiser now if
less petite, I landed here the other month ostensibly to teach
kiddie English at a local academy for the overprivileged (and
in fact to forget about the sinking of a beastly marriage). Had
heard you were in the vicinity, called your old home to learn
where, had a grand talk with your mom, an all-time charmer,
who provided the info. Would like to have dinner some time if
your life permits. Happily, I have no legal woes to burden you
with.

Cheers,
J. Lennox

That she had taken the trouble to write instead of coming
on with a call bespoke consideration that appealed to me. I
rang her up that night and arranged for dinner the next. She
sounded warm without waxing feverishly enthusiastic. We met
at Blessings, my Chinese haunt, and except for her hair, which
she wore much shorter now and in a page boy, and ten
pounds of heft, she looked much the same—long and ripe all
over, with a pair of rampant jugs there was no place to hide. At
least she did nothing to accentuate them. She was a genuinely
funny person whose feigned insouciance could not mask the
lacerations of insecurity left by her divorce. "Actually," she
confided with a readiness that unnerved me at first, "Donald
turned out to be such a raging asshole there wasn't anything
tragic about the thing—just relief. Can you imagine a guy who
has to hump every other night at precisely eleven forty-five and
insists that the Johnny Carson show stay on throughout the
proceedings? Fortunately, he only took five minutes to do his
business. I'm not even sure he took his shoes off."

But she did not harp on the subject or demand intimacies in
return beyond those I volunteered. Jessica Lennox was a thoroughly educated woman who had done graduate work in literature at Oxford and was capable of conversing briskly on a wide
array of topics from the state of contemporary fiction ("No
one under thirty-five is writing anything longer than a film
script") to the economics of oil ("Some day soon the Arabs are
going to pump out one barrel too many and the whole fucking

231

desert is going to cave in"). Her commitment to feminism, like mine, was undoctrinaire, and we agreed it was too bad that unsightly gays had occupied so prominent a position in the movement. "Not that I begrudge them their kicks," she said, "but I don't see how one brand of chauvinism is better than the other." What was particularly winning about her was the generous interest she expressed in my work and her recognition that it provided the main nutrient in my life. Her inquiries about my professional adventures among the bozos implied I was at least a mini-hero in her eyes, yet she was uncompelled to counter with claims of her own distinction in order to win my esteem in return. Only toward the end of the meal, and then I thought inadvertently, did she let out that she had been writing serious poetry for years and had had her first two pieces taken for publication only recently. "It's no big deal," she said when I congratulated her warmly. "What really knocks me out is how you have the balls to stand up in court and fight with all of them bruisers. It would scare me shitless."

"It did me, too, in the beginning."

"No, but I'd get sick to my stomach every time."

"Not if you enjoyed it," I said. "It's sort of like—like—um—" I stopped in mid-simile. "Would you believe I'm actually embarrassed?"

"Say it."

"I—don't actually talk with women very often about—private things."

"Try me."

Her offhandedness made me feel silly. "Okay," I said. "Have you ever swallowed semen?"

Her egg-yolk eyes widened. "That's what you're embarrassed about?"

"A little."

"Big deal," she said. "The answer is: Who hasn't?"

"I've never taken a poll," I said with a small laugh.

"Well, I can assure you on the highest authority that eighty-eight percent of sexually aroused females between twenty and forty have been known to go down. I never call it fellatio, by the way—that actually makes it sound dirty."

232

I smiled. "Do you remember what it was first like?"

"Of course. I died." It was so huge, ugly, choking, and otherwise hateful, she said, that the power of the thing completely eluded her. All she could think was to get it over with. Then she discovered how exciting it was and began to savor it. "I think you could call it an acquired taste."

"Exactly—and you've just recited the scenario for *Tabor Hill Goes to Court*. That's what it was like—point for point, so to speak."

"Well, that's graphic enough," she said. "Is it straining the analogy to ask if law and sex produce a comparably orgasmic effect?"

"I never thought of it quite like that. One is so mental."

"So is a lot of sex."

"I prefer mine to be mindless," I said. "Maybe it's because I think too much the rest of the time."

"That's a helluva time to stop thinking."

"When I'm thinking, I'm not feeling—not much, anyway."

"I see," she hissed and dropped into a Viennese accent: "And how long have ve been having dis problem, *fraulein*?"

"Forever," I said.

She rubbed her imaginary beard. "Sounds like dis patient I got who shwore off sex after shcrewin' vit' Secretariat. She kept thinkin' how much it vas costin' dat it vas over before she knew it."

We laughed away the rest of the evening at the three-room apartment she had taken in a handsome private residence on one of the more elegant streets in town. I left around one, feeling I had known Jessie Lennox well all my life.

I began to see her a couple of nights a week without either of us becoming the least beholden to the other about reserving the time. One of us just picked up the phone and called; if the other was busy or tired or plain not in the mood for company, she said so. Weekends, I explained, I spent with a man in the country, and she never pushed for details. In time, I offered some and heard a few back about her involvement with a science teacher at her school but never more than I cared to know. It was an instinctive thing between us, that level of self-

233

disclosure beyond which neither of us was comfortable. The heaviest talk to surface was the revelation that her marriage had disintegrated shortly after she had aborted a two-month fetus despite her husband's strenuous objection. "It wasn't his," she said, "but I figured telling him would be worse than killing it. It was definitely one of your no-win classics." I asked if her inseminator didn't mind. "He did the deed coming and going—it was my gynecologist. Claimed I had the lushest torso he'd ever probed in fifteen years of practice. It was a helluva come-on. And God, was he clean. You've heard of the Immaculate Conception? I mean for a while I thought he was going to come to bed with his disinfectant and rubber gloves." I said I thought I'd have difficulty balling my doctor. "So did I," she said, "but then he knew where everything was—and seemed so appreciative. He also happened to be better hung than any man I've ever seen. I asked him where he stashed it when the customers were in the stirrups. He thought that was obscene."

Most of our exchanges, even the more clinical ones, were as easy and unguarded as that, with no stakes and no risk. We said what we felt about whatever we shared, vaginal, visceral, or cultural. She came out of the latest Woody Allen movie with me, raging at the critics who had proclaimed it a masterwork. "He's a big talent," she said, "but I have seen him make this same fucking movie with the same goddamn *schleimiel* gags six times now, and it's not endearing any more. He's the Jew you love to hate—weak, homely, chicken, sexless. I think the Anti-Defamation League ought to be out picketing the theater." I said I thought she was taking the thing too seriously and that Woody was a sort of kosher Charlie Chaplin. "But that's the point," she said. "Chaplin was a universal Sad Sack. Allen's a parochial shmuck who confirms all the neanderthal stereotypes about kikes—except that he comes over dumb." I said I still thought he was funny and that she was over-intellectualizing it. "What do you know?" she said. "You probably think Hirohito is a laugh riot." I said not since he had his orthodontia.

One evening I joined Jessie at her place while she was grading compositions by her seventh-grade class at the Baker School, a learning environment free of subliterate blacks and the hoodlum element. I offered to read a few of the papers and recommend a grade but warned, "I'm death on the sequence of tenses."

"We're still working on the difference between 'it's' and 'its'," she said. "Besides, I think the sequence of tenses was ruled unconstitutional by the Supreme Court two years ago. But help yourself to a batch—and remember, they're only little punks."

The punks' assignment was to write a two-page composition on a true-life adventure they had had with some member of their family. The first two I read were thoroughly tame. The third was an eye-opener. It began:

My father is an expert archer. He can hit the bulls-eye at a hundred paces nine times out of ten. Once last year he took me hunting with him to learn how to shoot. It's very hard to kill a deer with bow and arrow because they hear you creeping up on them no matter how few crackles you make. Well, this is how we got one. My father said deers always look for a pond that . . .

And the lad proceeded to write a graphic account of how he and his sharp-shooting old man tracked a doe they had wounded for two days through the wilderness before bagging the forlorn thing. I half-expected the young author to wind up by telling how his father shot an apple off his head to celebrate the successful completion of the hunt. Instead, there was a brief postscript remarking that it was much more sporting to kill an animal with an arrow than a bullet, but the youngster didn't think he was especially cut out for either form of carnage.

"How much do I take off for lying?" I asked Jess. "This kid's a whale of a storyteller but I think he's got his father mixed up with William Tell. He also threw in a free commercial for the Wildlife Preservation Society. I'd give the brat twenty years reduced to a B-minus on account of he's got a good heart and fertile imagination."

"Who wrote it?" she asked.

I turned the paper over. In the upper right corner it said

"Roland Nightingale." Sam's son. "Very gifted boy," she said, "and he doesn't give me any grief. It's kids like him that make it a pleasure to teach at the place. I met the parents—I mean you can tell right away. The father's a lawyer—got brains written all over his face. The mother's some kind of painter, I don't know whether she does houses or pictures." She saw the look on my face and stopped. "You know them or something?"

"I know them."

"What's wrong—do they drop acid or what? They seem very respectable."

I explained my professional connection and let it go at that.

"And Pops doesn't fire arrows around the office when things get slow? I mean maybe that's his thing."

"He's not the hunting type," I said.

"What type is he?"

I paused revealingly. "Just—very nice. A little excitable on occasion but highly civilized most of the time."

"Smart?"

"Very. Also funny—you'd like him."

"You seem to."

"Sure," I said. "He's pleasant, brainy, moderately attractive."

"And you're hot for him."

"He's a guy in our office."

"I think you're hot for him."

"Why?"

"The way you looked when you found out it was his kid."

I tried to shrug her off. "It just surprised me, that's all. I guess the kid's fantasizing the father he wishes he had."

"The one he's got doesn't sound half bad."

"At a guess, I'd say he doesn't know how to relate to the boy. He's probably his mother's son."

"And you're probably his father's lover."

"Hey, fuck off, will you?" I said it so fast and so hard that she knew she had hit the mark or come close. Neither of us said anything for a while. It was the first time that our mutual wall of privacy had been breached. The room inflated with tension as she kept on grading the papers without looking up. I just sat there immobile, thinking about Sam. Why had the fee-

236

ble bastard run to his wife with his tail between his legs when he had insisted throughout our thing that it had nothing to do with her? How cowardly not to take his lumps in solitude, shake the whole episode out of his system, and turn back to his marital commitment with fresh heart. It was as if by confessing his transgression he were punishing his wife in place of me because she was the more accessible of us and the more vulnerable.

"I'm sorry," Jessie said finally. "I had no business saying that."

"You're right," I said. "You didn't."

"You just looked as if it was going to bust out of you."

"And you thought you'd help it along a little?"

She tossed her papers on the card table she used as a desk and came over to me in distress. I would not look at her. She sat beside me and said, "Tabor, I didn't mean to hurt you. I'm much too fond of you to be so callous—don't you know that? It was just something I blurted out."

"I know," I said and looked at her. "Unfortunately, you were exactly right."

"Yeah," she said. "I figured. You must have it worse for him than you want to admit to yourself."

"I don't think so."

"Then why the storm clouds—bad vibes?"

"Something like that."

"It screwed things up for you around your office?"

"Sort of."

"He didn't handle it well?"

"He didn't handle it at all."

"Your dignity was compromised?"

"Yes."

"The whole place knew about it?"

"Yes."

"You wanted to punch out the fucking bunch of them?"

"Yes, yes, yes!" I bit down on my bottom lip and turned away.

"Okay," she said. "Okay, okay."

"It's not okay. It's lousy."

237

"What I said?"

"Not you—him—it—them—the whole thing."

"What whole thing?"

"*L'amour.*"

"Oh. That. I didn't think you cared."

"I don't—except when I do. And when I do, there are always problems."

"Lovewise, you are fucked up—is that all?"

"Nobody's love-wise. Love is *merde*. *Merde* and pretty packaging. I'm not talking about hearts and flowers. I mean warmth —and sharing—and consideration—not ruling, not relying on. See, I'm dreaming, right?"

"Not really. You just want it on your terms or not at all."

I nodded. "I'm not even sure that qualifies as love. Whatever it is, though, it's rare. Maybe even extinct."

Jessie shrugged. "How about some wine?" I said just a little. She went and got it and a beer for herself. The best of the night turned into a painfully frank seminar on the libidinous needs and sublimating fantasies of women who lived alone and said they preferred it. Invariably, men scorned the likes of us as sere twats, asexual and forbidding, or dykes hardened beyond redemption. The injustice of such indexing galled Jessie. "Down with the phallusocracy!" she cried and emoted on the virtues of the cockless orgasm—of which, I confided, I had self-ignited several thousand without pain or reduced vision. Everyone else does, too, she said, and why not? Aside from the testimonials of fertility cultists, tribal ritualists, and Freudian fetishists, the penis is an exalted thing only to those who own one. That it should have been accorded a sanctified place among the bodily organs ever since the predawn of humankind had more to do with the blatancy of its function, we agreed, than any metaphysical design. Then why its totalitarian sway over morality? Why should its absence from a sexual context render its participants aberrant? For any purpose beyond procreation it was not remarkably better suited than, say, a Vaselined banana. "And a syringe can handle the procreative business quite nicely, from what I hear," said Jessie.

Which led us, eventually, to a consideration of lesbianism as

238

a legitimate alternative form of sexuality. The subject inspired neither enthusiasm nor revulsion in the pair of us. "It's just another human option," said Jess. "If sex is emotional release through bodily stimulation, then people are entitled to get off any way they can. To pigeonhole them as deviant because of one or another of their thousand traits is simplistic crap, not to mention dehumanizing as hell."

Still and all, I said, I detected a nasty defensiveness sometimes among militant gays—"as if to say the rest of us are missing something special if we're not at least bisexual."

"Maybe they're right," she said.

"To find virtue only in your own preferences?" I felt otherwise. What was not natural for me was, by definition, unnatural. Nor was I inclined to condition myself to see if I wasn't losing out on something grand. My life was not so devoid of highs that I needed to distort it in hope of purchasing a few extra moments sublime. Going against your own nature to prove a capability of doing so, I said, is just a lesser form of suicide.

"I never thought of it like that," said Jess. "Christ, you're fierce."

After that night, all barriers between us fell. We played out our hopes and doubts before each other in a spasm of disclosure. And in that joint confessional we exposed repressed fear and regrets that might never have been aired by either of us singly.

The physical side of the process was the less harrowing. We appraised our bodies and made a discovery. Where she thought her breasts too expansive and pendulous, I said mine lacked heft and symmetry. She wished her eyes were more expressive; I wanted a higher coloration for mine. She envied my round firm ass; I, her finely tapered hands. And yet each time we got to a new anatomical department, the complainant heard the other one of us say she would gladly settle for owning the offending part or parts—about as supportive an assessment as two people can provide each other. But that, after all, was largely a vixenish exercise in assuaging vanity; our bodies, if differently contoured, were both still ripe and shapely.

Our characters presented a different sort of trial. We convinced ourselves that unless our most grievous traits were faced down and their components isolated, we might never possess ourselves fully. While hardly holding myself fault-free, I had long before resolved, with precocious wisdom, not to dwell on my shortcomings; the world, I was certain, would soon enough find them out on its own. My job was to get out there so far in front of the pack that they'd never catch up with me when the worst became known. Not a bad strategy, but lately my timing had been off. Jessica thought it was more than timing. "You're hiding from yourself," she said. "I do the opposite—I sit in front of the mirror and chew out that fucked-up idiot I see in there."

Our conclusion was that Jessie and I were the opposite sides of the same coin. Neither of us was ever likely to sustain an intimate and loving relationship with another human being, we decided, until we learned to tolerate a common list of flaws that bugged each of us inordinately. The difference between us was that I could not stand them in someone else because I would not tolerate them in myself; Jessie did—and disliked herself for it and swore she would never cohabit again with someone not of far sterner stuff than her own. The sins we winnowed were: sentimentality, indecisiveness, self-pity, sloth, timidity, and insecurity. I said they all came down to the last one. Jess said maybe so but its various manifestations were instructive. If I had turned into a hard woman, bordering on the abrasive, in order to function effectively in rugged terrain, she had felt capable of no such denial of her nature. The resulting difference in our professional performances was revealing. But if in the process I had made some sort of monster of myself—cold, predatory, opportunistic—it was far from clear that I had come out ahead of her in the game.

One immediate outgrowth of our special brand of intercourse was the beginning of my direct involvement with feminist rights. Jessie, not inappropriately, was the *agent provocateur*. "You're all in favor of women's pubic hair, right?" she asked me beguilingly over the phone one night.

"Not any or all," I said, "but generally yes."

"It's God's gift for them to do what they want with, right?"

"Well—generally, yes."

"And does it matter what somebody else thinks about it?"

"Esthetically or legally?"

"Esthetics are subjective. I'm talking law now, kid."

"Pubic hair is not an area I've done much with, professionally speaking. From what I gather, though, it's quite a tangled thicket—to quote Justice Frankfurter in a slightly different context."

"One of your obscure judicial japes, no doubt," she said. "But listen, at my school is a guy named Womczuk, and he was telling me about the screwing his younger sister is getting at the Darlington Arms plant just because she won't shave her legs. She's a waitress in the company restaurant and her supervisor told her to shave or take a walk. He said hairy legs on a waitress were bad for business. The girl—her name is Mary, Mary Womczuk—isn't a womczuk a small Slavic amphibian with web feet and a bushy tail or something? Well, anyway, Mary is pissed off something terrible and says she'll sue if the company forces the issue. I told her brother I knew just the lawyer if it came to a showdown."

And so it did. Darlington Arms, a munitions maker that happened to have the biggest payroll in the Amity metropolitan area, did not take kindly to employees who balked at its regulations. Mary Womczuk, reporting to work with a profusion of wiry black growth on her piano-stout legs, declined to shave it off when ordered a final time and got herself fired on the spot. I was therefore obliged to inform the company that it had violated Ms. Womczuk's rights under Executive Order 11246 and Title VII of the 1964 Civil Rights Act—and unless it had required all workers, men as well as women, to shave their legs or could demonstrate some direct link between the condition of my client's legs and her job performance, I was prepared to move for a federal injunction against her firing and bring the entire matter before the Equal Employment Opportunity Commission. The company, in the person of the vice president for personnel, told me on the phone to do whatever I wanted, but that Mary was out of a job so long as she insisted on showing up shaggy. "Okay," I told the honcho, "but I want you to know it's also been called to my attention that there are a good many women on your payroll who've been receiving a substantially lower salary than men in the same job category—that's a violation of the federal Equal Pay Act of 1963, amended to expand coverage in 1972." He asked me what job categories I was talking about, and I said I was not at liberty to discuss the matter—which was certainly true since I had invented the claim just a moment before. The next thing I knew, I was on the carpet in front of Maynard Lamport.

"Having sued the bejesus out of the city," the elder partner began somewhat funereally, "you now appear to have locked horns with the largest manufacturing enterprise for miles. Is this some sort of elephantiasis of the litigious ego, Tabor, or do you just naturally attract mite-sized clients so ravenous they want to devour their host?"

"I think you've got the wrong party doing the devouring."

"Well," he said, uncranking his neck, "whichever way it is, you seem to have the Darlington people in quite a snit."

"They should think a little harder before acting so beastly. A woman is entitled to maintain her body the way she wants as long as she's not imperiling others. My Hairy Mary is not Typhoid Mary."

His upper lip quivered in reflexive imitation of a smile. "Hairy Mary indeed," he said. "It's not the hirsuteness they're exercised over, however. It's your accompanying threat of action over equal pay for their women."

"Oh," I said. "Well, I didn't exactly threaten them. I just said the subject had been called to my attention."

"And had it?"

"Not exactly."

"What does that mean?"

"It means no."

"Then say no when you mean no."

"No."

"So you were bluffing?"

"I—yes. But it was a calculated bluff. I figure every big company is probably underpaying its women—and will keep on doing it till they get forced to stop."

"That's a rather reckless way to proceed on your part, don't you think?"

"A little blustery, maybe, but not entirely reprehensible. Just because they're a giant, I don't think they should be able to get away with treating one not very important human being like so much dirt."

Lamport gave a small, cryptic grunt. "Well, I had a call from the president of Darlington a little while ago—we have many mutual friends, half of whom I should say the firm represents in one capacity or another—and he is alarmed that you're about to tip over his apple cart—unwittingly, as it turns out. Darlington is on the verge of announcing an equal pay policy in all job categories and as a show of good faith has allocated half a million dollars in retroactive back pay to the affected women. They're nervous that you're going to push for heavier damages."

"Sounds like a good idea," I said. "How long is the pay retroactive for?"

"Six months."

"The finks. They've been in violation of the law for years—and they're admitting it."

"I don't think they should get penalized for their candor."

"And I don't think they should get rewarded for their prejudice."

"I don't really see how that's your business. You're not actually representing any of the affected women."

"No," I said, "not yet."

"And what does that mean?"

"It means it wouldn't be hard to round up some."

"Tabor, that's highly unethical."

"Almost as unethical as Darlington."

"That's not your concern."

"I'm not so sure," I said. "I'll tell you what. Let's say they make it a full year's back pay for the women—and Hairy Mary gets rehired as long as she wears any shade of stockings darker than skin color."

He gave a single amused bark. "And who's going to make that outrageous proposal?"

"I was hoping you might."

"Tabor, that's preposterous—and downright devious."

"But I haven't done anything underhanded to get the information. They volunteered it. I'm just functioning as a sort of collective social conscience."

"And you think I'm going to be a party to bilking a major local corporation and potential client out of half a million dollars?"

"I don't view the situation in exactly those terms."

"Evidently not. But right is right."

"And is it right for the company to have bilked its working women out of millions for a good while longer than their settlement acknowledges?"

"Maybe not, but I must persist—we're not a party to that question."

"Perhaps you're not."

"Nor you. You can't go gambling your professional integrity on a lark."

"It's a lot more than that. It's a vital principle."

"In the proper context, yes. As a product of serendipity, no. And I for one won't play any such game."

"Blame it on me, then, why don't you? You could say you don't know how much I know exactly about their intentions to remedy the equal-pay grievance."

"But that would be dishonest. I know for a fact that you knew nothing whatever about their back-pay settlement proposal—you told me so."

"That's not quite true any more, though, is it? If you know what I told you, I also know what you told me."

"What the company said was told to me in confidence."

"And so was what I told you."

He thought about that a moment. "I think perhaps I was being somewhat careless," he said.

"I think something else," I said. "I think perhaps we were both being manipulated a little."

"How's that?"

"I don't see that you had much choice but to tell me what

the company was up to—how else could you have found out what I knew about the equal-pay business?"

"By asking you without mentioning the company's plans."

"But don't you see, that would have been no more ethical than what you think I'm proposing—taking advantage of confidential information. Just because I'm a member of the firm doesn't make it any less heinous. No, the company can't have it both ways—getting what it wants without any risk to itself by supposing its communication with you is privileged but mine with you is not."

He scratched his scalp for a moment. "Offhand," he said, "I'm not sure who's more cunning—you or they. What's plain is that I'm being used a bit."

"I didn't initiate any of this with you."

"Perhaps not," he said, "but you're picking up the game very rapidly."

"Isn't that why I'm here?"

"Yes-yes-yes," he said, more miffed at himself than me or the company for being outfoxed. "All right," he went on wearily, "suppose I tell them you were thinking about a year's retroactive pay, but I think you'd settle for nine months' worth without too much fuss?"

"And my client gets rehired in dark stockings?"

"Yes-yes—the Hairy-Mary protocol."

I had not before, and have not since, been the beneficiary of a purer piece of luck. True, I acted with unalloyed brass in seizing instantly on the opportunity, and that is something, but in my zaniest dreams I never concocted a scheme of such bluff and bluster against that grisly a foe. So formidable, though, was Maynard Lamport's standing that it was all arranged in a few hours. The resolute Mary Womczuk got her job back and became a kind of Che Guevara in black stockings among the now more amply remunerated working women at Darlington Arms. Mary credited me with the whole bonanza, and before long I had more female clients trooping through my door than any nonwelfare lawyer in the city.

The only price Maynard extracted from me, at peril of being

ingloriously deep-sixed, was that my lips remain sealed in the matter. How would it do for word to get out that the community's foremost barrister to the carriage trade had handled the workers' side in a labor negotiation—and not even been paid for it?

20

Sparky Grier was true to his word. He wore out incalculable quantities of rubber bands trying to arrange an attractive settlement with the city in my omnibus Fourteenth Amendment suit against it in behalf of the Boot Coop and, in that wonderfully archaic language of the law, "others similarly situated." The price he made me pay for it was almost unbearably cruel: I was to remain invisible throughout the proceedings, leaving the matter exclusively in his accomplished hands. "If you want to argue the case in the newspapers," he said, "there won't be anything to settle—the city will just dig in for the duration. If you'll let me go at it quietly, I think you'll be happily surprised."

"Is that a promise?" I asked.

"I don't make promises I can't keep. It's a pledge to do the best I can for all concerned."

I said the case had been docketed and any move to halt the trial would depend on the city's initiative in the matter. Sparky came back to me with word that the mayor's people would not negotiate with a pistol at their heads. "Tough," I said.

"Withdraw your suit for sixty days," he said, "and see what happens."

"And if nothing does?"

"What have you lost?"

"My clients' confidence—the initiative."

"Tell your people the court will look more kindly on their complaint if you've exhausted your remedies."

"All right," I said, "sixty days."

The reporters called me every day for word of progress or stalemate on what they assumed were head-to-head negotiations between the parties. With uncharacteristic restraint and growing apprehension, I steadfastly declined to comment. My resolve was not braced much by Sparky's repeated advisory that things were coming along and he would be back to me as soon as the package had taken firm shape. "Just make sure when it does," I said, "that it's got something besides horseshit in it."

In the event, there were no negotiations, only a unilateral announcement by the mayor of a far more thoughtfully conceived program than I had anticipated. Sparky had done his job well and preserved his franchise as municipal mover and shaker par excellence. The city's proposal to the Gully provided for stepping up police patrols by half, bringing garbage collection up to city-wide standards, repairing all broken street lights over a six-month period, extending the Seaview Avenue bus line to the city limits while increasing its frequency to half-hour intervals, and a major drive to improve housing by a sweat equity program enlisting many elements in the community. It was this last plank that was the most important and farsighted. The city was foreclosing on 157 restorable dwellings and 320 other rubble-covered building sites throughout the Gully that had been in tax arrears for eighteen months or more and making them available for the token price of one dollar to any area residents who wanted one. Forty-three other hopelessly blighted structures would be demolished at city expense and eventually added to the pool of available sites. Residents who chose to participate were to get a tax exemption on their property for five years—a gift from the city, in effect, of several thousand dollars per dwelling. Local banks promised to make fresh mortgage money available to Gully people who came in with specific building plans and high determination. Mather University said it would assign a special task force of faculty and students from its Center for Architecture and Urban Design to provide free professional guidance to Gully residents who asked for it during the next three summers. The building trades unions agreed not to interfere with the effort by any resident to build or renovate his or her own house. And the realtors promised to steer would-be buyers to Gully homes that their new owners had refurbished in the hope of selling them for badly needed income. Whatever might come of the plan still depended, of course, mostly on the sweat of the Gully residents, but now the rest of the community would, at least in the theory, be supporting their efforts instead of hobbling them.

"We'd rather have us the bread," Duckett said when I met with their tribal council on the night of the mayor's announcement. I said I thought that was probably being penny-wise and pound-foolish and that there were no guarantees they'd get even half as much if we fought the thing out in court. "But we got them on the run, it look as if," one of the younger men said. "What they really doin' when you get right down to it is givin' us back what they got no use for nohow."

That was not an altogether inaccurate reading of the proposal. By tax-foreclosing on the abandoned properties, the city was only doing what it should have done much earlier. By giving away title to them and granting a tax holiday to the new owners, furthermore, the city looked generous when in fact it was surrendering nothing in order to get a lot of presently worthless properties back on the tax rolls five years hence. The rest of the city's toothless gift horse required similarly close inspection. There was no way of telling for sure, as an example, how much money the banks would actually be willing to sink into the community venture or under what stringent conditions. The university people might have wildly grand ideas about what should be done to the Gully houses, and there seemed to be more than a little *noblesse oblige* about their participation. "It sound like they gonna tell us what to do and we do it or else," one of the black lady chieftains said. "This here's spozed to be our plantation." The crafts unions were even more suspect, based on their historic hostility to letting blacks aboard their gravy train, and there was no reason to suppose they had suddenly developed fraternal twitches. "They gotta be figurin' we'll be so busy fixin' up around here ain't no one gonna be bellyachin' about bein' fucked everywhere else in town," is how the Coop treasurer

248

put it. And the realtors, of course, were the grossest offenders of all, committed as they were for their livelihood to the supposedly divine maxim that birds of a feather ought to flock together, especially blackbirds, whose fouled nests they regarded as barely fit for habitation. To think they would somehow go out and plump for new residents of any and all shades to come to the Gully, no matter how attractive the housing values, struck my clients as wishful if not entirely unthinkable.

Even with these reservations, I argued, they ought not to spurn the proffered hand of city hall. Our sweeping complaint had been officially heeded, and there was a tempering of arrogance in that fact alone. The moment had come, I said, for them to decide whether they were after a propaganda victory or tangible improvements in the quality of their lives. To phrase the choice that way was to make it obligatory. We settled on a statement of commendation of the mayor's proposal and a private request for better terms—a ten-year tax-free respite on the reclaimed property, a collective commitment of at least two million in mortgage money from the banks, and a municipal grant-in-aid to the Boot Coop to serve as the nonprofit supplier of building materials to residents participating in the program.

"You're being greedy," Sparky said.

"I don't think so. My people feel the thing is very soft—very iffy."

"That's too bad," he said, "because I'm afraid that's all they're going to get. The mayor and his people don't like being backed into the corner."

"Those are quite revealing metaphors you keep using—pistols to their heads, being backed into the corner—that sort of thing—almost as if they think they're getting mugged."

"Not far from it."

"Then tell them to forget all about it, and we'll just let the suit ride. I wouldn't mind going down as the attorney of record in a landmark decision."

He stretched a rubber band almost to the breaking point and gave it a twang with one of his disengaged fingers. "As to that," he said, "I've discussed your complaint with three of the top people at the law school. They all give it high marks for ingenuity, but none of them thinks you've got a prayer. They say it's a high-class grab bag of grievances, and the stitching shows through. It's got a lot of little virtues but there's no real central thrust to it."

"Naturally," I said. "A woman wrote it."

He snorted. "Tabor, you are the most masculine woman I've ever met."

"Why—because I know what I want and go after it?"

"Because," he said, "you want the world—and mean to have it."

"Is that bad?"

"It's hard on most of the rest of us."

"It's hard on me, too," I said, and we both smirked at the not very coy pun.

In the end, he went back to city hall and got the tax-exemption extended from five years to six but nothing more. The banks were not prepared to commit their involvement in the project to a dollar figure, and the mayor said that funding the Coop's entry into the building-supply business smacked of socialism, especially since there were plenty of lumberyards and hardware outfits in the area hungry for business. I recommended to Duckett that he take the deal. He agreed, provided the city explicitly granted the Coop title to the vegetable garden that caused the whole fracas, along with the right to cultivate it in perpetuity. The mayor rejected the condition on the principle of the thing—the city would be acknowledging that wrongdoing pays, he said—but offered a similarly sized plot even closer to the Coop for the same purpose. "Honky principle," Duckett said, and the deal was clinched. Agreement was announced at a city hall press conference, and a new day in Amity race relations acclaimed. Sparky and I had a drink after work to mark the occasion. His picture, as usual, did not make the papers or television, and for a welcome change, neither did mine.

That night, still in a state of exhilaration, I phoned Sam Nightingale at his home. His wife answered. "I'd like a word with Mr. Nightingale if I may," I said.

"May I tell him who's calling?" she asked.

"I'm from the office."

"Very well," she said, "hold on a moment."

Sam came on with distant caution. "Yes?"

"I just wanted to thank you for all the help you gave me in the Coop case," I said. "It's all settled."

"Yes," he said, "well, that's very nice." His voice was solid ice.

"I guess you've got company."

"I think this can wait till morning," he said. "It shouldn't present any difficulties."

"I can't talk to you at the office—I can't talk to you at your home—what am I supposed to do, send you a letter care of American Express in Paris?"

"Yes," he said, "well, that's a possibility."

"Christ," I said, "you can't be that uptight."

"Thanks for calling," he said.

"All we did was love each other a little," I said into an empty phone.

The rest of that fall and winter, the Coop people were busy with planning and paperwork for a bootstrap operation that, come spring, would dwarf their earlier efforts. Duckett had become for all practical purposes the acting mayor of the Gully—"the jive-ass boss," he called himself—and the Coop council the only really cohesive organization in the neighborhood, and so local power flowed naturally to him and it. On my suggestion, which was eagerly adopted, a local young black lawyer of demonstrated competence named Geronimo Jones began to work closely with the Coop and other area residents to turn the sweat equity program into reality. I watched from the sidelines like a distant den-mother.

My diplomatic withdrawal from the affairs of the Coop did not leave me bereft of social causes to champion. In fact, I was even busier than I had been. That winter I challenged the Amity school board in behalf of a tenured teacher who had been required by regulation to take an unpaid maternity leave four months before delivering her child and prevented from returning to work for three months afterward. None of the mandatory layoff was chargeable to her paid sick-leave allowance. Since male teachers with temporary disabilities were permitted to remain on the job as long as they were physically able—and, when not, were allowed to utilize their accumulated sick-leave time and get paid that way—the regulation was in plain violation of the '64 Civil Rights Act, and so I wrote to my old antagonist, school board president Valentine. He wrote back that the maternity-leave policy had been modified a few years earlier in recognition of the better health care available to expectant mothers and the more sophisticated attitude of the community, but no further changes in the rules were contemplated. I gathered half a dozen articles from respected journals, saying there was nothing in a normal pregnancy that made it medically undesirable for a woman to keep on working until her delivery and to return to work two to four weeks thereafter, and shipped them off to Valentine and the six other board members.

They were unbudgeable. I suggested to the teacher who hired me that she gather the names of every other woman in the Amity school system who had been similarly victimized over the past three years by the board's maternity-leave policy and invite as many of them as liked to join in a Title VII legal action. To attract the maximum number of plaintiffs, I agreed to handle the case on a contingency-fee basis—an arrangement that scarcely pleased my superiors when the preparation of the suit turned out to consume some two hundred unrecompensed hours of my time before it was ready for trial. By then, the action had been joined by sixty-three women seeking back pay totaling well above three hundred thousand dollars—no small *cause célèbre*.

My other activist cases that season propelled me into combat with adversaries no less forbidding. The first pitted me against the Mother Church, which ran the big Sisters of Mercy Hospital in town, which ran the Mercy School of Nursing, which tossed third-year student Antonia Nesbit out on her can after she was overheard to say she favored euthanasia. The church's inflexible position that Our Maker moves in mysterious ways and nobody is incurable until dead required nurse-in-training Nesbit to recant publicly or leave. When she came to me for counsel at that point, I rated her cause as hopeless: The hospital school was a private organization, legally entitled to discharge whom it chose so long as its policies were administered evenhandedly. But when Ms. Nesbit asked the hospital to issue a transcript of credits for her first two years as a nursing student so she might apply for advanced standing at another school, the Sisters of Mercy showed none. I called the matter to the attention of the diocese, which supported the hospital's independence of action. Then I went to the archdiocese, which supported the diocese's independence of action. Then I sued the holy hypocrites. Only Gil Serini in our firm thought me rash. "Doctors shouldn't play God," he told me.

"If God wanted people to suffer," I said, "He wouldn't have let us invent vaccination."

"But you're talking about a mortal sin."

"Why does your church have to tell everybody else how to live—and how to die?"

"Whatever you think of it," he said, "I just don't think you should be suing the Catholic Church."

"It's no beads off your rosary."

"That's beside the point."

"I agree. The point is that the church is just as capable of being cruel as any other human institution—sometimes more so—and should be no more immune from temporal answerability than the ungodly."

"I still don't like it," he said.

"Then send my name in to the Inquisition. It's the time-honored way to deal with troublemakers."

Equally grievous in my view was the rape of Glenda Nossiter, officially adjudged a non-event by the Amity police department. Ms. Nossiter, who was separated from her husband and living with her parents at the time, worked as an assistant cheese at the main branch of the Amity Public Library. One night, while her folks were away on vacation, she was visited at home by the chief security guard of the library, who gained entrance on the pretext of official business. In short order the ruse was revealed, and she asked him to go. He refused, made improper advances, and then raped her, threatening afterward to accuse her of promiscuous behavior on and off the job if she reported the incident. She did, and he did, and the police declined to prosecute. She came to me. I appealed up through the ranks and was finally referred to the familiar precinct of City Prosecutor Schoonmaker. "Why are you in this?" he asked me. "The girl's not even black."

"I've got nothing against whites," I said, "except when they're brutes."

He gave a croaking, bitter laugh and reached for the Nossiter dossier. "Well, let me spare you an ordeal. There are about twelve reasons why this woman's charge is not actionable, in our opinion. To begin with, there was no semen in her, so there goes the *prima facie* case."

"She bathed right away—most women do when they're raped. Wouldn't you?"

"I'll let you know when it happens. But the fact stands. More to the point, there were no bruises on her or on the guy, suggesting the possibility of her complicity in the thing."

"He's a big mean bastard, she didn't want to risk disfigurement, and so she decided resistance was pointless."

"Maybe so, but that weakens her case."

"But you don't expect a robbery victim to resist—or any other kind."

"This is different."

"No, just more awful."

"And that's why we look for some small sign of struggle."

"Otherwise, she enjoyed it, right?"

"Or somehow brought it on herself."

"Like little old people bring muggings on themselves because they're not strong enough any more to fight back?"

"They shouldn't be out late or live in dangerous neighborhoods."

"Or get old."

"Look, how come this guy knew no one else would be home with her that night?"

"She thinks she showed a postcard from her folks to somebody at the library during that day and the guy picked up on it."

"Speculation," he said. "The fact is she isn't usually at home alone, and this time she was. Add to that a history of sexual aggressiveness on her part, and you begin to get the picture."

"For one thing, her sexual habits are irrelevant, and you know it."

"They're not admissible—that's very different."

"She is not a loose woman."

"That's not what her estranged husband told us."

"Sure, because the guy grabbed every skirt over twelve and under seventy he could get his paws on, and she threw him out."

"Her word against his."

I had only one trump card, and there would be no other chance to play it. "There's something else you're leaving out," I said.

"What's that?"

"The rapist worked in the police department for five years."

"So?"

"And he's got a lot of friends here still."

"So?"

"Including his brother, who I gather may be up for promotion to lieutenant pretty soon."

"So?"

"So I'd hate to have to blow the whistle on the department for a cover-up because some people here want to save the guy's ass."

Schoonmaker threw a great sigh that left his broad torso vibrating. "You have this curious little habit, Tabor, of threatening me with reprisals whenever I don't snap to. A less patient man might kick you the hell out of here."

"You're the soul of civility," I said. "Anyway, I never threaten —I just offer a sneak preview of what's coming. I'm trying to be considerate, don't you see, not pugnacious."

"Sure," he said, "and Muhammad Ali is really a Quaker at heart. You do what you want, but I think you'd be making a big mistake to take this thing public."

"Because the truth hurts?"

"Because you'll get a lot of people's backs up around here, including mine—and there may come a day when you'll need us."

255

"I need you now."

"There'll be other days."

"I play them one at a time."

"I'd think it over, Tabor. You've got more at stake than the wounded vanity of one alleged rape victim."

I called him on it. The press played the story big because the parties were on the public payroll. Schoonmaker was obliged to issue a denial of police indifference to the case and turned the matter over to the civilian review board for further consideration. Meanwhile, Nossiter and her accused assailant were suspended from their jobs.

"Your name is mud at city hall," Spanky reported after the thing hit the headlines.

"What's new about that?"

"Before, they used to think you were just annoying—'loud-mouthed ginch,' I think was the official term. Now they think you're a cop-hater—in the same category with snipers."

"They're paranoid."

"You would be, too, if everyone kicked crap on you all day."

"Maybe they richly deserve it."

"Why—for doing a thankless job?"

"For bullying us all in the process. They just can't handle anyone who stands up to them, legitimately or not. It's your classic authoritarian mentality."

"Maybe," he said. "All the more reason not to be surprised if next time you drive over thirty, they pull you in by your pretty little curls, frisk you undaintily, book you for resisting arrest, and toss away the key."

21

Of all the places in town I ever wanted or expected to visit, last on the list was the home of Dan and Sally Kettering. I had little admiration or use for him as a lawyer, and still less of either for her as a human being. It was with muted joy, then, that I received a call from Sally one snowy night in the middle of that cold winter inviting me to what she promised would be "a rather special gathering" at their place a week hence. "It's sort of a quasi-civic thing," she said, nothing daunted by memory of our last fanged encounter.

"Sounds like a reception for the last of the Hapsburgs," I said.

She forced a little laugh. "Not quite that tony, I'm afraid, but close."

I thanked her perfunctorily and tried to beg off on the ground of heavy office duties. She would hear none of it, though, adding that I ought not worry since all the brass from the firm would be on hand. "I don't generally travel in such exalted circles," I said. "What's the occasion?"

"You'll have to show up to find out—and do bring along your decorative architect friend; I think he'd be interested as well."

"I don't exactly have him on a leash."

"I'm sure you can remedy that. It's a buffet—come at seven. We'll expect the both of you."

Jonathan, to my chagrin, was glad to be asked. "Tonight's dinner is tomorrow's commission," he said.

"I thought you had all the business you can handle?"

"Yes and no," he said. "No one's asked me yet to do the Taj Mahal."

So we went, Jon in the name of enterprise, I out of sublimated loathing. It had not occurred to me when Sally said the firm would be heavily represented at the occasion that the men would bring their women. Perhaps I merely blanked that possibility out of my mind. More likely, I thought it inconceivable she would foster a meeting between Lee Nightingale and me. I had not sufficiently estimated her penchant for mischief. Within a moment or two of our arrival, my miscalculation was apparent. Maynard and Sparky and their wives waved me over warmly and in no time were extracting from Jonathan the story of his life. Out of the corner of my eye, I saw Sam Nightingale fetch a drink for his companion—a short, pretty woman with straight, dark hair. Dan introduced us a few moments later while Sam was off somewhere with the Lamports.

"Oh," Lee Nightingale said without a smile, "yes, of course." She glanced quizzically at Dan, then back to me. "I frankly hadn't expected the pleasure of your company."

Her eyes were curiously lusterless but they met mine and held firm to them. "Or I, yours," I said.

"No doubt—Sally's so very thoughtful that way."

"I see that."

Dan, with his characteristic obtuseness, missed the byplay and excused himself for other hostly pleasantries, leaving the two of us to stare each other to death. I think we both must have wanted to turn our backs and say not another word, but something held us there—pride, no doubt, and anger and the raw challenge of the encounter. I stood my place studying her and being studied in return, ready to parry whatever thrust was to come. It was clear, though, that she was no happier about the circumstances than I and not about to do the wounded woman's number or otherwise upbraid me. There was neither contempt nor fear in her small, well-organized face but what I took for a kind of morbid curiosity over what sort of unwholesome young woman had preyed upon Sam's staunch allegiances.

"I saw some of your paintings at the gallery a few months back," I said, grasping for any straw. "They're quite remarkable."

"How nice," she said.

"My friend Jon—that's he over there—bought one for his office."

"One might have hoped he bought it for its virtues." She smiled for the first time.

"Oh, he did. He's an architect, though, and I meant only that he liked it so much that—"

"I understand," she said. "I was teasing us both. Artists are notoriously ungracious about accepting praise."

"I hadn't heard."

"It's true. We hide from everyone ninety-nine percent of the time, and when we come out from the woodwork we want to be loved to pieces. If we are, we think it's due us. If we aren't, we curse the lot of you and slither back where we came from."

"Testy group," I said.

"To put it charitably. But I'm truly glad your friend took my painting. I hadn't shown before, and the first few sales are a great boost. He bought the blue one, if I'm not mistaken."

"I—I'm not sure exactly."

"You mean they all looked rather alike to you?"

"I—well—yes, rather. The graphic arts are not my special strength, I'm afraid."

"You have other gifts, I hear."

It was so quick a thrust, delivered with so little apparent malice, that I nearly failed to notice I'd been hit. "I can't vouch for what you've heard," I said, "not being privy to it."

She laughed and said, "Even away from work, you talk like a lawyer. Sam says you're absolutely marvelous at it."

"Does he?"

"Why, yes. He says you're undoubtedly the brightest young lawyer in the city."

"I'm afraid he's overly generous."

"Who can say? What's clear is that he went to bed with you as much for your intellect as for the usual reason."

The blow this time was frontal and full-bladed and nearly dropped me on the spot. In my lightheadedness I was grateful to her for at least killing with kindness. In defense I managed only the feeblest effort at disarming her. "And—and did that make it any—any less unpleasant for you?" I asked softly.

"More understandable—not less unpleasant," she said, hardly heeding my crumpled resistance. "I don't find you especially ravishing, to be quite honest."

"No—I wouldn't think so."

"Ah," she said brightly, "you think I'm being peevish. Nothing of the sort. I'm thoroughly objective, believe me. Your body's very good, I can see that. He must have liked it."

I was no doubt losing blood faster than I knew. The whole thing seemed a dream now. "I—I don't get you," I said.

She must have seen my dazed look. "Why—because I seem detached about you and Sam?"

"Yes—decidedly."

"You mean I should be tearing my hair and pulling yours?"

"I'd understand that better."

"Because you haven't been married," she said. "and because men must zoom in and our of your life."

"I don't know as they zoom out exactly."

"*Touché*," she said. "But any one of them more or less doesn't materially alter your inventory, I shouldn't think. My situation is not so fluid. I may lack your resources and energy, but one develops a sort of resilience and tenacity when one is in it for the long pull."

"But don't you care?"

"Care that he screwed someone else all last summer and hardly laid a finger on me? Of course I cared! But I know how much to care—and when. You were Sam's mid-life thing, Miss Hill, however demeaning that may sound. If it hadn't been you, it would have been somebody else, maybe even some chippy with a social disease, though I think Sam has more class than that. He did very well picking you, considering his inexperience at philandering. And I think he's done quite well exorcising the whole thing from his head. That's my point—it's something he had to get out of his system—something every man about his age has to prove to himself about still being virile and attractive enough to lay somebody he wants. It just took Sam longer than most. I can't say that I'm grateful to you, exactly, but I think you performed a highly therapeutic function in Sam's life and did it about as untraumatically as these things can be done. That's no small skill." She took a long sip from the scotch and soda she'd been holding since we were introduced and watched her words sink in with the force of a relentlessly twisted knife. Then she said, "I trust my information is right—it's a function you're no longer performing?"

So deftly and thoroughly had she dispatched me that I lacked the will to land even a consolation blow. "No," I said numbly.

"Good," she said. "And by mutual consent, I trust?"

"You'd have to ask Sam that. No doubt you already have."

"Oh, no," she said, "we've never discussed it—any of it."

"I thought he told you?"

"Not a word. It never happened as far as he's concerned."

"Somehow I thought he'd—"

"Spilled the beans? He's very guarded when he wants to be. He's recovering on his own. I guess he didn't want to hurt me unnecessarily. You can understand that, I think."

"Yes, of course."

"Did he tell you he'd told me?"

"No."

"Then why would you think that he had?"

"I—I was misinformed, I guess."

"Something tells me your misinformant is the same sweet stooly that let me in on the secret. She's rather willful about how she administers her venom."

"But why would she lie to me about it?"

"Who knows? To cover her own tracks—to get back at you in my behalf. We're supposedly friends, you know."

"Then why would she want to hurt you by telling you in the first place?"

"For my own good, of course—her very first words. The truth is that it thrills her to pieces to hurt people she envies—and she envies almost everyone. She hates Sam especially because he's twice as smart as her own dumb bunny. She hates me because I don't dance to her tune and have my own life to live. Can you believe that she got us to apply to that tennis club they belong to and then tried to get us blackballed because Sam was allegedly too left-wing? Sam doesn't know about that little intrigue, either, because I was afraid he'd never talk to Dan again and—well, they're partners, and I just didn't see the point of splitting them over something so petty. And as to you—I suppose she disapproves because you're young and bright and sexy and a threat to her somehow. No doubt she supposes you've gone to bed with Dan, too, or want to."

Here I had dishonored this woman by, as the Bible says, lying with her husband, and she would not even dignify me with the back of her hand. She transferred her scorn instead to a third party and made me out a minor miscreant by comparison.

"If she's so unscrupulous," I asked, "why are we all here?"

"I've been wondering myself. I can't answer for others, only guess. Fear, I suppose—you never know how she'll wound you next. That's why generally it's best to stay out of her range. She said tonight was something special, though, so I guess most of us are humoring her in a display of our own weak characters."

"Well, I think it's time somebody put her in her place."

"Oh, the time is past due," she said. "But I suspect it would be far more trouble than she's worth."

"It shouldn't be all that difficult."

"Perhaps you'd be better at it than most of us," she said. "But whatever you do, promise me you won't let Sam in on any of this conversation—will you? Since he's tried to spare me, I'd like to return the favor. If you cared for him at all, I hope you agree."

"I cared for him quite a bit."

"Then I hope we understand each other."

"I understand you love him."

"Good," she said. "Now take me to your young architect so I can compliment him on his taste in art and women—in that order."

Jonathan was as pleased to meet her as she him, and I left the two of them to talk about painting and architecture and the eternal verities while I circulated among the company till the roast beef and lobster thermidor were served. There must have been a hundred people there, some of them social butterflies, some social lions, and all connected somehow with money and power. I recognized a banker or two, some top people from the university, the doyenne of the women's club, one of the mayor's men, the owner of the art gallery where Lee had shown, and their ilk, and none of them knew quite what the gathering was all about. Sally, teasing and touching and generally playing the sly puss, kept everybody's curiosity simmering till after dessert when we were adjourned for coffee to the basement playroom, where folding chairs and a screen and slide projector had been arranged as in a little theater.

The secret was simply Sally's latest scheme to save her Amity Symphony, which had fallen on especially hard times of late and faced imminent extinction unless fresh funding could be found. The new brainstorm was an effort to tie the orchestra's fate to the city's tricentennial celebration, planned for the coming summer, and make it the primary beneficiary of a not altogether implausible piece of boosterism. The plan, she explained, was to create something called the Amity Heritage Preservation Society, the main purpose of which would be to save whatever cultural resources were deemed worth rescuing from the wrecker's ball throughout the city. The initial project would be the designation of a dozen architectural landmarks spanning the history of the city. Municipal funds would be allocated to restore the chosen sites where necessary and to keep them in perpetual good repair; if their current owners ever decided to give them up and no new buyer could be found, the city would buy them at a fair price and maintain them as a museum. A bus tour of the sites, with volunteer guides provided by the new society, would generate annual revenues that would go into a kitty supplemented by municipal grants, private gifts, foundation money, and special fund-raising galas to be held four times a year at appropriate spots. The society would be free to support whatever cultural enterprises it chose; the symphony, as the most immediately needy one, would likely be the first organization to benefit.

"I call the whole idea Project Panache," Sally said, winding up, "because it can work only if carried out with real flair and style—with the sort of sophisticated civic pride, taste, and imagination that I'm sorry to say public officials here and everywhere generally lack. My thought was that the people here tonight might form the nucleus of such an undertaking, which would be our collective gift to the city on the occasion of its three-hundredth birthday. All of our lives would be enriched for it." And then she ran through a slide presentation of thirty or forty buildings that she thought appropriate candidates for canonization as Amity landmarks, among them a rare seventeenth-century "stone-ender" farmhouse out near the bay, a pre-Revolutionary townhouse that had withstood shelling by the British, our firm's office as a superb example of early nineteenth-century Greek Revival, the Congregational church across from the green with its lithe steeple and splendid Federal portico, and of course city hall, that elegant pile of high-Victorian gingerbread rendered massively in red brick and brownstone. "And I haven't even touched upon the university buildings, which are surely a treasure in and of themselves," she said.

Jonathan groaned softly at that and whispered into my ear, "Panache, my ass." I asked him if she knew what she was talking about. "Not much," he said, excoriating half the buildings she had picked and commending the more obvious ones she had omitted. "Beware of official beauty brigades," he warned.

Sally, meanwhile, was taking her bows and asking the assemblage to speak right up with its thoughts on any aspect of her proposal. A few polite souls said that she had indeed given us all food for thought and something to sleep on. Nobody said she had wasted an evening's time for a hundred productive people in a pathetic effort to widen her bitchy sway. Then I stood up.

"On the premise that genuinely constructive criticism is not out of place," I said, "I'll volunteer to play the devil's advocate for just a moment or two—if that's all right?"

"Of course," said Sally, looking at me hard.

"The basic premise—that there are endangered structures and institutions in this city worth preserving—is undeniable and commendable," I launched in. "The question is how best to achieve that end. The method proposed seems an unfortunately elitist one. Any group of self-appointed cultural monitors, however public-spirited and high-minded, is bound sooner or later to collide with the needs and preferences of the citizenry as a whole. How much better it would be, I think, to conceive of this effort not as a private philanthropic gesture undertaken in the interest of a public that does not know what's good for it but as an open, democratically appointed municipal commission, representing a cross-section of the community. Undoubtedly, this is a more unwieldy approach but in the long run, I submit, a more candid and healthy one for educating the general population to its cultural responsibilities and opportunities. Ceding the problem to a local cultural aristocracy is at odds with American tradition—and, in a year when that tradition is to be much in our thoughts, seems an inappropriate and perhaps even tactless step. So I would urge, then, that if there is to be any such program to preserve our local heritage, the city itself is the proper agency to sponsor it, but with as much help and energy as possible, of course, from concerned friends like Mrs. Kettering and those who share her dedication."

Throaty murmurings and burblings clotted the room. I had dared to point out that the empress was naked as a jay. By the time order was restored, Sally had rallied a bit and remarked archly, "Thank you for your thoughtful views, Miss Hill. Is there anyone else who would like to operate on me?"

There was polite laughter, but the moment it subsided, I said, "I hadn't quite finished, actually."

"Oh," said Sally, "I thought you'd done it in rather well. Do go on, Miss Hill."

"I won't be long," I said. "But if I understood the somewhat general thoughts put forward on the funding of this venture, they all finally depend on the city. It takes a considerable piece of change to fix up and maintain and, if necessary, to buy these fine buildings, which after all really are a public trust that ought properly to reside with officials chosen by and answerable to the public. That being the case, I don't quite understand by what right any private individual or group can assign priorities to determine which shall be the first and foremost beneficiaries of this proposed program. Our symphony orchestra is an excellent institution, much deserving of wider support that it now receives. But the best way to rally behind it is not to penalize other equally worthy and needy cultural enterprises for its benefit—I think, offhand, of the city's rundown library system, the understaffed and undersupplied creative arts workshop, the languishing summer-theater-in-the-parks program, and the all but defunct children's museum—but to seek new support for all of them in a broad-based drive for higher cultural consciousness in this city. The proposal as framed, I'm afraid, is an elaborate and somewhat transparent bit of special pleading that would likely lose the symphony friends instead of assuring its survival."

Now there was no sound in the room but the echo of my

voice, harshly reducing Sally Kettering's vapid conceit to rubble. "Are you quite done now, Miss Hill?" she asked grimly.

"I have just one final thought," I said, as if oblivious to the general discomfort my butchery was causing. "I would hazard a guess that the process of picking a limited number of buildings around the city and tying a blue ribbon to each with the designation 'landmark' on it would prompt a great deal more dissension than satisfaction. Emotions run high in these matters, and even if objective standards were applied by a qualified panel of impartial experts, divisive controversy is hard to avoid. Perhaps one example will suffice. Among the photographs shown to us a little while ago of likely contenders for elevation to landmark status was the Congregational church. Unquestionably a noble edifice, and included in the presentation, I am confident, not merely because our hostess attends there and her husband is a vestryman. But such petty objections are precisely the sort that are raised when deep-lying allegiances are tapped. Why, for example, the Congregational church and not the equally eminent All Saints-on-the-Green directly across the street from it? Its soaring vaults and splendid proportions make it every bit as much a masterpiece—one of the first examples of the Gothic Revival style in this country, I believe—and I do not say any of this, I trust you will understand, because I have worshiped there on occasion. Nor would the vibrations stop with a clash between the Congregationalists and the Episcopalians over which has the more eminent structure. Even if one were to settle the issue by selecting both, what then of the Roman Catholics? And of the Greek Orthodox, of whom this city includes growing numbers? And there is the Lutheran church on Grove Street with its wonderful stained-glass windows. Or one fraternal group over another? Or one company over another? Or one fine old Amity family over another?" I swung my head in a slow arc and saw them all watching me, waiting for the *coup de grâce*. I made it short and swift. "No, I am afraid this intriguing but highly mischievous game would hardly be worth the candle." And I sat down.

Sally Kettering, for the first time in anyone's memory, was left speechless. Dan stood up and announced gamely that liqueurs were being served in the living room. But the air was so thick no one wanted to stay long and risk suffocation.

Jon and I were among the first wave to depart. Lee Nightingale caught me at the door. "They're still giving Sally smelling salts," she said, not distraught at the idea.

"She'll recover," I said.

"Not soon." She nodded approval. "Sam was right—you're very gifted. A bit prone to overkill, perhaps, but highly effective. I'll keep you in mind if I ever wind up in court."

"Please do."

"Yes," she said, "and even if I don't."

22

It became increasingly evident during the last part of my second year at the firm that I had developed into as much of a problem as a *wünderkind*. The partners found me less and less available for matters involving their paying commercial clients and more involved than ever with my own people. When called down for this disproportionate devotion to semicharitable business, I argued that my clientele would in time pay its way if I diligently nurtured it. If I were constantly being sidetracked on matters of the partners' dictate, how would I ever attain the breadth of experience and continuity of association so essential to my proper seasoning?

"I'd say you have it exactly backwards," Sparky Grier countered even after word came in that I had won my maternity-leave suit in behalf of the Amity schoolteachers and been awarded a fee of twelve thousand dollars and change for prosecuting the case. "These one-shot crusades are great adventures and no one begrudges you them, but it can be an awfully long cold wait out there before the next trolley comes along."

My trouble, though, was that the trolleys were careening my way so fast that it was all I could do not to get run over.

The carefully negotiated truce package that had been the basis for settling our massive stop-shitting-on-us suit against the city began falling apart as the warmer weather came on and the Gully blacks made it clear they expected the promises made them to be honored. But instead of viewing the moment as a rare reprieve from terminal social decay—instead of mobilizing the whole city behind a genuine self-help effort by one strongly motivated and ably led sector of the underclasses—the municipal squirearchy laid back on its fat duff and let the drowning needy go under a third time. The banks wrote cruelly few loans and mortgages on the properties turned over to the Coop people, and those that were extended carried with them interest rates fully one third higher than the going charges elsewhere in the Amity region. The realtors showed no enthusiasm whatever for bringing would-be buyers to the site of the proposed Gully salvage operation. Mather University attracted only a pair of architecture students to its promised summer counseling service. And the famously compassionate building trades unions, despite their pledge not to harass black participants in the sweat-equity enterprise, picketed half a dozen spots in force. Repeated episodes of scuffling and a batch of bashed heads followed as the union chiefs claimed the whole program was an end-run around organized labor, refused cooperation with it, and called on the community at large to share its disdain. The rougher things got, the fewer blacks who were inclined to risk physical and financial peril by angering white gorillas.

By the middle of the year, only a couple of dozen houses were in the process of being reclaimed from the ghetto flotsam, and the city-backed program to upgrade life in the Gully was being mourned as still-born. Though police and sanitation workers were more in evidence than before, those sorry streets seemed no safer or cleaner. As fast as street lamps got rekindled, others were shattered, and the shadows invited as much mayhem as ever. Even the stepped-up bus service on Seaview Avenue proved a fiasco when passengers failed to materialize in sufficient numbers to warrant the heavier schedule.

Because I had been a prime instigator of the Gully's legal maneuvers and a strong supporter of the settlement that many of its residents now said had been harshly imposed upon them, I could hardly turn my back on the disintegrating situation. Badly discouraged, Duckett and Lenore Washburn asked me out to a Coop planning council called to head off desperate measures by increasingly restless elements in the neighborhood. I hung back, listening mostly and fearing that I had already stuck my honky face too far into their affairs and not earned them anything but a new round of turmoil and dashed hopes. A contrary view was argued by Geronimo Jones, the young black lawyer who had replaced me as the Coop's principal legal counselor. "Hey, we're just gettin' goin' good," he said and insisted the whites would yield nothing of permanent value unless the Gully showed grit and persistence. The answer was not to falter and yield the important beachhead they had established with the creation of the Coop and its good works but to frame hard-hitting retaliatory litigation against the power blocs that had conspired to scuttle the widely ballyhooed settlement with the city. My hearty concurrence with Jones's view earned me the privilege of helping him draft the new round of legal action, though I insisted that my name be kept entirely off of any official papers and my participation go unacknowledged to the press. "When you guys show up downtown, they see black," I said, trying to rationalize gracefully my diminished identity with their cause, "but when I do, they just see red."

We picked fresh targets this time besides the city itself, which was attacked now only in a narrowly drawn suit for failing to provide adequate police protection throughout the Gully. The cops' countenancing of union hooliganism at the picketing sites all spring long was characterized as merely the latest example of their chronic indifference to the safety of area residents. Far more aggressive were the sharp complaints we brought against the local banking and realty interests. Using their own data on the geographic distribution of mortgages and home-repair loans, which federal regulations required them to make public, we charged the six flushest banking institutions in the region with redlining the Gully. The hard numbers could not be readily refuted: The banks funneled five times as many dollars per capita to suburban areas as into the core city, and the average Gully allotment was only half the citywide figure. The higher interest rates on those loans that were placed in the Gully reinforced the prejudicial pattern. Against the ten most actively regressive realtors in town we filed a comparably sweeping action for racial steering, a practice plainly outlawed under Title VIII of the blithely enforced 1968 Fair Housing Act. To document the case, we recruited a team of "testers," both black and white, who visited real-estate offices asking to see houses for sale in the forty- to fifty-thousand-dollar range without stating any preference for ethnically pure neighborhoods. None of the white testers was shown a home in a black neighborhood, none of the blacks was shown one in a white neighborhood, and none of either was taken within a mile of the Gully. A final suit was filed against the Amity Building Trades Council for its failure to rent apartments to qualified blacks who applied in a middle-income complex in Amity Bay owned jointly by the constituent union locals.

Our four-pronged legal assault brought scarlet faces and pained asses to the oligarchs of local Babbittry. It was that loftiest sector of the power structure, of course, whose silverware our law firm polished. Among the banks named in the redlining suit was the First Amity, to which Maynard Lamport had been chief counsel for several decades. Among the realtors cited in the racial steering suit were a number that Dan Kettering dealt with almost daily. The pension fund run by the truculent Building Trades Council had been restructured only recently by Gil Serini, growing in repute as a labor lawyer. And city hall, charged now with gross dereliction in its police department, regularly turned for guidance to Sparky Grier when a problem of high political volatility arose—and then thanked him with half the municipal bond business. Given such a stake in the foundations of the community, the partnership viewed with deepening displeasure any tie between me and bomb-throwing dissidents.

"Did my eyes deceive me," Sparky probed when we met on the second-floor landing on the morning after the new Gully suits were reported in the press, "or was your name missing from all those briefs?"

"They're handling it themselves now," I said.

"You seem to have trained them very well," he said, "because somebody over there has been drafting pretty damned professional complaints."

"They have their own guy—very competent."

"You don't say? I guess too many honkies spoil the corn-pone."

"That—and the fact that I wanted out. I'm extremely sympathetic but I can't devote my life to their problems."

"That makes sense," Sparky said. "I'd try to stick to a rooting interest if I were you." He headed off toward his office.

"Don't worry."

"Oh, incidentally," he said, stopping short, "you know that black fellow Geronimo Jones?"

"Sure—he's the one I was talking about."

"I know," he said. "That's why I asked."

"What about him?"

"He graduated next to last in his class from St. John's Law School."

"Who said?"

"The dean. He's my cousin. I thought I'd check out Jones after I read the excerpts from the briefs in the paper last night. Seems he couldn't write worth a damn as a student."

"That's fascinating," I said. "It just goes to show you how fast these people can grow if they're given half a chance."

Sparky gave me the meanest look I had ever seen on him. "Very funny," he said and disappeared through his doorway.

Lest doubts lingered about my impartiality toward the partners, I filed suit that spring against Mather University in behalf of a dozen women students who claimed the school denied equal opportunitites to females in athletics. The Title IX action charged sexist policies in every aspect of the sports program—too few facilities, inadequately trained and underpaid coaches, and no publicity for the intercollegiate teams. All lithe and pretty, my plaintiffs got their pictures plastered over the papers throughout the East Coast and a goodly number of points west. The university, in the closing stages of a three-year fund drive, was miffed at the rotten publicity and let its favorite off-campus counsel know. Sam called me to his office in white heat. "This is some shitty trick you're pulling," he said.

"I don't consider representing people with legitimate grievances to be any kind of trick," I shot at him.

"You know damned well how close I am to the university."

"I know you do work for them on an *ad hoc* basis and at the moment are not involved with them in anything."

"Who told you that?"

"Your secretary."

"That's not the way to find out. And she had no god-damned business answering you. You want to know what I'm doing, ask me, not anybody else, you got that?"

He was wondrously furious. Not since that first day when he came stalking out of the library had I seen him so ticked off. It was not an unattractive spectacle in so normally even-tempered a man. "I didn't ask you, Sam, because I knew what you'd say, and I didn't want to defy you."

"You knew what I'd say because you knew what you were doing was wrong," he barked.

"I didn't say that—and I don't agree with that."

"Come off it, Tabor! You know you can't play on both sides of the net at the same time."

"I don't play on their side."

"But you have. You were in very deep with the university on the power station acquisition—or was that someone else?"

"Just because I played with them once doesn't mean I got in bed with them forever."

The image stirred him to even higher levels of froth. "Sometimes I don't think you've got a single lawyerly principle," he said, "except to win at any cost. You'll take on any case that'll get your name in print!"

Now the spectacle was no longer pretty, just bitter. There was no point trying to debate the matter with him while he was in such a frenzy. I sat there with hands folded waiting for his splenetic reaction to wane. Finally he grew weary of tongue-lashing me and said quietly, "Tabor, I just don't understand how you could do such a thing if you care anything about me as a human being."

"And if you cared anything about me as a lawyer," I said, "you'd stop carrying on like a kindergartener who just had his blocks taken away. Don't you think I considered your position carefully before I took these women on? But I can't be emotional about my practice and hope to survive. If you'll recall, you're the one who taught me that quite a while back. My job is to weigh all facts coldly and then proceed as I think prudent. In this case the facts say you are not the university counsel. You are a consultant to them when they damned well feel like it. And you have never litigated for them and wouldn't be called on in a case like this. And they do not own your body and soul and have no right to limit what clients you can take on—and even less right to say whom your associates can represent." I wandered over to the window, where his small forest of plants was prospering. "As to my feelings for you as a human being, they haven't changed. When I care for someone, I care —and keep caring. It doesn't matter what else goes on in my life. There's a part of me that's reserved for you—that has been since we met—and I keep watering it because I don't want it to die, even though I should let it."

He looked at me hard. "Christ, you're devious."

"Then you should be glad you're done with me."

He gave a mocking grunt. "I'm not glad—I'm delirious. There's a whole slap-happy gang of us—the Dismissed Lovers of Tabor Hill. We hold annual conventions and put on funny hats."

"You weren't dismissed."

"No? What do you call it?"

"I stopped sleeping with you."

"You stopped everything with me."

"I—that wasn't my doing."

"No? Whose was it?"

I had said more than I wanted. I tried to recoup instantly, but nothing clicked. "It doesn't matter," I said.

"What are you talking about?"

"Nothing."

"Tabor, stop horseshitting. If something happened, you'd better spill it. Otherwise, you still rate pretty low with me, pal."

I narrowed the distance between us to a few yards. "Why do

the people closest to you keep treating you like an infant, Sam?"

"What do you mean?" His coloring rose.

"I mean Sparky told me to lay off or I'd be out on my ass."

"Lay off what?"

"What do you think—LSD?"

"Me? He knew about you and me?"

"Everybody knew, Sam."

His face suddenly drained and his eyes closed with grief. He slowly ran a hand over his forehead a couple of times before emitting a terrible sigh over the indignity of being the last to hear. "Why—didn't—somebody say something?" he finally asked.

"They did—he did—to me."

"Why not to me?"

"Exactly," I said. "Because nobody wants to hurt you. You're Mr. Pussycat in everyone's book around here. And I, plainly, was the temptress in our short-lived collaboration."

"Then why didn't you, at least, say something to me? Was it fair for you to take all the heat—and me to be left in the dark?"

"I didn't see any point, frankly. What were you supposed to do—punch Sparky in the snoot for abusing my honor? Or tell him it was all a mistake?"

"At least I would have understood more about why you backed off so far. But it was never more than an affair to you, was it?"

"Affairs can be pretty intense."

"But when they're over, they're over—aren't they?"

"I don't happen to work that way."

"Then you should have told me about Sparky."

"Maybe," I said.

"There's no maybe about it. You just took it as a quick way out of—of any complications between us."

"Hey," I said, "why are you laying all this on me? If I backed off, so did you—just as far—farther, even. You hardly spoke to me."

"I thought that was the way you wanted it. You made that pretty clear."

"And you didn't argue the point."

"What do you mean?"

"I mean you took no for an answer and let it go at that."

"What was I supposed to do—swing through your office window every Monday at noon and beat my breast with passion? And then let you kick me in the crotch the rest of the afternoon? I'm not a masochist, Tabor."

"If you cared so much, you wouldn't have given up."

"You mean faint heart ne'er won fair lady, for crissakes?"

"As a matter of fact, yes."

"Well, I happen to think self-immolation is a little too steep a price to have paid."

"Nobody's talking about that. You're over-dramatizing the thing, Sam. You've over-reacted to it all along, if you want the truth. You turned it into a much bigger thing than it really was for you, so at the end it was easy to blame it all on me instead of understanding how it looked from my side. I didn't have any choice except to pull the plug before it sucked us both under."

"Speaking of over-dramatizing—"

"Look, you didn't have any risk. You were a summer bachelor —a wheel around here and a pillar of rectitude. So what if you decided to grab a little ass for laughs—who was going to say anything? It wasn't exactly an even match, Sam."

"You weren't thinking about me at all, as a matter of fact, were you?"

"Because you didn't really want me or need me, Sam—not for long."

"How the hell do you know what I wanted?"

"Maybe I didn't—but you didn't, either. Carrying on with a new woman threw everything out of perspective for you. I became something in your mind I never was in fact. Besides which, you're a married man and not the sort who can just walk away from the fact. And having met Lee, I can't think why you'd want to. She's quite attractive, if you ask me. I can't believe deep down you wanted or needed somebody else."

"People believe what's convenient."

"She cares for you a great deal, Sam."

"Basically, you don't know anything about it."

"I've talked with her."

"It must have been quite an intimate conversation."

"My intuition is pretty good. She digs you."

"Yes—in her way."

"And that's not enough?"

"I—don't really want to go into it."

"Are you telling me she's a cold person?"

"I'm not telling—you're wheedling."

"Then tell me."

"It's none of your business."

"Tell me, Sam."

"There's no point."

"I'm asking—that's the point."

"Why—so you can instruct me further in the art of living?"

"Because I care."

"Oh," he said, "swell."

"Isn't that enough?"

He shut his eyes and pinched the bridge of his nose and sat there thinking for a long minute. "She's convinced herself I'm a failure," he said, "and she's got me half-believing it."

"You? I don't get it. You're a respected lawyer—with a lucrative practice."

"Those are relative terms. I'm a medium-size frog in a small pond. The money is all right, but she comes from money. I'm a piker by her family's standards."

"What does she want from you?"

"To go bigtime—New York or Washington or Boston—where everything is happening. She claims she's stifled by this town. She finds the university people smug and insular—and the rest philistines."

"Is that what you think?"

"I'm happy here."

"And she hates it."

"And resents me for locking her in the dungeon."

"Then why doesn't she split?"

"Because I'm not what's holding her back. It would be the same anywhere she—or we—went. The place doesn't have anything to do with it. It's what's inside her."

"And what's that?"

"Not enough. At least that's what she thinks. And it's easier not to face up to it in places where there are a lot of distractions."

"But she seems so confident—so—pulled-together."

"Sure. She can manage very well when she wants to."

"You mean it's a front?"

"It's an effort. Most of the time she hides out."

"From what?"

"From everything—herself, most of all."

"And you're the scapegoat for her own sense of inadequacy?"

"That's not far off."

"But she's got talent, doesn't she?"

"Some. But you were right: She only plays at it—because I think she's afraid to find out for real."

"And if she did find out and the answer was no—would that be your fault, too?"

"That's a distinct possibility."

"Sam, she sounds like a disturbed person."

"No, I'd say bitter."

"But she's got so much—"

"Except knowing what to do with her life."

"Why doesn't she just enjoy it?"

"I've suggested that."

"And?"

"She thinks it's a put-down. Most people try to reconcile themselves to reality. She just resents the hell out of it."

"Where does that leave the two of you—in an armed truce?"

He looked out the window. It was plainly a question he had been asking himself for some time. "I wouldn't call it that exactly. There's a real measure of affection—you're right about that, too."

"You never told her about us, did you?"

"No," he said, turning back to me. "Why should I have?"

"To be fair to her."

"I didn't see any point in hurting her. She would have taken it as an act of spite."

"But if she's hurting you?"

"She doesn't do it purposely."

"Does that make a difference?"

"I think it does. I want to help her, not punish her."

"But you don't help her by feeding into her—her problems. You both have to face up to it. Maybe you haven't worked on it hard enough together. Maybe you've both taken the easy way out."

"Tabor—"

"What?"

He folded his hands together with deliberation. "Stop horsing around with my life. Either you're a part of it or you're not. You can't just pop in when it suits you and tell me how to live and then buzz off on your superior way. That stinks." He turned to the papers on his desk and began to sift through them.

"Okay," I said. "Okay."

23

I marked time emotionally that spring. Weekdays I passed more and more of my spare evenings in the usually spirited company of Jessica Lennox, in whom I had come to confide as with no other person in my adult years. Weekends, I remained in companionship with Jonathan Kenyon, my moody stud, who by turns would possess me utterly and then fade off into his private nirvana, forgetting for hours that any other creature dwelled on his planet. By the ides of May, though, both arrangements had nearly run their course.

With Jessie, I failed to apply the brakes in time. I blame myself largely. Bit by bit, as her own life grew more ragged and trying, she extended her incursion on my psychic terrain, and I could not take being leaned on that way. Her school principal was not pleased by her work. She was having trouble controlling her classes and motivating them. By the end of the school day, she was all keyed up half the time from the extra effort she now put into the job and exhausted the rest of the time. Either way served as an excuse to have a drink, then two, then tank up. She was putting away more than she let on to me, and when I told her to lay off, she denied it. But in that stretch, she turned to me more than ever. She suddenly could not make a decision about how to dress, what to eat, where to go, without calling. Her sex life, for the moment, seemed to have evaporated. And she had no energy for writing. Which left her still more dependent on me and my declining good nature. It was not that I didn't want to help, but I could not live my own life and hers, too. And I will not humor people who have nothing better to do than feel sorry for themselves.

With Jon, the trouble was I had taken to following the path of least resistance, admiring his virtues to excess, discounting his limitations, forgiving his self-absorption—and failing to acknowledge that every path was supposed to lead somewhere and ours just seemed to spiral back upon itself. The more I knew him, the less I found. The trick was to extricate myself from both arrangements as painlessly as possible for all concerned. Unplanned, the perfect dual solution presented itself.

To celebrate the full flowering of spring, Jon had bought a motorcycle—a Honda 250 or 350 or something-50—and for me it was hate at first sight. He spent half the weekend toying with the oily stink bomb, rum-rum-rumming over back roads and country lanes to the general consternation of the residents and other forms of livestock, and returning in a cloud of smelly smoke from which he emerged like a goggled avatar inviting tribute from worshipful multitudes. At which point the aphrodisiac effect of the machine, having clanged his scrotum to the very brink of auto ejaculation, took command and he bore me off caveman-style for a besooted balling.

"And when do you chain-whip me?" I asked when we were done.

He laughed and said the chain came with the black leather jacket and he wasn't sure he was going that heavy into it. "But you ought to come out with me," he said. "It's an incredible sensation."

"I just had an incredible sensation—and it didn't stink out the joint or shatter anyone's eardrums."

"Shit," he said, "you're jealous."

"Of a motorcycle?"

"Yeah—because it's more fun than you are a lot of the time."

"Thanks," I said. "The same to you."

"See," he said, "you always do your defensive number the minute you get the least little dig. From you all I get are digs."

"How would you know—you're not here even when you're here most of the time."

"I'm here when there's a reason to be."

"Meaning what—that I'm only here to entertain you?"

"Meaning you don't share a whole lot of yourself."

"Because you don't."

"I share what I know how to share. But you think sharing is some sort of weakness—that everything really valuable in life is a solitary experience."

"Like fucking?"

"Even that," he said. "You're technically flawless—a vertible ballerina of the bedsprings—but you do it with an abstract air, as if you could be anywhere."

"Maybe I am—you usually are."

"Not then—not ever when I think I matter to you."

"You matter. I wouldn't be here if you didn't."

"I think you just like screwing with me."

"I can screw the milkman."

"Not like with me."

"How do you know?"

"You mean he's good?"

"If you like the cream all at the top."

"Gross," he said. "How come you're so gross?"

"Because you love it?"

"Tabor, come out on the Honda with me—it's fantastic!"

"I hate the goddamned Honda!"

"Just try it once."

"It'll make my ass spread."

"No, it shrinks asses—that's what it's for."

"You sure?"

"I'm sure."

"All right," I said, "once."

It would have been unballsy of course for me to insist on

anything as prophylactic as a helmet, so we went out half an hour later unprotected except for his goggles. The vibration was worse at first than I had expected and I latched on fiercely to that beautiful bulgeless midriff of his as we jounced over ragged roads, real ovary-scramblers, then steadied on to smoother local thoroughfares, picked up speed on the state highways, and took off into the wind on the interstate. Jon gunned it over sixty—how much over, I didn't ask—and it felt as if we were flying, were being clawed at by the rushing air, were being whipped back and off and away, were within one wrenching gust of being obliterated, and I screamed into Jon's ear, and he thought it was for joy like in sex and drove us faster still until I was practically gasping for relief and closed my eyes and prayed for it to end before our cells exploded all over the asphalt.

"Tell me you don't love it," he said when we finally took a break.

"I don't love it."

"Maybe I was going too fast."

"Oh, no—I usually turn green this time of day."

"I'll slow it down."

"Couldn't we just walk it home?"

"I get it—you don't want to give me the satisfaction of admitting what a thrill it is."

"God, what insight. Who ever said you were insensitive?"

"You hate it, huh?"

"I hate it. It's loud, smelly, dangerous, and unnatural. If I want a thrill, I can get it taking a walk in the woods—I don't need a machine to make one."

I would not ride on the noxious son of a bitch after that. Neither of us ever remarked on it, but the thing served as the final wedge in a relationship that was about to shear in two from its own dead weight. Some other object or incident would have done as well, for the time we spent together not in bed or pursuing our separate pleasures had become a drain on both of us, though neither was ready to say so straight out. It was a rupture that could never be repaired, and so we approached it, out of mutual appreciation for good times had, somewhat gingerly. But there comes a moment when past gladness can no longer justify present disaffection. I suggested we invite Jessica

Lennox and any friend she chose to join us for the following weekend, and he grabbed at the idea. Before, he would have resented house company as a confession of our incompatability; now, any intrusion would freshen the air.

"Hey, great," Jessie said when I asked her, "only there's no Mr. Marvelous just now. I—I've been distracted."

"Then come alone," I said.

"Three's a crowd."

"Not at all. Jon and I aren't exactly novices."

"I don't know. It seems odd somehow."

"Come on—it'll be fun."

"For who?"

"All of us."

"One of us won't get off."

"Who knows?"

"Oh, cut it, Tabor."

"Cut it yourself. I'm telling you something."

"What?"

"I want you there. Think of it as if I want to share the other side of me with you. Now that I think of it, he's well hung enough to take us on together—with something to spare."

"Sure," she said, "and I'm stacked enough for four busy hands."

"That's a fact."

"Hey," she said, "tell me you're kidding."

"I don't know. A picture is forming."

"Better leave me out. Kinky's not my thing."

"Kinky, hell. Anyway, I was only thinking out loud."

"I think you're off him," she said, "and you're pimping."

"Oh, thanks."

"I'm right, huh?"

"Not really."

"But partly?"

"Well—maybe. Look, just let him ride you on his Honda and everything'll be cool."

"He's got a bike?"

"Brand-new—and loves it to pieces. He drives with one hand and plays with himself with the other."

She laughed and said she was hot for bikes and if it meant all that much to me, she would come.

I picked her up right from work the following Friday. I could tell she had already had a belt or two of something, the way she launched in gabbing the second she got in the car and then sat as far from me as possible so I couldn't get a whiff of her. We stopped for some Beck's dark beer or maybe it was Beck's light, whichever it was Jon had called me about and said went beautifully with the blazing chili he was whipping together, but they had none at the two places on the way so I settled for four six-packs of Piel's, the cheapest stuff they carried. "It all tastes like horse piss, anyway," Jessie said and broke open a pack and helped herself to a can. And then another. I told her to take it easy, and she said that was exactly what she was doing but naturally I wouldn't know that, never having seen her tank up on Friday nights, the one time all week she permitted herself the luxury. The escape, I said, and she said to get off her back or let her out of the car right there. So I shut up and she was ready to start on a third can by the time we pulled up beside Jon's Victorian exquisitery.

"Piel's!" he groaned when I tossed him the groceries. "God, I'd rather have Ovaltine than this shit."

"Things are tough all over," I said. "That's Jessie—she says it all tastes like horse piss, which is why she's halfway through a pack."

"Hey, Jessie," he said.

"Hey, Jon," she said. "Your friend here's down on beer drinkers."

"She's got other saving perversions."

"I hadn't heard."

"Oh, yeah. No beer but plenty of pretzels. She can wolf a dozen of them in a row."

"Right," I said, "I'm hung up on big, salty sticks. Now if nobody minds, I'm going to shower and change."

"See?" he said to Jess. "Perverse."

By the time I rejoined them, Jessie had slipped into a leftover Holyoke sweatshirt that draped artfully between and around her cantilevered boobs and a pair of jeans that sculpted her ass and snatch no less fetchingly. Jon, barefoot and furry, was spread-eagled on the sofa in an open-necked T-shirt and tattered shorts that bulged uncoyly just left of center below the fly. Was anyone but me wearing a shred of underwear? For a moment I felt as if I were intruding on a mating dance the two of them were about to perform to the sweet Simon and Garfunkel sound swimming out of the stereo. Then I helped myself to some sangria from the small pitcher Jon always fixed for me on arrival, and everything improved.

Jon had us teary-eyed in no time with his run-through of a would-be client's plans for converting a large barn into his dream house. The guy wanted a library in his hayloft, a sauna in his milking stalls, a solar heat plant in his silo, "and red aluminum siding on the whole goddamn thing," he said, buckling an empty beer can with his thumb and sailing it toward the trash basket. "I said why not do the siding in tractor green instead, and he said that sounded great and very creative but he'd have to think it over. I told him to stow it." Jessie threw in her own asshole-of-the-week story about the parent of one of her students who complained bitterly because Booth Tarkington was no longer assigned reading. "She said we've got to get back of those good old Indiana values, and then I told her his writing was full of racist language, and she said that was just a reflection of the times and anyway that was better than all the smut the kids read now. I told her to stow it." I wondered aloud how Booth Tarkington and Idi Amin would have hit it off, which soon got us into a discussion of totalitarian types in general and the discovery, which seemed all the more astounding after we had shared a joint and begun a second, that none of us knew the name of a single reigning dictator in all of Latin America. "They're all the same person," Jessie said.

"No, they're different people but they all have the same name," Jon said.

"No," I said, "they're different people with different names but they keep changing countries every month."

I went to make the salad while I could still stand and Jessie joined me when Jon headed upstairs to wash and change. "He's some hunk," she said, "and about twice as smart as you let on."

I agreed. And while she was off peeing, Jon returned and said, "She's some piece—and about twice as funny as you said." I agreed with that, too.

We ate on the terrace and I think the two of them were beginning to play footsie, but I was well into my second pitcher of booze by then and missing a lot of the action. The talk turned more earnest after the subject of Jessie's marriage came up. Jon asked her if she thought anyone who was passionately committed to his or her work ought to marry and impose the burden of that commitment on a relationship that would inevitably prove secondary. Jessie said she supposed that depended on the couple and wondered why the two relationships had to be mutually exclusive. "I don't know," he said. "Ask Tabor."

"Isn't the real question whether two people passionately committed to their work can also be committed to each other?" I said.

"Yeah," Jon said.

"Then ask it," I said.

"You heard," he said to Jess. "Speak the wisdom of the ages."

"I don't think you can generalize," she said.

"That's crap," he said.

"Don't tell me it's crap, buster," she said. "I'm smart as hell."

"Then how come you married such a horse's ass?"

"I didn't know he was a horse's ass when I married him. He kept that part hidden."

"You're supposed to look first."

"I looked, I looked."

"Not hard enough."

"I was afraid what I'd find. Besides, I liked him. And I wanted to get away from home. And I didn't think I could make it on my own."

"Why not—you've got looks, brains, wit?"

"No character," she said. "A woman's got to be tough as shit to make it by herself. And why bother—if she can get a free ride? At least that's what I thought. Now I know there aren't any free rides." She looked over at me. "That's what Tabor

285

figured out a while back. She also isn't riveted with guilt about being selfish."

"Hey, thanks a bunch."

"It's the secret to everything," she said. "If you aren't selfish enough, you can't ever become much of anything. And if you're too selfish, you can't ever be really happy—you become your own whole world and that's craziness."

"See?" Jon said to me, nodding.

"See what?"

"What she said."

"About what?"

"You were right here—didn't you hear?"

"I heard."

"That's why you're so miserable—you're too selfish."

"*I'm* too selfish? Speaking of the snowball calling the albino white."

Jessie laughed uncomfortably. "Where'd you pick that up?"

"That's what we say in the Gully when someone mean starts hitting on us."

"Who's mean?" said Jon. "I'm trying to save your miserable life."

"Will you please stop calling me miserable? You're the only miserable bastard around here."

"I'm not criticizing," he said, "I'm empathizing. I'm sorry that you're so unhappy. And I think you ought to hear what Jessie is telling you—it's a genuine epiphany."

"I am not unhappy—who said I was unhappy? I'm happy as a clam. And Jessie doesn't make epiphanies in public, it so happens."

"You're not happy," he said. "I know when you're happy, and take it from me—you're not. You're all tied up inside yourself. You hardly know anybody else is alive except when you're getting good and humped."

"You cocksucker!" I yelled. "You're transferring all your own agony to me."

"Holy Christ!" Jessie broke in. "And you guys aren't even married."

I had to laugh and Jon laughed and we both told her we

were only fooling and that psychodramas were our little George and Martha thing but she knew better and turned the talk to something neutral and Jon broke open a new six-pack of horse piss and gave us each a can. I got almost all the way through mine without saying a word while they were agreeing the trouble with America was that there was nothing really excellent happening in it anywhere, at which point I keeled and didn't wake up till after noon the next day.

"Good morrow, Merry Sunshine," Jon piped as I appeared, all swollen and muzzy, on the terrace where he was doing some sketching by himself. "Want to go for a wake-up bike ride?"

"Up yours," I said. "Go take Jessie for a ride."

"I already did—last night, after you crumped. It's terrific with nobody on the roads."

"What else did you guys do without me?"

"Nothing we wouldn't do with you."

"I'm glad to hear that. You practically had your face in her jugs last time I looked."

"I'd say it was more her jugs in my face."

"Don't tell me you minded?"

"Just that you were watching."

I found Jessie stretched beneath a stand of birch. By then we each knew what the other was up to and did not disapprove. Arms linked, we came back to the house and spent the rest of the afternoon driving Jon's hormones wild. Our talk turned explicitly and then clinically sexual and it never stopped. Its high point was a mock seminar devoted to considering whether a meaningful correlation existed between the dimensions of the genitals, the frequency with which they were utilized, and the intensity of the sensations achieved.

"Are you going so far as to propose," Jessie asked as we wound up our number, "that the larger the uterus, the greater the ganglia, the longer and more intense the climax? Or the bigger the testicle, the stronger and more lavish the ejaculation?"

"Mmmm," I said, "other things being equal."

"Are there any studies?"

"Beats me."

287

"It sounds totalitarian."

"It sounds logical."

"It sounds simplistic."

"Ah, but I'm really thinking of more than mere physical prowess. The very sighting of large organs stimulates the libido more than smaller ones, making it possible if not probable the act will be performed with greater potency and inspire a bigger bang for the fuckee."

"I really wonder."

"Let me put it this way. Aren't you more likely to be turned on by the sight of a mammoth pecker than a wee nubbin?"

"Extreme cases prove little."

"Let me refine the point then. Whose chest would be more likely to stir a man at the root of his virility—your splendid endowment or my merely adequate set?"

"Well," Jesse said, "perhaps you have a point."

Jon did his best to remain oblivious to all this verbal masturbation, but after a while he fell in with the talk, the effect of which was evidenced by the rod he sprang and could not conceal. The sight of it drove Jessie to grosser and more vivid language, which in turn prompted the same in the two of us. It would have been hard to say who took off what in which order, it happened so mutually and inexorably and unreservedly. It was clear no bed in the house would hold us all, so with hoots and grabs at one another's gorged nakedness we dragged the upstairs mattresses down to the living room, made a giant playing field out of them, and somersaulted onto it with molten desire. The arrangement of all those thrashing limbs and so much turgid flesh was not gymnastically accomplished. Rollicking proposals and urgent directions were required to master the geometry of the human triangle. The thing was for each of us to be done while doing, a multilateral accord admirable in the abstract but demanding unaccustomed suppleness and infinite good will in the execution. Every orifice was occupied, and all hands were stroking any pliant part or saturated bush in reach. I feasting on him feasting on her feasting on me and then reversed and obversed and subversed in richly lubricated revolutions till he was in me and I on her and she was tearing at his seed and I felt him responding and responding and all at once I yanked away and changed us around and then his immensity that I knew sank deep down her glistening channel and he discharged and she shouted her throat raw and I saw them bursting and throbbing and felt them and they were my gift to each other and I was glad.

Only Jessica went out to Jon's place after that. I saw her in town from time to time and we spoke on the phone but were never again as close as we had been. As if to show he bore no hard feelings, Jon asked me to represent his firm. "Why hire someone who's so mean, selfish, and unhappy?" I asked him.

"You left out smart," he said.

"You're right—and smart?"

"Who wants a kind, generous, happy jerk for a lawyer?"

24

I always knew I would have to marry the law firm or leave it. What I had not anticipated was that the choice would have to be confronted at such an early date.

All five of the partners were on hand in dark-suited array when I was summoned without warning to the first-floor conference room one overcast morning hardly two years after I had first set foot in that noble house. Maynard Lamport, in his gaunt majesty, presided at the far end of the table. To his right sat that dogged pieface, Dan Kettering, and the cagey broker, Sparky Grier; to his left, my wry innocent, Sam Nightingale, and our ethnic diamond-in-the-rough, Gil Serini. I was directed to the lonely seat at the end opposite the senior partner. Their faces said at once that grave business was afoot. Had they been a jury, I would have bet a dollar to a penny that they had just voted me the guillotine.

But why? Hadn't I worked hard and well? If I had not serviced their commercial clients to quite the extent promised, what work I rendered was of a high and useful order. And my billings overall more than paid my keep. Still, it was no secret that my justice-for-all activities brought few patriotic thrills to the firm's principal customers. However principled my efforts, they were open to interpretation as ever more visible defiance of my superiors. Was some willful pathology afflicting me? Was a profound anxiety lurking within and driving me toward inevitable martyrdom so I would not be obliged to assume the full burdens of success? For the moment, I did not entirely trust my own disclaimers. From the firm's point of view, I clearly had to be curbed or disappeared.

The four younger partners eyed me sideways or not at all; only Maynard Lamport looked straight at me. He let me stew there a moment and leaned over to ask something of Dan, who brayed briefly before muttering an inaudible reply. Then the senior member of the firm tinked the water glass in front of him with a pencil, called us to order, and went for his prey.

"We are gathered *en banque* this morning to discuss the unusual dilemma presented to us by the activities of our associate Miss Hill," he began in monotone. "Without the usual jiggery-pokery, let me attempt to state the matter. In no more than twenty-five months of service with this firm, Miss Hill has demonstrated to us, individually and collectively, as well as to the local legal community at large, a notable precocity as a lawyer. She has proven herself not merely tirelessly dutiful in the pursuit of her work but quite passionate about her commitment to any assignment she has undertaken. She has displayed a marked gift for legal analysis, going to the heart of an issue and leaving subsidiary matters where they belong. She is not only clever and manipulative—qualities that are not in and of themselves unalloyed virtues—but she is also highly creative and sometimes even downright imaginative in developing strategies to meet problems that would confound less enterprising minds. She writes clearly and speaks forcefully—indeed I have not met a young practitioner so accomplished in both these basic skills for many a moon. In short, she is a rare combination of intellect, energy, and purpose, and under normal circumstances we should consider ourselves fortunate to have acquired all these resources in a single package."

I had been anointed with oil and brightly garlanded so my head would gleam the more brightly when severed. I held my breath.

"And how has Miss Hill applied these myriad talents," Lamport went on, pitching his words half an octave higher now. "Unquestionably, she has rendered valuable service to many of the firm's more substantial clients when called upon for assistance by the partners. Indeed, that assistance has at times been so sustained, resourceful, and successful that the clients may have gone off convinced that our profession is hardly more than child's play if so raw a recruit can master it nearly overnight." His look darted from face to face, pausing at mine no longer than the others, as if I were merely a witness at my own execution. "But alas," he said, with pained resignation, "we must turn over this rare coin if we are to assay its true value. Or to shift the metaphor a bit, let us consider to what purpose the bulk of this valuable commodity has been applied. Miss Hill, since coming here, has participated in—if not in fact been the architect of—a number of unusually aggressive legal actions aimed at winning a higher level of social justice as she and her often genuinely aggrieved clients have conceived that end. Now this is a worthy and honorable undertaking, and I do not gainsay it. None of us does. The question is whether such activity has occupied an undue proportion of Miss Hill's time in violation of the original terms of her employment with us. Even more to the point: Have her activities, under this roof and our auspices, redounded to the enhancement or detriment of the firm's position in this community?"

He paused for a sip of water. I could see the first signs of the strain this unwelcome task was causing him.

"As to the question of her time, that is an open-and-shut case," he said, proceeding a little more slowly now. "Her weekly logs, when they finally materialize, reveal that the preponderance of Miss Hill's billable time is going to service clients she has brought to the firm, few of whom are able to pay the going rate. But her occasional success in garnering a quite

291

large fee—as in the action this spring against the school board —as well as her willingness to work long hours makes it impossible to claim she is a financial drag on the firm. And in those instances where she has put herself at the disposal of our well-heeled clientele, the result has often been highly rewarding to the firm as well as beneficial to the client. So I think we can safely say we would not have assembled this morning if the first of those two points was the only one troubling us. At most, we would be beseeching Miss Hill to allot a more generous portion of her time to commercial work as she had promised to do in coming to us."

He leaned forward now and fixed his look steadily on me. "On the second point, however, there can be no such charitable a judgment. By my own observation and the accumulated intelligence reports reaching other members of the firm, Miss Hill's celebrated actions *pro bono publico* have earned not only herself but, by her association here, the rest of us as well the ill regard if not the outright enmity of powerful individuals and institutions in this community. To be precise, she has become the *bête noire* of the ranking officials of this municipality by virtue of the thundering indictments she has leveled at them in behalf of a veritable handful of indigent clients. She has, by several actions, deeply divided and antagonized the board of education. She has cast doubt upon the integrity of the leading banks and real-estate firms in the area and charged them with bigotry. She has made a lasting foe of the largest manufacturing company in town by casting it as callously antifeminist. She had attacked the Catholic Church for doctrinal intolerance. She has accused the police of cronyism and abdication of duty. And just lately she has challenged the most venerable and celebrated of our institutions—Mather University." He turned to the partners. "Now that, I submit to you, is quite an astonishing piece of work to have done in such short order."

I could see the sunlight glinting off the edge of the terrible blade poised above me. There was everything to say in rebuttal, and nothing. The evidence was conclusive. I had done all those things—how justifiably was beyond their immediate concern— and crossed a lot of people who did not enjoy the experience. It was too late for apologies, and I would not in any event have offered any.

"Now I do not propose," Maynard said, moving in for the kill, "that we debate the degree to which these various activities of Miss Hill's have jeopardized the reputation and future stability of the firm. Quite naturally, I prefer to believe we are strong enough to weather such adverse effects—and far worse ones if need be. The issue at hand is what to do with the skillful and charming perpetrator of these acts. In a less winning personality, such a performance would undoubtedly be rewarded with an invitation to resign. But we have far more complex considerations to sort out in this case. Miss Hill's extraordinary qualities make the prospect of her loss lamentable even when weighted against the most disagreeable consequences of her work. There is the added important factor that none of us is getting any younger and there is not an abundance of legal talent out there waiting to be plucked off the branches. How, then, might we resolve this dilemma?"

He pushed back his chair with a sharp, startling movement and hauled himself slowly to his feet. His unbuttoned jacket revealed the lower portion of his suspenders. I wondered if there were ten other men in the state who persisted in the style. He folded his arms over his chest, surveyed the rest of us for another moment, and then marched to his conclusion. "If I felt her total performance to date reflected a merely perverse personality," he said gently, "or that her preoccupation with clients of her choice was the mark of an incorrigible solipsist, I would urge—regretfully—Miss Hill's dismissal forthwith. But that is not what I feel about this outstanding young woman— that is not what I feel at all. What I feel is that she has not demonstrated an abiding loyalty to the interests and reputation of this firm because she remains deeply conflicted within herself about how she should best use her God-given gifts. Now it is not unusual for young people of high accomplishment to struggle with themselves in determining who they really are and what they want to do with their lives. Miss Hill's acting out of this difficult time of self-testing has been very nearly a public event, and I, for one, am not unsympathetic. But the moment has arrived for her to resolve these conflicts lest they consume her—and for us, to the extent we admire and care for her, to help her reach that resolution."

He moved out from behind the long oak table and began tacking by starts and stops toward my end of the room. "Tabor," he said, addressing me directly for the first time, "the decision you will have to make after we are done here is not so much one of alternative career routes but of a far more basic sort—and no one, I'm afraid, can make it for you, certainly not your working colleagues. But we have the undeniable physical advantage of being able to view you from a distance you cannot manage yourself. Much of what we see is exceedingly pleasing, and I have itemized a number of those goodly features. Yet for all your fine lawyerly traits of mental adroitness and articulation, we are moved no less by what seems an intolerance within you for the routine—by an impatience to put aside the boilerplate part of the business in favor of the more thrilling combat against the latest rascal to move across your horizon. Now that may be a suitable state of mind for a world heavyweight champion but it is not in character for a seriously dedicated attorney at law. To frown at the careful and orderly disposition of regular business is to persist in a career that ranks instant gratification above any other reward—a priority that is the hallmark, I am sorry to say, of a basically infantile and self-indulgent personality. True professionalism in the law is no such roaring adventure. It calls for commitment to a less spectacular style of service—for traversing long, steaming valleys as well as rarefied peaks—for a seasoned and at least moderately philosophical overview of society with all its imperfections. In return it provides a less scintillating but almost certainly far more enduring sense of satisfaction than the—forgive me, please—than the practice of lurching from one rodeo to the next that you appear to have adopted."

He was within a few feet of me now as he reached the pinnacle of his oration. "The one way to harvest a talent as rich as yours, Tabor," he said, his eyes only for me now, "is not to go charging off in a frenzy after the latest foul varmint in your bestiary. The way is to abide—the way is to persist—the way is to devote as much of yourself to the ordinary as to the phenomenal, and probably more. If no man is an island, dear Miss Hill, no woman is a garden unto herself. Do not cultivate your own flowering as if it were a solitary bloom. Lone blossoms are too readily obscured in the rolling countryside. And they do not last. Consider instead the virtues of contributing that loveliness to a wider field and thereby brightening the entire prospect."

He turned back partway toward the rest of them so we could all see about equal portions of that angular stalk. "I am therefore recommending to this meeting," he said with a closing Ciceronian flourish, "that, with the sole proviso she accept no additional cases in behalf of socially aggrieved plaintiffs, singly or in groups, but remain free on occasion to defend a destitute individual worthy of her services, Miss Tabor Hill be elevated to the position of full partner in this firm."

Christ.

They all applauded, and I was crying real tears and laughing at myself for them, and they laughed too but fondly, and I wanted to hug them but that was not what professionals did. I gave a mighty sniff instead and bobbed my head in thanks to the whole pack and grinned like an addled jack-o'-lantern. As through a mist, I heard Maynard saying how sharply at variance with the practice it was to elevate a young associate to partnership after so brief a trial but that under extraordinary circumstances such a step was not without precedent. But I must not accept the designation, he said, unless I was fully prepared to meet the obligation it would entail.

Each of the other men then offered a few sentences of commendation and welcome. In a few very well-chosen words, most of them monosyllabic, I thanked them for everything that had been said and told them that while they had indeed paid me a high honor, they had in so doing—if they would not mistake my meaning—honored themselves the more. "It would have been so easy to send me home," I said. I asked to have until the end of the week to think through all the ramifications of their offer, and everyone agreed that would be wise. My only immediate source of unease, I said, was the possible upset my promotion might generate throughout the office. Sandy Weiss had been presumed next in line for partner, and my officemate Steve Balakian certainly had seniority on me, I noted.

"That is not how we proceed here," said Maynard. "The firm is a meritocracy. We have no heirs apparent—only prospects." He assured me the matter I raised had been talked over and that if I elected to stay with the firm, the remaining associates would be advised that my new eminence in no way prejudiced their own chances. The partners had determined in any event to wait another year before deciding on Weiss, and Steve's incubation period still had a ways to run. Maynard commended me on my thoughtfulness and prepared to close the meeting.

"There's one other thing in this area," I said. "Well, two actually, if I may?"

"By all means," said Maynard, all gallantry.

"If I accept your generous offer, I wonder if Mrs. Pinkham's salary might be adjusted moderately?"

"Mrs. Pinkham? Isn't she still off in trust and estates. What has she to do with you?"

"Nothing directly."

"Then I don't quite—"

"It's a feeling I have."

"You're being too subtle for me."

"Maynard," Sparky put in, "Estelle and Tabor are both women."

"I'm on to that."

"Tabor no doubt wants to avoid earning Estelle's ill will," Sparky explained.

"Yet more of her ill will," I corrected him.

"You and she are on cool terms?" Maynard asked.

"Polar, practically."

"Odd—I should have thought just the opposite."

"I'm afraid she thinks I've set out to corner the ladies' concession around here. This news is not likely to disabuse her on that score."

"Oh," Maynard said, "I see your thinking now. Well, I'm not sure one can—or should—buy off resentment quite so openly. No one ever said the world rewards us all equally." He tugged his flinty chin a moment. "Still, I suppose a little solicitude might be politic." They agreed to take the matter under advisement. "Now was there something more?" Maynard asked, a hint of impatience creeping in.

"Just one thing, if I'm not pushing my luck," I said. "Could my office possibly be on a different floor from Mr. Potter's? It's a matter of our mutual well-being. My cigar smoke is terrible for his emphysema. And there's congenital anemia in our family that makes us a little edgy in the presence of vampires."

A bleak smile crept over his stony face. "Your charity," Maynard said, "is not one of the qualities that commended you to us, Tabor. Alva can be something of a trial to all of us from time to time, I grant you, but a little tolerance goes a long way."

"I just don't think every form of misery benefits from being dosed with indiscriminate kindness."

"Well," said Maynard, "then you'll be pleased to learn Alva's anticipated you. He's moving to Phoenix in the fall for his health—and yours, too, evidently. Frankly, I don't know how the place is going to run without him."

"Better," I said.

Maynard's smile fled. "I should think it a moot question from your end if you're not going to be around here. Why don't you settle that matter first and let nature dispose of Alva?"

I took off the next few days, driving up to Farmington, where my mother had decided to sell the house and wanted a little moral support in arranging things with the broker. It was not a particularly maudlin moment, but that sundering of my last physical ties to childhood was surely mellowing. Mother wondered if I could bear to throw away the doll house I had helped Daddy make so many seasons back. I said it would be worse still to keep it, like a girl's companion to Rosebud, collecting dust in the attic of a dear departed past. That inspired mother to trash 90 percent of her own mementos. Life marched on, or gimped or something, she said and drew herself upright. I helped her pick out paint and wallpaper for the condominium she had taken in Hartford—there was a spare bedroom for me any time I wanted it—and in passing I shared with her the news of my good fortune.

"You don't sound entirely ecstatic about it," she said.

"I'm not. It means giving up a lot of the work I care about most."

"Then don't do it."

"There are compensations—besides the compensation."

"At least you're not prejudiced against the money."

"*Au contraire*. It's how I know they think I'm real, not just bright and adorable."

"Good," she said. "Money can be useful."

"But I don't want to devote my life to collecting it."

"I shouldn't think."

"Not that I want to become a mendicant, either."

"I understand."

"You can starve saving underdogs."

"I wouldn't be at all surprised."

"They also turn around and bite you in the ass if you're not careful."

"Who does, dear?"

"Underdogs."

"Perhaps that's why the firm doesn't want you doing them any more?"

"Their motives are rather more crass, I'm afraid."

"And you resent that? Surely you knew what was foremost in their minds before you joined the gentlemen?"

"Yes, they made it abundantly clear. I just never wanted to believe that money and mercy were mutually exclusive."

"Perhaps if you weren't quite so good at both?"

"Then I wouldn't have been offered partnership."

"Curious," mother said. "Well, I still say it's a splendid tribute to you, and I'm not entirely clear why you hesitate."

"Because it seems so—final. I'm not at all sure it's what I want to do most. I might want to teach—or write—or go into government—or back to social work."

"One can't keep one's options open forever, dear, without sacrificing irretrievable opportunities."

"I know."

"Then choose. You always wanted me to. Perhaps if I had had the gifts you're blessed with, I wouldn't have hesitated."

But what good were my gifts if I did not savor the rewards they earned me? Or was the quest itself to prove my soul reward and all attainment but a lure to the bowers of dissipation? I had contrived the plausible enough premise, in coming to the law firm, that I could better reform the social order from within by guiding the control levers on a course of my selection than by stalking the gates with a bullhorn and denouncing iniquity until my lungs gave out. But now that those levers were within reach, the premise itself seemed dubious. Once I seized the controls, would I ever relinquish them willingly? Wasn't the kick all in manipulating the power? Would I ever again worry about who or what was being ground up in the machinery? Who had ever mastered the system without in turn being mastered by it? And so, why not avoid the terrible temptation? Why not be honest and admit that I had joined the firm just to prove a point? And now that I had been invited inside the locker room—all one hundred sixteen dripping wet pounds of me—and directed to suit up without the indignity of having to don a *pro forma* cup and jock, why persist? Why not leave and practice law as and when and where I wanted, as I lived the rest of my life, and remain answerable to no one? I did not need their money, and the other emblems of achievement were just so much tempting tinsel. What was integrity but the strength to say no when the world wanted to kiss you to death? I asked my mother that.

"Yes, dear," she said, "but people who win at solitaire never prove much of anything."

"Maybe I've proven all I ever wanted to?"

"I doubt it," she said. "What you've done is confirm all our suspicions that you could reach about any destination you wanted. And you got there with all your faculties intact and energies in gear, but you're just not sure how to proceed now. I don't deny that's a problem but you're a great deal more fortunate than most people with talent. They wear themselves out on the journey—and if they finally manage to get there, they've usually forgotten why they came. And even if they remember, they're generally too exhausted to do anything much beyond enjoying the view."

She was always surprising me that way. One did not hope for parables from a sounding board. "Maybe I've got a case of premature exhaustion," I said.

"Or perhaps what you're really doing is asking yourself if it's worth it."

"Are we back to babies again?"

"Did I say anything about babies?"

"No, but they rush to mind."

"Then I must be right or they wouldn't rush so fast."

"I've still got time for that."

"And love—what do you do for love, meantime—can you bear my asking? Good God, I'm turning into your classically meddling mother."

The point was that it was so unlike her I knew the question had to be heartfelt. I clamped a hand on her wrist and gave it a thank-you squeeze. "I love," I said. "It's just not the full measure."

"Can it ever be—if you keep running?"

"It's how I stay free."

"The question, dear, is whether you're running toward something or away from everything."

"You mean I should stop and find out?"

"I can think of worse things. You might even discover you've actually arrived and being there isn't nearly the constraint on your freedom you'd imagined. If it were me, dear, I'd grab the chance they've offered at your firm and commit myself totally to it for the time being."

"That's not what they mean by a commitment. They want me to declare the firm my whole professional life—now and forever."

"Nobody can make you do that—at work or in love. All life is only for the time being. Use it—don't run from it—and see where it leads."

I called Maynard Lamport the next night at his home and said I would accept the firm's offer. "With all your heart?" he asked. I said yes. "Be certain," he said, "because half won't do." I said I knew and he said he was glad for me and for the firm, and when I went back in on Friday, I found my desk and files moved into an unused former bedroom on the second floor across from Gil Serini's office. He had put my name up on the door in letters made from elbow macaroni.

25

My partner Sam Nightingale rarely appeared in court. And even less often argued in federal court. And had in fact never presented a case before the United States Court of Appeals before embarking by train for Boston that early June morning to try to persuade the First Circuit to reverse a District Court ruling against the son of one of his professor clients. My heart, for reasons I had not much examined, went with him. Then, on impulse—and because it was one of my rare slow days at the office and the skies were so blue and inviting—my head, too, decided to join him.

On the pretext I had to phone him on a question of law, I learned from his secretary that Sam could be reached later in the day at his hotel room, where he planned to hole up and refine his argument for court the next morning. After claiming that a backlog of research awaited me at the Mather Law Library and promising to call in from time to time, I gassed up my Rabbit and bounded off for Boston.

The drive seemed even quicker than the under two hours it took. Every minute of the way I devoted to unscrambling my motives for this headlong pursuit. The professional explanation was the more bracing. After all, I had been to court a lot more than Sam. And my year clerking for George Millis had taught me much about the mentality of the federal bench. True, I neither had ever argued before a Federal Circuit, had appeared actually just a few times in District Court, yet I held myself vastly more experienced as an advocate than Sam. His legal craft was beside the point. He was a bright enough man and more than competent office lawyer, but as with anything else, it took practice to excel on your feet in a court of law. And practice breeds confidence. Sam simply had had too little practice. His confidence, it followed in my view, could therefore not be high on this occasion.

Nor, from what little I had gleaned of the case itself, would his task have been easy even for a veteran advocate. His client was a young Tufts med school graduate whose education had been partially underwritten by the U. S. Naval Reserve, which expected two years of active duty for its investment upon the fellow's completion of his residency. Six months before he was due to report, however, the guy filed for an exemption as a conscientious objector. His sincerity was certified by a service psychiatrist and a navy chaplain, but the hearing officer found to the contrary, and a federal judge upheld him. Sam's hope for winning a reversal was complicated by the disinclination of the appellate judiciary to second-guess the duly conducted administrative workings of government agencies and tribunals. Perhaps I could be of help by sifting through the record at the last minute and spotting a thing or two Sam had somehow missed.

But Sam had not asked me to. Why was I volunteering, swooping down on him like a self-appointed *deus ex machina* so he might carry the day? The man, whatever his limitations, was no novice. Partly, no doubt, I was driven by guilt for having undertaken my sexist charges against the university. And partly, I supposed, because I was rooting for him to gain a grand triumph and maybe open up a career that had become too tightly chambered. That was begging the question, though. The question was why was I rooting so hard for him. The question was did he need me—or I, him. Or both. Or neither. The answers suddenly seemed important to me. Why had I dealt so sharply with him in our last encounter? Why had I defended my temerity in filing against the university by attacking the man for timidity toward me personally? He, after all, had been the one to declare his feeling for me at the end of the previous summer. What had I said back to him but thanks for the nice time? To have said more, it was true, would have encouraged him excessively, given his buffeted psyche at the moment, but to score him for not having persisted in the teeth of my icy gales was to discredit the man's pride entirely. His openness had been repaid once with rebuke; why had I tendered him yet another round? Out of perverted remorse, I concluded. How dare I blame the dear man for not trundling after me? If he had mattered as much to me as I required of him in reverse, why had I let Sparky Grier's ultimatum rule me? Why had I not come forward after his wound had had time to close and said he still mattered to me? Because there was enough else in my life not to tantalize the man that way. Now, all at once, there was not. I had arranged it that way. But why reach out anew toward Sam Nightingale when in theory there were infinite candidates for companionship? Because companionship did not begin to describe the quality of union I had been forming slowly but ever more certainly in my head. And because there were things about Sam Nightingale, for all his unrealized capacity, that had moved me more lastingly than I was willing to admit before to myself let alone to him.

He was staying at the Ritz-Carlton. I parked by a meter on the Common and phoned him from the lobby. I have had warmer receptions. "What are you doing here?" he asked straight off.

"I thought I could help. You've helped me in the past."

"I really don't need any help, thanks."

"Sure, I know. But I thought—you know—it's the Circuit—and maybe you could use a sounding board."

He didn't answer.

"I could be your go-fer."

There was no relieving laugh. "Why didn't you call before coming?"

"The same reason I didn't ask before filing my cases against the university."

"If you knew what I'd say, why drive all this way?"

"It's not so far. And it's a nice day for a drive. And I love Boston."

303

"Fine, then go see the sights. I'm working."

"You sound uptight."

"Tabor, I'm not on vacation."

"Me, neither. I won't be a distraction, I promise."

He sighed. "Go home, will you?"

"Do your argument for me—just once—and I'll make a couple of notes. How can that hurt?"

"Because you're so goddamned hard to please."

"Please me, and the judges'll be a snap."

"That's for sure."

He was wavering. "I came all this way," I said. "I'm entitled to a sneak preview at least."

"And then you'll beat it?"

"If you want."

"Oh, shit," he said. Some invite.

I checked into a room on a different floor from his, called the office to make sure nothing was doing, and then went to Sam. His papers were spread over everything, and the place was thick with pipe smoke. Plainly he was hard at his task: tie off, collar open, sleeves rolled up, underarms damp, brow rumpled with concentration. He studied me warily for a long moment and then gestured toward a chair. Christ, how I wanted to hug him, nothing more. Just a few short seconds to clasp and hold and say I was sorry without saying it and for his arms to answer. But neither of us moved to close the gap. I went where directed, then detoured to the window, which commanded a fine view of the Common, alive now with patchy urban green. "How about a little more air in here—it'll clear your head," I offered and reached for the sash.

"No! The wind'll scramble all the papers—"

Oh, was he ever clenched. "Sor-ry," I said and asked if I could read his brief till he was ready to perform his court presentation. His written work was, as always, of a high order. But since it had not won for him in the District Court, it needed a stronger tone than was his custom. Perhaps his oral argument would be more persuasive.

"All right, just listen and don't interrupt," he said after about half an hour of our working intently to the sound of softly flipped pages and the occasional distant honk of a car.

"But the judges'll interrupt you tomorrow."

"We'll do it that way later."

"But I thought I was only going to get one rendition."

"We'll see how you behave."

"Should I clap and hiss?"

"Just can the horseshit." And off he spieled, raggedly at first and then both more fluent and more strident. His substance was much better than his delivery. Throughout he avoided eye contact with me, preferring to consult a handful of index cards and the mirror.

"Not bad," I said when he was done.

"Not good, either."

"Mainly, you're just talking too fast—trying to jam too much in."

"All the points seem important, though."

"That's what the brief's for, sweetheart. The oral is just for the high points. You don't have to throw everything at them. And you certainly don't have to quote so much case law—just a line or two—let the citations do their own work. The judges can all read—at least most of them."

He nodded and sat down heavily in the chair opposite. "What else?"

"You want substantive criticism?"

"I guess."

"The main thing is I'd come down much harder and much earlier on your 'basis-in-fact' standard of review as the applicable one. It's not a matter of the court's judgment against the investigating officer's. What you're really saying is that the record shows the officer had no basis in fact for his finding of insincerity—and thereby denied your guy due process."

"I say that."

"Not in so many words—and not forcefully enough."

He made a note. "What else?"

"Well—you may be missing a bet by arguing that the officer distorted your guy's testimony in claiming that he favors abortion and euthanasia. The point is not only that your boy carefully qualified his position but that the examining officer was imposing his own moral standards in equating removal of a fetus and mercy killing, which are both very delicate and con-

troversial social questions, with the intentional and unambiguous taking of life in a combat situation."

Sam pondered that for a second or two and then shook his
head. "Yeah, that's good." He wrote it down. "What else?"

"You might appeal more directly to the judicial natures of
the judges by slamming the investigating officer for holding it
against your boy that he consulted with the ACLU before applying for C.O. status. I mean that's a neanderthal mentality at
work."

"I touch on that."

"Touch harder. It gives the Navy's hand away. What are
they implying except that anyone who seeks legal counsel before claiming exemption on grounds of moral scruples must be
faking it? That's just like saying every criminal suspect who
demands counsel before interrogation is probably guilty. Judges
don't like that."

He made another note and then went back to work by himself. He muttered softly every once in a while, trying out one or
another version of his new pitch. Then he ran through it again
for me. Some of it was better, some not. I made more sugges-
tions. He made more notes. Mainly he was too keyed up. We
did it again. And again. He was getting better as fatigue and
repetition softened his tone. The fifth time he let me interrupt
him with a couple of questions, the way the judges normally
did when they heard a point that troubled them. He handled
the questions well but lost the flow of his argument each time
and got angry with himself. I told him to take a break and that
he was exhausting himself. He agreed to a short one and went
to the bathroom, where he splashed water noisily on his face
and gurgled with satisfaction. He came out looking a little less
glazed and unhesitatingly took me in his arms for an ardent
hug. He was still steamy all over except for his cool, unlined
face with those strong, smart, mobile eyes that said so much
more than all the rest of him. "You're doing good," he said. "A
lot better than I am." I hushed him and held on and ran a
hand through his soft, clean hair. It was grayer close-up than it
seemed at a passing glance, and passing is all we had done since
I had last been this close to him. I brought my lips next to his
but his eyes were closed now so I kissed him gently. He smiled

that transforming smile that gave his whole face a sort of lantern glow and kissed me back with equal lightness. He disengaged a moment after.

We went through his presentation another time and honed in on one or two troublesome sections and then broke for a walk and an early supper before my announced departure. We tramped up and down and all around Beacon Hill for a time, thoughts and words meandering like our course through that maze of streets and alleys. We talked about anything but his case. Until I asked him if Lee would be coming over the next morning to hear him in court.

"Not to my knowledge," he said, eyes straight ahead.

"I should think she'd be pleased—your arguing a case this high—and in Boston. Isn't this the sort of thing she's wanted for you?"

"Sure."

"Then how come she's not coming along to cheer?"

He thought for a minute. "I guess she figures I'll be uneasy enough without her to worry about, too."

"I wouldn't exactly call that a vote of confidence."

He shrugged. "Presumably she thinks I'll tell her when I'd like her to come watch."

Presumably, my ass. After a moment I asked, "How is it with you guys?"

"Okay," he said.

"What's that mean?"

"It means okay."

"Tolerable?"

"Yes."

"And does that suit you? Can you go along that way?"

He did not answer. We walked on a while and then he said, "Tabor, why don't you say what you came to say instead of slicing me up? I thought I told you pretty plainly last time we talked that you don't have a license to go poking into my private life any time the spirit moves you. I meant it."

"Okay."

"Then spill it."

"It's not so easy. Coming here wasn't easy."

"Then why did you?"

"I'm not sure. I just wanted to be with you."

"Regardless of what I wanted—or what I'm here to do?"

"I thought I could help. Aren't I helping?"

"Yes, you're very helpful—so long as you stick to law."

"Sam, people change. Their needs and feelings change. Emotions incubate—that takes time. And then one morning you may wake up and know something in your head that the rest of you has been trying to tell you for a long time."

He chewed on that while we headed over to the river. A light wind came in off the water and swirled gaily around us, "Well," he finally said, "are you going to share this astonishing revelation of yours or am I supposed to consult the Delphic oracle?"

"I already shared it—and you know it."

"Cryptic bulletins are not full disclosure. If you want to say something real, say it in plain English."

He was making it no easier for me to re-enter his life than he had when I marched out of it. Could I blame him? "Sam— I want to give it a chance."

"What—us?"

"Yes."

"Then say it. It can't be that hard for you."

"It's harder than you can know."

"I can't know anything if you don't speak straight."

Worse than poison, I hated jumping through hoops at anyone else's bidding. But he was right, and I knew it. There was no oblique way to purchase his favor, no easy words or agile looks to substitute for a felt, forthright statement. That he might not reciprocate, even in part, was a risk I could no longer avoid.

"I care for you, Sam Nightingale." My throat was all gravel. The sounds came out so bare and flat. I could manage the rest only in short, painful spurts. "I've cared from the first day. And I've never stopped. More some days than others—sure—but it's always been there. I told you that—I said it would be that way when we parted last summer. I told you that's how it was last time we talked. But there was no reason for you to credit it, I suppose. You can't see inside my head. But it's as true now as ever. Truer, even. I've never known a kinder or more sensitive or more generous man. And you know my moods. I loved your being with me at the cemetery—you saved a part of my life by making me face up to it. I was so down. And alone. My father meant a great deal to me. And then you were there. And kept being there all summer when I needed someone special. I knew it would be as much a torment as a joy for you, but I couldn't live it through from your side. I mean the fact is that you're a responsible, functioning adult. I tried to tell you not to overinvest in me just then but you didn't hear it right. I wasn't talking about you so much as about where I was. And the truth is I couldn't be sure where you were. To this moment I don't think you know if you love Lee or hate her and won't admit it. She's not giving you what you want and need, that much is plain. I'm not sure I can, either, or should. But I want to try. Before this I've never trusted my own feelings farther than I can throw a—a breadbox. I always keep discounting them for sentiment. Unknown to the world, way down I am one of its most sentimental, jellyhearted creatures. Meantime, my rabid defenses put people off. They put you off. And I've always told myself what I told you—no guy who really cares enough is going to be fooled for long when I turn my back on him. I honestly believed that. But life's too short for making it all into some kind of game." I looked down and then back up into his eyes. They were studying every word as it left my lips and enveloping it and testing it. "Look, I don't know where it will go—or what damage it will do—to your life or to mine—but I'm willing to find out if you want to, too. I don't know where and when and how it can be worked out—all I know is I want time with you. The details are for the both of us to figure out—if there is any both of us. I'm ready to invest in a way I've never invested in any relationship before." I blinked back a storm of tears. Then I took his hand and said, "Is that straight enough for you?"

He spread his fingers and clutched mine almost fiercely tight as we walked and he tried to digest it all. "I have to think," he said finally. "This is a terrible day to spring this on me."

"At least it takes your mind off the law for a few minutes."

He smiled. "Comic relief it's not, though."

"Tell me you're not furious with me."

"Right now I'm not sure what I am."

We had a light supper at Locke-Ober's and kept the talk to the amenities of Boston and its advantages and shortcomings compared to Amity. It was, we agreed, a place we could both live with pleasure. But there was no portent in that—at least neither of us even hinted as much—and we headed for my car and send-off home. "Are you so sure you wouldn't like me around tomorrow morning?" I asked.

"I—hadn't thought about it."

"Think."

"I think I'd rather you weren't. Can you understand?"

"Sure. But I think you may be building the case into a genuine obsession. Just go in there and do your best."

"I'm saying I think I'll do best without my coach hovering in the prompter's shell."

"I dig," I said, but I did not love that weakness in him. "How about a little good-luck token, then?"

"Like what?"

"Like if you can stand to take your beloved papers off the bed, let's get in it."

"When—now?"

"Why not? It's marvelous for the digestion."

He gave a distracted little laugh. "I was planning on some work—I've got to pull it all together."

"Work after."

It was not a star-spangled screw. I think there was too much on both our minds, and our bodies and tempos were strange now to each other. But I gave myself to the act with as much dedication, if not abandon, as I ever had in my life. At the end we lay there entwined and speechless for a long time. I told him he did not have to see me to the car.

I slipped into the courtroom at the last moment, hoping he would not notice. But it was a small chamber and there were few spectators. He glanced around when everybody stood for the judges and caught me in the corner. I threw him a sheepish smile and a thumbs-up sign; he lowered his eyes. It was the only time I ever wore a carnation to court when I was not arguing.

It did not help Sam much. He did about a B-minus job of it.

He stressed some of the points we had discussed but a couple of the questions from the bench troubled him and he answered them evasively and had difficulty getting untracked after each. At best I rated his chances of winning at fifty-fifty.

He did not even glance my way as he left the courtroom. I had to hurry after him and didn't catch up until the courthouse stairs. "Hey," I said, "I'm not the enemy. Don't be sore. I didn't want to miss it."

"You wouldn't have missed much," he said, still not looking at me.

"I thought you did pretty well," I said, falling into step.

"I thought I did pretty lousy."

"You're hypercritical. Everyone is. It wasn't perfect, but you hit some of the key points hard."

"Thanks," he said. "G'bye—I'm hopping a cab."

"Why? I'll drive us back."

"I'm taking the train."

"Why? I don't understand."

"Because I want to take the train."

"But I have the car—"

"I don't want to go in your car." He looked at me hard now. "And I don't want you to be part of my life again."

It was turning into an ugly little sidewalk scene. I thought he was just overreacting to how his courtroom performance had gone, maybe even blaming me for it. "Couldn't we talk about it on the drive home?" I asked.

"Talk about what? You talked yesterday—I listened. And I appreciate what you said—it took courage, and I admire you for that. I've always admired your courage. That's not the problem, Tabor."

"What is?"

"You said it yourself once. We're made up entirely differently."

"But we mesh—we complement each other—that was your answer."

"And you didn't buy it. But now you're asking me to."

"I explained all that yesterday—or tried to."

"And I explained why I didn't want you in that courtroom this morning. But you didn't care."

"No! I cared so much I wouldn't miss it."

"Tabor, you're incurably selfish and insensitive. You can't dress that up with pretty words."

"You mean I'm insensitive because I felt enough for you to go against your orders?"

"But you didn't care enough to respect what I was feeling. The only rules you think you have to obey are your own. You know what you need? You need someone nearer your age who's strong enough to slug it out with you, and if you both survive, you'll grow old together biting and kicking all the way. Or you need another father—someone you can take turns teasing and venerating. I don't happen to be either one of those. I'm grateful to you for some of the things you've taught me about myself, but I've learned to separate the lesson from the teacher. Don't worry, though, you'll find someone someday who wants what you have to offer, which happens to be a lot. Only God help him if he doesn't know his own mind first." And he was gone.

I called in sick to the office and drove home through bleary eyes. Sam Nightingale was not the man I had thought. How I could have miscalculated him so, I was too hurt and angry to figure. All I knew for sure was that I had violated my own principles and been burned for it. By the time I reached the Connecticut border, I was blaming myself more than Sam. Pretty soon every car on the highway began passing me. Then I realized I was going slow because there was no place I wanted to be just then.

26

In the waning days of his tenure as manager and resident martinet of the firm, the hateful Alva Potter was visited with an untimely misfortune. The sparrowlike Mrs. Potter, while driving under the influence, rammed into another car and had the poor judgment to slip off without acknowledging her liability in the matter. Worse luck, someone took down her license plate and next thing she knew she had been invited to the Court of Common Pleas. Uncharacteristically Heepish, Potter asked Gil Serini to handle the matter, and ever the obliging soul, he agreed. At the last moment, though, a major client tangled in a major hassle required his services and Gil scrambled frantically among the associates for someone to take over the Potter appearance for him. He had had no success by the time he spotted me filling up at the coffee counter. His hesitation was apparent—both because of my new rank and my well-known lack of love for Alva—but circumstances gave him no choice but to blurt out his dilemma.

"Let me get this straight," I said, unable to resist protracting his discomfort for another moment. "You want me to go out of my way for Alva?"

"For Alva's wife, really."

"But it's possible he's friends with her, right?"

"I guess so."

"So it amounts to the same thing, right?"

"All right, all right—do it for me, then, maybe?"

"Now you're talking."

"You'll do it?"

"If his gruesomeness will have me."

"He doesn't have any choice. I'll go get you the papers—you're a doll—God bless." And off he scampered.

There was not a whole lot I could do to ease Mrs. Potter's plight except to ask the court's mercy in view of the lady's previously umblemished history. The judge, who had never fully appreciated my legal virtues and once made a crack about the carnation I always wore in court, responded with a fine of two hundred fifty dollars and a six-month suspension of Mrs. Potter's license, besides an order to pay full damages to the owner of the other car. In view of her imminent move to Arizona and her attendant need to be behind the wheel, I was able to persuade the judge to reduce the length of the suspension to Mrs. Potter's departure date. "Just remember when you get there," he said more gruffly than the occasion required, "those cactuses can't see you coming." Mrs. P. took it with better spirit than it was given, thanked me generously for my efforts, and said she would tell Alva I was every bit as good a lawyer as he had led her to believe. Clearly she was the diplomat in the family.

As I was packing up to leave court, the judge had begun the morning's arraignment hearings, a ritual I had not observed since quitting Legal Assistance. I lingered a few extra moments, perhaps to remind myself how fortunate I was to have fled that grubby, thankless branch of the trade. A couple of cases were routinely handled, and then a short, dark, unkempt man was brought on in a state of evident bewilderment. His eyes were peepholes in a web of crow's-feet, his ears large and jug, and he had a barnacled prow for a nose with an uncouth gray mustache fluttering beneath. His shapeless colorless pants were at least two sizes too big, and on top he wore an old denim shirt, and over it a still more worn leather vest with what must have been a sheepskin lining before time had fleeced it. His sleeves were rolled up to the elbow, revealing heavily muscled forearms, and both his big bony hands held on to a battered brown fedora as if it were a potent talisman. His name, according to the charge against him, was Gabriel Zampa, and his alleged crime was failure to obtain a building permit and violation of the city zoning regulations with regard to the height of structures.

What caught my attention was not so much the old man's bedraggled appearance, which except for the datedness of his dress was hardly peculiar among the hordes of near-derelicts hauled before that court, but the nature of the charges against him. According to the assistant prosecutor, the codger had been laboring for an undetermined period of time on three open-work towers in the middle of an old junkyard he owned about ten blocks beyond the Coop and just a block or two from the city limits. A building inspector had notified Zampa in writing five years earlier that he was in violation of the municipal code but to no avail. "And he has been in continuous violation ever since, your honor," said the law.

"For five years?" asked the judge.

"Yes, your honor."

"What's taken the city so long to bring an action?"

"Well—the place is pretty far off the beaten path, your honor—behind that old brewery way out there at the end of the Gully. It's hard to see from any of the main streets. Also, the towers were somewhat lower when the building department first became aware of the problem."

"And how high are these things now, counselor?"

"The highest, I believe, is about—a hundred feet."

The judge was more amused than distressed. "This gentleman, you're claiming, has built a tower one hundred feet high on the streets of this city and it's taken the building department five years to notice?"

"Three towers, actually, your honor. The other two are smaller."

"How much smaller?"

"I believe one is about seventy feet and the other is close to ninety."

"I would classify all three of them as quite large, wouldn't you?"

"Yes, your honor."

"Well, then, why the delay?"

"I'm not sure, your honor. Probably it's because the building department is extremely shorthanded and there's very little new construction going on out there."

"But you'd think someone in a responsible position—the police—somebody—would have called it to the department's attention."

"You'd think so, your honor. I can only surmise about it. It's a very dangerous section of the city, so not many people are likely to go wandering. And the junkyard is at the edge of a dead-end street, so you'd pretty much have to know what you were looking for to find it."

"I see," said the judge. "Well, let's get on with it." He turned to Zampa and asked if he were represented by counsel. The old man did not seem to understand. The judge repeated the question in Italian and got a glimmer and then in Spanish and got a more declarative shake of Zampa's gray head. "Do you understand any English at all?" the judge asked him.

315

"Sure t'ing," Zampa said.

"But you didn't understand my question about having a lawyer?"

"You call it somethin' else, judge—I don' know dat word. 'Lawyer' I know."

"I think you said 'counsel,' your honor," the prosecutor tried to help.

"I know what I said." The judge sighed and turned to consult some papers at his elbow, presumably for the purpose of assigning counsel.

"I done what he say," Zampa declared simply into the void.

The judge glanced up. "I didn't ask you that, Mr. Zampa."

"Sure t'ing, judge," Zampa answered in good spirit. "But I see you very busy—maybe it help I tell you de truth right away." He wagged his hat toward the prosecutor. "It's like he say."

"You mean you want to plead guilty to the charges?"

"Sure t'ing, judge. I did it."

"But you can't plead without a lawyer."

Zampa's brow became one fixed wrinkle. "How come, judge —if I did it like he say?"

"Because you may not be aware of all your rights and all the consequences of your actions."

"It don't seem such a terrible bad t'ing, judge," Zampa ventured quietly.

"Breaking the law is not nice, Mr. Zampa, whatever you may happen to think about it."

"Oh, sure t'ing, judge—I don't mean it's nice. It's not nice. But some kindsa t'ings is not nicer dan ot'er t'ings, huh, judge?"

"That's what the trial is for, Mr. Zampa—to determine just how bad a thing you really did."

"You don' know now?"

The judge studied the old man with benign interest. "No, Mr. Zampa," he said, "as a matter of fact I don't. It's hard for me to believe such a pleasant-seeming man could deliberately break the law for five years running."

"Oh, I didn' do it deliberate, judge. I jus' forgot afta' while, ya know how I mean? Like, if dey really care what I'm doin', I t'ink dey gonna come back and make me stop. But nobody come so what I'm sposed to t'ink, huh?"

He was a very appealing stump of a man, of the quirky, unpredictable sort who drives the courts daffy with a fearlessness born of ignorance. "You've got to have a lawyer, Mr. Zampa, because the law says so," said the judge.

"Sure t'ing, judge," he said. "I'm just tryin' to save money fo' de city."

"That's very thoughtful, Mr. Zampa. It's too bad you didn't feel that way when you received the notice of violation five years ago."

"Oh, hey, judge," Zampa said, "I figure I save de city by not doin' nothin' and den maybe nobody's gotta fuss 'bout me, you know?"

"Mr. Zampa," said the judge, "there are fifty other people waiting to see me, so I'm afraid we'll have to end this delightful colloquy."

"Sure t'ing, judge."

The judge scanned the room for a moment. "Ladies and gentlemen of the bar," he said, "I have a small predicament on my hands this morning and need your indulgence. The Public Defender's office has advised me that its caseload is so heavy at the moment that it cannot take on any but the most serious emergencies for the next week or so, at which time fresh recruits are due. By the same unfortunate token, the Legal Assistance people are shorthanded just now due to staff vacations. So what I need this morning are a few volunteers from among our selfless corps of private practitioners to help us over this brief spell. Will someone among you therefore be good enough to step forward and represent Mr. Zampa so we can proceed in an orderly fashion?"

None of the dozen or so lawyers in the room budged. It was rare, since the establishment of public and private agencies to represent the indigent, for the court to appoint counsel more or less arbitrarily, and it was rarer still that competent attorneys volunteered for an assignment. Most of them were busy people, not boy scouts seeking their good deed for the day. "All right, then," said the judge, "I'll resort to my military training and pick a volunteer." The first man he tried said he was due in Superior Court in half an hour. The next said he was leaving after work that day for a two-week vacation. Then the judge scanned over my way and his eyes brightened. "Ah," he said, "Miss Hill. We're graced with all too little of your attractive presence these days. Would you be willing to accommodate the court in this matter—or does your new stature prevent your mingling with us down here in the trenches every now and then?"

It was nice to hear that my elevation at the office was common knowledge among the city bar, but I had the immediate sense the judge was rewarding my arrival at the upper echelons of the fraternity by dropping a soggy bag of garbage on my head to see how I would react. In fact, I was doubly annoyed. The only reason I was in the courtroom at all that morning was to do a favor for a hard-pressed colleague. To be saddled with yet another involuntary duty was irony enough, but for it to be one of the sort that my partners had explicitly insisted I avoid accepting on all but the rarest occasions seemed a particularly snickering trick of fate.

"Of course I'll bow to your honor's wishes," I said, "although a number of my office confederates have upbraided me rather severely for taking on too much volunteer work in other arenas of the law. Perhaps your honor would consider a few other candidates in the room and come back to me if no one else is available?"

He gave me a fishy eye. "Is that a yes or a no, Miss Hill?"

"Both, your honor."

"Miss Hill, have you ever pleaded a client both guilty and not guilty?"

"Not that I can recall, your honor."

"Then perhaps you'll spare me the privilege of your first such maneuver. I don't have time to poll the courtroom. Why don't you just say yes and tell your hard-shelled office colleagues you certainly did not volunteer for the task? Perhaps you'd like me to write you a note for them?"

There was a round of nasal clucking in the room of the sort I had not heard since my first year of practice. No longer was there any question, though, whether I was the object of sexist derision, professional envy, or repressed lust. I had taken my place beside the best of them and could join in the laughter now as its inspiration, not its butt. "The note won't be necessary at this time, your honor," I said when the snorting had died down, "but I'd like to feel free to accept your gallant gesture at some later date if the need arises. Meantime, I'll be glad to represent Mr. Zampa."

"That's very fine, Miss Hill," said the judge. "Why don't you and he step into one of the conference rooms and then notify the bailiff when you're ready to enter a plea."

"Fine, your honor," I said, gritting my teeth.

"Judge," Zampa suddenly put in, "I don' want no girl lawyer."

The judge blinked a few times. "Why not?" he said in a voice harder than it had been toward the old man.

"Girls shouldn' be no lawyers," Zampa said flatly. "It's what I t'ink, judge—you know?"

"What have you got against girls, Mr. Zampa? They make up half the world."

"I got nothin' against girls, judge, excep' dey got t'ings dey gotta do in life and some t'ings dey gotta leave de men to do, you know?"

"Mr. Zampa," said the judge, "we're getting near the twenty-first century. Women have been doctors and scientists for a long time. They also fly planes, climb mountains, fight bulls, and—and—"

"Govern states," I offered.

"Yes," the judge said. "And more and more of them are becoming lawyers—and even judges."

"Dey got lady judges?" Zampa asked.

"Yes, they do, Mr. Zampa."

"How dey stack up wit' you, judge?"

"Several of them are supposed to be excellent."

"But you ain't so sure?"

"Mr. Zampa, Miss Hill here happens to be among the most

gifted young attorneys in this city. She was recently made a partner in one of Amity's most respected law firms. You're lucky she's agreed to take on your case."

"How come I'm lucky, judge, when I didn' want no lawyer in de firs' place—an' in de second place you make me take dis young girl one? I ain't got nothin' against her, judge, but maybe you got an old man like me could do it?"

"Mr. Zampa, I'm afraid you're a little prejudiced against the fair sex," the judge said, "and this court isn't going to cater to your bias."

"I got no prejudice, judge. I love de ladies. But ladies an' men are different, is all." He threw up his hands to stress the obviousness of the point. "Tell me somet'in', judge—how come dey ain't got no lady priests?"

"Some churches do, Mr. Zampa."

"Not de Cat'lic church, judge."

"You'll have to take that up with a different authority, I'm afraid," said the judge.

"But see, lawyers an' priests, judge—dey do de real heavy business in life, you know what I mean?"

"Haven't you ever heard the expression 'The hand that rocks the cradle rules the world,' Mr. Zampa?"

"Sure t'ing, judge. An' dat's what I'm sayin'—who's gonna run de world if dere ain't nobody home rockin' de cradles?"

As theater, it wasn't bad vaudeville; as law, it was appalling contempt of court, women, and reason. "In light of Mr. Zampa's plainly expressed views," I said, "I think justice would be better served in this case if I gracefully withdrew, your honor, and made myself available for any other case you'd care to volunteer me for."

"You surprise me, Miss Hill," said the judge. "I think we both owe it to Mr. Zampa to raise his sexist consciousness."

"I think we both probably have more urgent business, your honor."

"Don't tell me you've resigned from the feminist cause, Miss Hill?"

"Women lawyers can't if they want to," I said. "It's a matter of saving the ammunition for battles worth fighting. Some are hopeless, your honor."

"Perhaps," he said, "but this is one I'm in on, too. Why don't you get on with it?"

Zampa would not look at me as we marched side by side to one of the cubicles off the courtroom corridor reserved for client-attorney meetings. I noticed as he stood waiting for me to sit first that his left arm was a couple of inches shorter than the right one. He sat as soon as I did and yawned largely, revealing barely half a mouth of teeth; half the ones he had were gold, the rest brown from tobacco. "Oh, 'scuse me, miss," he said. "I didn' sleep so good last night, you know? I never been in court for nothin' before dis."

"That's good," I said. "That'll help."

"Help what?" he asked, slipping his wilted hat on.

"With what happens to you."

"How come anything gonna happen if I got a lawyer now?"

"How come anything happens if you got a priest?"

"Aah—dat's different." His gold mouth glittered with appreciation of the reply. "Anyway, de truth is I ain't got a priest. I quit de church way back, miss."

"That's too bad."

"No, it ain't bad. You wanna know why I quit?"

"Not particularly," I said. "I'm trying to read these papers to see what they can do to you."

"What could dey do—gimme a little fine, maybe, huh?"

"How come you were ready to plead guilty in court without knowing what they could do to you?"

He shrugged. "I figure dere ain't nothin' I can do about it so why make a—how you say it?—helloblue."

"Hullabaloo."

"Yeah."

"But why are you so sure you did something wrong?"

"'Cause I don't know de laws an' de city people do."

"You mean you just want to take their word for it?"

"What choice I got?"

"That's what I'm here for. So let me just read through this stuff for a minute."

"Oh, sure t'ing, miss. You read. Read all you want. I got all day." After closing his face for a couple of seconds, he began to whistle a few not immediately identifiable bars of something operatic. Then he said, "He's a nice judge, dat judge. What's his name, miss?"

"Lombard. Harris Lombard."

He chewed on that a little and when it wouldn't go down, he said, "'Scuse me, miss, but what kind name is dat—Lombard Harris Lombard. He got de same first name an' last name?"

"His name is Lombard. Harris is his first name."

"Ohhh." That held him for a moment. "He's a good judge, huh?"

"He's all right."

"I t'ink maybe he t'inks you a better lawyer dan you t'ink he's a judge, huh?"

Whatever his intellectual limitations, Gabriel Zampa was a pretty crafty coot. "Could be," I said, flipping to the last page of the arraignment report.

"What kinda name is dat—Lombard? He's Italiano, huh?"

"I don't know," I said. "I never asked him."

"Oh, sure, dat's Italian—dat's a part o' Italy—Lombardy—like de baseball player wit' de big nozola, like what I got."

"Schnozola."

"Yeah, dat's what I mean."

"There was a baseball player named Schnozola?"

Zampa laughed. "Dat's what they call him on accounta his nose."

"You sure you aren't thinking of Jimmy Durante?"

"Who?"

"Durante. He was a comedian with a big nose. They called him The Schnoz."

"I don' know him. I know Lombardi—Ernie Lombardi. He used to play catch for de Reds, you know? Almost the same name as de judge—"

"I'm afraid he was before my time."

"Yeah, you just a kid, huh?"

"Maybe not so young as you think."

"A gentleman ain't sposed to ask a lady how old she is."

"You want to know how old I am, Mr. Zampa?"

"It ain't none o' my business, miss."

"I'll tell you how old I am if you tell me how old you are—okay?"

"Suits me."

"I'm almost thirty-one."

"No-o-o."

"Sure—what'd you think?"

"I dunno—maybe twenty, twenty-t'ree—like dat."

"Thank you very much. Now you."

"Me?"

"You promised."

"Sure t'ing. I'm 'bout seventy—maybe seventy-two—aroun' dere."

"You don't know?"

"I neva' got no birth license," he said and told me he had been born in Haiti of a poor fishing family for which official records were not kept. His father, he said, was part Italian, part Greek, and a little Syrian. "My mama, she was mixed Spanish an' Indian wit' a little nigger in de woodpile, too, you know?"

"Why do you call it 'nigger'?"

"What do you say?"

"Nigger isn't a nice word. You didn't use ugly words for the other parts of you."

"Why you t'ink? 'Cause I don't like dem people. Dey take stuff from me all de time—dey take from ever'body—an' dey beat me up two times, de nigger kids. Dey like little animals, you know?"

"They're poor and ignorant, Mr. Zampa, and they haven't got any hope."

He nodded and then looked down at his own worn clothes. "Poor ain't reason enough."

"They can't get work. They live on drugs to forget their troubles."

"An' den dey beat shit outa me for fun, huh? No, miss, dey mean, lazy bastids, you want my 'pinion. I spit on dem all."

Brotherhood was not his long suit, and I was not about to

convert him to it by forensic passion. Gabriel Zampa had plenty passion of his own to meet it, and my business with him was not to conduct an introductory course in the dynamics of urban sociology. Besides, he could have written the book—if he had known how to write.

I finished scanning the legal papers and gave him the report. According to city law, each day of the continuance of the original violation after he had been notified of it in writing by the building inspector constituted "a separate and distinct offense," calling for a fine of not more than twenty-five dollars or less than ten. "Let's see," I said, whipping a pencil and a pad out of my bag, "they claim they notified you five years and two months ago—which is five times three hundred sixty-five—which comes to one thousand eight hundred twenty-five—plus one day for leap year—plus, let's see—sixty-one days of the sixth year—making a total of one thousand eight hundred eighty-six days they can fine you for. And since the fine for the original violation is not less than twenty-five or more than a hundred, that means the least—the least—they could fine you for is eighteen thousand, eight hundred eighty-five dollars for each violation. They're charging you with two violations—no permit and building your towers forty feet too high—so that brings it up to a minimum fine of thirty-seven thousand, seven hundred seventy dollars." I glanced up from my figuring. "You still want to plead guilty, Mr. Zampa?"

The numbers were sheerest fantasy to him. His pinhead eyes, dark and watery, seemed to spiral with disbelief. He put his large horny hand against his cheek as if to soften the blow. Finally he said, "How could such a t'ing be?"

"It's a law," I said. "They don't want people building whatever they feel like anywhere they feel like it. Does that seem so strange?"

"But why so much money fo' such a small t'ing?"

"Because you didn't stop when they told you to."

"'Cause I didn' t'ink dey really care. If dey care, how come dey let me go all dis time? It can't be such an awful t'ing if dey didn' stop me."

"The judge asked the prosecutor the same thing, didn't you hear him?"

"Sure, I hear—but how come it's my fault I live way away from where dey can see what I'm doin'? Dat's jus' why I do it dere—so I don' upset nobody. It's differen' if I do it in de middle o' de city green, huh?"

"We'll have to say that in court."

"Sure t'ing—I tell 'em dat. Dey unde'tand—dat judge, he's good—better'n you t'ink."

I told him there might be lots of things we ought to say to the judge and then we could both tell how good he was but first I had better see for myself exactly what the violations were all about. I requested and won a twenty-four-hour postponement of the arraignment and drove Zampa home. He was surprised I knew my way in and out of those scarred streets so little traveled by people of influence. I said my work had caused me to pass a fair amount of time in the Gully, and he said I should know then to lock my car door or they'd steal my back teeth at the next red light. But I knew a lot of these people, I said, and he said he knew them, too, and he was even part black but that never stopped them from robbing and beating him. I told him he could lock the door on his side, and he grunted but didn't.

For the last few turns I needed his guidance. Left, right, left, left, and the huge brick bastion of a brewery loomed out of nowhere, a boarded-up sarcophagus that memorialized the once churning life of the neighborhood. That two-block-long tomb so commanded the vista that no eyes were drawn past it. But my passenger had me thread down the alley at the far end of the idled factory, cross the railroad siding behind it, and follow the narrow street till it skidded to a dead end. On one side of the last block five ramshackle houses clustered, vying for oblivion. Across from them was a sprawling junkyard fenced off from direct view by a curtain of doors that had been scavenged from extinct tenements, linked side by side, and painted gaudy colors to brighten the local scenery. There, a little like slender oil derricks springing incongruously out of a debris-strewn prairie, stood three tapering towers of almost cobwebbed delicacy. The closer we came to them, the more intricate the crisscross of tracery that formed the spires. I wondered how anything so tall and fragile could stay up.

As we pulled alongside, the sun, which before had been silhouetting the implausible construction, fell upon it full force and turned it into a bejeweled mirage. The whole thing seemed to have been dusted with sugar, baked white and hard, and sprinkled with a million sequins of different shapes and sizes and colors—anything that would catch the light. Swept up by the grace and glitter of the giant curios, I felt for the instant that I had been propelled to some faraway lotus land and fallen under the spell of its emblazoned dreamscape.

"Dey almos' finish' now," Zampa said. "I was fixin' de tops when de city guy come."

I hardly heard him through my drugged haze. "You—did—this—all this?" I finally managed.

"Sure t'ing."

"Just you?"

"Jus' me."

"How?"

Zampa grinned. "How you t'ink?"

"I don't have any idea."

He fanned open his massive hands. "Wit' dese, miss."

"But how did you get the machines up that high?"

"I didn' use no machines—jus' dese."

"You did the whole thing by hand?"

"Sure t'ing."

"But how did you rivet the pieces together—or screw them or whatever you did to make them hold?"

"Dere ain't no rivets—dere ain't no screws."

"You welded it all?"

"No welds."

"So what's holding it together?"

"Cement," he said, "an' chicken wire. C'mon, I show you."

The true height of the towers was not apparent until you stood directly under them, and then they looked gigantic and far more substantial than I had supposed. None of the struts, including the dozen or so main vertical supports, was more than three or four inches wide, but the gridwork of the super-structure seemed to gain strength from its remarkable intricacy. Every few feet up, the towers were ringed by a horizontal band that was yoked to the upright legs and a center post by a

326

profusion of connecting rods like spokes on a wagon wheel. And at every conceivable juncture, inside and out, vertically and horizontally and diagonally, bowed protrusions of framing reinforced the principal form in a random interplay of arcs and loops that no engineer would have blueprinted without being delicensed on the spot. The skeleton, Zampa explained, was made mostly from steel reinforcing rods that he bought or found, but he also used piping and bed frames and any other cast-off lengths of metal that came his way. Every joint he wrapped in wire mesh and packed down with cement and a trowel. From the joint he worked outward, coating each strut with cement and implanting it with pieces of junkyard jewelry until the towers resembled one vast lovingly inlaid mosaic. He used whatever he could find to achieve the sparkle—pieces of glazed yellow tile, chips of floral crockery, whole clamshells, porcelain shards from old sinks and bathtubs, bits of broken mirror, glass slivers from blue milk of magnesia bottles and ruby-red drinking goblets and brown quarts of milk, and whole bottoms of Seven-Up bottles fitted flush to the surface like so many sea-green polka dots. Nor did the decoration end with the bangles. In between he had imprinted the drying cement with a dense intaglio of humble iconography—there were tulip shapes and rosettes, snowflakes and stars, shamrocks and pineapples and butterflies, hearts and teardrops and sunbursts, all looking as if they had been engraved by a giant with a cooky cutter. There was hardly a square inch of those three clustered minarets or the spars and ogee arches lacing them together that was not somehow festooned. And yet instead of standing there simpering like a trio of rhinestoned harlequins, those towers soared and shimmered—a marvel of fluid forms and rhythmic lines, raised implausibly high into the air and patterned charmingly throughout by a single possessed old man. It was nothing less than a miracle—a wholly unexpected flower of delight thriving alone in a jungle of despair. To my knowledge, I had never seen a miracle before.

The work had taken him close to eighteen years to build or maybe it was twenty-three, Zampa told me, and he had made it all up as he went along. "Once I t'ink maybe I hire a man to help but how's he gonna know what to do next when I don' know myself, huh?" Besides, he didn't exactly have money to give away. Not having worked steadily as a bricklayer in more than twenty years, he scratched what income he could out of the junkyard and lived alone in the small shack at the end of the yard farthest from the street. His whole life had become this isolated labor of love, and now that it was all but done, the city authorities had descended like the furies and contrived to celebrate the achievement by pillorying its lowly creator.

"Mr. Zampa," I told him, "I'm going to do some homework tonight to see if there isn't some way we can plead you not guilty tomorrow."

"You t'ink we gotta chance?"

"I don't know. It's worth trying."

He took his hat off and wiped his hairline. "Suits me," he said.

I told him I would be back the next morning to pick him up and drive him to court. But he said not to bother and that I wasn't running a taxi service and I was helping him plenty enough as it was. I smiled and he did back and we shook hands. On the drive downtown my head swirled with visions of Gabriel Zampa's junkyard gems. In my wildest imaginings I could not have conjured a more unlikely client or a less promising case.

At the office there was a box of flowers waiting for me with a thank-you note from Alva Potter. The day had been just one miracle after another.

27

In the clean soft light of early morning, his small dark form was easy to follow way, way up there as he hopped like a spider monkey from perch to perch and paused periodically on a crossbar of that fantastic trapeze to attend to what needed doing.

His ancient fedora was jammed tight on his head to keep the breeze from whipping it away. Over his shoulder was slung a bucket of cement that must have been a formidable cargo at that altitude. When we arrived, he was lathering on cement very near the pinnacle and dipping into his vest pocket for bits of bangle like those with which he had encrusted the whole height of his sky-spearing creation. Between dollops with his trowel he pulled his head back a little to study the effect he was creating, though no one but a feathered creature, a wayward steeplejack, or he himself would ever come close enough afterward to pass esthetic judgment on the arrangement.

Every second we watched I knew could be his last. He was an old man with gnarled muscles and joints that would not likely let him recover from a misstep. And he took no safety precautions at all that I could see. Yet as I contemplated him hanging free up there a hundred feet off the earth I was as certain as I had ever been of anything that he would not fall. Providence had hooped him to that exotic gridwork of his own devising, and I guessed that he knew its every length and ring and joint with such total tactile command that he could have negotiated its entire surface as easily at midnight as at noon.

"Outasight!" Jonathan sang in a husky vibrato as we stood at the junkyard gate watching Zampa perform his aerial handiwork. Jon had said nothing at all at first, keeping me in suspense over the validity of my own instinctive response to the towers. Not that I needed him or anyone really to tell me what I felt was justified. But my investigation of the old man's legal problem the night before had convinced me his best defense lay in the claim that these were no ordinary pieces of construction, susceptible to the usual strictures of the building code, but works of art of a high order and therefore exempt from prior restraint like any other constitutionally protected form of personal expression. Such an argument, though, would need authentication by professionally qualified observers. Less sensitive ones, like the bureaucrats charged with monitoring the building industry, were likely to see only a junkyard jungle gym—and, at that, one that could come crashing down in the next stiff wind. I thought it best to proceed from the start with the assurance that my own eyes had not deceived me.

Around midnight I called the only professional esthete I knew. Jessie answered instead. I had not known she had moved in. "For the summer," she said. I explained the reason for my call because I thought she deserved it, but she cut me off saying that Jon was out for his midnight bike ride. I knew that meant he would be all hot and bothered when he came back, so I asked if she would just get him to pick me up in front of my apartment at seven in the morning for the emergency mission. She said she would and I said to tell Jon I'd even ride out to the towers on the back of the goddamn Honda so he'd under-stand how important this thing was to me. "That's all right," she said. "I'm sure he can manage to follow you."

"Jess," I said, "this is strictly business."

"Oh, right," she said. "I forgot."

"You really dig him, huh?"

There was a pause, and then she said, "I've never had any-thing like this before."

"Great," I said, "but can I give you one small piece of ad-vice?"

"No," she said.

"Don't be so possessive about him or you'll be out on your ass."

"Thanks," she said.

"Have a good one for me."

"I'll do my best," she said.

I had trouble sleeping in my excitement over the towers but was still supercharged by the time Jon showed up in the morn-ing, ten minutes late and not at all certain his leg wasn't being pulled. I sketched out the background for him, and he snuffled and said, "The guy sounds spaced." I said that's what I wanted him to help me decide.

Jon must have stood gazing motionlessly upward five whole minutes while he drank in the size and brilliance of the feat. I yelled up hello to Zampa and said I had brought a friend, and he yelled down hello and said he would be working up there for a while. I asked if he minded our standing there in the meantime and he shouted back no and went about his busi-

330

ness. Snatches of song were the only sound that came wafting down from him as Jon and I moved in closer and inspected the three glittering masts in detail. The more he saw, the greater Jon's astonishment. "And he did it all himself?" he asked, running a hand over the heavily inlaid surface at ground level.

"That's what he says."

"Jesus! And no plans—just off the top of his noggin?"

"That's what he says. You think it's impossible?"

"No, it's probable—you see how the main tower tilts right a little?"

I had not noticed it before. "Is it going to collapse?"

"You say he's been working on them twenty years?"

"He's a little vague on details but something in that vicinity."

"If they were going to fall, they probably would have a long time ago."

"Why? I mean isn't the danger greater the taller they get?"

"Not necessarily. The center post looks pretty solid and the uprights are probably buried three or four feet in the foundation. Anyway, the whole design is highly redundant."

"That's engineering jazz, not a value judgment, right?"

"Yeah," he said, "it means it's overbuilt. Everything is supported and reinforced more than it would ever need—the stress is spread over the whole thing so the bearing load is negligible at any one spot. It's probably a helluva lot safer than the Empire State Building."

"You're kidding."

"Do I ever kid this close to sunrise?"

"You think it's really something?"

"Shit, yes!"

"What is it, though?"

"What do you mean?"

"I mean I see it but I don't know what it all is—or means."

"What do you mean what is it? It's what it is."

"But nobody not off his nut spends twenty years screwing around by himself with a thing like this."

"Why not—if it makes him happy?"

"Is it art?"

"Does it move you?"

"Yes—greatly."

"Then it's art."

"Just like that?"

"You can see it as well as I can."

"But you're the expert."

"It's not a question of expertness."

"It is for me. I've got to go into a court of law in a couple of hours and say it's art. I don't want to get laughed out on my fanny."

He squinted back up at it. "Now that I think of it," he said, "it's highly reminiscent of Gaudi's cathedral—in Barcelona."

"There's a far-out cathedral in Barcelona?"

"*Sagrada Familia*. It starts out Gothic and just keeps soaring and turning into fairy-tale weirdness as it rises—a kind of Jesus and the Beanstalk. Only there are four beanstalks, each an open-work tower like these here, and ringed and irregular and surreal like these are, with mosaic decorations on top, too."

"And they love it in Barcelona?"

"Even Franco gave it three *Arribas* and a castanet. It's generally considered an Art Nouveau masterpiece."

"You're beautiful," I said and dug out my notebook and pencil. "Now hit me with it slow."

"Gaudi," he said, "Antoni Gaudi," and he spelled out the name of the cathedral and gave me the guy's approximate dates and a few pieces of technical information. I was in clover. If something so quirky could qualify as sacred art in the heart of Torquemada country, how could it not here, in the cradle of New World enlightenment?

Zampa scrambled down his tower with the agility of a bow-legged acrobat. Jon studied the speed with which the old man moved and suggested that the dimensions of his physique must have dictated the ad hoc design of the whole thing. "See," he said, "each ring of the tower is only as high above the one below as he can comfortably reach. It's just like a big ladder to him." Which explained how the danger of his falling had been minimized and each heavily laden trip up and down was not so severe an ordeal for him as it looked to me. Still, he was reeking from the exertion as he landed, dumped his trowel and bucket on the ground, and lit up the stub of a used cigar he fished from one of his pockets. His arms were coated to the elbow with glinty specks and plaster dust that nothing under a month in a Turkish steambath seemed likely to remove. He tried to look stern with me for coming out there against his specific edict, but I said I wanted my friend to see what he had built and the old man relented. "Who's he—yo' boss?"

"My maid," I said and explained to Jon that Zampa was a bit of a male chauvinist, and we all had a laugh. Then I told him the truth and that Jon greatly admired the towers as a work of art. Zampa nodded stiff thanks and puffed away on his unsightly cigar butt. Jon said it looked as if he had just been putting the finishing touches on the towers.

"Almos'," Zampa said. "I gotta get de tops done befo' dey make me take it all down."

Jon's eyes flashed. "Who's going to make you take it down?"

"De city—all dem basta'ds down dere."

He had plainly had a bad night of it, and the buoyancy I had seen in him the day before had fled. Jon looked at me. "Is that true?"

"I think Mr. Zampa is just a little depressed today."

"I got a feelin', miss," Zampa said.

"Get rid of it," I said. "We're going to fight and we're going to win."

He looked at me with his plaster-caked brows askew. "I t'ink you jus' sayin' dat, miss."

"And I think you're feeling sorry for yourself all of a sudden, Mr. Zampa." I waved toward the towers. "Anyone who had the strength and the courage to build these," I said, "is a very special human being. Don't start giving up now—after everything."

He waggled the cigar around in his jaw awhile and then looked at Jon. "She some tough lady, huh?"

"Very," Jon said soberly. "She also happens to be right."

Zampa shrugged. "Maybe," he said. "An' maybe I been blessed to get dis far, huh? Maybe dey catchin' up wit' me late 'cause so far I got an angel up dere helpin', huh? And now de angel say, 'Okay, Zampa, you done, so time you gotta pay up,' huh? You know what I'm sayin'?"

"Sure," I said, "but what kind of angel makes you suffer for doing something wonderful?"

Zampa took out a small clamshell from his vest pocket and fingered it carefully. "Maybe he don' t'ink what I done is so nice, huh?"

"We'll show him he's wrong," I said.

"What'sa matta'," he asked, "de judge ain't enough—you gotta fuss wit' an angel, too, huh?"

I smiled and took his arm. "The devil used to be an angel before he got to be the devil," I said, "did you know that?"

"Sure, I know," he said.

"Well, maybe your angel isn't such a peach, either."

It took him a couple of seconds to catch and then he smiled and then he laughed out loud until he began to cough from his cigar and he coughed worse and finally he threw the sodden stem away in disgust and began walking toward his shack. We tagged along and I explained the legal strategy I had in mind for him and why I thought he had nothing to lose by pleading not guilty. The idea—that the towers were art and not commerce and therefore subject to higher if not heavenly license—appealed to the spiritualist in him. Besides, he said, it was true: he never intended the towers to serve any purpose beyond his own amusement.

In court a couple of hours later, he looked more presentable than when we had left him and the rankness about him had faded. He was not exactly ebullient but his heart had plainly returned. He sang out "Not guilty" in full throat. Judge Lombard, already weary at the prospect of so contentious a prisoner in the dock, set the pre-trial hearing for the following week.

On the drive back to the junkyard—to which he reluctantly consented in response to my claim that we needed to confer—I asked Zampa how he was going to crown his towers or were they just going to end in a point. He said he wasn't sure but would decide soon, and anyway what was wrong with just points. I said I wasn't competent to answer that but my instincts told me the towers wanted something a little special to signal their completion. He said maybe—and the only thing he knew for sure was that they weren't going to have any crucifixes on top. Actually, I had thought that might be just what he was considering—or perhaps I'd hoped so because my job in court might be a good deal easier if I could claim that this humble artisan had rendered a towering tribute to the blessed Trinity. I said to him I supposed the Church would have to approve any crosses he might want to install and I could understand how, having invested all those years in the work, he didn't need the priests to certify it. That wasn't it, he said. "I ain't no real Cat'olic no more, see? De priests, dey don' care 'bout people—only sin. Dey hate sin plenty but dey don' love de people who do de sinnin'." I asked if he was speaking from first-hand experience. He said, "Sure t'ing—I ain't de angel Gabriel."

While I never promoted Gabriel Zampa to membership in the heavenly host, I suppose I began to suspect subconsciously that there was at least a touch of the divine about his extraordinary handiwork. Miraculous may have been a bit too heavy a judgment, but for an unschooled and virtually penniless man to have worked that hard that long and fashioned something that glorious, a kind of visionary compulsion well beyond inspired habit must have taken possession of him. There was the temptation, in presuming that his gifted hands had been mystically ordained, to hope that an allied force would energize my defense of him, but I did not wait to be smitten by a burst of choral guidance performed at the decibel level of the Mormon Tabernacle Choir. I checked out every angle, pure and simple, and was as thoroughly prepped as I had ever been for a pre-trial session.

This disproportionate outlay of effort stemmed in part, no doubt, from the nature of my work since I had renounced charity cases in behalf of the public good. I had honored my pledge to the firm in that regard quite to the letter, and no one questioned the circumstances that had brought me the Zampa assignment. And while I had not attracted corporate or commercial clients of any substance—and was not likely to until my reputation as something of a headline-luring hellion subsided—I was summoned now to virtually every major transaction framed by the firm, ostensibly to assess the impact of the tax laws on the arrangements proposed, but in fact to detect any other legal booby traps in whatever merger, leaseback, spin-off, write-off, or sell-off was contemplated. It was not creative work for the most part but it was essential stuff, the grist of dynamic enterprise, and I knew it. To the uninitiated client, I sometimes appeared to be drowsing at the edge of a two-hour conference, obscured from the action behind pyramids of paper. But the first instant the proceedings hit choppy water in zones of my special competence, I sent up a warning flare and proposed a course that would avoid all shoals, or at least minimize the risks of running aground. Vigilance rather than ingenuity, rhetoric, or a quick lay was what I was there to provide. It was my final season of grooming for the high stakes, and I did not resent my temporary role as a vital accessory or fret any more whether profiteering clients were morally deserving of my prudent counsel. Indeed, I blocked out every urge to calibrate the worthiness of the clientele, telling myself that all organisms do what they must to survive and grow. I was not above grading them, however, for intelligence, civility, and traces of lambent humor that surfaced with exceeding rarity during those generally dour discourses. Thus, to strut my stuff in behalf of beleaguered Gabriel Zampa, as remote and unprofitable a departure from my daily rounds as the practice of law could provide under my newly prescribed regimen, seemed positively recreational as well as an act of kindness.

My first aim at the pre-trial, of course, was to have the case thrown out. I gave it a good run. "I would submit, your honor, that the statutory requirement under which my client is attacked does not apply—and was never intended to apply—to metalwork sculptures such as these," I began and handed up to the judge photographs of the towers. The allegedly violated paragraph of the building code stated that

> a building permit shall be obtained before work is commenced upon any excavation for a building, structure or wall or upon the erection, construction, extension, alteration, repair, moving, removal or demolition of any building, structure, foundation, sign, marquee, billboard, wall or any part of same. . . .

"In defining these terms, your honor, Paragraph 401 of the code describes a building as 'a structure enclosed within exterior walls . . . and designated for housing, shelter, and support of people, animals, or property'—and Mr. Zampa's towers are plainly not buildings under that definition," I said. "Nor are they even classifiable as a 'structure,' which the building code defines as 'an assembly of materials forming a construction for occupancy or use'—let me stress those words 'for occupancy or use'—'including among others, buildings . . . reviewing stands, platforms, staging, observation towers, radio towers, water tanks . . . shelters and display signs.' Mr. Zampa's works are plainly not observation towers—there are no stairs to the top and no one is invited on his private property to scale them— and they are not radio towers nor do they have any other utilitarian value."

"You're not denying that they're towers, are you, Miss Hill?" asked the judge.

"They are works of art, your honor, which you or I might describe as towers, but the artist or any observer might just as readily conceive of them as representing something else."

"Like what?"

"Oh—perhaps the masts of three ships—say, the *Nina*, the *Pinta*, and the *Santa Maria*—or perhaps the Holy Trinity."

"But objectively speaking, they're still towers," the judge said.

"However they're perceived, they were intended as works of art—and as such are neither buildings nor structures according to the definitions of each in the building code. These are not— and have never been—intended for occupancy by people or animals or for any commercial use. They are strictly a form of personal artistic expression and thus fall beyond the city's legitimate police-power interests."

The judge turned to the assistant prosecutor, a boyish beanpole named Drutman whom I had not confronted before. He hurriedly re-examined the statutory language I had cited and waded in. "Counsel is seeking dismissal on mere semantics," Drutman said. "Whatever else it is, the thing in question is undeniably 'an assembly of materials forming a construction' and therefore, a 'structure' under the statute. The list of structures cited in the code is by way of example and not intended to be a limitation, as indicated by the operative word 'including.'"

"Mr. Drutman is avoiding the restrictive words I emphasized in the statute," I countered. "It says '. . . forming a construction for occupancy or use' and goes on to give examples, all of which are plainly different in kind from Mr. Zampa's sculpture."

Drutman paused a moment before the unforeseen obstacle I had thrown up and then he saw his route around it. "Is counsel suggesting the defendant's artwork is useless?"

"In the sense the statute employs the word 'use'—yes."

"Counsel cannot have it both ways," said the young prosecutor. "To the extent the defendant's handiwork constitutes art, it presumably brings feelings of pleasure, delight, inspiration, or what-have-you to the onlooker, and that is hardly a useless function. On the other hand, counsel's proclaiming these large metal objects as sculpture does not necessarily make them so—any more than I can escape liability under the law for driving my car into a fire hydrant by claiming the resulting mess is an act of self-expression. The city's position is simply that the esthetic content of Mr. Zampa's structures is irrelevant to the statutory requirement that anyone building anything of any size has to get a permit so that the public safety can be assured."

Very good, Drutman. But he was playing into my hand. "The esthetic content may be of no relevance to the city," I said, "but it has been of the essence to Mr. Zampa. Perhaps our position will be illuminated, your honor, by reference to Paragraph 202 of the code which points up the basic—I am tempted to say absurdity—of the city's position." The law said:

With each application for a permit the applicant shall file two complete sets of acceptable blueprints of plans drawn to scale and two sets of specifications for the work. Such plans and specifications shall show clearly and fully all dimensions, and give a complete description of the kind and quality of materials, the method of construction, the sizes of all structural members, thickness of walls, piers, buttresses, etc., the purposes of which all parts of the structure are to be used, the width, depth, and height of the structure, story heights, exit facilities and any other information which may be required by the building department.

"It is inconceivable, your honor," I said, snapping shut the municipal code, "that the defendant could have provided such information in such a form to any city bureau—and unthinkable that he or any artist be asked to do so before the fact—or after it, for that matter. Gabriel Zampa had no more idea of the eventual form that his works of sculpture would take—or their extent or their materials—than Mr. Drutman over here can predict what I'm going to have for lunch tomorrow. This requirement most assuredly does not apply to works of art that cannot be rationally and statistically prefigured on blueprints or any other way. Spontaneity is the essence of the creative process, and in moving for dismissal of the charges, I respectfully ask that the city not be permitted to confuse prior restraint of artistic expression—which enjoys a privileged position under the First Amendment among the most cherished rights of Americans—with zealous enforcement of the law."

Drutman was perplexed by this frontal assault. "I don't quite understand," he confessed. "Is counsel suggesting that the building and zoning codes under which these charges are brought are unconstitutional? If so, that's patent nonsense. There is a truckload of case law to the contrary. The state's power to regulate building activity has long been established."

"But not its power to regulate personal expression," I jumped in. "We're not arguing that the statute is unconstitutional on its face—it clearly is not—but only if, as, and when it is applied to works of art or other protected forms of expression."

"That's complete and utter nonsense," said the young prosecutor, a tremor of panic in his strident voice. "In order to exist, the state has to curtail everybody's liberties to a certain degree —otherwise every wild-eyed defendant could come in here and claim that every statute on the books is an undue restraint on his freedom to run amuck. The plain fact is that Mr. Zampa chose not to obey a perfectly justified ordinance, and Miss Hill here is attacking the law instead of defending her client."

"I'm inclined to agree," Judge Lombard said. "This is not the place to challenge a long-standing municipal statute on constitutional grounds, Miss Hill. I'm denying your motion for dismissal."

"I am not challenging its constitutionality, your honor, only how the city seeks to apply it in this case."

"I don't see the distinction," said the judge. "Your client built something—whatever it is—and that's what the building code exists for. I won't hear any argument on federal grounds, Miss Hill. Now may we get on with it?"

It was about what I had expected. Local magistrates are not precisely famous for their zeal in protecting First Amendment freedoms. But I had put the point into the record and would pursue it at the trial, however briefly Lombard let me, by way of paving the route to more sensitive tribunals. I had not shared that somewhat obscure intention with my client, who sat at the table trying to follow the byplay between the lawyers and understanding—by the wounded look on his face—only that he had not won the opening round.

But I had another arrow in my quiver that suddenly seemed far more promising in its trajectory than the first. The city, I now claimed, had no authority to go after Zampa because the state criminal code plainly stated that "a prosecution for a petty offense or one not entailing a jail sentence must be commenced within one year after the commission thereof." The city building code provided, moreover, that no offense to it was recognized until ten days after a written notice of violation had been served upon the offending party by a building inspector; prosecution could follow only upon failure to comply with the ten-day notice to remedy the violation.

"Therefore, your honor," I said, "when the city duly handed Mr. Zampa its notice of violation five years and sixty-eight days ago, it had to wait ten days before it could proceed with its prosecution. After that, it had exactly three hundred fifty-five more days to prosecute. The record shows that it did no such thing. State law indisputably holds that an action at this late date cannot be countenanced, and I ask dismissal on this unambiguous ground."

Drutman, having prevailed in our first skirmish, was calmer now. He was also prepared for the issue I raised. "The building code is equally unambiguous, your honor," he replied. "It says that 'each day of the continuance of said violation, after having been notified by a building inspector in writing, of said violation, shall constitute a separate and distinct offense, for each of which offenses said person shall be punished by a fine of not more than twenty-five dollars nor less than ten dollars.' Now the facts are not in dispute, I believe. Mr. Zampa was duly served in writing—a precondition of prosecution by the city. He had ten days to apply for his building permit. At the same time he would have had to seek a variance for a nonconforming use from the zoning board of appeals because his towers had already exceeded the height limit under the building code. But Mr. Zampa did neither of these things. And he has not done them since. And each day that he has failed to do so since the initial ten-day grace period is, according to the law, an entirely new and fresh offense, punishable by a fine. The city has been lenient—till now—but now the law's command must be executed."

"No," I said, charging out from behind our table, "the city has not been lenient—it has been negligent. Even if we assume —which the defense does not—that Mr. Zampa's artwork was a cause of action under the building code, the city failed to act within the statutory period provided. All other factors must fall before this governing rule of law."

"Mr. Zampa's actions," Drutman came back, "constitute a continuous crime, not an isolated incident. The most prominent case on point defines a continuous offense as 'a breach of the criminal law not terminated by a single act or fact, but which subsists for a definite period and constitutes successive similar breaches. . . .' Now I submit to your honor that such a definition sounds as if it had been composed with our very case in mind. Mr. Zampa continues to be in violation of the law on both counts—he still has no building permit and his towers are still taller than the code permits. His is an ongoing crime, and no legalistic sleight-of-hand can relieve him of his failure to act within the law."

Drutman was making all the properly implacable noises prescribed for fledgling prosecutors but he kept leaving the door open a crack. "Just who is acting outside the law," I declared, "seems plain enough. Surely the assistant prosecutor recognizes that the state criminal code supersedes any municipal ordinances in conflict with it. He seems, moreover, to suppose that the Amity building code is self-executing—and that is exactly what it is not, according to its own internal language. On the one hand, the code says that every day a violation persists constitutes 'a separate and distinct offense.' On the other hand, it says no offense can be prosecuted except on written notice of the violation. Therefore, in order to bring an action against Mr. Zampa, the city would have had to issue a new notice of violation for every single day that it wished to claim he had committed an offense. It never did. Can it plausibly appear here, in this late season, and claim that a single notice of violation—issued more than five years and two months ago—covers nearly two thousand ensuing 'separate and distinct' offenses, not one of which was called to the defendant's attention in writing as statutorily required? That is not due process of law, your honor. That is bad government." To bring any action at all against Zampa, I concluded, the city would have had to serve him with a notice of violation no longer ago than one year prior to the date of his arraignment—and it had not done so. The court therefore had no business entertaining the city's action on any count.

Drutman looked as if he had been skewered. He took a moment to catch his breath and consult his notes. Then he tried a more subdued approach. "Counsel is again trying to escape the city's legitimate jurisdiction by wriggling off the hook on a technicality."

"Your honor, Mr. Drutman seems unaware that due process is no mere cosmetic. What he calls a technicality means the law is to be followed as written, not on the prosecutor's whim."

"Your honor, Miss Hill is being preposterous," Drutman said, retreating to the abusive language that is the sure sign of an advocate's dwindling confidence. "Two provisions of the building code had been violated in this case—pure and simple —and have never stopped being violated. The statute of limitations was never intended to cover such instances of repeated and unceasing lawlessness. And it is nonsensical to suppose that the city government can employ enough people to keep inspecting the site of every building code irregularity on a day-to-day basis and issue fresh notices of violation. They would have time to do nothing else. In this case, the perpetrator was required to apply to two municipal bodies—the building department and the zoning board—in order to have the violations lifted, and his continuing failure to do so was, *ipso facto*, all the proof city officials needed that he was not yet in compliance with the law—and is still not."

Judge Lombard parted us. "All right," he said, "I think there is merit on both sides. If I take your position, Mr. Drutman, that Mr. Zampa has been sinning non-stop for all these years, I cannot escape Miss Hill's point that the code defines his action not as one big long sin but as a series of consecutive separate and discrete sins. And even if we discount, for the moment, her argument that the city failed to provide daily notice of these sins—since, as you suggest, this is rather an impractical requirement—we must still face the state criminal code, which gives you only the one year to prosecute following notice of violation. I will therefore hold that the city's failure to prosecute before now has fatally damaged its claim to fines against the defendant for any period beyond one year. I will accept the city's theory of a continuous offense, however, and hold that the original notice of violation was sufficient to permit the prosecutor at this time to ask a year's worth of fines. I think that should be enough to satisfy you, Mr. Drutman."

In splitting the difference between us, the judge had of course ruled inconsistently, but that was routine for the Court of Common Pleas. What mattered was that Zampa's maximum exposure to city fines had been reduced massively. The remainder could still doom him to perpetual pauperdom but at least we were no longer locked in a nightmare of Kafkaesque justice. Zampa's eyes, like gleaming pinpoints, told me he knew we were rallying.

All that remained that morning was for me to win him a jury trial, and I so requested. The city, no doubt fearing a swell of sympathy for the old man, said the crime was not serious enough to warrant a jury and thought the judge could readily decide since no facts were in dispute.

I asked the prosecutor what he meant by a "serious" crime, and he said any one punishable by a jail sentence. The federal courts, I suggested, thought otherwise. "You will recall, your honor, that the Supreme Court, in *Duncan v. Louisiana,* looked to the severity of the punishment authorized as the most relevant indication of the seriousness of the offense in a given case—not the sentence finally meted out. And the Sixth Circuit held a few years later that a fine of five hundred dollars in a criminal contempt case against a company worth twenty million was no petty matter and warranted a jury trial." I turned toward my tatterdemalion client. "Now while the line between what is a 'serious' crime and what is a 'petty' one has not been sharply drawn by the courts, I submit, your honor, that the astronomical fine to which Mr. Zampa is statutorily subject, even under your humane ruling of a moment ago—no less than seven thousand dollars and possibly up to eighteen thousand—would make this a very serious case indeed to almost anyone save an oil sheik or a baseball star. To a man of virtually no means, it would mean ruin for the rest of his life."

Lombard bought it. Jury trial was set for the following month.

"We done okay, huh?" Zampa asked, clamping his hat on the moment we got beyond the courtroom door.

"Not bad," I said.

He hung by me as we threaded through the courthouse throng. "You believe all dat you say in dere?" he asked me only when we reached the outside steps.

"Every word," I said.

He nodded. "I t'ink you done real good, miss."

"For a girl—"

"For anyt'ing," he said. "Dat boy, he didn' know nuttin' like you do."

"Thank you, Mr. Zampa," I said, putting my arm through his before he got run over in the traffic, and steered us to my car. I asked if he wanted to drive home. He said he had never learned. I offered to teach him some time. When he was finished with the towers, he said, meaning, I suppose, that given a choice, he'd rather break his neck vertically than horizontally.

344

28

Jonathan willingly accepted my invitation to lunch as soon as I told him I needed his help to save the old man. We met in our old Greek haunt—because it was out of the way, I explained, not for sentimental entrapment. He said he didn't doubt it and that emotional scenes had never been my theater of operation. I asked after Jessica, and he said she was warm and funny and terrific. I said that was good and he should be nice to her. "I'm always nice," he said.

"When you're nice," I said.

He pinched his lips together in feigned contrition, which was about as close as he had ever come to conceding that conditional judgment of him. "There's only one thing about Jessie," he said, deflecting my aim.

"She's flat-chested?"

"I hadn't noticed."

"She's ugly?"

"No, I think she's great-looking—in a sort of Rubensesque way."

"I would have said Renoir, myself. She always makes me feel scrawny. Well, I know she doesn't have B.O., so what's the problem?"

"She hovers," he said.

"What's that mean?"

"I mean she always is there—any time I turn around."

"Where did you want her to be?"

"Well—around, more or less—in the vicinity—but not *right* there, almost on top of me."

"Maybe she likes you. Maybe she thinks you like her?"

"Sure," he said, "but not every minute. I mean, doesn't she have anything else to do?"

"She writes poetry."

"Not when I'm around."

"Then ask her to."

"I'm afraid she'll take it wrong."

"I'd risk it. She's a big girl in more ways than one. I think she'd respect you for being straightforward."

"I'm not so sure."

I told him not to underestimate her but acknowledged I hadn't ever been very good at advice to the lovelorn, having as I did a different counseling specialty. That got us to Zampa and my little stratagem. I asked him if he didn't agree that the towers ought to be called to the world's attention and the old man granted a measure of recognition for his achievement.

"Of course," Jon said.

"Good," I said, "because you're going to be privileged to direct the show."

"What show?"

"We're going to put Gabriel Zampa on the map. He's going to become a genuine culture-hero overnight—an impoverished folk-artist who worked twenty years in the wilderness creating a masterpiece that his callous and ungrateful city wants to punish him for now. It's a heart-gripping story—and it may just help me get him off. But I can't do the p.r. on it myself because I'm his lawyer. What we need is a Zampa Defense Committee—a small group of humane art lovers dedicated to spreading the word about this savage injustice. It's got to be a kind of media blitz so every potential juror in town will know all about Zampa and think the city's persecuting the bejesus out of him instead of chasing junkies and hookers."

Jon looked a little glum at the prospect. "I don't know," he said.

"Why not? If you believe in him?"

"You make it all sound like a hustle."

"Only because I'm under the gun. The fucking bureaucrats are trying to kill him."

"Who says the old man wants to become a culture hero? I mean, how do you know that won't kill him as much as the city assholes? The guy is totally off the wall, he can't speak the language, he's practically a hermit—why bother him if that's the way he likes it?"

"Because he can't hide out any longer. They've caught up with him, don't you see? You and I can look at what he's done and cry for joy, but these other shitheads decide he's just an idiot tinkerer in a junkyard and want to stone him. Somebody has to mobilize an effort in his behalf or they'll get the poor bastard for sure."

He saw the point. "But why me?" he asked. "You ought to get someone famous."

"Because I can trust you. Because I can tell you what I need. Because you're an up-and-coming local architect known for your commitment to high standards. And because famous people won't break their asses to save him—and that's what has to be done for the next couple of weeks."

Jon nodded and thought about it another few seconds. Then he said okay but that he'd never been a flack before and he wouldn't know where to begin. I leaned across the table and kissed his face and promised to help. On a hunch I recommended that he enlist Lee Nightingale for starters since she was a bona-fide artist and he liked her work. And maybe she could get the owner of the gallery that showed her paintings to join the effort. And maybe her husband, with his university connections, could bring in a professorial bigwig or two. "But he's in your firm," said Jon. "Why don't you just ask him?"

"Because I've got to keep at arm's length. The firm's already got me down as Clarence Darrow in drag."

"Not to mention Sam Nightingale's ex-lover," he said.

I felt a small shiver from public overexposure. "Not exactly," I said.

"Close enough, I gather."

"Who from?"

"Who do you think?"

"The hoverer?"

He laughed. "I thought you dug her."

"I do. But she talks too much."

"She thinks you're Wonder Woman."

"She's gonna get one of my miraculous bracelets as an I.U.D. if she doesn't learn to hush her yap."

We agreed the first two steps were to form the defense committee and have it put out a short descriptive brochure on the towers. Meanwhile, I would prepare Zampa for the coming glare and try to interest Duckett Washburn and the Coop people in embracing the towers as a community landmark. Despite all setbacks, the Coop's hegemony had widened steadily, encompassing several dozen block organizations now, and its growing discipline and purposefulness made ultimate reclamation of the Gully no longer seem quite such a fool's errand.

The old man's back was bothering him when I drove out through the Gully the next day to see him. I had looked in vain for him in the upper reaches of the towers and decided to try his shack. He asked who it was without opening the door and when I told him, he came and unlatched it and, looking more peaked than I had seen him before, invited me in. It was close and dank and dark. He dusted off the single chair in the room with his hand and presented it to me as if it were a throne while he sat nearby on the edge of the small metal cot he slept on. Water was boiling on an old wood-burning stove and he offered me a cup of tea which I said would be fine, thanks. He reached for a few chunks of a chopped-up door from the wood bin and shoved them in the burner to hurry the water along. The stove, it was clear, doubled as his furnace, the way the deep kitchen sink beside it must also have functioned as his bath. An empty can of sardines sat on the sink edge—a vestige of his lunch or maybe dinner the night before. A towel and a shirt and a pair of pants drooped from hooks in the corner next to a tiny w.c. There was no electricity anywhere I could see—only a couple of candlesticks, one on a low metal cabinet that served as his dresser, the other on the round wooden table where I was sitting. On it lay open a volume of the *Encyclopaedia Britannica*—he must have found it somewhere in his scavenging since none of its companion volumes was anywhere in view; it was turned to a color plate showing precious gems. How he could make out much of it I didn't know, for the two skinny windows in the shack were boarded up three quarters of the way—to keep out the thieving kids, he said. Last time they had taken his portable radio, the only pawnable thing he owned, so he decided to barricade the place. The effect was not what you would call cozy.

"Used to be diff'ren'," he said. The children in the neighborhood, when there was one, would bring him old glass and busted crockery for the towers, and he would pay them a penny or two for each offering and got to be not exactly a beloved figure but an admired one among the small fry. He would let them hang around the yard, playing whatever make-believe games the current crop of junk parts inspired, and sometimes they were even allowed to dangle off the lowest rungs of the towers if they took care not to damage the inlay. But then some of the parents found out that kids were stealing perfectly good glassware and china and breaking it to peddle to the tower builder and they stopped it—"an' den I run outa money so dey got no use fo' me no mo' afta' dat an' curse me, like dey say I'm a spick-nut an' dirty dago cuckoo an' all like dat, you know? An' dey break t'ings off what I make, dey bust de shells an' de glass, an' dey come in here afta' anyt'ing dey t'ink I got." There were rumors he had hidden away money in the walls of the shack and even that he had buried his wife under the main tower which he had built as a kind of pyramid to her.

"Did you?"

"What?"

"Bury your wife under the big tower?"

"Hey, what do you t'ink—I'm crazy?"

"Then where is your wife?"

"Who knows?"

"You mean she's lost?"

"I'm de lost one. I leave her fo'ty years ago in Mass'chusetts."

"Forty years—and you haven't seen her since?"

"She write me once."

"And?"

"An' nuttin'."

"You didn't write back?"

"I hate her."

"Why?"

"She crabbed all de time—said I drink too much, you know?"

"Did you?"

"Yeah, sure—f'om listenin' to her. She make me crazy."

"Is she the reason you don't like women?"

"Who say dat?"

"I'm guessing."

"Dat ain't nice. I like de women—de nice ones. Dey jus' like men, you know—some nice, some bitches."

"I know," I said. "Don't you miss them?"

He shrugged. "How you mean—in bed?"

"Every way. I live by myself, too—don't you ever get lonely?"

"Sure t'ing," he said. "I got peace, though." The largely Italian and Greek composition of the neighborhood had broken down twenty years before, he said, and it was true that most of his friends had gone, to be replaced by blacks and Hispanics among whom he remained a distant curiosity, neither of them nor against them. But he had his yard and he had his ever-rising towers and somebody or other was always coming by even if it was usually nobody he much wanted to see, and he had had his radio till they stole it. He sorely missed the radio, he confessed, for the music and news and he had been saving to get a new one but the junk business was very bad just then—he'd sold only a claw-foot tub and some copper tubing all that week for a grand total of twelve dollars—and he was low on groceries so the radio had to wait.

It seemed an appropriate moment to present him with the gift I had brought. He was not in the habit of getting gifts and looked perplexed when I handed him the flat tin of Schimmelpenninck cigars. He examined the box with care, caressing its rounded corners and dwelling upon the curlicued pattern imprinted all over it as if it were a rare lithograph. "What's dis?" he finally asked. It was for him, I said. He opened it cautiously and I watched his eyes devour the ten slender cylinders packed tightly inside. I told him they were my favorite brand. His eyes dilated still wider. "You smoke dese?" he asked.

"One a day—maybe two on Sunday. They're very nice."

He shook his head a fraction, restraining his disapproval, and then gave the box a sniff. "Ver' nice," he agreed. "Where dey from—Tampa?"

"They're Dutch—from Indonesia, I think."

"Asia?"

"Well, sort of."

"Nothin' good come f'om Asia," he said.

"How about your tea?"

"It ain't good—jus' cheap."

I smiled and urged him to try a cigar. His stubby, grime-darkened fingertips had trouble dislodging the first one. When he finally freed it, he spun it a few times and savored its shape and aroma like any connoisseur before wetting the tapered end and sticking it in his mouth. I lit it for him and he drank in the taste with great relish. It was hot and it was dry, he said, but it was also sweet and delicious. He thanked me for the cigars and then remembered to offer me one but I would not deprive him of that one extra treat, so we sat there having tea while the little room soon filled with his pungent smoke. He asked me why I had given him a gift when I was the one who deserved it. To lift his spirits, I said, but he said that except for a slight sprain in his back he was feeling good and for me not to bother about him so much and to mind my paying customers. But he was not ungrateful. He extended the cigar sideways toward me in a gesture of tribute and puffed away for a while with such contentment that I would not disrupt his hazy reverie with conversation. Finally, I told him that I was making plans for the trial and might want him to testify even though he didn't have to. He said he would if it would help but he didn't speak the language so well and besides, what could he say? "You could say why you built the towers," I said.

"Why I build 'em?" He squinted at me hard through the wreath of smoke. "Who knows?" he said.

I smiled. "That won't help much in court."

He shrugged. "What am I s'posed to say?"

"The truth."

"De trut'? I done it 'cause I like to build t'ings—dat's all."

"But why these things? And why so big—and so fancy?"

"'Cause eve'yt'ing aroun' was gettin' ugly—an' I wanna make a beautiful t'ing."

"You were fighting back, sort of?"

He consulted the ember of his cigar. "I neva' t'ink of it like dat 'zac'ly," he said, "but maybe you right."

I asked him to think harder about it and said I'd be back in a few days to let him know how everything was going. Only when I left and he doffed his hat did I realize that he had had it on the whole time I was there.

On the way back downtown, I stopped by the Washburns' place, hoping to catch Lenore for a few minutes. To my surprise, and subsequent chagrin, Duckett was there as well. He had been laid off from his hospital job a few days before on suspicion of having helped himself to some drugs again; in fact, he said, word had come down that his sacking was a straight reprisal for his role as instigator of the Boot Coop's running guerrilla tactics against the city. I said all they probably cared about downtown were the lawsuits and he should have blamed them on me. "He did," Lenore said, "but they can't get to you, honey."

It was not the ideal moment to ask for a favor, but the timing was out of my hands. I had a client in need. After commiserating with them a few moments over the backward turn in their fortunes and urging that Geronimo Jones do battle in Duckett's behalf, I told them about Zampa.

"The junkyard spick?" Duckett asked.

"I don't think of him quite like that," I said.

"Oh, right," he said, "shut my racist face. But what're you doin' with that dirty ol' bum anyhow? I thought you retired from the do-good line o' work."

I explained how I had been drafted for the job and the nature of the unjust charges against the old man. Duckett said it was no surprise because the city had been hauling in not only the Coop ringleaders but everyone in the Gully they could find lately who made a habit of flagrantly flouting the law. I asked him if he'd ever had a good look at Zampa's towers, and he said he had always thought they had something to do with the power company and steered clear. I said that was a shame because the towers were by far the most beautiful thing in the whole city and they were just about completed and I thought a wonderful way to call attention to the Coop's efforts to rebuild the Gully might be to make a big occasion of it when Zampa put on the finishing touches. And if we could drum up enough acclaim for the towers as works of art, the city might be persuaded to create a park or build a playground or somehow mark the site and acknowledge the community's pride in so unique an achievement—"like a symbol of resurrection, sort of," I said.

"And that way," Duckett added, "they'd stop tryin' to put his dumb ass in hock."

"You got it," I said.

He looked at Lenore with a leer as if to say I was up to my old tricks again. Then he said, "First off, this cat ain't no brother. He's just an old loon an' from what I hear he gives the kids a bad time when they go by his yard."

"First off," I said, "he's your neighbor and he's lived here most of his life and he hasn't split like every other non-black— that should tell you something about whether he's a brother."

"He's just screwy, honey—that don't make him a brother," said Lenore.

"Whatever he is," I said, "he's never bothered anyone—it's the kids who are hassling him, the way he tells it. I'm not sure whether he hasn't called the cops because he's afraid the little sweeties'll carve him up for it or that he'd remind some city hall asshole he's doing his thing out there without their permission. The point is that he's not the enemy—and you might do him and yourselves a very big favor—not to mention me—by making a hero out of him, at least for a little while."

Lenore offered a sour look that said they already had quite enough problems, thank you, without my embroiling them in one that seemed this removed. I read that chilled silence of hers and said I never would have bothered them if I didn't think this was something important. "Depends whose ass is gettin' gored, honey," she said. I told her I thought it was a mistake to take a narrow view of the thing, and she said any other kind was meddlesome and sure to backfire on them. I told her to suit herself and got up to leave when Duckett finally said he figured they owed me one but he wasn't sure this was it. I said they didn't owe me a thing and I thought what I was proposing was as much to their advantage as Zampa's. All I wanted them to do was have a look at the towers during the next day or two—while I was checking out what could be done about getting Duckett his job back. That was when Lenore saw the light.

29

The gears began to mesh. Within forty-eight hours, my chief field officer reported in with good news. Jonathan said I had guessed right about Lee Nightingale, that she had been flattered to be asked in as part of the Zampa rescue mission, and when he drove her out to see the towers, was totally smitten by them. Lee, in turn, enlisted Michael Tillinghast, the owner of her gallery, who could not believe his eyes; he, in turn, touted the towers to Cyrus Bellevue Brady, Mather's sterling architectural historian and one of the nation's ranking figures in the field. "I studied with him," Jon said. "He's a howitzer. Lee says he told Tillinghast he'd help us write the brochure if we want him to. I think maybe we're in business, kid."

Gabriel Zampa was no longer my personal property—or wouldn't be for long. I felt a little like Margaret Mead must have among the aborigines: eager to have her news spread but fearful the exposure would devastate the specimens. I asked Jon what the old man had made of all the comings and goings. He said there was no sign of him outside when he and Lee had gone up, and the others probably didn't know he lived in the shack—and, at any rate, were undoubtedly eager to make a getaway before the muggers caught their scent. It was possible, then, that Zampa had no clue yet of what was brewing. I told Jon to give me another couple of days to accustom our uninitiated recluse to the idea of celebrity.

When I appeared the following noontime toting one of the red-and-blue-striped shopping bags I saved from the Mather

University Store, Zampa eyed me cagily and asked, "What're yo'—Miss San'a Claus or somet'in'?" I laughed and said hardly, but that I had passed an old antique shop on State Street the day before and something caught my eye that I wanted him to have for the towers if he thought they belonged—and if not, I would keep them myself. I set the bag down carefully on his table. All he could see was the crumpled tissue paper on top cushioning its mysterious contents. "What's in dat?" he asked with the directness of a threadbare Dickensian waif.

"See for yourself," I said.

The bag was plump and appealing. He circled the table cautiously as if trying to decide on just the right angle to attack it. As he was about to spring, he checked himself and looked over at me. "Why you do dis, miss? I ain't done nuttin' fo' you."

What to say to someone so little surfeited with kindness? Each time I saw him, this untidy, inarticulate, malodorous old baggage managed to move me deeply. But it was essential that I not let on. "You've done a wonderful thing for everybody," I said and motioned toward his towers.

"I done dat fo' me," he said. "Nobody gotta t'ank me fo' it."

"I know—but I want to. You can't make me not want to."

He shook his head a lot while making one last slow, complete circle around the table. Then he took off his hat and held it next to his heart and gave me a supple little bow of thanks. I responded with a full flowing curtsy that made him smile and then we both closed in on my package. The stuffing flew out every which way till I told him to be careful. With a delicacy surprising for such large steely fingers, he fished through the tissue paper till he produced a small round corrugated bottle in cobalt blue. It was about the size of a Christmas tree ball with a similar little neck but much heftier. His hand closed gingerly about it as he tested its tensile quality. The thing almost disappeared within his palm but proved no fragile geegaw. "I neva' seen nuttin' like dis," he said, closely inspecting its cross-hatched surface.

"Keep looking," I said, inviting him to dip back into the bag.

He brought out two more of the little globes, a white one embossed with the scene of a hunter cocking a rifle skyward and a dark red one showing a vee of geese or some general-purpose waterfowl darting for the horizon. He regarded the new pair as well as if they had come directly from King Tut's tomb. "Vera', ver' beautiful, miss," he said, arranging them together on the table. "Hey," he noticed, "dey red, white, an' blue—you know?"

"I know." It was hardly an accident. I explained that they were called target bottles and used to be made a hundred years ago for hunters to practice their shooting.

His brow became a single thick furrow of puzzlement. "Dey made dese t'ings jus' to break 'em?"

"I'm afraid so," I said. "That's why they're not many left."

He picked the blue one up and fondled it. "Dey strong," he said, "an' t'ick." I could see his brain cells percolating. "I t'ink maybe I use 'em, huh?"

"I'd like that," I said.

"Maybe on top, huh? One fo' each—like fo' de United States of America, huh?"

I just nodded.

"Dat's what you was t'inkin', maybe, huh?"

"Yes."

"I cement 'em in good 'n' tight—way up so none o' de kids can get 'em, huh?"

"Yes."

"Only one t'ing, miss."

"What?"

"I gotta pay you fo' dem."

The shop owner had asked for fifty bucks for the set; he took my thirty-five without arguing. The target-bottle market must have been down. "No," I said, "I want you to have them."

"Sure t'ing—only I'm gonna buy 'em. How much dey cost?"

"I—I can't remember."

"How much, miss?"

"I—gentlemen don't ask questions like that."

His head recoiled. Then he thought for a minute and said, "An' ladies don' smoke no ciga's. How much dey cost, miss?"

"I—a dollar each," I blurted.

"Okay," he said and reached into his back pocket, carefully

extracted three singles, and placed them on the table beside the bottles. "We got a deal," he said.

"Sure thing," I said and, exploding happily into tears, gave him a fast hug that seemed to startle him. I had never come across so much pride in so unprepossessing a package.

He put on the tea kettle and we talked. He was confused by my first name and I explained it to him and then he told me he used to have an odd nickname himself when he was a boy—Starfish. His father had been an oyster fisherman when the family moved from Haiti to Amity before the country got into the First World War. Amity Bay was still clean and quiet and shallow then—perfect for the bivalve crop—and oysters were a major export item for the state. As a boy he would go out sometimes with his father in a "sharpie," he recalled—a flat-bottomed single-master built for both speed and cargo. It was so low in the water, he remembered, you could reach over the side and rake in the oysters by the bushel or lift them up with tongs or hand-hauled dredges farther out in the Sound. They would gather as many as two hundred bushels, making for one very heavy boatload, and sometimes they'd be out there ten or twelve miles ready to come in when the wind would die, and guess who got to row them back with the single scull aboard? He'd ache so much after that he wouldn't ask his father to take him out again for weeks. But since he craved the taste of oysters, he would wade out from shore at low tide and scoop up a bucketful as if he were a human version of the oyster's most relentless natural predator, the starfish. "Dey was millions of 'em," he said. You could dredge up a cartload of seaweed and the starfish would come tumbling out by the hundreds. For hours at a stretch he and his childhood chums would watch the sea stars moving in on pincer-like feet to engulf their prey. The memory was still quick in him as he recounted how a starfish would attach a couple of its sucker arms to one valve of the oyster, then a couple to the other valve, anchor the leftover arm to a rock or a plant to give itself maximum leverage, and then slowly, slowly, but ever so relentlessly, begin to straighten out its rays. The oyster was good at defending against a strong sharp pull but not a long steady one, and the starfish, said

Zampa, "he wasn' in no hurry." Sooner or later the oyster would yield, and once the shell was partway open, other starfish swarmed in to help with the kill, the whole mess of them rolling over and over like a spiny ball, all fighting for a piece of the booty.

"So you were a starfish, too," I said and he nodded and said he was also very skinny then and could squeeze through narrow spaces the same way starfish did. I said what a fitting name it was for him, considering how adept he later became with his arms and hands. "Maybe only a human starfish could have built the towers," I said and he gave a concurring laugh.

I felt by then that he trusted me enough to consider my plan for publicizing the towers. It would help his cause a great deal, I said, if art experts and the press and the other media were asked to come and see what he had made and proclaimed what a wonderful thing it was. I told him about the small committee Jonathan was enlisting to organize the effort if Zampa had no objections and even raised the possibility of turning the topping-out of the towers into a community event and trying to get the television news people to film it. You would have thought I had asked him to address both houses of Congress buck naked, from the look that came over him. "I don' wan' none o' dat stuff," was all he said at first.

I told him I understood how he must have cherished his privacy while constructing the towers but wondered why he objected to sharing the completed work with other people. "They're a beautiful thing," I said. "They'll make a lot of people happy."

He shook his head. "Lotsa people come hea', dey gonna break it," he said. "Nobody know about it, dey don't make no fuss—an' eve'yt'ing be okay."

"But the city is suing you, Mr. Zampa, for thousands of dollars, and unless the public decides you've done something really grand out here, you could very well lose the case."

"How could I lose? I got such a good lawya'."

"You could lose because you broke the law—unless we can convince them you're a remarkable artist and answer to a higher law. You understand?"

358

He thought about that awhile and came out confused over the signals I was giving off. "You really t'ink we gonna lose, miss?"

"I didn't say that. I said we *could*. My job is to do everything I can think of to help us win. Getting the towers recognized as art is the most important thing. And you'd be famous—would you hate that so very much?"

"I ain't nobody," he said.

"You're wrong—you're the man who built the towers—the Zampa Towers."

"Once dey done, dey ain't got nuttin' to do wit' me," he said. "Dey jus' t'ings."

"No—they're alive. That's what art is. They'll always be you because you made them, don't you see?"

He went over to his cot and slumped down on it. "I don' know," he said, "you talkin' rings aroun' me."

"I'm not trying to."

"Sure, sure—I know, mis. You tryin' t' do de best fo' me."

"Look," I said, "I'll help you. My friends will help. We'll see that it's all done with dignity. Nobody wants to hurt you. All we want to do is pay you honor—everybody except the dumb fucking department of buildings."

It slipped out in a spasm of ardor. He glanced up sharply. "Dat ain't a nice way fo' no lady to talk."

I sighed and said, "Oh, for crissakes, are we back to that?" Which only made matters worse. He sat there stonily silent till I said I was sorry and hadn't meant to offend him, but nobody thought twice about using rough language any more. He considered that and finally said he supposed that if I was doing men's work, I had to use men's language, and if I really thought he should let the towers become an object of public attention, he would do it because he wasn't going to stay around there much longer anyway. "Dis ain't no place to live," he said.

The thought of his just upping and leaving the object he had worked on longest and hardest in his life—the one thing that distinguished his days on earth—saddened me terribly. I had the immediate sense the towers would be vandalized the very hour he decamped. I asked him where he would go. He said he didn't know and it didn't matter—New Bedford, maybe, where he thought he had some relatives still around. Didn't he care what happened to his towers? "Nah," he said, "you gonna make 'em famous—an' you see what happens den. I don' wanna. I got it all in my head, you know? Dat's enough."

Under ordinary circumstances, I would have dismissed as simple client paranoia Zampa's conviction that my scheming would surely hex the towers. But on his auguring tongue, private neuroticism seemed to escalate to an oracular fatalism. Yet I could not hesitate before that nearly mystic invocation and still pretend to practice my trade diligently. He was just being a superstitious old screwball, and I knew it. I called Jonathan right afterward and shifted our save-Zampa campaign into drive.

The five of us sprang out of the station wagon that bright September Saturday like a production number at a casual-wear convention—our chauffeur, Professor Brady, in properly aged tweeds, Jon in his wide-wale corduroys, gallery-owner Tillinghast in nubby Irish woolens, Lee Nightingale in expensive high boots and a dirndle, and me in jeans and a poorboy—and attacked the towers with cooing admiration. Jon and Lee drew sketches. Tillinghast took pictures. Brady made notes. And I went to drag Zampa out of hiding. He came ungrumpily, to my surprise, lifting his hat to Lee and shaking hands energetically with the men. A chorus of hosannas arose from them, and everyone wanted to know how he had built this superb thing. He gave us a tour.

A padlocked tool shed at the rear of his shack was crammed with the secrets of his art. A few leftover steel tee and angle beams were wedged into the corner behind a couple of sacks of cement, coils of chicken wire, and a pair of heavy buckets. He never kept more than a day or two of supplies on hand, he said, for fear the shed would get broken into. Scattered on a flimsy but serviceable shelf were a family of trowels in varying sizes and a batch of bric-a-brac he used to pattern the cement surface of every rod and beam and arch in that fantastic filigree he had concocted. An outdoor faucet handle produced the rosette design; a small iron gear with long sharp teeth, the sunburst effect; an old door hinge, the butterfly outline; a rusty latchclasp, the head of a tulip. There were wooden kiddy blocks with stars and hearts etched on them in relief, tin stencils of pineapples and snowflakes, fragments from grillwork gates featuring graceful swashes and exuberant curlicues, and underneath the shelf a severely dented garbage can still half-full of shattered seashells and crockery and glass. He led us to the towers, narrating en route how he had been a master bricklayer in his day, laboring on many buildings both plain and fancy, and later became a telephone lineman in rural parts of the state when building jobs grew scarce. He was accustomed to working well above the ground, so the higher his towers rose, the more they reminded him of his younger days. He had used a pickax and shovel and wheelbarrow to excavate the foundation, he explained. Jon wanted to know how deep it went. Zampa shrugged—maybe a foot and a half or two feet, he guessed with his hands. Jon gave a little gulp. But the base was filled with broken concrete under a two-inch-thick cement patio that the old man said was plenty strong enough to anchor the footings of the central tower. Brady wanted to know how he had shaped the steel struts that ringed the towers and gave them their other-worldly aspect. "I show you," Zampa said and paraded the clucking entourage of us back to the shed, where he grabbed one of the last of the steel angles, and then on a brisk two-block walk outside the junkyard to the railroad siding that once served the brewery. He pushed back his fedora an inch or two, clamped his cigar butt more firmly in place, jammed the steel rod well under the iron rail, took a deep breath and a firm grip, and then wrenched the rod upward with a mighty heave. The angle yielded so slightly that the bend was almost imperceptible at first. But he kept heaving—with such force I thought his heart would come rocketing out of his chest cavity the next instant—and the metal began to buckle and then bow and then arc gracefully. Then he took us back and showed us how he fused the beams by wrapping them tautly with chicken wire and packing the joint with as much cement as he could force into it. No nut or bolt or solder or acetylene had braced a single centimeter of the construction; it was hardly less an act of handcraft than the pyramids, Professor Brady suggested, and all the more heroic for the solitary labor of its creator.

We camped out all day Sunday at Jonathan's house thrashing over our visit with Zampa and trying to translate the essence of it into a twelve-page brochure that would serve as the centerpiece of the publicity drive. Lee designed it, Jon refined some of the sketches he had made on the site, Tillinghast contributed photos and a knack for description as a veteran composer of catalogues, Brady churned out a few cosmic insights in appropriately dense academese, and I added a shot or two of orgasmic prose at critical interstices. Mostly, it was an account of the old man's odyssey through urban desolation—forever rummaging among the detritus of the tenements for his materials, straining to shape them to his needs and sweating to haul them to cruel altitudes, toiling alone and ignored except by the wind for unreckoned thousands of hours alchemizing dross into glitter. The result we collectively hailed "an exultant phenomenon of surreal folk art that, assembled bit by bit from small salvaged things, reached a triumphant crescendo of form and texture and color; once seen, it cannot be forgotten." Authorship of the pamphlet was assigned to The Committee for the Zampa Towers, for which I filed papers the next day as a nonprofit corporation. Each of the charter members gave two hundred dollars to the cause, and most of the kitty got allocated at once to print the brochure on quality stock, run off a covering letter on appropriate stationery, and mail out the proclamation of genius to every newspaper, magazine, and television station within the fallout radius. Leaving nothing to chance, we made follow-up calls to be sure our broadside had been received.

The undergraduate daily at Mather was the first to pick up the story. Tickled by the unlikelihood of such a remarkable thing having risen unnoticed in a modern city of the electronic age, the student writer came and rhapsodized: "Just before sunset, the towers shimmer and quiver like a fantasy from all our childhoods—enchanted stepping stones to the Milky Way and galaxies beyond. They are playing the sweet music of the firmament. . . ." The local counter-culture weekly, pandering to the crafts, waterbed, health food, and drug communes, was more interested in the human gesture than the inanimate object. "This amazing thing, whatever the hell it is," crowed the scribe from ersatz bohemia, "renews the faith that a single being, of however little wealth or learning, persisting long enough, defying materialist values, may yet make a statement that can be heard, and create an object that can be seen, above the din and dinge of modernity. You are far, far out, Gabriel Zampa, whoever you are and whoever sent you to us." By the time the Amity *Light,* the city's monopoly daily, caught up with the towers, its interest was less in Zampa's esthetic genius than his legal woes. The story contained a generously long biographical sketch of the old man's life and recollection, including how he got the nickname Starfish during a more colorful era of the city's past. Accompanying the piece was a photograph of the quintessential Zampa, his stubby, age-webbed face lifted toward the towers, his heavily dimpled hat hugging the back of his scalp like a helmet, and the habitual cigar butt in process of getting chewed to shreds. The prosecutor's office was quoted by the *Light* as calling the city's action against the poor craftsman "unfortunately necessary enforcement of a vital municipal code." Zampa was quoted to the effect that he just wished the city was as earnest about trying to catch the scum that regularly robbed him as it was about punishing him for an innocent hobby. Maybe he didn't need a lawyer, after all.

Soon the publicity was feeding on itself. The local television station took some footage of Zampa explaining in his flavorful dialect how he had built the towers, and it turned out so well that ABC put it on network news the next night. New York editors saw it. *People* magazine came out and did a page on Zampa, dubbing him "a junkyard Giotto" and his creation "Starfish Towers." Hartford, Boston, and Providence papers dispatched stringers to do weekend pieces. And *Artforum* sent us the advance text of the first real review the towers received as art rather than curio. It began:

> There is a rapturous quality about Gabriel Zampa's thoroughly unexpected open-work sculpture that comes over you after the

initial suspicion subsides that you have come a very long way only to find three enormous upside-down ice-cream cones encrusted with costume jewelry. But they cast a spell by their visual tintinnabulation, and the closer one looks, the more one is charmed. Here is an oriental splendor of demotic motifs and improvised designs, endlessly varied yet somehow integral, that suggest nothing so much as the golden stupas of Siam. . . .

One of us on the ad hoc committee always tried to be on hand when the press came by in case the interviewing got sticky. But Zampa, while ever wary, proved a voluble enough ham to supply the writers with all the quotable lines they needed to turn him, with a bit of embroidery, into a homespun sage. They had him saying he liked but did not understand modern young women (I took that personally), that prices were so high he thought he was buying caviar instead of sardines on his last trip to the grocery, and that he had never voted because he couldn't tell the parties or the candidates apart except for Franklin D. Roosevelt, who he wished had not been assassinated at Yalta. As to his opinion of modern architecture, he didn't think he had ever seen any, except for the glassy First Amity Bank building, which he didn't like because the windows couldn't open, and the poured-concrete Mather Gymnasium, which from the humpback look of it he thought had just collapsed the day he wandered past. Will Rogers he wasn't, but what did anyone ever build with a lasso?

By the time I got back to Duckett and Lenore Washburn, the fame of the towers had spread citywide and a trickle of sightseers had actually begun risking the trip through Amity's most harrowing ghetto to take them in. That Zampa's works might serve to spur the city's consciousness of the Gully and encourage the hope of resurrection, the Coop leaders now readily grasped. They were, within reason, at my disposal, but only after I reported where things stood with Duckett and his hospital job. At my request, Sparky had made tactful inquiries at city hall, where the message came flying back that the nigger first had to stop biting the hand that fed him. Sparky relayed the added intimation that the mayor, facing re-election, might be open to a new action program for the Gully—one with teeth in it—provided the blacks dropped their hectoring lawsuits for good. I passed the message that Geronimo Jones ought to make an appointment to explore the fluid situation with the city's corporation counsel. Meanwhile, to advance the spirit of revival in the area, the Washburns agreed that the Coop would sponsor a community festival to mark Zampa's completion of the towers the next weekend. An open invitation was extended to all Amity residents to witness the event. But any chance that a mammoth crowd might have accumulated was squelched when city officials, from the mayor down, said they could not attend in view of Zampa's pending trial and that lawlessness, however attractively cloaked, could not be openly countenanced. Accordingly, the police were not assigned in substantial numbers to secure the area around the junkyard, and few from beyond the Gully turned up. Multitudes, while they would no doubt have heightened the occasion, were not essential to substantiate the claims I planned to make in court; a token showing of community approval was.

Mike Tillinghast and his wife picked me up in their wagon, and on the way we stopped for Lee and Sam Nightingale, who as a twosome were nothing if not cordial toward me. Perhaps I had been a tonic to their pallid relationship after all. Jonathan and Jessica had arrived at the junkyard ahead of us on the Honda, along with perhaps two hundred other people, most of them black, and a flying wedge of white newsmen including half a dozen paunchy photographers and a squad of TV honchos with hand-held cameras. A table and three folding chairs had been set up in front of the central tower where Duckett and one of his Coop lieutenants presided. Cables had been strung out to the street to bring in power for the p.a. system, and a young local rock group took turns performing with a quartet from the choir of the nearest A.M.E. congregation as the crowd slowly collected. Hot dogs, soda, and balloons were being hawked, an American flag was undulating midway up each of the towers, and the whole scene had as genuine an air of impromptu civic hoopla as I could have asked for.

At the shack, Zampa seemed a little mesmerized by the tumult outside. Of even greater distraction was the appearance of two long-lost boyhood friends who had heard about the towers and come from the other end of Amity Bay for the occasion. That meant more than anything else to the old man, who had shaved close and cut his hair that morning and even made a pass at reblocking his hat over the tea kettle. I took him aside for a moment to see how he felt and he said never better. Having fixed the red and blue target bottles on the tops of the two smaller towers the day before, he had only to climb the main tower, cement the white bottle to the pinnacle, and come down to accept the congratulations of the community leaders. "Dey all nigga's, huh?" he asked. I said that was unkind of him and then asked if he wanted to say anything to the crowd when he was done. He shrugged. "I do whateva' I feel," he said and went back to his friends for a few more minutes of reminiscing before gathering up his trowel and stirring his bucket of cement.

When the combined singing groups struck up a rock gospel rendering of "America the Beautiful," Zampa strode from the shack with as much dignity as his compact shape could muster, waved his hat to the assemblage, and began his ascent. The crowd offered a perfunctory cheer as the music stopped and watched the climber's progress almost sullenly; most of them were there on Duckett's direct orders and I supposed half of them were hoping the old man would fall and splatter his brains all over the junkyard.

"Good Christ," Lee Nightingale said to me as the committee people clustered up front, "how could you let him go up there?"

She had not ever seen him make the climb as I had. "He's been doing it for twenty years," I said, "give or take five. Now's no time to stop."

"But he's never had an audience before, has he?"

"And he never will again," I said. "Relax—I was inside with him. He knows exactly what he's doing."

Her eyes were fastened to the speck in the sky. "I guess there's no such thing as an indispensable client," she said after a moment of low breathing.

"Hey," I said to her, "I love that old man."

"Then you shouldn't have subjected him to this," she hissed out of the side of her mouth.

"Nobody forced him," I said. "It's the biggest day of his life —can't you see that?"

"I only see an old man in mortal peril."

"Then close your eyes."

She turned to me. "Aren't you at all frightened, even?"

"I'm scared shitless," I said, "but I'm not the one up there."

Zampa soon gave a big wave of his left arm—the shorter one —to signal that the last bit of his masterpiece was in place, and a volley of astonishingly ardent cheers went up to meet him. It was impossible to watch him scampering high among those gleaming spires without thrilling to the superhuman dimension of his feat. As pre-arranged, he uncoiled a special tape measure till it reached Jonathan, who was waiting at the bottom of the central mast. From the ground to the bottle its builder had just put in place, Jon reported to the assemblage, the tower rose one hundred four feet and seven inches. Another cheer was airborne.

Cameras whirring all the way, Zampa's final descent was recorded for posterity. He lowered himself very deliberately. I had no doubt he was saying goodbye to a treasured friend. At the end he looked like what he was: a short exhausted old man who had had no business building a dizzying monument to man's everlasting spirit—not there, not then, and not he of all the unfavored innocents on earth.

The group of us surged forward to embrace him. I skidded a kiss off his cheek and he gave me one back and our eyes were wet when they met. At the microphone Duckett was already well into his number, declaring how proud the surrounding community was of Gabriel Zampa and grateful to him for beautifying all their lives. In dedicating the towers to the proposition that every American of any station could rise to acts of greatness, he orated, the Gully was simultaneously asking the city to grant perpetual protection to so splendid a work by designating the area a public park, badly needed in that neglected and forgotten neighborhood. And he flourished a petition to that effect signed by the Coop leaders. It was all I had asked.

The gospel singers offered a couple of verses of "Way in the Middle of the Air," and then Zampa was brought to the microphone. You could barely see him amid the cluster of well-wishers but his voice boomed out over the loudspeaker: "I wanna say t'anks to eve'ybody fo' comin'—an' whoeva' took my radio should give it back an' I wouldn' be angry."

After all the excitement, I thought he might be lonesome by himself that night, so I drove up there, not without trepidation, and spent an hour with him by candlelight. I asked him if he regretted all the fuss and he said no, except for one thing. He was sorry the press had taken to calling them Starfish Towers. I said I thought that was rather endearing but he said I didn't understand: He had fudged the story about his nickname. It had not derived from his fondness for oysters but from a childhood accident that had mangled his left arm in an oyster-crating machine and permanently disfigured him. He stretched both arms in front of him so I could see the discrepancy. I said I had noticed it but not thought much about it since whatever had caused it seemed not to have disabled him noticeably. He nodded that that was true but it had taken him years to overcome the effects of the injury and a resulting shyness over the nickname his heartless peers soon pinned to him. The oyster fishermen, it seems, used to catch starfish for fun and tear them in half to register dislike of their predatory manners. The two halves would then be tossed back into the sea and most of the torn starfish would naturally die. An occasional strong one would survive, though, and grow new arms, which were never as big as the originals but sufficed. They looked unbalanced, something like comets, propelling themselves freakishly through the brine. Add to the frequent sight of such creatures a general awareness among seafront folk that starfish made excellent fertilizer, and small, crippled Gabriel Zampa was doomed to suffer a psychic wound that endured longer than the physical one. It made him sad being called that, he said, and being thought a misfit of no more value than shit. But then his arm got better and he grew stronger and more determined to work as any man, and when he thought about it at all in later years, the nickname seemed providential.

368

I drove home through the cool autumn night thinking that if there were no horrid handicaps to be overcome in life, there would be few great deeds and fewer impassioned doers. Too bad most of the ripped starfish just sank.

30

The first sign that the city was not going to treat the Zampa trial as a trivial matter reached me only a few days before the jury was due to be picked. Gil Serini came across the hall from his office after lunch and said he had heard that morning at the courthouse that Prosecutor Schoonmaker had taken the case away from his assistant Drutman and was going to argue it himself. That seemed odd, given what I hoped had become the city's distinctly unpopular position in pursuing the case. If ever there was an instance when I would have expected Schoonmaker to reduce his broad beam to a low profile, this was it. I asked Gil why the substitution.

"Don't say I told you," he said, "but I got the distinct impression that Schoonmaker—and a few other heavies at city hall—want your ass."

"In a sling, you mean?"

"Well—yes. Lust is the least of your problems."

"Damn," I said.

"Hey, I'm glad you're loose about it," he said, "because they may really try to do a job on you. They think all the fuss in the press about the old guy is a patented Tabor Hill production."

"Why, the nerve of them."

"Actually, someone said if they didn't shoot you down now, 'that brassy broad is going to be running this town before long.'"

"How flattering."

"Only they didn't say 'broad.'"

"What did they say?"

"You know."

"No, I don't. Tell me."

"It was bad, that's all."

"Tell me, Gil."

He was flustered. "Forget I said a word."

"Gilbert!"

"Cunt!" he said. "They called you cunt—okay? Is that a big lift for you?"

"Those dumb cocksuckers!" I yelled. It echoed out the open door.

He looked stunned. I had always spared him my choicest expletives on the theory that anyone who believed literally in the virgin birth shouldn't have to know grossness was a human and not exclusively masculine characteristic. "Do you have to say that?" he asked.

"Hey," I said, "how would you like to be called a prick behind your back?"

He was flame orange around the gills now. "Not much," he admitted.

"Well, a cunt is a lot worse than a prick."

"I—hadn't heard."

"It happens to be true," I said. " 'Prick' is a term of semi-endearment around the locker room, isn't it?"

"Well—I don't know—sort of, maybe."

"You can call a woman a twat in that same palsy Rabelaisian sense—or even pussy or snatch. I mean, they're degrading but not without a certain horny affection implied. A cunt means just plain wicked. There's no real male equivalent."

"I can't say I ever thought of it like that."

"Why not? Didn't they teach you anything at that seminary?"

"I didn't go to a seminary."

"Then you've got no excuse. Didn't you ever hang around the gutter with the other guys?"

He laughed finally, ending the porn lesson, but the news he brought was no cause for merriment. My father had told me the more success I won among men, the more scorn I would suffer as a woman. Here was the surest evidence to date that I was prospering. And there was more to come.

Geronimo Jones called later that afternoon to say that, on his advice, no one from the Coop would be testifying for Zampa despite a promise to do so. In fact, he said, Lenore herself was going to testify for the city and say the towers represented an attractive nuisance and potential danger to children from the neighborhood who might climb it. I asked how she could do that when the Coop had sponsored the ceremonies honoring the old man.

"You'll see," he said.

"You mean they bought you out?"

"I mean they're finally dealing—for real. They'll hang tough with the sweat equity program and start putting up city money as loans or outright grants. They're talking three million a year —at least half for the Gully. We're asking for five. And the mayor is talking about going to Washington to ask HUD to guarantee local mortgage money the banks wouldn't risk otherwise. He wants black votes next year. I said there wasn't any other way to get 'em."

"And p.s.—Duckett gets his job back, right?"

"If Lenore testifies against your guy."

"What's one thing got to do with the other?"

"You're their new number-one bad-ass nigger."

"I see," I said, "and so the old man's got to pay for it because city hall has a hard-on to put me in my place?"

"You might say that."

I confronted Sparky with the intelligence. "I wouldn't be surprised," he said, "and you shouldn't be, either. You've been pushing their face in it for a long time."

"But I'm out of that line of work now. Isn't that what the partnership is all about?"

"They don't know that, though."

"Couldn't you tell them—somehow?"

"What—that we didn't want you playing Joan of Arc any more, so we promoted you?"

"I'm sure you could word it more felicitously if you tried."

"It's nobody's business outside this building. Besides, no

matter what you said, all they'd see is your making a celebrity out of this geezer and leaving them red-faced one more time."

"They should be red-faced. They're being assholes about it."

"Tabor, they don't like you, or anyone, telling them that. And they don't like you pissing on the town's reputation."

"I just represent my clients."

"Too well," he said.

"What am I supposed to do—take a dive?"

"No—just not try quite so hard—at least once in a while."

Now they told me.

Another vital part of my case was lost to treachery the next day when Professor Brady backed out of testifying. Jonathan said he had heard that Brady was up for a major departmental grant to study the architecture of Venice before it sank, and the pipe-sucking pooh-bahs in Sachem Hall led by President Prettyman had put the screws to him after getting the word that city hall would look with great displeasure on any faculty participation in the Zampa case. In view of the city's threatened challenge to Mather's continuing tax-exempt status, the university was walking on eggs to avoid riling the town fathers. That meant I would almost certainly be unable to get any other Mather authority on art to testify, either, even if there had been someone in Brady's league.

Still another blow fell when the third of my four expert witnesses, a friend of Jon's who was the head of the local chapter of the State Society of Architects and Design Engineers, was muscled out of appearing by the none too subtle advice not to bother applying for any future work on municipal building projects if he persisted in testifying for Zampa. My carefully constructed case was getting gaping holes shot through it. I made a last-minute effort to have the critic who had written about the towers for *Artforum* come up from New York and testify, but he had a teaching commitment most of the week and I couldn't pinpoint when I'd need him. The Somebodies Up There were not liking me a whole lot.

I woke up with cramps the morning of the trial, which was rainy to boot, and then my car wouldn't start and by the time a cab came and I went for Zampa, who I was afraid would get soaked walking to the courthouse or waiting for the undependable Seaview Avenue bus, it was too late for me to buy my customary courtroom carnation. All the omens were dark. But Jon and Lee were there to urge me on when I straggled in with the old man, and by the time Judge Lombard convened court, I had been supplied with a yellow rosebud, courtesy of my erstwhile lover, who had never been so thoughtful out of bed before.

Prosecutor Schoonmaker did not bother to show up and spell his underling till we were halfway done selecting the jury, and then he was all smiles and unction; having stacked the deck, he could afford to be. I nodded to him once and then never let my eyes cross his again throughout the trial. There must have been eight or nine reporters on hand—which was seven or eight more than for any other case I had ever argued—and only a few empty seats remained in the back rows. None of that did wonders for my gastrointestinal tract.

Before the Coop crowd turned its back on me, I had wanted at least two or three blacks on the jury—in the hope they could be appealed to on the ground that Zampa was being roundly persecuted—and a couple of professional people or creative types likely to be sympathetic to what Zampa had actually achieved. But now that self-interest had ranged the black leadership in the Gully against me, I probably stood to lose from heavy black representation on the jury. And the other side used all its challenges, of course, to prevent anyone suspected of an esthetic quotient much beyond Archie Bunker's from being impaneled. We wound up with a jury of a retired postal clerk, a black window washer, a supermarket assistant manager, a secretary at an electrical equipment company, a bus driver, a bank teller, a black saleswoman at a fabric store, an attendant at a dog and cat hospital, a restaurant cashier, an appliance repairman, and two housewives, one of a garage owner, one of a high school science teacher—six women, six men, two blacks. I figured it a draw.

Each side waived an opening statement, and growly Kenneth Schoonmaker went right to work as if the defendant had been charged with ax-murdering a kindergarten class. I saw then that it was I and not Zampa who was on trial. I wondered what the sentence was for shitting in public on male chauvinism.

The prosecutor first called the building inspector who had served the original notice of violation on Zampa five and a quarter years before. A balding, mousy man named Howard Sweet, he testified to handing Zampa the written notice in person and explaining to him exactly what his two offenses were. "And did you tell Mr. Zampa that he could not continue work on his—his structure—until he brought in blueprints and obtained a building permit?" Schoonmaker asked, and Sweet said yes and that he even told the old man the exact address where he could apply. Then I exercised the witness a bit.

Q. Mr. Sweet, you never thought Mr. Zampa would actually reach the point of applying for a variance, did you?
A. As a matter of fact, no.
Q. Why not?
A. Because I could tell his construction would never pass the safety requirements.
Q. Which ones, for instance?
A. Well—the code says that concrete-support columns have to be at least a foot wide.
Q. And how wide were the columns in Mr. Zampa's towers?
A. A good deal less than that—four or five inches at most, and less in many spots.
Q. In fact, they're not really columns at all in the conventional sense, are they? They're more like struts, aren't they?
A. Yes.
Q. Did it occur to you that since Mr. Zampa was building an open-work tower—that is, a hollow structure that was not going to have any floors or occupants or utilitarian purpose—it may not have needed to have columns of such thickness?
A. That's not the sort of thing I consider. The code is plain.
Q. You mean you have to go by the book, even if a structure may be perfectly strong enough for its particular design?
A. That's right.

374

Schoonmaker followed with the manager of the department of building and safety, a debonair sort named Peter Shanley, who explained the rationale behind the code—namely, to prevent any construction, under the municipality's general police powers, that imperiled the health, safety, or morals of the community. It was unfortunate, in this case, he said, that so much time had elapsed between the initial notice of violation and its prosecution, but his staff was severely overtaxed and budgetary cutbacks had made it impossible to enforce the code as stringently as it should have been.

I asked Shanley why his office didn't have a procedure for double-checking on structures once they were charged with being in violation of the code. "Even if you're shorthanded," I pressed, "I should think it would be the highest priority of your people to pursue known violators of the code."

A. We do have a procedure to follow up on violations—and usually they are at the top of our agenda.

Q. How does that work? Do you take the earliest violations and press them hardest—or what?

A. More or less. It depends somewhat on the seriousness of the case.

Q. Oh, I see. You mean there is no set procedure?

A. No.

Q. Some violations are more serious than others?

A. Yes, of course.

Q. If Mr. Zampa's violation was a serious one, why wasn't a stop put to it long ago?

A. It was just one of those things. Our people were occupied elsewhere.

Q. Why wouldn't Mr. Zampa then be free to presume it was not a serious violation?

A. For the same reason he wasn't free to put up his building without a permit in the first place.

Q. But now you're presuming that he thought he was putting up a building and not creating a work of art—aren't you, Mr. Shanley?

375

A. Whatever he thought or didn't think is beside the point. The point is that it is certainly a structure and therefore subject to the building code, which states that things more than sixty feet high can't be built without a permit, whatever they are.

Q. Even if there is no legitimate reason to limit a work of art to that height?

A. The legitimate reason is to inspect the plans to make sure the thing won't come crashing down on anyone below.

Q. And is that what your inspector indicated might happen in the case of Mr. Zampa's towers?

A. It didn't get to that stage of the enforcement process.

Q. Then the inspector couldn't possibly have thought that was an imminent possibility, could he?

A. I suppose not.

Schoonmaker took him back on re-direct to establish that structural safety was a matter to be determined not after the fact of construction but before the public might be endangered. I had to go to the toilet too badly to bother with a re-cross, and the judge mercifully recessed us for lunch.

Jon and Lee, full of encouragement, urged Zampa and me to join them for a bite, but I was too tense and settled for a mouthful of the cheese and tomato sandwich my client had brought with him. The old man, who by now fancied himself an authority on courtroom procedure, said he was afraid a few members of the jury were catnapping during the best parts of my performance but otherwise we seemed to be doing fine. I told him to keep his eye on the jury for me and his fingers crossed.

The prosecutor, looking as if he had just been bolstered by a steak and two or three bottles of beer, launched his afternoon program with one Lorenzo Giles, who identified himself as the art critic of the Amity *Light*. Schoonmaker asked him if he had ever seen Zampa's towers in person. Giles said he had. "And have you formed a professional opinion of these towers?" the prosecutor asked. Giles said he had and, invited to give it, stated that he thought they were "a large pile of junk," utterly without redeeming value as works of art and of curiosity value only because one man had apparently made them from neighborhood debris.

I eyed the philistine with disdain for rather a long moment before going at him. "No doubt, Mr. Giles, you studied the history of art at college?" I asked. "A bit," he said.

Q. How much is a bit?

A. I took an art appreciation course.

Q. I see. And where was that?

A. At Paterson State Teachers College—in New Jersey.

Q. I see. And is that what qualifies you to be the art critic of our daily newspaper?

A. Well, I've studied the subject quite a bit on my own.

Q. That's very enterprising of you. Tell me, do you make your living as an art critic?

A. No. I'm actually the obituary editor on the paper.

Q. Oh, I see. *Vita brevis, ars longa,* eh, Mr. Giles?

A. Yes—I suppose.

Q. What is it I just said, Mr. Giles.

A. I'm not sure exactly.

Q. It's Latin. It means life is short but art endures. I should think even a part-time art critic would know the expression. Tell me, Mr. Giles, do you know the publication *Artforum?*

A. Certainly.

Q. Isn't it one of the leading art journals in the country?

A. I believe it is.

Q. What would you say if I told you that *Artforum's* critic wrote a review of Mr. Zampa's towers and said they were quite remarkable works of art?

A. He's entitled to his opinion.

Q. And is it any better than yours?

A. I wouldn't like to think so.

Q. Would you say the same thing if I told you he was an associate professor in art and archeology on the faculty of Hunter College in New York?

A. Well—yes.

Q. Mr. Giles, do you know what a collage is?

377

A. Yes.

Q. Would you call it art?

A. Some people would. I don't happen to care for it.

Q. It's really just little pieces of junk stuck together, isn't it —no matter what the esthetes call it?

A. I think so.

Q. Not unlike Mr. Zampa's towers—which are just junk in three dimension, aren't they? Isn't that what you said?

A. Yes.

Q. Mr. Giles, would you agree with the statement that Pablo Picasso was a great artist—one of the greatest of this century if not of all time?

A. Certainly.

Q. Isn't it also true that Picasso did some of his most important early work in collage?

A. I think so. Yes, I believe that's so.

Q. So it's possible, then, to make art out of junk, isn't it, Mr. Giles?

A. If you're a genius. Picasso was a genius.

Q. Some people think Gabriel Zampa is also a genius. That's all, Mr. Giles.

Schoonmaker was starting to get edgy, I could tell by the unaccustomed rapidity of his questioning. He followed the dismantled Giles with a far bigger gun, Lionel Olmstead Marsh, chairman of the department of art at the University of Connecticut and contributor to a long list of professional journals and textbooks. He chose his words with care. Zampa's towers, he said, were not even folk art, which generally had a certain vibrant if unrefined quality to it, but the merest sort of Erector Set *kitsch*. "The world of art is too ready today to embrace every new sensation, thanks to the promoters and gallery owners and patrons who have nothing better to do with their money," he said. "I'm afraid that eager impulse is what is responsible for the flurry of enthusiasm for these grotesque structures by Mr. Zampa. Their size does not make them any the less tasteless."

Without an academic authority to call in rebuttal, I had armed myself for combat with just such a grandiloquent adversary. "Do you know who William Dean Howells was, professor?" I began.

A. Yes, of course.

Q. Would you mind telling the court?

A. One of the most prominent men of American letters during the latter part of the last century. I believe he was the editor for many years of *The Atlantic Monthly*.

Q. Thank you, professor. Now I'm going to read you a brief passage by this worthy gentleman, if I may?

A. By all means.

Q. I am quoting now, sir:

. . . the mass of common men have been afraid to apply their own simplicity, naturalness, and honesty to the appreciation of the beautiful. They have cast about for the instruction of someone who professed to know better, and who browbeat wholesome commonsense into the self-distrust that ends in sophistication.

Do you find any merit in such a view, professor?

A. Some, of course. But the implication is that such experts are self-proclaimed. Many are not. Some work all their lives to deserve that honorable status.

Q. And are you such an expert, professor?

A. There are certain objective standards for determining that.

Q. Does that mean you are or aren't an expert on beauty?

A. My field is the history and theory of art and esthetics. Nobody is an expert on beauty as such.

Q. I see. Then if you say such-and-such a painting is beautiful and I disagree, neither of us is necessarily right or wrong. Beauty, as they say, is in the eye of the beholder, is it not, professor?

A. So they say.

Q. Thank you, professor.

Schoonmaker wound up his case with Lenore Washburn, whom he put on to testify that the surrounding neighborhood viewed Zampa's towers as a menace to the safety of children. He established, before I could, that the Gully had only recently honored Zampa for his work and petitioned the city to turn the junkyard and its environs into a recreational area. But she claimed—to my burning disbelief—that a number of youngsters had begun playing in the towers as a result of the great amount of attention drawn to them and it would be only a matter of time before someone was seriously injured. Several people in the area had also told her they thought they heard the towers creaking when the wind rose and there were widespread doubts about their stability. "In short, Mrs. Washburn, aren't you telling us that your neighborhood—of which you are a prominent civic leader—regards Mr. Zampa's structures as a hazard to life and limb?" She said she was, and he let her go.

She had testified rather mechanically and, it was plain (to me, anyway), under duress, but she had done the dirty deed and I could not love her for it or, just then, in spite of it. No doubt she had agonized over it—or so I wanted to think—and decided the self-interest of a lot of hard-pressed folk required this moment of disloyalty to a staunch friend. And I, of all people, she must have thought, would understand, having been as responsible as anybody for advancing their cause to the point where gains could actually be bargained for. And I did understand. But I was not grateful to her except for not calling me ahead of time to apologize. She did what she had to do—and would go on living. It took a woman's strength. Men, in the same fix, pretend there's no price to be paid for minor treacheries and holler honor all the way to the deathbed.

Lenore's eyes did not flinch from mine as I moved toward the stand. I said hello and she nodded. I felt more empty than vengeful.

Q. Mrs. Washburn, these towers have been under construction for some twenty years. I wonder how it is that the children of your area have only recently taken to playing in them?

A. Well, like I say—all the noise over them lately has got everybody around knowing they are there—the kids especially since they don't have a lot of places to go and play except the street.

Q. I see. The children are attracted to the towers?

A. Yes.

Q. Are you aware, Mrs. Washburn, that the towers are on private property—which means that any youngsters who have been playing in them are guilty of trespassing and punishable by law?

A. They're just little kids. They weren't doing no messing.

Q. That doesn't change the fact they were trespassing, does it?

A. I guess not.

Q. Since the children seem to be attracted to the towers but the site is potentially dangerous, as you see it, Mrs. Washburn, wouldn't it be better if the city secured them and turned the area into a genuine playground—as your petition asked—with the towers left to stand apart as a work of art, bringing delight to the youngsters and inspiring them with the thought that one man made them all by himself?

MR. SCHOONMAKER: Objection. Counsel is making a speech, not asking a question.

THE COURT: Sustained. Rephrase.

Q. Wouldn't you like to have a park up there if the towers were proven stable and fenced off from the kids?

A. I'd like a park outside my front door.

Q. But that's not likely to happen, is it?

A. I guess not.

Q. Thank you, Mrs. Washburn.

A. You're welcome, Miss Hill.

Before I could open for our side, Jonathan came to the defense table with the disastrous news that my last and only expert witness, Mike Tillinghast, had scratched. The fire marshal was threatening to close up his art gallery if a sprinkler system wasn't installed within forty-eight hours—which would have necessitated pulling the whole place apart and canceling the big fall show he had just hung. By now Tillinghast understood the pattern of intimidation—and how to avoid the city's booted heel. The economic survival of his gallery was at stake. He promised not to testify if the fire people would relent. They gave him six months' grace.

"I'm going to have to call you," I told Jon. "There isn't anybody else." He said he wasn't sure he could do it without preparation. I told him just to answer the questions and not think cathedrals. He smiled and said sure.

On the stand, he was nearly the perfect expert witness—knowledgeable without being arrogant, informative without getting long-winded. I quickly put his outstanding academic credentials on the record and some of the better known buildings in town he had designed or converted. Then I asked him to trace his involvement with the Zampa committee, identify its other members, and comment briefly on some of the articles that had been written about the towers. It was my only way to get on the record that Zampa's handiwork had been widely publicized and authoritatively admired. At the wind-up Jon added a quiet bit of eloquence of his own. "It's worth remembering," he said, "that almost everything else we're surrounded by now—from whipped cream to fireplace logs—is mass-produced and artificial. Not this thing, though. This is unique. No machine could conceive it. No computer could explain it. It reminds us we're human. One man thought it up in his head. One pair of hands made it—all million pieces of it—and one soul sustained it over many years in as bleak a setting as this city—or any city—can offer. For these reasons alone—even if it were not a work of exquisite ornament and thrilling proportion—Mr. Zampa's towers are rare and beautiful."

If I ever forget what there was about Jon Kenyon that had prompted me to entwine a part of my life with his, those words of his that day will remind me. Whatever it was that caused his flame to burn so inconstantly, there was no denying the lovely glow it gave when all the chemistry was right.

The prosecutor, however, saw something less than poetry in Jon's testimony. "I have two questions for you, Mr. Kenyon," Schoonmaker said, almost licking his chops with anticipation. "First, did you hold any of these views about Mr. Zampa's quaint project before his lawyer asked you to organize a committee in his behalf?"

I objected, of course. Jon had not said that I asked him to form the group, only that we had consulted on the idea. "And just how Mr. Kenyon learned of the existence of the towers is entirely irrelevant, your honor. His judgment of them—and his credentials to make that judgment—are all that can concern the court." The judge agreed.

The prosecutor turned his back on Jon and faced the jury now. "I'll move to my second final question, then, Mr. Kenyon. Isn't it true that you and the defendant's counsel have been intimate friends and, for several stretches of time, cohabited?"

I was not willing to concede, before that instant, the full measure of virulence I had earned for wearing a skirt and daring to win. Sexuality is the last refuge—as well as the first—of the threatened male ego, and this big bastard couldn't stand the challenge. I did not reply with a wounded whimper or a tremulous whisper. I raised my objection like a battle cry, and no other sound competed with the echo. "Counsel's private life is no more the province of the court," I stormed, "than the frequency with which the prosecutor picks his teeth, clips his toenails—assuming they are in reach—or performs his other bodily functions."

The judge could hardly ignore my fury. "What is the purpose of the question, Mr. Schoonmaker?" he asked.

"The usual one, your honor—to impeach the purity of this supposedly disinterested expert. Paramours are notoriously unreliable witnesses, and the jury should be spared their partisanship."

There seemed to be no limit to how foul Schoonmaker could play, and in a game without rules, I wasn't going to stand there and scrimmage by the book. I asked to approach the bench. The prosecutor's perspiring bulk shadowed me. "Mr. Schoonmaker and his minions have worked overtime, your honor, conniving to keep every other witness I had intended to call from appearing here," I said as softly as I could manage, which was not very, "and I am prepared to try to prove it, however long it takes, if he persists in this line of questioning. I am going to put Mr. Schoonmaker himself on the stand next and ask him why he feels obliged to stoop to cheap calumny to discredit the one witness he and his people didn't bother to intimidate. No doubt he knew he could always smear Mr. Kenyon—and me—in open court."

"What's this all about, Ken?" Lombard asked him.

"I think Miss Hill's just getting a little emotional. If she can't stand the heat, she ought to get back to the kitchen."

"Very funny," said the judge, "only I think the lady's got you just as hot under the collar." He turned back to me. "Are you saying there's no basis in fact for Mr. Schoonmaker's question about your relationship to the witness?"

"I'm saying it's a cheap shot—and he knows it and your honor knows it and everyone in the room knows it. And if he doesn't take it back, I'm going to make it my business to let the world know what's behind it."

"And what's that, Miss Hill?" the judge asked.

"A ten-thousand-year-old castration complex."

Schoonmaker shook his head. "She's hysterical, your honor—in more ways than one."

"I don't like the sound of any of this," the judge said. "If the prosecutor's office has acted improperly, this isn't the way to let me know about it," he told me. "And if you don't want me to call a mistrial, Ken, you'd better get out of the lady's boudoir before the witness over there puts his knee in your groin."

"I've got knees, too," I said.

The question was withdrawn. Jon grasped my hand as he left the stand.

There was only Zampa left to be heard.

The old man looked exhausted from the day's proceedings, although he had not been an active participant. I asked him if he was ready to go on and he said yes. My only instruction to him had been not to volunteer more than I asked him. There was no need to detain him long up there. I asked if he had ever drawn up any plans for his towers before he began working on them. He said no. I asked him why he hadn't stopped building the towers when the city inspector gave him the notice of violation. He said he thought it was just a warning to be careful—and that if he had really been doing anything wrong, they would come back and make him stop. And when nobody came back, I asked, what did he think?

"I didn' t'ink nuttin'," he said. "I t'ink dey all got betta' t'ings to do dan worry what I'm makin'."

At the end, I asked him to tell the court why he had built

the towers. I had put it to him once before, in private, and it seemed to have thrown him, almost as if I had asked why he walked on his feet instead of his hands. I had told him I would ask the question when he took the stand but didn't want to know what answer he would give. Generally, that is a poor courtroom tactic. Better a canned answer than a damaging surprise. But the whole case hinged on the sincerity of an unworldly old man, as I saw it, and if the answer came out rehearsed and contrived, he was done for.

Zampa twisted the brim of his hat through one full revolution while he pondered the question in front of the jury. "I don' know 'zac'ly," he said. "How come anybody eva' done anyt'ing? I done it 'cause it make me happy, you know? Like I always got somet'in' to do de nex' day, you know? I done it 'cause it's a free country an' nobody stop me—not all dat time I was doin' it—so I t'ink maybe I make somet'in' beautiful to say t'ank you—you know?"

I asked him if that was why the glass globes on the tops of his three towers were the same colors as the American flag.

"Sure t'ing," he said and gave me a wink.

"Your witness," I said.

Schoonmaker asked him only if he denied building the towers or receiving the notice of violation, and Zampa said no. I took him back and asked if he had meant to break the law or known he was breaking the law, and he said no. Then he got up and walked away from the world.

"There was a time in the march of Western civilization," I began my summation, "when a man like Gabriel Zampa was warmly welcomed in any community to which he might travel. Such men were called freemasons, and they wandered throughout Europe bearing their precious skills in their heads and hands. It was they who, with their instinctive knowledge and simple tools, built the great cathedrals and palaces, who brought the beauty and grace that ended the dark and dreary prospect of medieval life. Today, when so much of what typifies modern society is made badly and works poorly and brings small delight to the eye or the soul, a man like Gabriel Zampa is a troubling throwback. Without meaning harm, he depresses us because he is a reminder of how much we have lost in the name of progress—of how little room we allow for truly personal expression—of how low we now value fine design and durable materials and careful workmanship. Profit and utility are all that count with us, and so a man like this seventy-five-year-old craftsman is viewed as an eccentric who must be penalized by our city officials because he cannot be made to fit into the usual bureaucratic pigeonholes. I say we should be striking a medal for this man and declaring his towers a municipal landmark for all the world to come and admire, not trying to figure out a way to punish him. We can line up art critics and learned professors and run them in here in relays for the next month and probably no two of them would agree on just what beauty is or whether the Zampa towers are works of genius or piles of junk. The wonderful thing is that you ladies and gentlemen of the jury have eyes and feelings of your own and you do not need anyone else to tell you whether what this one man, laboring by himself, has created is something remarkable that deserves your praise—or something loathsome that requires you to shame him."

The municipal building code was a perfectly good law, I said, but it was never intended to regulate works of art. How many artists achieved memorable work when first required to submit detailed blueprints for it in duplicate? There was no way Zampa could have applied for a permit without killing the creative spirit inside him. The only legitimate question the city might now raise was whether the towers were structurally safe —and that subject was not involved in the case since no charge to that effect had ever been made. To insist that the towers were too tall without establishing a rational basis for a height limit under an up-to-date statute was to place a prior and arbitrary restraint on Zampa's freedom of expression as guaranteed by the First Amendment. Finally, how was it serving justice to let a man create his monument for more than twenty years— and go on creating it five years after discovering what he was creating out there, in the open air, where anybody could see what he was up to—and then finally decide he was really a criminal? "What the city seeks," I concluded, "is a cruel and unusual punishment for a man who has harmed no one and intended no offense to anybody. By any standard of common sense and fair play, Gabriel Zampa is a truly innocent man. You may not choose to give him a medal, but do not, for God's sake, flog him for trying to bring you—and me—and anyone with eyes to see—a little joy."

I had held their faces, and that was all I wanted. Whether they grasped this or that point precisely or followed the logic of my flow did not matter just so long as they got the overall sense of it. And of me. No more did I worry if the women of the jury might favor me because I was a woman or spurn me because I had outdone them. No longer did I speculate if the male jurymen ached with desire for me or with fear I would unman them. Which is not to say I had become oblivious to my femininity, any more than I wanted them to be. But I sought no more advantage from it than my opponent deserved deference for his authoritarian mass, his wrathful voice, or the potency of what hung between his legs. We each were entitled to proclaim our presence any way that served to gain our will. And Kenneth Schoonmaker, subtle as a blacksmith, was long practiced at the art.

"Miss Hill has plucked at our heartstrings," he began, "and the sound is quite beguiling. But you ladies and gentlemen are not here to be serenaded. You are here to uphold the laws and public safety of our city, and these are not to be charmed out of your thoughts. A lady of the night may be done up in an alluring outfit and painted in fetching cosmetics, but her appearance does not change the fact that she is degrading the act of love and the rule of law. And that is very much what we have here, I'm afraid—illegality masquerading as righteous beauty."

Gabriel Zampa had violated at least two provisions of the building code, the prosecutor said, and no one was denying it. Nor could he, or did he, claim ignorance of the law, which at any rate would not have excused him; the city had indisputably put Zampa on warning that he was breaking the law. Nor did the lateness with which the city moved against this unlawfulness alter the fact of it nor did it confer upon him any rights or the privilege to pursue his unsanctioned activity. "Unceasing violation of the law," he rumbled, "does not grant one immunity from it." And if the city had been understandably dilatory in enforcing the law in a remote and virtually unoccupied corner of the city, the defendant had been even more so for failing to come forward and ever to claim that his work was exempt from city regulation. "It is a late—and highly suspicious —hour for his attorney to assert that what Mr. Zampa has been up to is mere artistic expression and not the building of a large and—in some people's opinion—highly unsightly object. And even if we were to grant, for argument's sake, that it is art, the basic question in the case has not changed. A good many architects believe the buildings they design are artful as well as useful and constitute a form of personal expression—yet they are not exempt from the scrutiny of the building code. Why should Mr. Zampa be? No, I'm afraid Miss Hill cannot dodge us by hiding behind the First Amendment, which was not written to license antisocial disregard of the community's health and safety."

He had them—you couldn't miss it. He greased the skids by telling them that enforcing the law is never much fun and that while they might sympathize with Zampa and envy his perseverance, they must do their civic duty lest the laws thereafter be broken with impunity and chaos follow. The jury deliberated just over half an hour before agreeing with him.

At the sentencing the next morning I appealed for leniency on the ground that the city had been manifestly unjust in prosecuting at so late a date and that the defendant had not been shown to have harmed anyone. Instead of the statutorily prescribed minimum fine of more than seven thousand dollars, Judge Lombard invoked his equity powers to reduce the penalty to a thousand dollars and gave Zampa up to three months to pay it. Since that was still a thousand dollars more than Zampa could lay his hands on and I thought the verdict unjust, I told the inquiring reporters we might well appeal after studying the transcript. I told Zampa not to worry and that if all else failed, the money would be raised in his behalf. He thanked me but said he wouldn't accept any more charity and would work it out by himself somehow.

On my way out of court, the judge called me aside for a moment to say he thought I had done the best anyone could with the case. On our glum ride back to the junkyard, Zampa said the same thing. That meant more.

31

I had not asked to handle Gabriel Zampa's case and had never really expected to win it. All the court had wanted of me was to provide him able counsel, and by any standard I had discharged that responsibility. Why, then, did I persist in the matter and appeal the verdict against him to the state Superior Court? Part of it, no doubt, was my metabolic reflex to losing —especially after I had gone to the trouble of inventing a plausible First Amendment defense that the judge had smothered *in utero*. And no doubt part of it was anger over having been jobbed by the prosecutor's office. And part, the novelty of the case and the relief it offered from my regular chores. But beyond these was an emotional investment Zampa had wrung from me without trying.

During the early months of waiting before the Superior Court ruling came down, I drove out to the towers every few weeks or so just to see how he was getting along. In the cold weather, when his junk business was virtually nil, he scraped by on his Social Security, most of which had gone in warm weather for supplies to build the towers. His sole winter activity, so far as I could tell, was trying to survive. Given the absence of amenities, it was no easy job. He had absolutely forbidden me, on pain of instant banishment, to bring him gifts. My coming at all was kindness enough, he said. In fact, it may have unwittingly brought him discomfort.

On the face of it, we shared nothing except being alive in the same place at the same time. He was old, and I was ripe.

He had no money; I had all I needed—and then some. He survived by his hands; I, by my wits. He was unschooled, unwashed, and unlovely. I was learned, finished, and—well—comely enough. Nothing really good had ever brightened his life; nothing dreadful had darkened mine. He had no expectations; I was full of them. And yet we connected. For there was a quality to that man that drew me to him and made me meek. I could not isolate it for the longest while. It was not merely that he had constructed a great thing but that he had done it for the sheer joy of the process and, having finished, did not need the world's validation. I did not understand how any envelope of mortal flesh could so contain itself. We were each willful in our way but only I was obliged to be wily. It is the vertical way women prosper in this man's universe. Prospering, for him, was beside the point.

All my wiles were required to persuade him to take the portable radio I brought him the week before Christmas. It was not a fancy model and I told him so, clicking it on to a staticky reception of "I Saw Mommy Bleeping Santa Claus," but so far as he was concerned it was a quadrophonic space satellite. Finally he relented on condition that I come back the following week, which of course I did, and was presented with a gorgeous little table he had made for me with leftovers from the towers, including bits of colored glass, shells, china, and tile he had inlaid on top in a free-form pattern. I hugged him for it and we had tea and the two buns he had let me bring to mark the holiday and I read him a short piece about the towers that had just appeared in *Art News*. He was becoming more famous all the time, I told him. That was too bad, he said, because the kids were sure to peck his work to pieces when the warm weather returned. Fame had not greatly altered his outlook on the sweetness of human nature.

The intractable old man was not the only swain of my life that season. I was wined and wooed in a rabid fashion to which I was thoroughly unaccustomed by Terry Alan English, Jr., one smooth article. The kewpie-faced, honey-lunged, custom-tailored manager of station WAMY-TV, the only show in town, Terry had clout—and if you didn't know it, he told you.

We met at the office in October during marathon negotiations that one of Dan's real-estate clients was holding with the station to lease it space for expanded studio facilities. It was a complicated, long-term deal that Dan had asked me to help him superintend. Despite my all-business deportment, I could not altogether repulse the wanton microwaves beamed at me throughout the session by Terry's hot orbs. In the interest of good client relations, I accepted the inevitable lunch invitation and heard more than I wanted, starting with his premature birth in Akron, Ohio ("I couldn't wait to get going"), and ending with his current six-month separation from the decorative but dimwitted Mrs. English. In between he worked hard to wow me with tales of heroism and intrigue from the dark heart of the electronic jungle. First it was how he had foiled the network brass when they pressured him to take an unspeakable sit-com about an Indian reservation where oil is discovered —"the laugh track went wild over some crack about the tribe not having to worry any more about dry scalps," he said, "and it was all downhill from there." Then it was how he had hustled a big film star into his private office shower when the guy showed up absolutely sizzled the week before for the noontime interview show. And when the mayor had pressed him for Sunday adjacency to the Washington press-panel programs for a projected weekly report-to-the-people, "I told him the only sustaining time available was the Hour of God—and if we bumped it, he and the station might both have Someone beyond the viewing public to answer to. He crossed himself and settled for Saturday afternoon after college football." It was the sort of nonstop egotripping that usually inspired only puke from me, but his routine was so uncoy that somehow it failed to nauseate. Everything about Terry English said: I am hot shit and going places and if you're smart, you'll be my friend, and if you're not, you're missing a bet. Charm was not exactly the word for it.

We began to date once a week and sometimes twice but never more and when after a month I had not been to bed with him, he grew testy and asked why. I told him it was because he was all seamless plastic to me and kept the inner part of himself carefully hidden—and I did not sleep with friction-free mannequins. That was being both candid and not. The truth was I had no idea if he had any inner parts. What was clear was that he collected power and people like so many trophies, and I had no great enthusiasm for being added to the lot.

"Why the tough-guy act?" he asked me after I laid my charge on him.

"It's just a turn-on," I said. "I'm really all butter."

"No, seriously, Tabe." That was what he called me—it was meant as an endearing cross between Tabor and "babe" only I hated it; that I had not told him yet was a sign of my muddled fondness for the guy.

"I'm not tough—I'm honest," I said. "You're just not used to women talking back. Some of us are even marginally competent human beings."

"See," he said, "you've always got an answer. I've never seen you at a loss for words."

"Is that bad?"

"It's like you're always trying to top me."

"Maybe you need topping."

"See? You do it every time—as if you've got to prove yourself whenever you open your mouth."

"And you'd rather I prove myself spreading my legs?"

He laughed and said I was impossible and if I didn't like him enough to get in the sack that was all right, but it said more about my anxiety than his character. "Which anxiety is that?" I asked.

"Sort of an all-purpose one," he said, "as if you're panicked someone's going to discover a chink in you somewhere if you let them come too close and then they'll bore in and blow you away."

It was the first moderately astute thing he had said to me, and I didn't like it much. He saw me brooding a moment and said to think and not get defensive about what he had said. "I'm thinking," I said.

"Going to bed with someone is just a more intense form of interaction," he pattered on. "It opens you up emotionally and

392

physically—it leaves you vulnerable, literally and every other way. And that's just what you can't bear, Tabe."

"Call me Tabor for short."

"Tabor," he complied and flashed his pearliest smile. "Hey, relax—be human. Mannequins don't bite."

"Some try." Then I said it was funny how I had wanted to tell him the same thing since we had met: relax, open up, not everybody's the enemy.

"Then why didn't you?"

"I guess because it was easier to put you down instead."

"Because I'm such an insufferable prick?"

"I didn't think you knew."

"But you suffer me, anyway."

"Yes. Puzzling, isn't it?"

"No. Shall I tell you why?"

"Please."

"Because we're so like each other—only you don't want to admit it. So you've got to show me you're even better. And that's just what you do with the rest of the world, too, every way you can. You try to dazzle it so it can't get a really good bead on you. It makes you superhuman—but not very lovable."

"You don't think I'm lovable?" I asked in feigned horror.

"Not very."

"Then why do you want to go to bed with me?"

"Because you probably screw as well as you do everything else."

That was when I started liking Terry English more than I was put off by him. Even at his shallowest, he was diverting. And he had a good lean body that he applied fluently though hardly thrillingly in bed, where we wound up once a week all that winter after he monitored the late evening news, told me whom his anchorpersons were balling, and insisted his was the best weather report on any station in New England. "Whippy-do," I said. "Why don't you just tell us what it's going to do tomorrow instead of giving all that shit about what the humidity was twelve hours ago and the low over Montana?"

"That's show business, shweethaht," he said in his bad Bogey monotone.

"Television sucks," I said.

"Television is the pervasive medium of our time, shweet-haht."

"Pervade me," I said, and he did and stayed the night. He never said much about the backstage part of his life, about his wife or family or youth except that he'd been a stellar boy disc jockey at Lehigh and started out in the industry that way until he figured out the power was in being an impresario, not a performer. He'd risen in the field as a modestly clever local programmer and an ace pruner of managerial deadwood. He said he doubted if there was a more profitable station the size of his anywhere in the East, and at thirty-seven, he expected to be summoned to a place in the network sun before much longer. Meanwhile, he ran his fiefdom like Simon Legree—and was about as interested in the civic welfare of the community. "You're just a goddamn mercenary," I told him.

"And what are you—the Mohandas Gandhi of the courtroom?"

"I care about this town."

"Oh, I do, too. If it goes down, so do my billings."

He talked about shifting the station's legal business over to us, but I said only prostitutes took money for sex. He said wives did, too, which got my feminist enzymes churning. "Only my ex-lovers are allowed to be clients," I said, "no present ones."

"How many present ones have you got?" he asked.

"I forget," I said. "How many have you got?"

"Is anyone I ball my lover?"

"For statistical purposes, yes."

"Then the answer is one."

"One? What kind of stud are you?"

"A rusty one."

"You're not counting the missus."

"I don't ball the missus. She went home to mommy in Louisville."

"What about the anchorpersons?"

"I've done the anchorpersons. And it's bad policy."

"And now you're doing me once a week. What do you do the other six nights—jerk off to Carly Simon records?"

It took him a while to answer. "Does it matter?"

"Only if you're lying."

"Why would I lie?"

"Out of habit. Or maybe to keep me in line."

"Can anybody keep you in line?"

"I don't encourage the practice."

"Tabor," he said heavily, "have you ever really loved any-body and got hurt even a little from it?"

My antennae started wigwagging. "Sure I've loved—to one degree or another."

"But no one's ever really wounded you, have they? You won't let anyone, will you?"

"I'm cautious about investing emotionally, if that's what you mean."

"You're not cautious—you're petrified, if you want my opin-ion."

"I don't think I do, actually."

He rode right over me. "And if you're not deathly scared of being hurt, how come you're floating around loose and getting it only once a week?"

I was trying to avoid a complete collapse of our postcoital comity but he seemed bent on a confrontation. "Haven't you heard that abstinence makes the heart grow fonder?" I asked.

"Colder, I'd say."

I turned my head sideways toward him on my pillow. "Has it ever occurred to you that maybe the 'it' I'm getting the other six days is highly compensating in a noncarnal way?"

"Oh, sure," he said. "So steady lovers need not apply because it might screw up milady's plans to rule the world, is that it?"

"Maybe not the world, exactly."

"But as close as you can come?"

He was acting out his own fantasies and laying them on me, and all at once the whole subject seemed terribly tedious. "Sure," I said, "only you happen to be wrong about my interest in a consort. I review all applications with great care and dis-cuss them with my cohabitation committee."

"Tabor, I'm serious."

"No," I said, "that's just what you're not. You're fun, you're pretty, you're successful, you're a jolly good lay, and I love you for coming courting, Terry—but what you're not is serious."

"And why's that?"

I was down to my last rounds of ammunition and still he was coming on. "Because," I said, firing point-blank, "you don't know who you are. You may be a high-class operator and very dynamic, but that's different—that's not real—that's just flash. And you're the classiest flash on the beach. But I don't fall hard for that—if you really have to know."

No sound came out of him for so long that I lifted my head to assess the damage. He was just lying there staring up at the ceiling with glazed eyes. I folded an arm across his chest as if it were a bandage for the wound. He flicked it away and said, "Now I know who gives lessons to the black-widow spider." And he turned his back to me and went to sleep.

Over dinner the next night I traded confidences with Jessie Lennox, whose own alliance with Jonathan had turned sporadic, much to her sorrow. He stayed the night at her place irregularly, and she went out to his house only for occasional weekends now. It was his work, she thought. His head was very much caught up for the moment with the grammar school he had been chosen to design in a nearby suburb—he was determined to demonstrate that grace and function could be happily married on an austerity budget. "I also think he hates my cat," Jessie added. "He drop-kicks her into the bathtub every time she jumps into bed with us."

"The insensitive brute," I said. "Men are all alike."

"Yours isn't moody, at least," she said.

"Only because he doesn't have soul."

"Oh, fuck Jonathan's soul! It's his excuse for everything."

"Is it that bad?"

"It's not good. A manic-depressive lover is not what I need, exactly."

"Then forget him."

She threw me an ironic smile. "Not everyone's like you," she said. "You quit while you're ahead—or at least even."

"It's not a high-art form."

"But it takes balls—and I don't have them."

"Me, neither—just exquisite character."

She laughed and then sighed. "I keep thinking I'm just on a losing streak with Jon—that the thing'll turn around, the way it has before. I tell myself the easy thing is to walk away from it, and what really takes guts is to hang in there till the clouds part."

"Maybe you're right."

She picked up on the veiled doubt in my voice. "You think I'm wimping out, don't you?" she said.

"I think you're hooked on a sting ray—and I feel guilty as sin for having baited the line."

"Christ, no!" she said. "It doesn't matter if I bomb with Jon —I've had a helluva good time with him—sometimes. You have to take what comes if you're going to get involved."

"Maybe you do," I said. "I play the game different."

"No," she said, "you just never go beyond spring training."

"What's that supposed to mean?"

"It means you like to go through all the drills and the warm-up games, but when the season starts you'd rather coach than go out there and maybe get your ass busted."

Dan Kettering couldn't have put it more graphically. "And you disapprove?" I said.

"Hell, it's your life, kid," she said. "I just don't understand how you manage. You don't smoke much, you don't drink much, you don't eat more than a large sparrow—and you only make love when you've got nothing better to do. I mean that's inhuman, Tabor. Nobody's got that much self-control. Don't you just want to throw all the crap on your desk out the window sometimes and scream at the top of your lungs?"

"Sure," I said, "but it's easier to masturbate in the shower."

That stopped her short. "Really?"

"Every night—sometimes twice or three times—with Ivory Soap. It's gentle."

She gave a supercilious little sniff. "But not very rewarding, I shouldn't think."

"At least it's painless."

"That's your trouble," she said. "You don't know the pleasure of pain."

397

The Superior Court judge on the Zampa appeal must have been listening to Jessie. He doled me grief the following week by upholding the verdict of Judge Lombard's court. I went through the motions of taking it to the state Supreme Court but they refused to certify. That exhausted the old man's remedies within the state judicial system. The federal route was the only one left. It would be a long, slow trip at best, and the odds were hardly favorable. But what was there to lose? Sparky suggested an answer. "Everything," he said. "You fought hard and well, and the town beat you because you had no case. Now let it go and do a little fence-mending. The boys just wanted to show you you're only human. Give us all a break, Tabor."

"I think I've got a chance on the First Amendment angle," I said. "I may petition for a special three-judge court." Meaning if I lost, I could appeal straight to the U. S. Supreme Court.

"You're dreaming," Sparky said. "It's an open-and-shut case."

"I don't happen to think so," I said. "I see a basic conflict between my guy's freedom of artist expression and the city's effort to censor him by a crabbed application of the law."

"But you've tried all that already—and it didn't fly."

"Because Lombard wouldn't hear argument on it—that's way beyond his depth. Superior Court just said we got due process so what were we squawking about—which avoids the constitutional point entirely. And the state Supremes didn't want to be bothered. That leaves the whole question of Zampa's protected status under the First Amendment totally untouched."

"He doesn't have any protected status," said Sparky, heating up, "except in your city-baiting brain. The building code meets every reasonable and valid standard you could ask. It's a basic police-power regulation."

"Reasonable and valid aren't enough. The city has to show a compelling interest in regulating Zampa's freedom of expression by prior restraint—i.e., a building permit. It never has— because there isn't any. All it knows is that the bureaucracy has to be served. Well, it's about time city hall learned a little humanity and humility. It's supposed to serve the people, not clobber them. I'm going in with it."

398

Sparky's skin glowed the russet of his hair. "You're going to burn up a lot of people in places that count around here," he said. "Why bother?"

"I have a client to protect."

"You've also got a law practice to protect," he said, his mood darkening. "I thought we'd all gone down that road with you?"

"Sure—and I'm sticking to the road faithfully. I didn't go out looking for the old man."

"But you're riding him as if your life depended on it."

"Not mine—his."

"But you've done what you can."

"Not everything."

He looked grimmer than I had ever seen him. "Tabor, hasn't anyone ever told you discretion is the better part of valor? Do you know what that means? It means having the maturity of judgment to know when to pick your fights and when to back off if the other side's loaded for bear."

"I didn't pick this fight."

"Then why can't you stand to lose it?"

He needed to be defused. "I don't know," I tried. "Maybe I've got a phallic fixation for towers."

He wasn't about to be jollied out of it. "Goddamnit, Tabor, you're being an obstinate kid about this whole thing. Let well enough alone, why don't you?"

I thought of Jessie then. Was I, in this instance, letting myself be ruled by passion and blindness just as she did by hanging in a loser and getting trampled for the effort? But if my way of cutting losses was the more prudent, hers of enduring them was plainly the more courageous. Now I was in her place, and for once I was willing to try it her way and ride with the sensation. "How come," I asked him, "the boys can't stand the thought of my winning this one?"

"Because you don't deserve to," he said, "and because you've kicked shit on the city's linen—and because you're not very endearing about it."

"Why do I have to be endearing—because I'm a woman?"

"Out of respect."

"Respect for what—male tyranny? You mean it's all right for a broad to win but only if she wiggles her can and makes kissypoo to all the honorable officers of the court? I'm just as adorable as the men I deal with—no more, no less."

"You're also something of an overbearing bitch—in the eyes of a fair number of impartial observers around town."

"Impartial, my foot." I picked up one of the tangled paper clips that littered his desk, armed a rubber band with it, and fired it across the room. "Anyway," I said, "you know where nice guys finish, don't you?"

"Yeah," he said, "and supercunts get gang-banged."

For the instant I could not believe that a man of his quality had said anything quite so vile. "I didn't hear that," I said.

He saw my sudden anger and lowered his eyes a fraction. "You know what I mean."

"I must be hearing things. I could have sworn you just said something I wouldn't expect to come from a gutter rat."

"I didn't mean you—I meant in general."

"I'll consider an immediate apology."

"I'm just trying to be helpful."

"Do I get an apology or not?"

"You're acting infantile. You're supposed to be a partner here, Tabor, not a teenage hysteric."

I reached out with both hands and clutched the large electric typewriter moored beside his desk. "I'm counting to three," I said.

"You've got to be able to take constructive criticism if you want to grow in this business."

"One."

"Being petulant is the sign of insecurity."

"Two."

"Oh, please."

"Three," I said and shoved hard. The typewriter crashed to the floor with its bell going off in a startled frenzy.

Sparky sat there stunned, eyes riveted to the smoking deadweight on the floor. "That's lovely," he said quietly.

"You're lucky," I said. "Next time it lands in hernia country. I don't deserve that kind of talk from you or from anybody, Mr. Grier." And off I marched, trailing vehemence.

He was right, though, about what lay in store. Forty-eight hours after I filed Zampa's complaint with the Honorable

George H. Millis in United States District Court, the city slapped a tax foreclosure notice on the property; the old man was $6,700 and six years in arrears. And for good measure, an order to demolish the towers as structurally unsafe was issued the following day. Who would buy the property knowing the principal asset on it was in imminent peril of destruction?

One of the city marshals delivered me a copy of both legal notices a few days after their date of issue. "Your client's not around," he reported. "We've gone up there three times a day for the last three days."

"He's wintering in Palm Beach," I said. "He can't worry about little things like taxes."

I drove out to the junkyard to see for myself. The shack was shut so tight I thought he must have hammered up the door from the inside to match the boarded windows and materialized out through a crack in the floor. Or had he decided his usefulness on earth was at an end and fallen on his favorite trowel, Nipponese style? Surely there would have been a telltale whiff if he were decomposing in there. No, he had just migrated. Without him around, the towers looked an icy sepulcher that somber March morning. It did not take much to imagine how, in their sleek winter husks, those three frosted spires could come tumbling down any moment, as much from remorse as from their own unsupportable weight.

I called TV Terry and asked whether his station might help with an appeal for funds to head off the tax foreclosure. "But you said the old guy's flown the coop," he said. "Just showing the towers is pretty grim footage."

"What do you want me to do—strip and climb them halfway?"

"Hey," he said, "terrific. WAMY goes to pink! What a shot that'd give Action News."

"Terry," I said, "please."

"You know, we're not exactly flacks for the Hundred Neediest Cases?"

"That's showbiz," I said, "all heart."

"Look, I'll suggest it to my news director, but I don't order him."

"Except when you want to."

"Who said?"

"You did, El Macho. You told me anyone who gives you grief gets sacked on the spot."

"Don't believe everything you get told in bed."

"Some of us don't believe any of it," I said. "Now how 'bout it?"

There was some muffled growling of instructions on the other end. Then he came back on and said, "Okay, they'll get on it. My guys want to know where you want the money sent. We're not against giving an occasional transfusion to bleeding hearts but a collection agency we definitely are not."

I blew him a kiss and said I'd get right to work reactivating the Save Zampa Committee only now it would be the Save the Towers Committee. In high excitement, I phoned Jonathan's office, to be told that he was working at home all day. I suppose I should have respected his privacy enough to phone ahead, but I thought it might dramatize the urgency of the situation better if I just appeared on his doorstep and urged him to drop everything for this critical mission of mercy.

I drove out to his place fast, my head full of ways to rescue the towers and turn the property into an appropriate shrine to the old man—maybe as an arts workshop for ghetto people funded by municipal and foundation money and the Friends of Gabriel Zampa Society, Inc. In my distracted state, I nearly skidded the last quarter of mile over the snowy rutted road to Jon's hideaway and came jouncing to a halt in front of the small barn he used as a garage. The doors were open and the usually vacant space next to his car was taken up by a familiar-looking Saab. A glance at the license plate confirmed it was the one in which Sam Nightingale had squired me our summer together. But it was not Sam who had driven it out there that day. I didn't bother to get out of my car.

32

Only her high burgundy boots in soft Italian kid proclaimed that Lee Nightingale could afford the best. Everything else she wore—and the jewelry she didn't—bespoke frugal taste and disdain for the trendy. She spent but carefully, and it was not clear to her at the luncheon I had summoned her to at Annie's Soup Kitchen that the cause I had in mind was worthy. "But shouldn't we make sure that the towers are safe," she asked, "before we go trying to pay off the tax bill?"

"That's exactly how the city skunked us," I explained. "The foreclosure date comes before the demolition hearing. Unless somebody pays off the tax bill, there won't have to be any hearing— the city can pull down the towers ten minutes after they take title—and we won't have any legal standing to stop them." Which was one reason the appeal for funds on Terry English's TV station netted us exactly $74.68 and some food stamps.

"So we have to pay for the privilege of trying to prove the towers are safe even though the city has already decided they're not?" Lee asked.

"That's about it."

She shook her head sadly. "Not a very appealing prospect."

"No," I said, "that's what they had in mind."

"I just don't understand why the city is being so cruel."

I offered her four theories. One was embarrassment at so much attention being focused on the worst part of town. A second was that a deal had been struck between city hall and the blacks in the Gully who had no love of Zampa and found his towers were an irritating distraction from the real needs of the area. A third was galloping dislike of me, especially now that I had insisted on carrying the fight into federal court. And maybe—just maybe—the city really thought the towers a hazard or at least a potentially chronic headache that was better removed.

She patted her wide thin mouth contemplatively with a napkin and tried to sort it all out. "Well," she asked after a moment, "wouldn't we be better off trying to determine for ourselves if the towers are safe—or if not, maybe how they can be fixed—before we go paying through the nose for the right to preside at their burial?"

"Sure," I said, "and Jon's trying to round up a structural engineer to get right on it. But even if we decide they're safe to our own satisfaction, the appeals board could still rule against us."

"What are the odds?"

"Beats me. You've seen the towers. Frankly, I don't understand how he got them up in the first place. But Jon seems to think they're absolutely safe—just ask him the next time you see him."

Addressing her soup when I said it, she chose not to look up. I felt like a *picador* sinking the first infuriating shaft in the animal's hide. If it hurt, she was not showing it. All she said when she glanced up was, "How much do you want from me?"

"You make it sound as if I'm their proprietor. I don't have any more vested interest in the towers than you do."

"No more financial interest, perhaps," she said, "but there are other kinds—I think we both know that."

I nodded briefly in acknowledgment. "Look," I said, "I'm willing to put up a couple of thousand dollars of my own, but to meet the tax bill and do the safety tests and maybe hire a guard for a while or build a really secure fence, it's going to take another seven or eight thousand. Mike Tillinghast says he'll put in a few hundred and try to get Professor Brady to match it, but there isn't a lot of time to pass the hat. Any prudent soul is going to ask the same thing you did—why throw money away on the towers if they've already been condemned?"

"But you think I'm rich enough not to mind, is that it?" she asked.

"I think you care because you're an artist and recognize the old man's achievement."

She gave me a short half-smile. "I forget how quick you are with the answers."

"It's my profession," I said.

She was still troubled by the apparent perversity of the city's position and wondered why Sparky or Maynard Lamport or Dan Kettering couldn't use their drag to have the tax foreclosure deadline put off until after the demolition hearing. I felt I owed her an honest answer. At risk of sounding paranoid, I told her city hall was determined to beat me; Zampa was of minor concern. "Why the vendetta?" Lee asked.

"I'd say because I'm a spunky lady and they can't bear it. If you ask them, they'd probably call me something else."

"You mean to say it's a straight-out sexist thing?"

"At bottom, yes."

"You're sure that's not just a wee bit self-serving?"

"Maybe a little," I said. "I suppose they wouldn't like me a whole lot better if I were a man."

"Then maybe in all fairness to Zampa, you ought to step aside," she said. "I know you're deeply committed to this, but your very fervor may not be in your client's best interests. I'm sure it would be a painful step for you, but I suspect it would be the responsible one—and all the more admirable."

"I can't do that."

Her eyes skimmed over me. "Can't—or won't?"

"Won't," I said. "I don't run from fights."

"Pyrrhic victories don't get you very far."

"Neither do strategic withdrawals when the war's nearly over."

"Don't you think it's worth a try?"

"No," I said, "I think I have to tough it out."

Her arched brows told me she was not convinced. "And the old man's not to be consulted about any of this?" she asked.

"Of course I'd consult him—if I had a clue where he is. He mentioned something to me once about New Bedford. I've got the police there checking on him, but so far there's been nothing. He's an official missing person."

"Oh, my," she said and then fell pensively silent for a few minutes. Finally she looked me in the eye. "What would you say," she asked, "if I told you I'd write you out a check for ten thousand dollars before getting up from this table—which is the least I happen to think it will take to keep the wolves away from the towers—provided you get out of the case?"

I rubbed my neck for a few seconds and studied the fixed purpose on the face of this woman whom, against all expectation, I found myself admiring each time we met. There was a quality to her manner and intellect that did not correspond to the peevish and disconsolate person Sam had drawn for me. Was she so skilled at covering the scars? Or had he miscalculated her mettle? Or deciphered wrong the messages she sent him? I could not tell where, between them, the strength—and truth—lay. "And what would you say," I finally answered, "if I told you I'd retire from the case provided you get out of Jon Kenyon's bed?"

There was just one delicious instant of advantage in it for me while she recoiled and calculated. Then she said, as if I had noted merely the imminence of the vernal equinox, "Frankly, I don't see what one thing has to do with the other."

By being direct she had at once reclaimed the edge she seemed always to have on me. "Only that each is a thing we've invested in heavily," I said.

"So if you're to be deprived, I ought to be, too?"

"I hadn't intended it as a *quid pro quo*. I was just trying to make a point. Your proviso would hurt me as much as mine would you."

"Leave that aside," she said. "My condition has a point to it —yours is pure pique."

"Not at all. Why should I care who you go to bed with?"

"Exactly," she said. "But you do or you wouldn't have brought it up."

"I brought it up because you made an unreasonable proposal."

"And so you made an irrelevant one to let me know you're bargaining from strength—do I have it right?"

"I'm not bargaining any which way. I'm trying to save a work of art. What are you trying to save?"

406

She folded her hands on the table and studied them. "A large part of my insides," she said evenly, "so long as you've chosen to make the subject your personal business."

"Friends of mine are getting hurt by it," I said. "That's why I take it personally."

"What friends are those?"

"Who do you think?"

"I can't imagine."

"Jessie, for one. Sam, for another."

"Sam doesn't know a thing about it. I can't vouch for Jessie."

"Not knowing doesn't mean they're not getting hurt."

"But the problem in each case existed before we—beforehand."

"Is that any reason to make it worse?"

"I don't think that's what I'm doing."

"You don't want to think that," I said, "because you've never been screwed before by anyone like Jon—and you don't want it to stop."

She brushed a hand through her hair. "I forgot for the moment that I was talking to an authority on the men in my life."

"If that's supposed to embarrass me, save yourself the trouble."

"It was an aside," she said. "I take you to be invulnerable to insult or you'd never have got this far. As to your other friend, your concern is misplaced. Jessica, from what I gather, was never emotionally equipped to deal with Jonathan's temperament."

"And you are?"

"Oh, yes. I don't put up with nonsense."

"He respects your age, no doubt."

"Now who's trying to embarrass who?"

"No, I'm serious."

"Oh, that's bullshit, Tabor," she said with almost savage bite. "And being three years older doesn't exactly make me his mother. He's laboring under the delusion I'm savvy, gifted, and quite a good lay for an old warhorse."

"I don't doubt it. He's had a yen for accomplished older

women—and I don't mean doddering ones. He left me for one once—or did I throw him out first? I can't remember now."

"A little of both, is how he tells it."

"I see—you two have no secrets?"

"I'm not sure I'd go that far. But he's made it plain you're someone who mattered to him rather a lot—more than he did to you, from the sound of it."

"That's news to me."

"I'm not surprised."

"Why is that?"

"Because you're too busy using people and discarding them to notice how they feel."

For all her cushioned phrasing, she could deliver a direct blow that injured bloodily. "That's unkind," I said.

"On the contrary." She maneuvered the salt and pepper shakers between us. "I think somebody who cares even a tad had better tell you that before you mash up the emotions of a few dozen more people—and kill what chance you have left for genuine love. You don't know about love, Tabor, and I don't think you want to. You've got so much else going for you that you decided somewhere along the line loving is more trouble than it's worth, and so you don't love—you use people to gratify you as the need arises—and then you toss them away—the way you did Sam and the way you did Jessie and the way you did Jon—and Jon's friend Jeff—and whoever you were with before, no doubt, and whoever you're with now—this pretty television fellow, I hear."

Anger churned through me. Who in the Christ was she? A failed, frustrated, wilting rich bitch, trying to salvage a few pelvic thrills before she dried up. I wanted to smash that pert face and tear that bobbed hair. She had me in turmoil. "Sam!" I said so loud half the place must have heard it. "How did I use Sam?" I pitched my voice softer now but the frenzy had not left it. "I tried to give Sam something he wasn't getting from you. I tried to save Sam—and you—if you really want to know."

"You didn't save him—you tormented the man. You used him to pump you full of sperm when you were in heat and after you'd had your fill, you douched him right out of your life—the way you do everyone who threatens your flaming free spirit."

"That's—that's—just totally absurd!"

The woman had reduced me to sputtering incoherence. To compound the pain, she had a hurried sip of water and looked at her watch, as if to say there wasn't time to debate the matter further. "Whatever it may sound like, Tabor, I'm not trying to hurt you," she said, reaching into her bag for her purse. "I didn't bring this whole thing up—you did."

I put my hand down heavily on her bag and stopped her fussing with the money. "I won't have you thinking that about me and Sam."

She threw me just a glance. "Forget what I said. I'm only a jealous wife."

"He's a lovely man with all kinds of virtues you seem to have stopped noticing. I don't understand for the life of me why you're tossing him away for a moody stud like Jon."

She gave a sigh of resignation and finally looked at me. "I know all about Sam's virtues," she said. "Why do you think I married him? But he lost something vital back there somewhere—I can't pin down when it happened but it did. He stopped growing—and I've just begun. What am I supposed to do? You're an emancipated woman—tell me."

"Help him—not become someone else's mistress out of desperation."

"I've helped him all I can, but he thinks I'm only carping. The man's found his niche and he's locked into it. Now I'm trying to help myself—is that so terrible? Life's not long enough to turn down the chance." She gently disengaged my hand. "And Jonathan is a good deal more than a stud, as you perfectly well know, so there's no point in your being abusive about it. Now while we settle up, suppose you decide whether you want my ten thousand dollars."

I left her sitting there and went straight to the bank. The woman downstairs in charge of the safety deposit boxes had to ask me three times for my name before I focused. In the privacy of the little booth, I managed to cool off enough to count the stocks my father had left me and I had hoped never to have to sell. But there was enough there for an occasional invasion of capital if my salary would not cover an irresistible cash purchase. And who knew—maybe Gabriel Zampa's towers would appreciate a lot faster than AT&T? All I had to do was save them from the clutches of everyone else in the world. Them—and me with them. I had felt so ganged up on and bruised. By acclamation I had been found loveless, unloving, unlovable, and inhuman. The illegitimate daughter of the Wicked Witch of the West. Fit companion to the Loch Ness Monster. Condemned as mineral by a jury of her peers. Hailed as mechanical marvel and sub-being. Could none of them understand? The price of glory was overloaded circuitry. Surely someone might have sympathized a little. Did they know how much I yearned at times to vegetate? Did they think I truly aspired to permanent unembraceability? Or had my act been so good that I had begun to live the part without realizing? Tabor Hill, shooting star. Was there ever a heroine more marvelous or meteoric? She of the fearless visage (and the knotted colon). She of the dazzling intellect (and the protean principles). She of unbending resolve (and towering ambivalence). She of—of —of all these goddamn fucking tears sloshing down my cheeks and spattering the shiny tin box that holds what tangible security I have in this world. Why are half my parts voting to abandon ship? But oh, how tackier than polyester to come unglued in the corner of a bank vault? The middle of a summation, maybe, or an obligatory orgasm but not the bowels of a bank. Especially one that was a client. I sniffed and snabbled, bottomed out of the self-pitying downer, glugged my secret stabilizing potion, got up, nearly fell but kept going. And going.

Lee Nightingale called me at home that night to say she had contributed five thousand dollars without strings to the fund Jon was gathering for the towers. And that she was sorry if she had upset me at lunch but I should nevertheless think hard about what she had said. I told her I thought she must have had enough going on in her own life just then and not to worry about mine. "You're probably right," she said. After a moment's hesitation she added, "May I presume our conversation was a private one?"

"Presume what you like."

"Tabor," she said, that iron in her voice, "I'll tell Sam myself what has to be said if and when it's necessary. I don't expect to make a career out of Jonathan."

"Well, I'm glad to hear I'm not the only one who uses people like Kleenex."

"Everybody uses everybody," she said. "The venal thing is not giving as much as you get."

"Sure, but that comes down to who's measuring the portions."

"Not always," she said and let it drop. "Are we agreed, then?"

"On what?"

"On the nature of our conversation."

"I gather that's what the five thousand dollars is for."

"What do you mean?"

"To seal my lips."

"Oh, God," she said. "I never intended that."

"Then your timing is off."

"Yes," she said, "I see that." She was silent for a moment. "Would it prove anything to you if I took the money back?"

"Only that you're an Indian-giver," I said and told her the secret was safe and that I understood and that I even forgave her the vicious slanders from lunch which I hoped would prove as therapeutic for me as infidelity seemed for her. She could easily have snarled at that but she laughed instead because she guessed I meant it, and somewhere far down, at a depth so dark and cavernous I feared to visit even in a dream, I loved her intensely.

33

The best Jonathan could come up with in the way of an expert to test out the safety of Zampa's towers after we had rescued them from tax foreclosure was a scrawny, balding, whispery guy named Ross Otis, who had all the medals for the job but hardly inspired confidence on first sight. Appearances aside, he also happened to be out of work.

"Temporarily," Jon assured me after phoning the news. The fellow had been highly recommended by someone who had worked closely with him at Sikorsky before he had been let go in the post-Vietnam slowdown, and before that he had been well regarded by the NASA people at Houston until the phaseout took effect down there. For a year, he'd been scraping by as a consultant on odd jobs—"but none quite as odd as ours, he said when I told him about it," Jon added.

"If nobody else has hired him, why should we?" I asked.

"He has exactly the qualifications we need—he's licensed as a mechanical engineer, a structural engineer, and an aeronautical engineer. That's a lot of know-how—and he happens to be available when we need him."

"We're not claiming the towers can fly—why do we need an aeronautical engineer?"

"They know all about stress and metal fatigue. Look, believe me, he's a real find. He's just had some rotten luck. People do, you know?"

In the flesh, what there was of it, Ross Otis looked decidedly malnourished. He was only a couple of inches taller than I and couldn't have been more than twenty pounds heavier. He showed up at the office wearing a windbreaker and khakis and linked to his big-eyed, seven-year-old daughter Valerie, who had come along because it was Saturday and the towers were the sort of weekend diversion usually available to children only in their fantasies. Valerie's mother, I was shortly to learn, had died of leukemia two years earlier. Ross Otis had not exactly been a favorite of the Lord. Still, he appeared to be unafflicted by brooding, even if he did not qualify as sunny. Outfitted with a slide rule strapped to one side of his belt, a miniature calculator to the other, a small tool kit in the hand not clasping his daughter's, and a spiral notebook wedged in his hip pocket, he seemed anything but listless about the assignment. Maybe it was just the high forehead or the ascetic quality his gauntness gave him, but I had the hunch that three quarters of the guy's internal organs were brains. Almost none of him was mouth: I had to crowbar every word out of him, and his daughter was hardly more of a chatterbox—a pleasingly modest trait in an age of ferociously demonstrative urchins. At the towers, though, they both grew immediately animated. Jon, I sensed, had not erred in his choice.

That first afternoon Ross did nothing but look and touch and measure with a big reel of industrial tape he had packed in the trunk of his car. Next day he left his daughter with friends and went scuttling like a human fly almost halfway up the towers, which had shucked their icy coat only a few days before. I watched with prayerful fixity. Stealth and sureness marked his movements among those crisscrossing struts. He poked and pulled each overhead member before exerting his full weight upon it and hoisting himself to the next higher level. At each stop he hunched beside the nearest ring joint and, balancing with apparent fearlessness, scribbled notes on what he had found. Could the builder have hoped for a more kindred spirit to certify his handiwork?

I asked Ross afterward over coffee at my place why he hadn't become petrified on the towers as I would have been. "I never look down," he said, and that was it for derring-do. As to the state of the towers, he couldn't tell much for certain yet, although they felt solid enough. The cement skin showed some cracking from the weather and spots of corrosion here and there underneath, but the acute angularity of the structure meant that what water seeped through to the metal framing probably had little chance to collect before coursing earthward. "It's horizontal configurations that get you into trouble," he said with a straight face. I said I couldn't agree more. He thought about it some and then permitted himself the first smile I had seen brighten his generally cloudy countenance.

During the next several days, he worked up at the junkyard alone, exposing the struts in one or two places on each tower, chipping off samples of the plaster for laboratory analysis, making a test-boring of the foundation, and taking a core sample of the center post in the main tower. Most important of all, he said, was the careful uncovering of one of the joints to see just how skillfully Zampa had spliced the metal members together with mesh and pressed the mortar in. While the lab tests were being completed, he made dozens of diagrams and hundreds of computations, the point of which he shared with me in something approximating plain English. And when I didn't understand something—which was almost everything at first—he went over it again and again until I had it. If there was a grain of impatience in him he kept it hidden.

When the lab results came back, he ran through one last batch of figures and then announced, "I'd say it'll withstand any hurricane up to a hundred miles an hour—and in a century there's been only one around here anywhere near that." I asked him how he knew that for sure and he said he'd checked with the state meteorological service. "Actually," he said, "with a really big wind, the grave danger is from downed power lines and falling trees—not things like this." I remembered how Jon had been fearful the foundation was too shallow when the old man told him about it. "No sweat," Ross said. "Zampa must have forgot, he did it so long ago. It's four feet, most of it masonry rubble. The footings are in like Flynn." He actually blushed after he said it. I asked if there was any likelihood the towers would collapse of their own weight. "No way," he said, "but it needs upkeep. The corrosion should be stopped." He seemed so calm and thorough and matter-of-fact that I never doubted him.

The hearing on the demolition order was before the Amity Building Code Enforcement Committee, which functioned as a quasi-judicial appeals board. It was composed of a consulting engineer, the owner of the largest optical establishment in town, and a plumbing contractor, all of whom had been selected by the city administration and none of whom could be considered likely prospects to buck it. The optician, a hobnail type named Charles Rudolf, served as the chairman, a responsibility that left him heady. For no sooner had we assembled than with classic star-chamber form he ordered the proceedings into executive session on the ground there was no room for the press and interested public inside the cramped quarters reserved for the board's deliberations on the third floor of city hall. I rose at once to tell him his ruling violated state law and the due process clause of the Constitution against the unlawful taking of property. An accompanying howl went up from the attending press corps, which included reporters from half a dozen papers, the wire services, and TV Terry's blown-dry Action News crew.

While Rudolf was scurrying around to find us a larger hall, I had my first glimpse of the rumored secret weapon the city had commandeered to smite me. Instead of Kenneth Schoonmaker or one of the prosecutor's sturdy men or any of the milquetoasts from the corporation counsel's office, the authorities went out of town for special counsel to represent the building and safety department in this momentous matter. Her long lines accentuated by a two-piece maroon knit dress with a wide hem that swirled dramatically as she moved, Ellen Trask mingled easily with the pack of municipal officials who had imported her from Hartford to teach me a lesson in lady lawyering. If not for that purpose, why range so far afield for an attorney? Her light hair was pulled severely back to lend a teardrop shape to her pale, stately face. I had heard about Trask from my mother, who had worked with her on some civic function and thought we would hit it off together, given our similarities. At each successive rung on the early-career ladder, she had in fact narrowly outdone me, serving, in turn, as a ranking editor on the *Harvard Law Review*, a clerk on the First Circuit, an assistant to the United States Attorney in Hartford, and lately a fast-rising associate in the glossiest private firm in the capital. Just because she was younger, rangier, prettier, and conceivably even brighter than I gave me no reason at all, I told myself, to take this immediate, childish, and intense dislike of her. That would be playing directly into the hands of my massed enemy. No doubt they had me down as fiercely combustible tinder, likely to go up at the first touch of competitive fire from a sister-in-the-law. I would undercut the premise at once. "Good morning, Miss Trask," I said as her corporal's guard moved past me to the door en route to the city council chamber where the hearing had been transferred.

She looked up crisply. "Good morning." Her eyes were uncertain.

"Tabor Hill," I said, extending my hand.

She took it, still looking quizzical. "Have we met before, Miss Hill?" she asked regally.

"I believe we have a mutual acquaintance," I said.

"And who might that be?"

"It might be my mother, Meredith Hill?"

"Oh, yes," she said tentatively, awaiting a further clue.

"She says you're an excellent organizer."

"How nice," She was still in the dark. "And where was it again that we two met?" She had one of those haughty, hot-potato mouths you wanted to flush out with borax.

"Mother is vice chairman of the American Nazi Party for the state."

Her face froze. "You must be mistaken, Miss Hill."

"I'm joking, Miss Trask. I don't honestly keep close watch on Mother's civic enterprises. Next time I speak to her, I'll check it out."

"Do," she said. "I don't like being impolite, but one meets a great many people."

"One does," I said. "Well, I hope you enjoy our local hospitality."

"I'm sure I shall," she said. "Are you involved in any of the Zampa business?"

"I'm only his attorney."

"Oh, of course—forgive me. The name didn't register. I'm afraid there's been so much technical material to absorb I've

overlooked the human element somewhat. So nice to see you—
and, well, good luck." And she was swallowed up again among
the men who had hired her. Break a leg, lady.

She ran through her presentation nicely, sparing the bombast
but not the clinical details. Three officials from the department
were called in ascending order of authority, starting with the
senior building inspector, an open-collared stalwart named
Mongillo, who said he has spent two full working days examining the materials and workmanship that had gone into the
towers. And to my surprise, he added that he had spoken for an
hour or so with Zampa, apparently just a few days before the
old man had taken off, about his methods of construction. It
was an advantage I would not have ceded them. In general,
Mongillo testified, the stuff that had gone into the structure
varied in quality from very good to very bad—an unacceptable
range—and it was difficult to pass blanket judgment on any
one aspect because of the extreme irregularity of all the components. "And is such irregularity desirable?" Trask followed
up rhetorically, "or are uniformity of materials and consistency
in craftsmanship considered essential to sound building? Isn't
that in fact why we have building codes, Mr. Mongillo?" He
did not debate the point.

Methodically she led him through a damaging recitation
on the state of the cement-encrusted framework. From what he
himself could see and what the builder had told him, the metal
members that composed the intricate strutwork were made out
of, among other things, steel tees and angles, flat concrete reinforcing bars, galvanized water pipes, rigid electrical conduits,
rolled sheet metal, bed frames, and automobile exhausts—and
just how much was made of which, he could not say. He had
detected exposed corrosion in some sixty spots on the three
towers, and in one of them he said he had pried off a piece of
rust that was nearly a quarter of an inch thick. "Almost all of
the members, horizontal and vertical, are so cracked in my esti-
mation that there are very few places where water and moisture
have not penetrated and flowed down the entire length of the
structure."

Q. Now, Mr. Mongillo, did you actually touch these cracked and corroded members?

A. Oh, yes—in a number of places. I wanted to see if they were rigid or not and could support a man of my weight.

Q. And what did you find?

A. In many cases the cement covering was loose and so I wouldn't risk climbing on them. It didn't look as if they could hold me, and I'm not all that heavy.

Q. Could they hold a hundred pounds, say?

A. I wouldn't bet on it.

The quality and strength of the cement holding the towers together was likewise highly suspect, he said. "In some places you can see where he had so much sand aggregate in his mixture that now it's crumbling away," he explained. "You take your hand and just rub it and it falls off, so apparently he didn't have enough cement mixture in the total batch. No less of a problem, the inspector said, was the apparent lack of density to the cement, much of which had been casually mixed and then applied without any compacting tool, according to Zampa's own description of the process. My head throbbed. This was an especially troubling disclosure because, having seen the old man work with a trowel, I had made the unwarranted assumption that he always operated that way. As if sensing my carelessness, the tenacious Miss Trask zoomed in on the point:

Q. And what happens if the plaster is not properly compacted as it is applied?

A. The strength of mortars and concretes depends to a large degree on the denseness of the mix and the proper blending of the aggregate with the cement paste. This is usually accomplished by the application of pressure—say, by a hand tool—or by a vibrating machine so the mix is more thorough and even and compacted. For much of the cement work, Mr. Zampa used no hand tool—just his hands—and he prided himself on never using a vibrator or any other kind of machine.

Q. And what is the result of such improper compacting?

A. You get voids—holes or spaces, you would call them. They might be too small to be seen by the naked eye, but they would definitely contribute to a weakened finished product.

Worst of all, Mongillo reported of his findings, was the state of the tower joints. In several of the locations where the members lay exposed, you could see that the metal elements had been wired together. "Now a proper structural connection can be made in several ways," he said, "but wiring is not one of them. It can be made by welding. It can be made by riveting. It can be made by bolting. It can even be made by laps or splices—which is what the builder came closest to accomplishing in these towers. But a lap splice has to be properly designed and the bonding agent between the two metals must be strong enough to transmit the stress. In a reinforced concrete structure, which is what these towers pretend to be, a properly designed lap should be no less than twelve inches—and there aren't any that size in these towers."

Q. Aren't these joints reinforced by chicken wire, though, Mr. Mongillo?

A. Chicken wire is not recognized as a suitable construction material—it stretches like a rubber band. And Mr. Zampa used a wide variety of materials for the joints—almost any kind of wire mesh he could lay his hands on, including what's called hardware cloth. In a few places you can see where this wire, which is very thin to begin with, has eroded away but the imprint is still there.

Q. You say these towers are only pretending to be reinforced concrete. I thought any combination of concrete over metal qualified as reinforced.

A. No, ma'am. By accepted engineering standards, a reinforced concrete column contains not less than four bars, tied or hooped together with very specific spacings in between. This is because these columns are under heavy compression loads, and a slender steel element has little or no lateral support value on its own. Only when you tie them precisely can you prevent the concrete columns from buckling.

Q. And these members that make up the towers, they're not tied like that?

A. They're not tied at all—they're just bound up with mesh, something like a bandage, without any concern that I could see for proper design or stress factors.

Q. Are you saying, then, they lack strength?

A. They lack all load-bearing strength so far as I can tell.

Q. And what is your overall evaluation, Mr. Mongillo, of the structural stability of these towers in view of your two-day inspection of their materials and workmanship?

A. They are deteriorating rapidly. I expect they will disintegrate before much longer and collapse if not taken down, possibly on the row houses across the street.

Q. How much longer can they stand?

A. There's no way to say for sure.

I never interrupted her. It was all so smooth and effortless—and lethal. Maybe her sweat glands had been surgically removed or she had sponges for dress shields, but I had the unnerving impression that Ellen Trask excreted no bodily moisture of any sort before, during, or after her legal exertions. Like a reptile. By the time I took over against Senior Inspector Mongillo, I felt five touchdowns behind with only one quarter left in the game. But in the immortal words of Grantland What's-His-Face, it wasn't the winning or losing that counts but letting the bastards know you were there.

Q. Mr. Mongillo, didn't you tell us that because some of the cement covering felt loose in a few spots where you touched it, you never actually climbed up on any of the struts—or members, I guess we're calling them—of these towers?

A. Yes, I didn't think they would hold me.

Q. You were just being naturally cautious?

A. That's right.

Q. You didn't think they would hold you?

A. No, I didn't.

Q. But since you never really tried, you don't know that for a fact, do you?

A. Well, you could just tell by looking at them.

Q. You can? You're able to just look at a piece of construction and determine its support strength, are you?

A. Well—in some cases. Maybe not exactly, but more or less.

Q. So you're just making an approximation in saying some of those members couldn't even hold a hundred pounds —you didn't actually test any of them, did you?

A. No, not actually.

Q. And if you didn't climb up on any of them, can you tell us how you were able, Mr. Mongillo, to evaluate the workmanship and materials in a hundred-foot-high tower without ever leaving the ground?

A. Well, I used a ladder to go up about ten or twelve feet.

Q. But you didn't go any higher?

A. No.

Q. Then how do you know the condition of the cement and the metal above that level?

A. I used binoculars.

Q. You used binoculars to determine the physical state of these towers?

A. Yes.

Q. You evidently have bionic eyes, Mr. Mongillo. Are you telling us you can determine if cement will crumble—or the ratio of aggregate to cement paste—at a given spot simply by looking at it?

A. To a certain extent, yes. Anyone with experience in the construction industry can.

Q. And is that the way you usually inspect the structural safety of the buildings you're sent out to evaluate— through binoculars from fifty feet away?

Miss Trask: Objection. The witness has already explained the special circumstances preventing him from making a closer inspection of these structures.

Miss Hill: And that, gentlemen, is precisely the point. Mr. Mongillo thought the towers were unsafe, therefore he didn't bother to inspect them except casually. In other words, he didn't let the facts interfere with his preconceptions.

Chairman Rudolf: Go ahead, Miss Hill.

Q. You say there was exposed corrosion in sixty spots in the towers, Mr. Mongillo. Do you know how many of those occurred at joints?

A. Not very many.

Q. How many?

A. I'm not sure.

Q. Were there in fact any exposed joints?

A. There was cracking and spalling around quite a number of the joints.

Q. But no exposed corrosion?

A. I don't remember.

Q. Wouldn't you have included it in your report if you had found such rusted joints?

A. Yes.

Q. Now I'm sure you noticed, Mr. Mongillo, that the cement covering of these towers is decorated with thousands of small objects—glass and shells and tiles and so forth?

A. Yes, of course.

Q. And did you notice, Mr. Mongillo, that in quite a number of places these decorative objects have been pried off by vandals, leaving little craters where moisture might enter?

A. In places, yes.

Q. Isn't it possible that these spots where such unfortunate mischief has occurred coincide in large part with where you found corrosion and exposed metal?

A. I suppose so, but that really doesn't matter. My job is to determine the condition of the towers, not try to guess how they got that way.

Q. Yes, but if the corrosion were largely the result of vandalism and not poor materials or poor workmanship, that would suggest the trouble spots could be patched and, if the towers were protected from malicious mischief the way other works of art usually are, there would be little likelihood of such exposure and corrosion occurring spontaneously—isn't that distinctly possible?

MISS TRASK: Objection. The witness should not be required to answer a strictly hypothetical question based upon a mere supposition.

MISS HILL: Gentlemen, if we're going to throw out hypotheticals and suppositions, I don't see how any of Mr. Mongillo's testimony can stand. We heard him testify to the hypothetical strength of these towers based solely on the power of his own eyeballs, and if that's not supposition, I don't know what is.

Right in the ask, Trask. She took it without protest, and the chairman instructed the witness to answer. He said maybe I had a point but there was no way to tell for sure. Well, then, I asked him, could he tell me if the struts evidencing corrosion were load-bearing members or not? He said he wasn't an engineer and couldn't be certain. I asked if he knew, then, how to calculate stress in structural members, and he said no. I asked if he knew how the weight-bearing capacity of a metal member was affected by the degree of rust corrosion it had suffered, and he said, "Well, the department doesn't recognize any such metal as what's been used in these towers, so how could I compute such a thing?" I said that was exactly right, and if he could not make such computations and did not know for a fact, by first-hand or first-foot experience, what weight any part of the towers could bear, how could he possibly say they were about to collapse? "By general experience," he said. I picked up a plaster chip Ross Otis had taken from the towers and asked Mongillo if his general experience qualified him to estimate the ration of sand to cement in it.

A. Just by looking at it?
Q. Yes.
A. No, I couldn't just by looking at it.
Q. And did you do anything more than look at the cement covering in the towers besides touching it in a few places and deciding not to risk your neck on it? Did you submit any of the cement to a laboratory test to determine its exact composition?
A. No. We don't have such facilities in the department.
Q. Did you submit any of the cement to a compression test to see if your instincts about its density were correct?
A. No, we don't have those facilities, either.

Q. Mr. Mongillo, you've said that the members and the joints of these towers are deteriorating so badly that you doubt if the struts could support a weight of one hundred pounds. How do you explain that the man who built them climbed all over those towers for many years without any apparent ill effects to himself or to the members?

A. I wouldn't know. Maybe he knew where to step. And I'm not sure I'd agree that his movements or those of others didn't weaken or damage the members.

Q. Well, did you find any evidence of buckling in the members, Mr. Mongillo? I don't see anything in your report to that effect.

A. No, I can't say there was any actual buckling.

Q. Or crippling? Or bending?

A. Bending, yes.

Q. Oh, where was that?

A. In Tower A, the smallest one—in a horizontal member at the north side, about six feet high.

Q. How bad a bend was it?

A. Not severe.

Q. Could a falling object have dented it?

A. Possibly.

Q. There are 2,130 members in those towers, and you found only one with a slight dent in it. Does that suggest anything to you, Mr. Mongillo, about the structural soundness of those towers? I have no further questions.

Miss Trask: Hold on—let him answer the question.

Miss Hill: He's already answered it.

Miss Trask: No, he didn't—you did. Give the man a chance.

Miss Hill: I've been giving the man a chance for an hour, and all he's been telling us is that he's not really qualified to pass any of the judgments he did and that he didn't obtain any outside corroboration. I think that's an eloquent answer.

Miss Trask: Mr. Chairman, a question was asked, and I believe the witness should be allowed the courtesy to answer it.

CHAIRMAN RUDOLF: Please answer the question, Mr. Mongillo.

A. I think the towers are structurally unsafe. Just because nothing terrible has happened to them yet is no indication that they don't have very serious problems.

MISS HILL: And just because some of the cement is flaking off and there are a few spots of rust on these towers doesn't mean they're about to fall down. Their real problem, I submit to you gentlemen of the commission, is that they are of unconventional construction and don't conform to Mr. Mongillo's—or anybody else's—expectations. And things that are strange or new make us uneasy, but that is no justification for destroying them.

Trask looked me a dagger as we broke for lunch. I ducked. Was that perhaps a pearl of dew I detected beneath her plucked right brow?

In the afternoon she started clobbering me again with the head engineer of the building department, a low-key, by-the-book operative named William Wilbur, who sounded distressingly as if he knew what he was talking about. His remarks were directed largely toward the design of the towers, which he said was pretty well guaranteed to cause their destruction before long—only instead of just collapsing from rot the way Mongillo had predicted that morning, Wilbur thought they would fold upward and inward at the first strong gust.

Q. And why is that, sir.

A. Because of the improper shear transfer element.

Q. And what does that mean in layman's language?

A. Well, suppose you have a vertical pole with a horizontal element extending from it in mid-air and you put a hinge at the connection, as was done in the towers. And suppose you had a great many of these horizontal elements radiating from that pole, as in the wagon-wheel configurations in the towers. Now under the application of a lateral load, such as a strong wind, these elements are going to fold up because, in non-technical language, they are improperly braced and overstressed. The proper design in this case would have been to install diagonal

425

bars linking the horizontal elements to the center pole and thus transferring the horizontal shear to the next lower level and on down into the base.

I turned to Ross Otis, who was stationed beside me to ward off the effects of all such technological voodoo. He drew me a quick sketch showing how the horizontal rings were in fact braced at the perimeter by arcing vertical bars, creating more than enough tensile strength to avoid the peril the engineer was citing. And the hinges linking the horizontal struts to the center pole, Ross whispered, were probably a lot stronger than Wilbur credited them for. Still, I was uneasy with the conflicting testimony of technocrats; no wonder needless hysterectomies were said to be mounting into the tens of thousands a year.

The city engineer plowed ahead under Ellen Trask's deftly flicking lash. The building code, he explained carefully, called for structures designed to resist a wind load of twenty pounds per square foot above sixty feet high and fifteen pounds below that level, but he had modified those standards in view of the conic shape and open-work construction of the towers, which gave the wind a smaller target. And he even assumed, he added, that all structural elements in the towers were straight and true and properly connected "and that in all cases the triangular- and elliptical-shaped elements present their least dimensions to the wind—assumptions that fly in the face of good engineering judgment. Now following the accepted formulae where combined axial and flexural stresses exist in a member, we calculate that the maximum allowable stress in pounds per square inch—the p.s.i., engineers call it—is ten thousand for these towers. And that's pushing it some, in view of the miscellaneous sizes, shapes, and grades of material in them." Translating that computation via seismic coefficiences and other cabalistic devices, Wilbur concluded that a wind of seventy miles an hour, exerting a load of ten thousand pounds on the towers, would send them toppling—and a lighter blow might do the job as well.

Stomach jumping again, I consulted Ross, who was already manipulating numbers at the speed of light. By his reckoning, a ten-thousand pound tug on the towers would produce stress of a little over half of the city's estimate. The discrepancy, Ross advised, lay in Wilbur's unwillingness to acknowledge that the towers qualified as reinforced concrete and that the joints could dependably bear any real load. That, I decided, was the place to attack. I double-checked my terminology with Ross and then glided into the fray.

Q. Mr. Wilbur, how heavy a load would you say the chicken-wire splices used in the joints of these towers can bear?

A. I haven't any idea. I haven't ever computed a piece of chicken wire.

Q. So what would you say if I told you the wire used most commonly throughout the towers was ten-gauge good for ninety-six pounds per longitudinal strength?

A. It wouldn't mean a thing to me.

Q. You couldn't say whether it is a fair and accurate statement that a strand of chicken wire can carry ninety-six pounds in tension?

A. I haven't any idea whether it could carry one pound or a thousand pounds. It's not a customary engineering material.

Q. So you're telling us that these towers can't possibly be safe because such wire will not bear a load. But how can you and your people be positive until you make an analysis and pursue your calculations? You can't just tell by looking, can you, that a structure is overstressed? A lot of calculating goes into it, I would have thought.

A. I don't think it took me more than five minutes with a pencil and slide rule to conclude that these towers are unsafe.

Q. Five minutes?

A. That's right.

Q. Five minutes to seal the fate of a work of art that a man spent twenty-five years building?

A. I sympathize with him, but I have my job to do.

Q. Suppose, Mr. Wilbur, you found other elements in these structures that the building code did not permit but you nevertheless tested and discovered could carry the load they were required to bear—would you not come to the conclusion that, however peculiarly constructed, they were safe?

A. If they depended on chicken wire, I could never come to such a conclusion.

Q. But you modified the code requirements in calculating the wind load the towers can surely bear, didn't you, in view of their particular configuration? Why, by the same token, can't Mr. Zampa have used materials not specified by the code so long as they do the job?

A. It's a matter of engineering judgment, in the last analysis, and Mr. Zampa is no engineer. Furthermore, I would question the intelligence—even the sanity—of an engineer who attempted to build with chicken wire.

Q. In view of everything you've told us here this afternoon, Mr. Wilbur, I wonder how you explain the fact that these towers are still standing?

A. I can't explain it.

Q. Do you think they're perhaps a miracle, Mr. Wilbur?

A. That's not my line of work, madam. All we can tell you is that by the known principles of science, they shouldn't be there—and aren't likely to remain for long.

To close, Trask put on my suave antagonist from Zampa's trial, Peter Shanley, manager of the building department, who stressed how painful a duty it was to issue a demolition order. "But when there is overwhelming evidence of poor materials and poor design, as we have in this case," he said, "the department is left with little choice." Trask got him to explain why the builder was not invited to submit plans for repairing the structure, as was usually done. "For one thing," Shanley said, "we couldn't find Mr. Zampa by the time we decided how severe the problem was. For another, we couldn't conceive of any way the towers might be made structurally safe without materially altering their appearance—in effect, rebuilding them from scratch."

"They're a terminal case, in your view?" Trask asked with what struck me as misplaced puckishness.

Shanley, though, thought that was rich. "As a matter of

fact," he said, smiling, "our people feel that up to half of the cement covering would have to be removed to check for corrosion." And the only way the towers could be safely anchored, he said, was to thread a pipe of about eighteen or twenty inches wide down through them as the central structural element and drive it twenty or thirty feet into the ground. "Of course, some of the interior strutting would have to be removed and replaced to accommodate such a column. You might avoid that by putting a structural steel corset, so to speak, around the towers on the outside and then anchoring it somehow—only there wouldn't be much left to see of the towers, I'm afraid. We even toyed with the notion of stabilizing them with guy wires, but the closer we looked, the more obvious it was that there are no structural elements strong enough to connect the wires to. We tried to think of everything to salvage them, but nothing made sense."

Q. Your inspector and engineer have told us that no tests were undertaken, as Miss Hill has proposed, to determine the exact strength and specific composition of the materials in the towers. Can you tell us why that was, Mr. Shanley?

A. Surely. First, the visible evidence of the inferior quality of the materials is unmistakable. As Mr. Mongillo explained, the plaster is just dropping off in places. More to the point, these things are so irregular in terms of design and workmanship that we have nothing to guide us—there just aren't any plans or specifications—and so we couldn't make the assumption that if they met the standards in one joint or member, they also would in the next. We'd have to test absolutely every stick and stone in the things—and we're just not equipped to give the necessary time and energy that would require.

Trask had effectively undercut my ground. I had only one question for Shanley. "Can you tell us," I asked, "what you think of Mr. Zampa's towers esthetically?"

"Esthetically? I can't say that I've given the matter much thought."

429

"Suppose you try to now."

Trask objected that the question was irrelevant to engineering considerations. "But not to human ones," I said. "I think an official who orders the demolition of a structure that a considerable number of people have found to be a work of art owes it to the creator and his community to acknowledge the gravity of his act."

"Mr. Shanley has explained in detail," Trask countered, "how he and his colleagues tried to figure out a way to salvage these towers. They would hardly have done that if they were totally indifferent to the point Miss Hill is raising. Unfortunately, we're not running a beauty contest here but a hearing on the structural safety of some highly idiosyncratic and illegally built metal towers."

"Have you seen them yourself?" I suddenly asked her.

She was taken off guard. Colloquy between counsel without reference to the presiding official is highly irregular at a judicial proceeding. But this was no hidebound tribunal and the question could not be airily waived on procedural grounds. Well, yes," she said after hesitating a moment, "in pictures. I've seen dozens of pictures."

"But you haven't seen them in person?"

"I don't live here. I haven't had the chance."

"And from the sound of it, neither you nor Mr. Shanley wants anyone else to have it, either."

She turned angrily to the chairman. "I think that sort of comment is unwarranted," she said.

"So is this demolition order," I said, bringing a call to order from Chairman Rudolf. Trask looked heated.

After adjournment I took Ross to the office where we reviewed the day's testimony and compared it page by page with the department's demolition report, searching for inconsistencies and dubious mathematics to bring out in our own presentation the next morning. It was a grind, relieved only by a hamburger break and my suggestion that we work afterward at my place to be more comfortable. He was not enthusiastic about the idea. "Why drag all this stuff around?" Ross said, indicating the pictures and charts and reams of paper swelling around us. Translation: more comfortable for you, maybe. I did not push it, and we stayed in the office till midnight rehearsing how we would lay out our story to the commissioners. Only when we packed it in did he confide that he was jittery about his assignment. He was not very good or very quick on his feet, he said, and was afraid Ellen Trask would pull him to pieces. I told him he knew all the material inside out and had nothing to worry about—and anybody who had climbed nervelessly all over those towers as he had was undoubtedly being watched over by a strength-giving power. He thought seriously about that for a moment and then said, "You don't really believe that?"

"Why not? You heard them say there's no earthly reason for the towers to still be up. That narrows the sponsorship down to heaven or hell and hell isn't heavy into arts and crafts."

He smiled. "You know, you're amazing," he said. "I would have crumped hours ago, but you're still going. You're not on anything, are you?"

"Just adrenalin. I don't like these guys a whole lot."

"Or the lady, either."

"You can tell?"

"Just by the whites of your knuckles whenever she's speaking."

I laughed and gave his wrist a pat and sent him off to his motel to catch what sleep he could manage. "And don't worry —you'll do fine," I said. So long as I showed up, he said.

Lee Nightingale reached me at the apartment first thing in the morning with the news that she had driven to New Bedford the day before and, helped by the police, had managed to locate Zampa. He was living in a mildewed rooming house near the waterfront under the name of Emilio Sampo. She had gone on a whim, she said, and because she wanted to help somehow. If I needed to ask him anything technical about the towers, she had arranged for him to be summoned to a telephone at a grocery near his room. "He doesn't know anything technical," I told her. "If he did, the towers wouldn't ever have been built."

Still, her news lifted me. The old man, even *in absentia*, stirred something in me well beyond sympathy. He was too mindless to be an inspiration, so what was it exactly? Maybe just plain love of his simplicity—and the courage to do his eccentric number and then turn his face to the wall with dignity and tell the world to screw itself.

I gulped coffee and a glutenous bun to sock up my energy level and sailed down to city hall on fluttery wings. The morning *Light*, which I grabbed from a vending machine, offered little encouragement. It bannered the details behind the towers' death sentence as pronounced at the hearing the day before and cast me as a shrill mouthpiece with slim chance to win a reprieve from the historically obdurate appeals board. Ross was waiting for me in the lobby, not cowering precisely but appearing anxious and fatigued in his rumpled herringbone jacket and skinny dark tie. We went upstairs together to the council chamber, where Ellen Trask, having changed dresses (swishy brown today) and regained composure, did not acknowledge my presence. The commissioners, I sensed, were irritable because the hearing had spilled over to a second day. But however dreary the prospects, as they had always been for him, I was not about to let the old man get railroaded.

Pinked by my press notices, I pitched my voice lower and spoke more slowly than usual. There were three points to be made, and I made them as briefly as possible: First, that in recommending demolition, the city had relied on prejudicial assumptions about the strength of the towers instead of testing them objectively as we had done; second, that no structural member had failed during the twenty-five years the towers were rising and, with minimum expense, steps could be taken to repair corrosion and prevent its recurrence; and third, that the towers were a priceless art monument in the view of many people competent in the field and to demolish them would be an act of official and shameless vandalism. Then I called Ross Otis, looking more emaciated and ineffectual by the moment.

I qualified him at length because our case depended almost entirely on the resonance his testimony managed to generate. At first he answered my questions about his extensive schooling and professional experience in a voice so diffident I had to remind him there was no microphone in the chamber. The problem was he thought it was fatuous to go into all that about himself when it was the towers alone that mattered. I finally got him to open up some, but the contrast between his subdued manner and the trumpetings of infallibility by the building department yahoos the day before did not work to our advantage. And more than once during his presentation, he bollixed up explaining the arithmetic and geometry, as Euclid might have in the face of such adversity. But what he lacked in presence and fluency Ross made up for with earnestness.

He had spent five days climbing over those towers, he said, without any mishap to himself or damage to the structure—in itself, a far more revealing test than any the city had bothered to undertake, I pointed out to the commission. While it was true that the cement plaster was loose in places, Ross said most of those where corrosion had set in were indeed traceable to the removal of decorative elements. I asked him how he could be sure it wasn't due to poor cement, and he said the quality of the cement was really the key to the structural soundness of the towers, so he had made a number of tests to analyze the bond for its chemical properties, strength under compression, and power of adhesion. He produced photographs of three little cubes of cement that he had cut from the towers with a diamond saw—one from a support leg near the base, one from the central support column, and one from a splice between two members about forty feet up on the main tower—and circulated them among the commissioners along with a drawing of the whole structure showing the precise spots where the samples had been extracted.

"The ratio of cement to sand for all three samples was 1 to 4.23 by weight and 1 to 4.14 by volume, and the sand weighed 96 pounds per cubic foot," he recited. "This is regarded as a good mortar mixture anywhere in this country and well within the code regulations for this city." Then he distributed a sheet providing the numbers for each sample in each category, as determined by the testing laboratory. The crushing strength of the three compression cubes was even more revealing. The sample from the splice, he said, registered a 3,206 p.s.i., the one from the central column was 3,446, and the one from the leg at

433

the base was 9,604. And how strong did that make the cement? "Very," he said. "Anything over 3,000-pound mortar is considered acceptable by the most stringent construction codes in the world." As to the bonding quality of the cement, he handed around serial pictures showing the effects of successive chisel blows when he had tried to expose the metal in the support leg. After half a dozen blows, the mortar had come loose from only one of the five faces of the T-shaped steel member and it was evident that the job could not be accomplished with hand tools.

What, then, was his overall evaluation of the strength of the Zampa towers? "With a minimum of maintenance," he said gently, "they'll be standing when the American tricentennial is held—and if I had to guess, by whatever you call the one the century after that."

After two hours of testimony, they gave Ross five minutes for a glass of water before committing him to the clutches of Ellen Trask. She, too, had done some homework the previous night, most of it apparently of an *ad hominem* sort. "Mr. Otis," she began, "did you leave the employment of NASA in Houston of your own will or were you dismissed?"

A. A lot of people were let go when the space program was cut back.

Q. But not everyone, by any means, isn't that so?

A. Well—no. They kept some of the senior people.

Q. But you were not a senior person?

A. No.

Q. And did you leave Sikorsky Aricraft on your own or were you dismissed by them, too?

A. I was furloughed when their volume of business dropped during the slowdown after Vietnam.

Q. What does 'furloughed' mean, Mr. Otis?

A. Let go for the time being.

Q. And have they called you back?

A. No.

Q. Did they furlough all their engineers, Mr. Otis?

A. No.

434

Q. Didn't they keep the ones they felt were most knowledgeable in their field?

MISS HILL: Objection. Mr. Otis cannot be expected to evaluate the criteria for the company's hiring practices.

CHAIRMAN RUDOLF: I think we can skip over that, Miss Trask.

Q. Mr. Otis, aren't you in fact unemployed?

A. No—not exactly. I do consulting work.

Q. How much consulting work?

A. It varies.

Q. From what to what?

A. From a lot to a little.

Q. But it's not really full time, is it?

A. When I'm working it is.

Q. How much have you worked in the past year?

MISS HILL: I object to this entire line of questioning. It's unkind and indecent. If Miss Trask has any evidence for us regarding Mr. Otis's competence to perform his work, let her present it, but to belabor him for economic circumstances entirely beyond his control that have limited his working time of late is unconscionable. A good many well-qualified engineers have had a hard time of it for the past several years, especially in the fields in which Mr. Otis is knowledgeable.

MISS TRASK: Unfortunately, gentlemen, this line of questioning is unavoidable. The testimony of this witness directly contradicts the collective wisdom of an entire department of this city's government, and if it is to be taken seriously, his qualifications and brilliance as an expert must be put under the sternest scrutiny. What meaning the commission wishes to read into his employment record is not for me to say, but surely you gentlemen are entitled to obtain the facts in the matter.

Did I hate her because she was so good or because she was a woman—or because of both? It was the combination, without a doubt, that was intriguing—and intimidating. She had the granite purpose that for so long only men had deemed their proper possession. But the package she bore it in met the classic standards for feminine form at its loveliest. Somehow it seemed unfair. It was as if nature had unaccountably decided to experiment with a superior breed of hermaphrodite: mentally keen, physically firm, constitutionally sanguine, and sexually capable of fucking not only itself but with everything else that moved. Such creatures are fated, till their numbers multiply, to earn more loathing than affection from the less generously endowed. I would have had to be totally blind not to see myself, perhaps a better self, reflected in Ellen Trask. I bit my tongue.

They let Trask go on cutting up Ross, as she was being paid to do, but after a while it began to work against her. Meek and mild as he was, Ross did not relish being used as a punching bag. Cautiously at first and more aggressively as the cross-examination lengthened, he swung back:

Q. Now are you actually contending, Mr. Otis, that these three little cubes you say you took from the towers—and, by the way, did anyone witness your taking these samples, which no longer exist?

A. No. But I brought them straight to the laboratory.

Q. So you say. The fact is they could have come from anywhere, couldn't they?

A. But they didn't.

Q. We have only your word for that, Mr. Otis.

A. I've lived my whole life believing my word means something.

Q. No doubt, Mr. Otis. But there happen to be some unscrupulous people in this world, even if you are not among them. It's my job to point out to the commission that your evidence is unverified.

A. The city can take whatever samples it likes if it doesn't want to accept my word for it. I've also brought photographs to document my testimony.

And when she asked Ross how he as a scientist could reasonably claim his findings were typical of any object so irregular in terms of materials and construction, he said, "Irregular, but not inferior."

Q. But you took your samples from only a few spots on these very large structures. That doesn't prove much, does it?

A. I think it proves a lot more than no samples—or just looking at the towers through binoculars.

Q. Mr. Otis, three is not a very extensive sampling, is it?

A. Actually, after the compression test results came in, I went on down the vertical support leg trying to expose the metal and looking for soft spots. But it got harder as we went toward the base, and I had to abandon the chisel.

Q. But if you kept going higher—or tried a different leg or member—you might have found soft cement.

A. But I did go higher. I went forty feet up—I testified to that—that's where I undid the splice for one of the sample cubes. If what you want me to say is that the more specimens you take, the more reliable the findings, I'll agree. But selective sampling is what the scientific method is all about. And that's all building inspectors ever do—except when they choose not to do any because they have their minds made up beforehand.

At the end, Ross had left me little to add. The whole issue, I said, came down not to whether the towers were an unconventional structure unconventionally made—nobody contested that—but to whether a bureaucratic system could tolerate such deviance. In a land of free expression, the only reason not to was the public safety. The burden to prove that the towers were a menace rested with the city, and the city had not proven any such thing. All it had to show the commission were a few spots of corrosion and one slightly bent strut out of more than two thousand. Destroying a beautiful thing under such circumstances was more than mean-spirited, I said; it was a blow to life itself.

Ellen Trask was unchastened. Sentimentality, she said, would make heartless ogres of devoted civil servants. Why should the commission ignore the judgment of the city's duly appointed and fully qualified experts on the subject for that of

437

one not very senior and only occasionally employed aeronautical engineer? "The only reliable way to test these towers and prove to the city's satisfaction that they are strong and stable," she said, "would be to exert a ten-thousand-pound load directly on them and see if they survived. Anything less would be meaningless. And we have to assume that their owner would hardly agree to submit his quaint handiwork to such an ordeal."

I glanced at Ross. His eyes met mine and locked there while his brain whirred. An instant passed. The device flashed green with a shrug of its shoulders. "As a matter of fact, gentlemen and lady," I said, rising in place, "the quaint owner very well might."

34

The hearing chamber had nearly emptied when Lee Nightingale came barreling in on me in a corner. "You've got one helluva nerve!" she snarled. "Since when do you treat a work of art like a piece of hardware?"

"When there's no other way to save it."

"You think shoving it over is saving it?"

"It's not supposed to move—Ross says so."

"And suppose Ross is wrong?"

"Would you rather I just let these guys vote to tear the thing down tomorrow?"

"Who says they were going to?"

"I do."

"Why? I thought you were going just great."

"Thank you. But you didn't see the look on those cookies. Believe me—hearts of pure obsidian."

"I guess it takes one to know one," she said.

I just looked at her coldly for a moment. It had not been my easiest day in court, and the last thing I needed just then was needling by a second-guessing camp follower. "How would you like a punch in the nose?" I asked.

My spent state must have finally registered with her. She apologized at once and hugged me for my effort and said she supposed I knew what I was doing. That was her second mistake.

They gave us forty-eight hours to devise what the engineers called a proof-load test to determine if Zampa's handiwork could meet the city's prescribed safety standard. Ross and Jonathan spent the first of those hours comparing notes and numbers with chief building department engineer Wilbur, the bristling gray crewcut whose obstinance in testifying to the rickety state of the towers was matched only by his eagerness now to be proven right—and at our expense: The commission said it would consider accepting the results of a test only if we paid for it ourselves. Also, I would have to get Zampa to consent to the undertaking—hardly a more pleasing prospect than the test itself.

Jon took Ross home where the two of them labored the rest of the day and well into the night to figure out how best to engineer the test with minimum risk to the towers. Meanwhile, I put in a couple of hours at the office to see what procedural alternatives we had in the event the test fizzled and the commission upheld the demolition order. Our options, as I read the city ordinances, would have been reduced to one: an appeal to the Court of Common Pleas, where the whole thing had begun. The appeal had to be limited, moreover, to the question of whether the commission had acted arbitrarily, illegally, or in abuse of its discretion—without due process, in other words. The odds of our winning a reversal on that ground I rated as astronomical. Convinced I had seized upon the only chance open to us, I went home for a shower and then picked up Lee on the drive out to Jon's house. When we got there, the fellows were hard at work perfecting their three-stage whiffletree.

"What the hell is a whiffletree?" I asked, surveying the litter of schematic drawings piling up beside Jon's drafting table.

439

"It's a floating or pivoting dingus that you use for controlling tension." Jon directed us to the drawing board and laid it all out in a flat clinical voice. "We'll apply the load with a hydraulic jack actuated by a hand pump supported on a scaffold here —at the thirty-three-foot elevation." He circled the spot with a blue grease pencil. "The load distribution is accomplished in three stages—that's the whiffletree. The main member is this ten-inch, wide-flange vertical loading beam, which is linked top and bottom by horizontal members to the midpoint of these two vertical eight-inch I-beams, which in turn are joined at each end to six-inch horizontal beams, four in all, see?—which are attached to six-inch-wide cotton slings that will be looped around the tower at four elevations—fifteen, twenty-seven, thirty-nine, and fifty-one feet high. The slings will rest against two-by-fours attached to the nine rear support legs of the tower. Under the two-by-fours we'll wedge rubber pads that will distribute the horizontal load from the slings to the tower joints and protect the mosaic ornamentation on the cement surface. The load reaction is supplied by a winch-truck cable— we'll use the winch only to remove cable slack in this case." He looked back at both of us. "You got all that?"

"Sure," I said, "I deal with loads all week long. I just want to know if it's going to work."

"Beats shit out of me," Jon said.

"I think it's pretty sound," said Ross.

"But didn't you design it?" I asked him.

"Well—mostly, yes."

"Then what good's your opinion?"

The poor guy was too tired to smile. I patted his head in commendation a couple of times. Lee was less trusting. "These big vertical beams," she asked them, "are they made of steel?" Jon said it wasn't rock candy. "But then how do they stay up like that?" she wondered. "They look suspended in space, the way you've got it drawn."

"They're supported by cables to the scaffolding," Jon brushed her off.

"Oh. Why didn't you draw in the cables?"

"They're understood."

"Oh," she said, "forgive my ignorance."

"Forgiven," he said. "Could you fix us a couple of drinks?"

"I'm not done with my questions," she said.

"Christ," he said.

"Christ yourself," she said. "I'd like to know how you can be sure that one tug isn't going to send the tower sprawling."

Jon deferred to Ross and went to get himself a drink. "There isn't going to be any one big tug," Ross explained. "The loads will be applied gradually in increments of a thousand pounds. We'll be monitoring the effects of each increment on a transducer we're going to build especially for the test. We'll use three of them, actually—two to measure the bending deflections at the fifteen- and fifty-one-foot elevations and one to measure overturning movements at the base. I'm thinking about a light panel that will show deflections in increments of one thirty-second of an inch. We'll be able to see the slightest movement every step of the way. And to be absolutely safe, the hydraulic cylinder is only going to permit a six-inch stroke."

"I know some people," I said, "who've suffered quite a lot of damage from a six-inch stroke."

"Can it, Tabor," Lee said. Her intensity was showing as she turned back to Ross. "Prurience aside, what's a six-inch stroke?"

"It's a safety device we'll build into the test rig. A six-inch movement of the tower at the thirty-three-foot elevation will bottom the short-travel hydraulic cylinder and block any further load application." On top of which, he said, the big ten-inch beam—the primary member of the whiffletree—would be set up to yield by bending if the load exceeded the agreed upon maximum of ten thousand pounds that the city was insisting be sustained for a full five minutes.

"How come you're so sure the tower can take it," Lee asked, "when the city people are so sure it can't?"

Ross began to pelt her with numbers till she threw up her hands in self-defense. "Just tell me what they mean," she said.

"Now you're getting the idea," I said.

"The heart of it," said Ross, "is that I credit the towers with being reinforced concrete. The city people just assume that the cement doesn't contribute to the bending moment of inertia of the cross-section—so my figures say the towers can handle two to three times as much stress as theirs do."

"So you could be wrong?" she asked him.

"I guess it's possible."

"But not very?"

"I'd say it's unlikely."

Ross's diminuendo was hardly more compelling in private than it had been in public earlier in the day. "But why?" Lee insisted. "Because you're much smarter than they are—or what?"

"It's not so much that—although frankly I wouldn't rule it out entirely—but that we each approached the problem totally differently."

"I don't follow."

Ross picked up the grease pencil and started doodling stacks of overlapping boxes. "Public officials don't get paid to make imaginative leaps," he said, addressing the sketchpad in front of him more than us. "They're hammerheads—I've been surrounded by the type my whole professional life. They go by rote. Authority to them means the power to say no. It's so easy —and makes them feel big and strong. They think if you just go on saying no long enough, everything will work out. And they get very jumpy when they're faced with anything that won't take no for an answer. It's like what Tabor was driving at but couldn't come right out and say at the hearing without sounding like an overage hippie. The towers are a standing refutation to bureaucratic mentality—the kind that insists that something built without a plan and without a permit and without the usual materials and without official inspection doesn't really exist at all. And if someone calls it to their attention— and it turns out really to exist despite the impossibility— they're preprogrammed to wipe it off the face of the earth as fast as they can. Otherwise there isn't any point to their own survival. So they look at these strange towers and, like Wilbur admitted, in five minutes they've figured out ten good reasons why the things ought to fall down. I look at them without the same sort of institutional investment, and I can see what they're not willing to. It's as simple as that."

It was the most consecutive words I had heard Ross Otis utter—maybe the most he had ever said in his life. But then this had been his day to face down the dragons, and we happened to be the only ones still around for his peroration. I wondered how many years would have to pass before he expressed himself so freely again. Did he understand that his disinclination to project himself had made his career a losing proposition so far? Was it possible no one had ever told him that talent is nothing without the attendant strength to assert its presence and claim its due? Could he not have noticed in a world teeming with talents—and no-talents laboring overtime to gild their ineptness—that the prizes falleth not like the gentle rain but must be wrenched from the jaw of the tiger? Or perhaps he knew all that but was constitutionally unequipped to promote himself. Would it benefit so frail a creature to isolate the cause of his failing?

Lee turned to me when Ross had had his say, as if to ask whether I bought it. "You heard the man," I said. "Have you got any brighter ideas?"

She shook her head and crossed herself semi-seriously and drifted off to the kitchen to help Jon throw together some stale delicatessen sandwiches for our supper. Ross stepped out to the foyer to telephone his daughter, who was being cared for by relatives during the Zampa crisis. It was impossible to miss the warmth in his voice as he spoke to the child. I envied him for the instant and felt thoroughly drained as I sat there by myself in the core of that picturesque house of assignation where I had once reigned and now entered as an alien. Jessica would have to be told where things stood.

All evening the men kept refining their drawings and refiguring their data for presentation the next day at city hall. Lee and I looked over their shoulders periodically, urged them on with a dumb question or two, and then retreated to the living room where we sat side by side and talked with an easy openness absent from our earlier exchanges. The longer we spoke, the more I was moved by how canny and contained she was capable of seeming one moment and how riddled by doubt and discontent the next. She was not a person at ease with confidences, either her own or those of others, but she was

443

drawn to me quite as irresistibly as I to her. An instant came when so much had been communicated that I thought we might touch. How I wanted to clasp her piquant face and tell her I understood so much more than she imagined because I was under assault by my own set of warring demons—who with fiber was not?—but that for her to let the clash go on unreconciled within her was to invite permanent disability. Perhaps she knew. She knew so much. And had read me so well. Nobody was much good, though, at attending to self-inflicted wounds.

When we rose at midnight, she slipped her arm through mine in a way so effortlessly companionable that I had to beat back an urge to embrace her. She neatly disengaged as we came upon the men and announced, in the interest of their survival, that the night's work was done. I offered Ross and her a lift home. Ross said he would as soon sack right there in the living room if Jon didn't mind. Lee just said thanks but no.

Jon called me at the office a little before noon the next day to report that the building department had agreed to the test plan. We had two weeks to prepare. The next step was mine.

Every monster truck on the thruway must have tried to run me off the road on the endless drive to New Bedford. My mind was so totally preoccupied with Zampa that I never noticed the asshole teamsters until they had roared right up my fender. The old man, I was certain, would be out roaming the city when I finally got there—down where the fishing fleet docked, probably, if there still was one. But he was right where Lee had told me I would find him—in a tiny cell down a dark corridor on the second floor of a clapboard boardinghouse. He seemed to nest in lightless places. The lone window in his room was partly covered by an army surplus blanket serving as a combined drape and shade, and a single bare bulb dangled overhead at the end of a series of fused sockets. The rest of the interior was equally dispiriting: A narrow bed, a folding chair, an overturned wooden Seven-Up case that held his radio and lone volume of the *Britannica*, a small cabinet for his clothes, and a couple of hooks for his hat and pants and a fly swatter. The window looked out on a flat gravel roof and the backs of half a dozen tenements whose distended TV antennae were the only skyline.

444

His face brightened on seeing me, but behind the smile he did not look at all well. His two-day stubble was no help, any more than the frayed flannel shirt and the oversized denim pants and the canvas shoes with slits in them. It was his eyes, though, that saddened me most. Small as they were, there had always seemed to be a glint in them, and now I could detect none. Still, he doffed his hat properly enough and dusted off the chair with it and motioned me to sit. We spoke a little about how he was getting on and had found a distant cousin living a few blocks away. People in the neighborhood were agreeable enough and the radio reception was much better than in Amity, he said and thanked me again for the gift. Then I told him what had happened with the towers, and he said he didn't want to discuss them. I said I could understand that but he was still their owner and was entitled to be consulted about their fate.

"No," he said, "I ain't de owner no more. You an' de udda' lady who come by—she say you pay de taxes so dey yours now, huh? I ain't got nuttin' to do wit' 'em." I said that wasn't so, that he was the owner of record, and what had been done in the name of his artistry did not change his legal standing in the eyes of the city. But he did not want to hear, and when I told him about the test, as I had to, he listened only long enough to show he was not at all happy about the idea. I said it was the last thing in the world we would have considered if there was any reasonable alternative. He shrugged and looked out the window.

"I need you to sign this," I said after a while and handed him a paper I had drawn up waiving all claims against everybody in the event the test did any damage to the towers. I explained what it said and why there was no chance of saving the towers without it, but he just shrugged and turned toward the window again. "Are you angry at me?" I asked.

"No, miss," he said. "All dis hadda happen some time."

"It can still be all right," I said. "There's a group of us. We have plans—"

He put up his hand to hush me. I asked him if he didn't care what happened to the towers and he said he cared but he wasn't going to do anything about it. I said he didn't have to do anything but sign the paper. Finally he confessed he didn't know how to write—only print. I said he could print his name and we would get it notarized, but he said his not being able to write was nobody's business. I sat there despairing for a while until I thought of asking if he would sell me the towers. He said as far as he was concerned, I already owned them. That wasn't good enough for the city, I told him, so he said to draw up a bill of sale on the back of the waiver and he would go with me to get it signed. "For how much?" I asked.

"How much what?"

"How much do you want for them?"

He seemed dumbstruck at first by the very thought that his work was negotiable. Then he shook his head. "Fo' you, dey don' cost nuttin'."

"Then it's not a real sale," I said.

He kept shaking his head and saying I had paid for them already by settling his tax bill and giving him my time and services and that he would not hear of my paying him another dime.

"Then how about a nickel?" I asked.

He thought I was joking till I explained a nickel was all right so long as the title transfer indicated the sale was also based on "other considerations." He smiled and said he would accept a nickel, and we spent the next half hour practicing how to print his name. When he had it down cold, we went out driving till we found a notary, who let me type up the bill of sale and then witnessed the old man's giant zed at the bottom. On the ride back to his room, I made him direct me to the grocery where he shopped on the pretext that I wanted to buy a snack. While he struck up a conversation with one of the customers, I gave the old woman who ran the place my business card and a check for a hundred dollars and asked her please to make sure Zampa never went hungry. Then I walked him to the front door of the rooming house, gave him a quick kiss on the cheek, and said I would let him know what happened. He told me not to bother.

I have not seen him since.

On the ride home I began to grasp how I had sentimentalized Gabriel Zampa all along. He was never the noble

446

primitive I had supposed, his hard hands and untroubled soul assigned by some higher power to undertake his improbable masterpiece. No, he had built the towers simply to shut out the dreariness from his lonely life, and he had expected to earn neither grace nor serenity for his effort. The miracle, if there was any, was that he had been granted just enough strength and time to finish. The cruelty was that having finished, he might now outlive the product of his prodigious labors.

All the equipment for the test and the work to assemble it came to eight thousand dollars, rather more than Lee and I, even as the co-proprietors, felt we ought to invest. Lee was able to get Sam to persuade the Mather School of Engineering to make a small grant in exchange for using the test as a seminar in stress analysis. And the Mather imprimatur helped us attract a few other donors, who were promised charter membership in the Zampa Foundation if the towers survived—and a tax write-off, at least, even if they didn't. We were still several thousand dollars short when I proposed to Terry English—*in flagrante delicto*, I will confess—that his station buy the exclusive right to televise the test live. I said maybe *Nova*, the science series, would do a show around it later and the station could earn syndication royalties. Terry liked my enterprising spirit but not the rationale. "To hell with *Nova*," he said. "We'll sell the air time if you'll run the test during one of my sustaining slots on Sunday." I couldn't see what difference it would make and said it was a deal. Lee, naturally, was put out with me for turning the ordeal into a media event, but I said that barring a last-minute rescue by the National Endowment for the Arts, we had no choice. Terry agreed to pick up the balance of our bill for the test rig and in no time lined up a clothing store, a discount hardware chain, an insurance broker, a pizzeria, and an exterminating service as sponsors. I wondered whether we ought to invite clergymen of all faiths to pray on camera for the towers.

Blithe as I tried to stay, my anxiety level shot right through the roof the week before the test. Probably it was due as much to my being a fifth wheel during all the preparations as to my uncertainty of the outcome. I could concentrate on nothing at the office. Even my period refused to arrive. I divided the days between watching the workmen put up the stick-like scaffolding around the towers and socializing with the Washburns and other blacks in the neighborhood. Slowly interest built throughout the area until a dozen or two Gullyites could be found there at all hours to witness the beehive stirrings at the junkyard. Betting action was lively among the onlookers who were about equally divided in their expectation of the test results. The pro-tower adherents exhibited a certain pentecostal fervor toward Zampa's mission on earth. The doubters noted that the rig had been positioned to pull the towers away from the street and the houses on the other side—an arrangement seen as more prophetic than cautionary.

Ross supervised the contractors' crew every step of the way, even tying the rubber pads for the slings in place himself lest the mosaic surface of the towers be damaged by less loving hands. Each segment of the whiffletree had to be positioned as precisely as possible, so Ross was forever measuring every part of the setup after the latest component was installed to make sure it had not disturbed the equilibrium. Head all but vanished inside his hard hat but magpie voice never ceasing, he hectored the workmen for a thousand tiny modifications— move this girder a few inches higher and that one a few inches lower, and now the first one a little more to the left and now a touch more to the right and on and on until even the steeliest-nerved galoot among them was ready to pitch Ross overboard. And still he persisted. Had I confused a mild manner and soft looks for irresoluteness? The more I saw of Ross Otis in action, the plainer it seemed I had convicted him of watery character on circumstantial evidence. His habitual avoidance of exhibitionism could have stemmed as plausibly from full faith in his own competence as from its opposite. In his modulated way, the man was consumed by the task before him, and though his entire professional standing was at stake, he never hedged his conviction that the towers would withstand the strain. Whether I could was more doubtful.

So contagious was Ross's commitment that he all but won over chief engineer Wilbur when the haughty official drove up one morning in a building department truck to survey the scene. Every detail of the rig conformed to the schematic, Wilbur noted with high approval, like a grade-school teacher hearing a star pupil recite flawlessly from an old McGuffey's reader. The civil servant registered frank fascination when Ross undid the cover for the measuring gadget he had designed and assembled himself during the evenings—"a linear deflection transducer," he called it and Wilbur nodded sagely and asked what such-and-such a part was and Ross said "that's the excitation and digital output plug" and Wilbur nodded some more and Ross said, "This is the torque stabilizer and this is the zero adjust and this is the contact wiper assembly," and Wilbur never stopped nodding, though I'd swear he had not the faintest clue what Ross was jabbering about.

The weather forecast was good, and the TV people came up to the junkyard the day before to plan all the camera angles. Ross brought his daughter along for the dress rehearsal, and I offered to take charge of her at the test itself the next day so Ross would not be distracted. To my surprise, the little girl said she was not going to be there but would watch it on television. I asked Ross why later. "I don't want her to see my face if we flop," he said.

"But we're not going to," I said.

"Right. But just in case we do."

"You mean you want to hide her from the real world?"

"As long as possible," he said.

Sunday came up spring-soft and cloud-dappled and my heart was in overdrive the second my eyes twanged open. Jon and Ross stopped in for coffee but none of us could say anything we were so souped up. The two of them went on ahead to get things moving while I went to pick up Jessie. Lee and Sam Nightingale arrived at the towers almost the same moment as we did; the tenseness of the occasion dictated a civility between Lee and Jessie that neither felt. The cops were out in force this time, as they had not been at the dedication ceremony. They were needed, too, because by the time the test was ready to begin, a crowd of about five hundred threatened to spill over into the area roped off as dangerous if the towers broke apart. Everyone was waving for the cameras, but they were installed in the test rig and scaffolding, each assigned a spot to watch for bending or cracking on the main tower. Ross manned the load-applying jack himself while Wilbur relayed the instrumentation readings to the ground. At maximum load of ten thousand pounds, the city had predicted the towers would theoretically undergo stress of 15,875 p.s.i.—theoretically because that was more than twice their rated resistance. Ross had predicted a stress of 5,210 p.s.i. under maximum load. Both sides agreed that if the tower moved the six-inch maximum allowed by the hydraulic cylinder any time during the test, whatever the load or whatever the p.s.i. reading, the experiment would end and demolition ensue the following week.

At eleven o'clock, WAMY-TV was on the air. The station manager was there beside me. I know because he told me later, but I have no memory of seeing him. I was looking up. Everyone was looking up. No one on the ground moved. "Okay," Wilbur boomed into the p.a. hookup, "we're ready to roll." There was a whirring noise and the cable tensed. "Here's the first run—we're loading on a thousand pounds." The sun faded. My world stopped. . . .

Nothing.

Good God in heaven. . . .

"Okay, we're going at it again," came the rasp. Another whirring. Two thousand pounds pulled on the tower. A full ton. You could see the giant loading beam jiggle.

No movement.

Oh, my palsied stars. . . .

A whirring for three thousand pounds. I could see nothing. But Wilbur's hoarse voice crackled. "We've got a movement!"

No!

"We've got deflection of six thirty-seconds."

Oh, oh, oh—

The whirring again. Four thousand pounds. "More movement!"

Every atom in me locked.

"Deflection is ten thirty-seconds of an inch."

I cannot watch.

Whirring. Five thousand pounds—halfway there. "A lot of movement!"

Someone yelled.

"Deflection is eighteen thirty-seconds."

More, it was more. It was moving more each time. . . .

Whirrrrr. Six thousand pounds. "Slight movement."

Hold, goddamnit, hold!

"We're at twenty thirty-seconds."

Whirrrrrrring. Seven thousand. "Twenty-four thirty-seconds."

Eight thousand. "Thirty thirty-seconds."

Nine thousand. "Thirty-two thirty-seconds—we have deflection of one inch."

I thought of father, a man who adored thirty-seconds of an inch. And my mother, who would have found the concept pointless. And my brother, Brownie. And Miss Terhune. And my beloved Tambourine, with his steaming flanks and telescopic pud that terrified and fascinated me. And the first boy I kissed. And the first I touched. And the first I slept with. And first I loved. Who was that? I have loved them all. At least a little. Why is loving all or nothing? It is too precious not to ration. I will not be robbed of mine. It will be there when I choose to bestow it. This instant I am beaming all I can spare to that small quiet man in the yellow hard hat crouching up there above me operating this gigantic torture device that is grinding up both our insides. . . .

"All right, we're going on the maximum-load run and holding."

Whirrrrrrrrrrrr. Ten thousand pounds. Five tons. A hurricane of seventy miles an hour. Tearing at every joint and mooring in the hand-spliced filigree. No toy was meant to bear such a burden. No art was asked to prove itself so terribly. . . .

"We have deflection of one inch plus six thirty-seconds. We have stress per square inch of four thousand seven hundred pounds."

Ross had been conservative by more than five hundred pounds of the p.s.i.! But could the towers hold out five minutes?

"We have no additional deflection at one minute."

No one breathed.

"The linear deflection is stable at two minutes."

A tiny chip of cement landed at the tower base.

"Three minutes—no more deflection."

The main I-beam seemed to quiver. And then it stopped. And then it bent. The steel beam bent. It was ten inches wide and twenty-something feet high and it yielded to the load. But the tower had not yielded. At thirty-feet up, it had moved one inch and not quite a quarter under maximum load. The tower stood.

Wilbur was saying that although the buckling of the main loading beam had prevented application of the maximum load for the prescribed full five minutes, he had seen enough. He shook Ross's hand and lifted it to the crowd. A roar went up.

The test was over.

In the afternoon Ross and I drove to New Bedford to tell Zampa. The landlady said he had moved out four days before and left no forwarding address. She hadn't thought that was strange, she said, because he never got any mail anyway. Not even his Social Security check? No, she thought he had said something about his government money going straight into the bank. What bank? She had no idea. All that mattered to her was that he had left his room neat.

35

Maynard Lamport died the following month. His passing was not altogether unexpected. He had never really regained full strength after his stroke, his claims to the contrary notwithstanding.

I felt the loss doubly. It was he who had hired me in the face of storm warnings, and I had remained his special protectorate more or less throughout my uneasy career at the firm. I had tried to repay his kindness with respect. When he taught, I listened. When he requested my help, I put everything else to one side. His stature was too great for him ever to have felt bedeviled by the purportedly disruptive antics of the office hoyden—and the difference in our ages had insulated him from the baser of my charms. To me he seemed as crisp as he was dry, as fair as he was stern, and as much in love with his profession as he was removed from the rest of the world. Without him, the place was not just poorer but paltry. I felt myself reduced accordingly.

And vulnerable. Dan Kettering was technically the senior partner with Lamport gone, but Dan Kettering was a horse's rectum, and the whole stable knew it. The firm belonged to Earl Grier now, and Sparky's ascension, I sensed at once, marked my days there. If Maynard Lamport had been my patron saint, and Sam Nightingale my lover, and Dan Kettering my mark, Sparky Grier had been my watchdog and my nemesis. He alone was my exemplar in guile; I alone menaced the security of his power. That we had escaped a direct collision until then was astounding; that we would not much longer was as certain now as Maynard Lamport's non-intervention in the destined event.

As always, I precipitated the crisis in the name of principle. Arnold Berenson, my old boss at Legal Assistance, had decided to try to grab the Democratic mayoral nomination from the incumbent. He understood the workings and problems of the city probably as well as anyone in it and could be counted on, if victorious, to address its needs with energy and compassion. His chances, however, were only slightly above hopeless. Which was why he summoned me, of course.

"It's not all that crazy, baby," he said, "and don't tell me you're not my baby, baby, or I'm gonna make legalized chastity belts the cornerstone of my platform and sweep the male-pig vote." Arnold had always been up front with me. His campaign plan was no more subtle. His natural appeal was to the liberal community and what remnants of the activist and radical movements he could reach. His targets would therefore be the blacks, the university, the Jews, feminists, and dropouts of every stripe if he could just get them to the voting booth. His own years of work with the ghetto poor put him a large leg up in that department. Arnold's bluff ways may not have inspired folk-hero status, but he had befriended a great many friendless souls over time and some of them at least remained grateful. As a Jew himself, he thought he could attract the allegiance of most of his co-religionists, though they were no longer the solid ten percent of the city population they had been through the mid-Sixties. He doubted if half that many remained since the white flight to suburbia had become a stampede. For the rest of his target groups, as well as to solidify his position with the Coop leadership, he said he badly needed my help.

"Sure thing. What do you want me to do?"

"Run my campaign," he said.

"No way."

"Why not—because you're in bed with the plutocrats?"

"My bed is my business."

"I hear it's all over the air waves."

"You know about that?"

"That gentleman is no gentleman. You're the highest rated beaver in town."

"He's very insecure."

"Oh, I'm not knocking him. In fact, I was hoping you could get him on my side. We'll need every bit of coverage we can scrounge."

"That may be the least of your problems. My running the show for you is out, though. I'm supposed to stay the hell out of *pro bono* business and make money for a while."

"This isn't *pro bono* business—it's partisan politics. What did you do—hock your citizenship rights to make partner?"

He was gaining. "Look," I said, "maybe I can help behind the scenes."

"I need you out front, Tabor. You stand for something in this town."

"Me?"

"You, baby."

"For what?"

"For guts—for the struggle against injustice—for the strength of the modern woman."

Oh, was he gaining. "Thanks," I said, "but it's no-go. Sparky would break my ass."

454

"Just tell him I'm going to win and if he doesn't want to get tossed out of city hall face first when he shows up, he'd better give you his benediction. Besides, he's smart enough to butter both sides of his bread. This way the firm can't lose."

There was an element of plausibility to that argument. The only thing wrong with it was that if Arnold happened to win by some fluke, I'd be the back-door power broker and not Sparky. "He'll never buy it," I said. "And the clientele doesn't dig political activists. We—that's the royal 'we'—are discreet, don't you know? I'll help with your platform, I'll write speeches, I'll do what I can to persuade Duckett and Lenore Washburn that you're really black at heart, and I'll even bake butterscotch cookies for your telephone squad, but I am not going out front and twirl the baton for you."

"You drive a hard bargain, baby."

"That's what makes me a strong modern woman, honeybunch."

He grinned. "Just one other thing."

"As long as it isn't money."

"Why, have you got some? I'm doing this on string and chewing gum."

"First of all, no one asked you to run, so don't plead poverty. And the pittance I put away for my old age has been badly depleted by my patronage of the arts. Haven't you heard—I am the joint owner of the largest free-standing sculptural construction in the Western world? And it is not exactly a moneymaker. So that's out. Now what else is it that your omnivorous heart desires?"

"Can you deliver Sam Nightingale?"

"For what?"

"I need the university community. He's got clout there."

"I don't think he'd risk it. And city hall's already trying to put the tax screws to Mather. If they got wind that the university's fomenting political insurgency, they might tighten those screws something awful."

"Christ, the university owns this town—what there is to it worth owning."

"But the proles have the votes."

"I'd make Sam the corporation counsel."

"That might interest him, I suppose, if he thought you had a real chance."

"Tell him."

And I did. Surprisingly, he took to the idea. An intra-party contest would give the university more leverage, not less, with city hall for the remainder of the campaign, he said. And his own efforts in Arnold's behalf among the intellectual elite would be mostly a matter of fertilizing natural affinities. Besides, he added, city hall needed a housecleaning; the city, a new purpose and sense of dedication. Besides that, I offered, the firm would benefit from a second sphere of influence. Translated, that meant: Don't let Sparky walk all over you. He said he supposed there was something to that.

What most attracted Sam Nightingale to the semiweekly brain-trust sessions I ran throughout Arnold Berenson's primary campaign, though, was the presence of Jessica Lennox. Thinking that a little community involvement would do both her psyche and vulva a great deal of good, I brought her into Berenson headquarters to help write Arnold's daily press handouts. She became so good at it that Arnold soon invited her to join his inner council, where Sam performed with a wry courtliness that decidedly captivated her. She flexed her own considerable funnybone in response, and he reacted as one might expect of any proud, sensitive, potent man in the throes of cuckoldom. Because of me the two were not strangers, and Jess had taught English to Sam's son the year before, so they shared at least that frame of reference. Whether Sam knew that Jess and his wife had also shared the same lover for a time, I never asked. If so, he surely never learned it directly from me. I had pledged Lee my silence on that score. But nothing had been said of Jessie. Perhaps I strained the spirit of my pledge by telling her of the intensity of Jonathan's alliance with Lee, but I felt a prior obligation to Jessie to minimize her internal bleeding from a pointlessly broken heart. As it turned out, she had guessed about Jon and Lee almost from the start. The clues had been unmistakable. Their mutual fondness was fueled at the Zampa committee gatherings, after which he sometimes spoke warmly to her on the phone within Jessie's earshot. Then he moved the painting of hers that he owned from his office to the house. And Jess found a lipstick of hers behind the living-room sofa one weekend. Thinking for a time that it would dry up between them, she settled for being his consolation lay until Jon started abusing her about her roundness. "Tubs, he called me—the shit," she confided to me after starting up with Sam, "so I called him Elephant Balls and he called me Whale Tits, and I packed it in. Some day I'm going to find out what whale tits look like—prettier than elephant balls, I'll bet."

Sam's new romance proved no more a secret around the firm than the one with me had been. But I had not expected to be blamed this time. To Sparky, the distinction was hazy. "Aren't you the little matchmaker, though?" he asked upon calling me into his newly expanded office suite and probing into the relationship.

"Not guilty," I said. "They're both grown-ups who happened to be in the same place at the same time."

"And who brought them there?"

"They weren't there to socialize."

"But who brought them there?"

"It's irrelevant."

"Isn't the Lennox girl your good friend?"

"She's not a girl—she's a woman."

"And your very good friend."

"Yes—so what?"

"So you thought she'd hit it off with Sam."

"Everyone hits it off with Sam—he's a very fine man. Does that disturb you?"

"I'm among his most ardent admirers."

"Then what's eating you?"

"I don't like seeing him led astray. I told you that once—and that I didn't want it to happen again."

"You make him sound as if he's in diapers."

"Don't con me, Tabor. That era is past."

"I don't know what you're talking about."

"I'm talking about Arnold Berenson for mayor."

"Oh. I thought it was about Sam's philandering."

"They're part and parcel."

"You mean you think Arnold's campaign is a sex ring?"

"Very funny."

"I'm not being funny. I'm trying to figure out what in the hell you're talking about."

"You know goddamn well what I'm talking about. This firm has been on close terms with city hall since the day I came here. And that closeness has been a big factor in our prosperity. There's not a client on our list who might not benefit some time or other from those ties. But you did your best to screw them up till we put a stop to it. And now you're trying again, head-on—and dragging Sam along in the bargain."

"Sam does what Sam wants to do."

"How come he's never been into politics before this?"

"Beats me. Maybe he was just waiting to be asked."

"That's the point—you asked him."

"No one ever told me I couldn't participate in politics if I took the partnership."

"And no one ever told you not to jump out the window, either, but I don't see you doing any jumping."

"You know," I said, "I think we've played this scene one time too many."

"I think you're right."

"Everything would be back to sweetness and light without me around, wouldn't it?"

"I don't know about the light," he said.

"But it's what you want?"

"It's not just me."

"You've polled the partners?"

"Except for Sam and you."

"Why not Sam?"

"It wasn't necessary."

"You got Dan and Gil?"

"Yes."

"I see."

"It was different when Maynard was alive. We could afford a little dissension in the ranks with a figurehead like him to—"

"He was more than a figurehead."

"Not lately."

My throat felt parched suddenly. "Dan I can understand," I said, "but Gil surprises me a little."

"Gil's people are not for Berenson. They're against everything he's for."

"That's no reason to vote me out of the firm."

"No," he admitted, "my strong preference is the reason."

His tufted red hair never looked more fiery. "You know," I said, moving closer to his desk, "I actually feel sorry for you. No grown man should become so insecure over a younger woman."

"It doesn't have anythng to do with insecurity."

"Then how about intolerance?"

"How about impudence? Tabor, you've been given every conceivable opportunity to play ball with us. We even made you a partner by way of recognizing your talents. Now you're a smart girl—"

"Woman, baby, woman."

"Maybe that's the point. Maybe I don't see you as a woman because you don't behave like one."

"And how does a woman behave? Decorously, right?"

"Well—"

"Compliantly, right? Obediently, humbly, and walking with God, right?"

"Well—"

"You can't write all the rules any more, Sparky. You own the ball here now, so I guess you can say who plays with it, but that doesn't change you into any paragon. You're still vain and petty—and you'll never hold Maynard Lamport's jock until you learn how to live with other people's legitimate ambitions without having to destroy them."

He moved forward, as if to protect his typewriter from renewed assault by a deadly woman. "Don't make this hard, Tabor," he said.

"What do you expect—a passionate kiss of gratitude?"

"I expect adult understanding."

"You're pompous, too—I left that out. Maynard, for all his starch, was never pompous." I drifted to the window behind him and looked out blankly for a moment. "Do you think it's adult to turn the other cheek?" I asked him softly.

"It's adult to recognize mutual incompatibility."

"That's begging the question. The question is why are we incompatible."

"I thought that had become apparent by now."

"To you, maybe. To me, all that's apparent is you think the fault is entirely mine. You're not willing to look at yourself—really and truly look—and ask what it is about me that bugs you so much. I'm just an irritant that has to be removed."

"You're awfully good at that maneuver, aren't you—turning your own willfulness into the other guy's character flaw?"

"I'm not willful—I'm purposeful."

"Sure, but the purpose is your own self-aggrandizement."

"And what's yours?"

He had no comeback.

"The most I'll admit to," I said, "is moderate rambunctiousness. But that's more than you can bear in a woman." I turned from the window and looked at him a final time. "Now you're sure about wanting me out of here?"

"Positive," he said.

"Okay, then. I'd appreciate it if you had my personal clients told I can be reached at Legal Assistance for the time being. And please have whatever I'm owed sent to my apartment."

"Sure."

"Well—I guess it's goodbye time, then." I gave his hand a perfunctory pump.

He looked surprised. "Yes—well—goodbye, Tabor. Good luck."

"And do me one last favor, will you?"

"If I can."

"Let your hair grow. Christ, if I had hair that color, it would be down to my fanny."

He smiled.

Always leave them smiling.

Three months passed before I saw Sparky again—this time opposing me in federal court. He had been hired to defend the city against my complaint that it had violated Zampa's First

460

Amendment right in prosecuting him. Of course, Sparky. Who else should they have got?

The occasion was still further heightened by the presence on the bench of George H. Millis, whom I once served so ably. Too ably, I should say now. Fortunately, it was the special three-judge district court I had petitioned for, and George Millis was not presiding. Everett Osgood of the First Circuit, a competent though pedestrian intellect, had been assigned that job. The third jurist on the case was a butcher-boy from Willimantic not known for latitudinarian readings of the Bill of Rights. If George Millis was against me, I had no chance. How could I really expect him to be for me on the merits? Because I thought him a man of principle. And because if he harbored animus toward me, he would not have sat on the case. Unless, of course, he was not a man of principle.

Sparky had outdone himself on the briefs. While I had always known his main talent was as a backroom bargainer, I never assumed he was a hack litigator. He just hated going to court if there was a way to avoid it, and generally he found one. But in the Zampa case, there were no peace overtures; clearly, he was itching for a tussle with his chief tormentor of the past three years. And since he had told me from the start that he thought my First Amendment plea in behalf of the old man was a sham, I was not surprised at the vigor and sweep of his answering brief for the city. The case law was overwhelmingly on his side. But I wanted him to sweat to prove it.

"The right of self-expression has long been recognized by our courts as fundamental in constitutional contexts," I opened. "The only condition attached has been that the form of expression should not collide with some pressing regulatory responsibility of government. Under the growing doctrine that the First Amendment holds a preferred position in our constellation of freedoms, government at every level in this country must heed a higher standard of due process when issues of free speech and other forms of expression are at stake. It is to such a standard that I now appeal."

Testimony at the trial had made clear, I argued, that Zampa would not have been granted a building permit even if he had applied for one unless he had first submitted plans and specifications in duplicate of the work he was about to create—a prior restraint on his First Amendment rights. Such a restraint, moreover, flew directly in the face of a 1958 Supreme Court holding that

> . . . It is settled by a long line of recent decisions of this Court that an ordinance which, like this one, makes the peaceful enjoyment of freedom which the Constitution guarantees contingent upon the uncontrolled will of an official—as by requiring a permit or license which may be granted or withheld in the discretion of such official—is an unconstitutional censorship . . . upon enjoyment of those freedoms.

The only legitimate ground for prosecuting Gabriel Zampa, I insisted, would have been that his towers endangered the public safety—a contention that was not made at the time he was served with a notice that he had violated the city building code, and one that subsequent engineering tests had shown to be unjustified. "The complainant never should have been made to stand trial," I concluded, "but his artistry was so inventive, so nonconformist, and so grand that it could not be accommodated by the tight little world that city officials inhabit—and so it had to be attacked. It is to ward off such arbitrary and one-sided attacks by government that we have a Constitution."

Then I sat down and watched Sparky Grier tramp through all my flowers. The bastard had a field day.

"First Amendment rights are not and have never been absolute," he began, "because we live in a real world with many contending, and often equally compelling, interests. Always, the rights of the individual must be balanced against the obligations of the state to maintain an orderly society. And while freedom of expression is a cherished right among the American people, it does not follow that it can be practiced in total disregard of all other considerations. Our legal annals are full of justified limitations." Sirhan Sirhan was undoubtedly expressing his political ideology, but who would contend he was free to choose the means he did—namely, the assassination of Robert Kennedy—to express himself? "You can never wholly separate the expression from the means," Sparky thundered. There were even some well-understood circumstances in which the very utterance of certain words constituted a crime. The communication of state secrets to other governments, for example, was an unsanctionable form of expression, as was the racial characterizing of a neighborhood by a realtor to a would-be home buyer. "Always the courts must balance the interests," he said.

Not in fifty years, Sparky reminded the judges, had the Supreme Court felt obliged to hear a case like Zampa's on the constitutionality of zoning and building codes because the right of municipalities to ensure their own orderly growth had been so long established. Police-power enactments such as the Amity building code and zoning laws were in no way unconstitutional so long as they "serve a public, not a private interest, are rationally formulated and administered, and are enforced by a mechanism reasonably related to the desired public purposes." The requirement to present plans for any sizable structure before it is erected—in order to make sure it will not endanger the lives of anyone occupying or approaching it—unquestionably constituted a rational mechanism to serve such a public purpose. "There was no antispeech intent in the formulation of these codes," he insisted, "and any claim to that effect is palpably absurd. If Mr. Zampa's muse felt unduly restricted in this city, then he was free to take it somewhere else —like the desert—where it could create whatever it wanted without regard to the rest of humanity."

No doubt he would win, given the composition of the court, when the decision came down in the fall. I congratulated him afterward. He thanked me and said I had done well to make so much out of so little.

"That's what I get paid for," I said.

"I thought you weren't getting paid for this?"

"Not in money," I said. "There are other ways to sell yourself—you should know."

"Always the charmer," he said.

I noticed that his hair was longer and complimented him on it. "Keep it that way for me," I said, "even when you lose this decision. You can always appeal—but at your age the hair may take forever to grow back."

"Oh, I'm not going to lose."

"Sometimes you lose," I said, "even when you win."

36

Why, O Lord, is this fanatically scrubbed man I visit with once a year standing here talking politics and hurricanes with his finger up me?

It is not the finger I mind—it moves gently and has a glove on it—but the inappropriateness of his chatter. Why is he talking at all? Why are we pretending this is a social occasion when I am in fact hoisted in the stirrups, bereft of dignity and everything else, with my prize poop exposed to the whistling wind? Doesn't he know little girls grow up being told to keep their legs crossed at any cost? It is not a reflex easily unlearned even under pleasurable provocation. An invasion is an invasion. Why else do I sweat, even in my thirty-third year, when required to present my equipment for clinical examination? It is no small matter to me—I do not care how many other muffs you have inspected this week—so let us, please, have no trivializing talk, Doc, while you are immersed in my pink heaven. If I wanted to be entertained, I would have gone to Danny Kaye. Just look, as fast as you can, and tell me what you find.

But I know already. That's why I've come, ahead of schedule. The consequences of Terry English's farewell squirt. He is six weeks gone to Boston, swaggering through the higher reaches of videoland and probably grabbing all the ginch he can. He will be in touch whenever the schedule permits, he promised. No rush, I said, and give my worst to all the Nielsens. He said not to be bitter. I said I was anything but. What

I was, was a little bit pregnant. Tension over the fate of the towers had thrown my ovaries into turmoil—I probably skipped a pill I shouldn't have, and Terry was not to be denied his bye-bye bang. At least it was one of his more balletic efforts. He must have thought they were filming it for a pilot.

Well, well, says the doctor, you have a little something growing up there.

Shit, I say.

He says nothing but glances at the nurse. I do, too, and catch the flicker of displeasure in her eyes. What do they want —whoopee and fireworks? I am not thrilled with this confirmation of a consummation devoutly unwished. The doctor detects my distress. He is only half as cold a cod as I supposed. What am I going to do? The question is crouching above the examining table like a small mushroom cloud. He has the grace to see I need a few moments by myself. They will be back shortly, for a Pap smear, he announces, gives me a reassuring pat on the arm, and disappears. Nurse Persimmon trails.

I am alone. I and my seedling. I reclaim my crotch and dismount. And wrap the sheet around me tight. It is only the end of September, why am I so cold? I curl up and think. My mind and body seem unattached. All the other casualties of the past few weeks have numbed me somewhat. The toll has been so heavy that I am not myself. Must I add to the list? It is hard to think straight. . . .

First there was Jonathan Kenyon. On his way to see Lee Nightingale in Niantic, where she was avoiding Sam for the Labor Day weekend. Someone up ahead had tossed flattened beer cans onto the thruway, and Jon came vroom-vrooming along on his Honda bike—that dumb fucking machismometer of his that I hated with fury the moment I saw it—and caught one of the cans and wiped out at a catastrophic speed. Only the grass saved him from pulp. He is recovering steadily, the hospital says. Except for paralysis from the lumbar vertebra southward. He who moved so well in that region can no more. There is no reason, though, they say, why he won't be able to resume his career—with certain modifications.

The damage suffered by the towers appears, however, to be

irreparable. There is no point in comparing the afflictions of the flesh with those of inorganic compositions, but if you are of the view, as Jonathan is, that art is not altogether inanimate, the impending loss of Zampa's masterwork is a tragedy hardly less appalling than his own.

Word arrived the last part of August, when the weather was most torrid, that three leading insurance companies had refused to renew their homeowners' policies in force in the Gully. And other companies were sure to follow. It was massive abandonment by the financial establishment. The message might as well have been written in the sky: YOU LOW LIFE CANNOT PAY US ENOUGH TO PROTECT YOU FROM YOURSELVES. Neither the mayor nor the governor nor any of the area's legislators was sufficiently distressed by the development to intervene forcefully in the residents' behalf, and their black anger soon boiled over. And what more tempting target than the towers—well-publicized alien property deep within the ghetto? For a time, the Zampa Foundation, meaning me, Lee, and a few other mad benefactors, had kicked in for a round-the-clock watchman at the junkyard, which had long since been picked clean of everything but the towers themselves. Even wino watchmen cost a lot of money, though, and we had to cut back. What if we had not—could one measly guard have halted the rampage?

They drenched the lower reaches of the main tower with gasoline, and even though we had had the cracks in the plastic covering sealed with epoxy, enough fuel clung to the surface to feed the hideous blaze. By the time the city engines showed up, the framing had been sufficiently melted and weakened to cause a fifteen-degree list to the spire. Only the remarkable strength of the hand construction kept it from crashing over. Curiously, more people than ever have been out to see it. It is a deathwatch. Any day now the building department will have the last laugh and issue a demolition order that only the second coming of Zampa—trailing clouds of machinery and materials—might stave off. But the old man is nowhere, and determined to stay.

Lenore Washburn called me afterward to say how sorry she

466

was about the fire and that she hoped I didn't think it was something personal. Why should I, just because I had over-invested myself in that strange creation and its eccentric creator? It had become my private fetish, as it had been the old man's before me, but I saw a world too full of lost causes to think this one had been hatched especially to do me in. That way lies the booby hatch. Yet I could not help wondering what the outcome might have been if the resident blacks had appropriated those towers as their own—had proclaimed them, as I proposed, a folk symbol of their unquenchable yearnings—instead of pawning them for cheap promises by faithless politicians. I did not ask Lenore that. I just thanked her for her concern. In the urban wasteland, cheap promises are sometimes the only shreds of hope.

The man who taught me that truth even while lamenting it—Arnold Berenson—was added to the casualty list three weeks ago when he lost the mayoral primary and every cent he had in the bank. The mid-life crisis strikes again. Actually, Arnold did better than anyone had predicted: 42 percent of the turnout. Against an entrenched enemy. They will have to hear him out now at city hall when he speaks. In defeat he has become the reforming conscience of the community. In the Gully he polled 77 percent of the votes, although officially the Coop leadership spurned my impassioned plea to endorse Arnold as a white nigger. "Oh, hey, no," said Duckett, frowning gravely, "that's the baddest kind." But he passed the word.

The effects of the election are still battering me. For one thing, Arnold has resigned as director of Legal Assistance, and invited, of all people, Sam Nightingale to succeed him. And for another, Sam has said yes.

I told Arnold, when he asked my opinion, there was no chance Sam could be persuaded. The man had found his station in life and manned it cheerfully. And while he was an accomplished legal craftsman, I doubted he had the temperament or will to endure the daily chaos of a *pro bono* shop and all the grubwork keeping the assembly line operative. But I had badly miscalculated the effect on him of Sparky's high-handedness in the wake of Maynard's death and my unceremonious expulsion.

467

More affecting still was the traumatic end of Lee's affair with Jonathan, who had been reduced in that one crushing moment to a sexual vegetable. If Lee had deluded herself into believing Jon supplied her with something beyond his musk in reawakening her carnal appetite, his disfigurement broke the spell with cruel speed. In its sobering aftermath, she is persuaded that her estimate of Sam's genial virtues has been decidedly uncharitable and warrants reconsideration. On his part, the whole searing episode has prompted a similarly fresh assessment of the state of his union with Lee and of his involvement with the rest of humanity. His preliminary findings, ratified by Lee and open to amendment by them both, are that each of them has risked too little for too long for fear of losing too much. His legal practice, Sam admitted, was invisibly asphyxiating him. His plunge into Arnold's campaign at least partially freed him from the paneled rooms and dispassionate people that had constituted his whole world since shifting from the Mather cocoon. The experience proved invigorating. He is convinced, as I had tried to impress upon him during our time together, that life is more than the care and feeding of ungrateful clients; chronic solicitude is the mark of an uneasy character, not a noble one. To live more, he will give more, whatever the risks. Lee, weary of lacerating both him and herself, feels the same. The plan is for them to make the effort in each other's company when not proceeding in their necessarily separate ways. She has begun painting every day now, and long hours. And Sam is phasing out of the firm by day and orienting himself at night to ways of coping with the law of the jungle. Lee tells me she is more than happy, under the circumstances, to make up the imminent loss in Sam's take-home pay—which means, unless I am mistaken, that they are screwing better already.

All of which might have left Jessica Lennox in the lurch once more—except for the interim appointment to an associate professorship at the Mather School of Engineering of the unsinkable Ross Otis. His work on the towers kindled high admiration among the students who worked with him on the stress analysis project, and their enthusiasm was relayed to the dean, who knew where to turn when he had an emergency vacancy to fill in midsummer. Ross's permanent status will depend on how this academic year works out, but he is overjoyed at the chance to pursue his profession free of fear the federal budgeteers will make him walk the plank yet again.

I invited him and little Valerie out horseback riding one day at the end of summer and had Jessie come by afterward for pizza supper. Val fell at once for her. Jess is a smash with kids, who love her firecracker laughter. Ross is more overwhelmed than beguiled but very interested, it is plain. They are dating. She brings him out of himself, and he likes the ventilation. Jessie is shedding pounds—one a day, every day, she says—so he will not feel so outbulked. Whatever course it takes (and I have urged her to go easy for a change), this is the first relationship Jess has launched since our re-acquaintance that has not seemed marked from the start for early extinction.

I have not been indifferent, through all these convulsions, to my own survival. Soon I must decide on Arnold Berenson's appealing offer of last week to form a law partnership with him.

"We'd starve," I said.

"We're starving now," he said.

It was true at least that I had not had a paycheck since Sparky showed me the door. I had volunteered my fulltime services to Arnold's campaign for the duration—which he says is why he did so well—and promised myself a sabbatical till the end of the year to decide what I should do next with my life. But Arnold is persistent. He calls every morning to ask if I've decided. When I say yes and that the answer is still maybe, he says I have only twenty-four more hours to decide. "I don't understand the stall," he said yesterday. "We've worked so well in the past—hey, we'd be dynamite together."

"That's what I'm afraid of," I told him.

"No-no-no," he said. "No touchy-feely. This is strictly professional."

"You tried once."

"So I'm not gay—shoot me."

"I may yet," I laughed. "Now just tell me one thing—what would you call this mythical firm of ours?"

"Hell, I don't care. There aren't a lot of options."

"Try one on me."

"I guess it's either Hill & Berenson or Berenson & Hill."

"Which one?"

"I don't care—whatever you want."

"It's your baby—you name it."

"Okay. Hill & Berenson."

"Why that?"

"Why not?"

"Because you're the senior member."

"Ladies first," he said.

"Since when?"

"Since always."

"Oh, horseshit, Arnold. That's only when the ship is sinking —and then it's to lighten the load. Otherwise, we get hind tit, as you chaps so lyrically put it."

"Don't sermonize me, baby. I am the most active male feminist in this town—and you know it."

"Sure—because you couldn't find any male lawyers to work at your wages."

"Is that my fault?"

"I'm fooling, Arnold. You're a prince. And I appreciate the gesture, but if it's going to be anything, it's got to be Berenson & Hill. It scans so much better."

He said it over a few times. "You know, I think you're right. Okay, Berenson & Hill it is."

"Good," I said. "The other way is such an anticlimax."

He shook his head, smiling. "I can tell who the straight man is going to be in this outfit."

But I do not feel like joking just now with this unsolicited fetus in me. No, it is not yet a being, and no, it does not yet possess a soul, and no, I am not at all Catholic, but the thought of killing this speck of life thoroughly depresses me. Will God know? Will God care? Will God smite me in return? Will God scrape me barren? I know better. There is no universal moral order, just germs and molecules and cosmic cataclysms. Only life's vanquished think otherwise—that powers beyond us oversee our acts and divine our fates accordingly.

But there is nothing metaphysical inside me. Just a little sperm a guy deposited. He was not even someone special. But I am. And life is. And this thinglet would be, wouldn't it? And I am crying. . . .

Shall I have it? And do what with it? Give it to Albert Schweitzer? No, he's dead. Present it to the Pope with the compliments of a friend? Hell, no. That sanctified sexist would just feed it wafers, make it burp in Latin, and consign it to celibacy. Maybe my mother? No, she's served her time. I could always keep it. And hug it and squeeze it and milk it—how long are your nipples raw?—and love it to shreds. And would it love me back? Love me, dammit. Love your smother, baby, or she'll stick a tuna sandwich into your teeny fist and pack you off to whelp with the coyotes. One endangered species is as good as another. Would you turn out smart and pretty? Probably. And I would teach you values. And fortitude. And cunning. And you would grow up and run the world. Instead of me. No, they are not going to let me run it, I can tell. I bother them too much. And why? You tell me. It's more their problem than mine, I think. That's why I don't overly mind de-escalating. The truth is I am less ambitious than last year. I have receded to playing star witness at my own trial, not the scintillating defense counsel as well. And world-beaters can't afford to settle for bit parts. Or have fatherless babies. Should I go get this one's father? He would no doubt have me if I came in pursuit. I would rather slit my throat first. He is unworthy.

And who is not? To find him I have not hunted hard or displayed my wares. The Law is my shepherd, I shall not flaunt. But someone splendid shall come soon. My womb, never gravid before, is telling me. Meanwhile, doctor, I will need minor surgery. And do be careful. If not, I trust you have an able attorney.

AUTHOR'S NOTE

I am grateful to Joseph W. Bishop, Jr., Lawrence G. Good-man, Joel Kluger, Arthur R. Riccio, Jr., Carol Eisen Rinzler, Diane Daskal Ruben, John G. Simon, Lawrence Turk, and Jon D. Wright, who helped in various ways in my research. I owe a special acknowledgment to N. J. Goldstone, who kindly made available to me his paper "Structural Test of a Hand-Built Tower" delivered in 1962 before the Society of Experimental Stress Analysts, and to the lucid and instructive writings of Professor Boris I. Bittker of Yale Law School, particularly his splendid satire "Tax Shelters for the Poor?", appearing in the February 1973 issue of *Taxes*.

R.K.